Praise for internationally bestselling author Julie Kagawa and The Iron Fey series

"This many books in, Kagawa is entirely at ease
in her invented world, and her ability to create strong, intriguing characters
has improved noticeably since *The Iron King*. Knowledge of the previous tales
is helpful but not necessary—fans will feel right at home,
and new readers will have no trouble finding their way."
—*Publishers Weekly* on *The Lost Prince*

"Kagawa's fans will enjoy this expansion of her world."
—*Kirkus Reviews* on *The Lost Prince*

"Julie Kagawa's Iron Fey series is the next *Twilight*."
—*Teen.com*

"Kagawa pulls her readers into a unique world of make-believe with her fantastic
storytelling, and ultimately leaves them wanting more by the end of each book."
—*Times Record News* on *The Iron Knight*

"Fans of Melissa Marr—and of Kagawa—will enjoy the ride,
with Meghan's increased agency and growing power showing the series' maturity.
Finally more than just a love triangle."
—*Kirkus Reviews* on *The Iron Queen*

"This third installment in the series is just as compelling
and complex as its predecessors, and wholly satisfying."
—*Realms of Fantasy* on *The Iron Queen*

"A full five-stars to Julie Kagawa's *The Iron Daughter*. If you love action,
romance and watching how characters mature through heart-wrenching trials,
you will love this story as much as I do."
—*Mundie Moms* blog

"*The Iron Daughter* is a book
that will keep its readers glued to the pages until the very end."
—*New York Journal of Books*

"*The Iron King* surpasses the greater majority of dark fantasies,
leaving a lot for readers to look forward to.... The romance is well done
and adds to the mood of fantasy."
—*Teenreads.com*

"*The Iron King* has the...enchantment, imagination and adventure of...
Alice in Wonderland, *Narnia* and *The Lord of the Rings*, but with lots more romance."
—*Justine* magazine

**Books by Julie Kagawa
available from Harlequin TEEN**

**The Iron Fey series
(in reading order)**

*The Iron King**
"Winter's Passage" (ebook novella)****
*The Iron Daughter**
The Iron Queen
"Summer's Crossing" (ebook novella)****
The Iron Knight
"Iron's Prophecy" (ebook novella)****
The Lost Prince
The Iron Traitor

*Also available in *The Iron Fey Volume One* anthology
**Also available in print in *The Iron Legends* anthology

**Blood of Eden series
(in reading order)**

The Immortal Rules
The Eternity Cure

And coming in May 2014

The Forever Song

THE IRON TRAITOR

JULIE KAGAWA

THE IRON FEY

CALL OF THE FORGOTTEN

HARLEQUIN°TEEN

Recycling programs
for this product may
not exist in your area.

ISBN-13: 978-0-373-21091-6

THE IRON TRAITOR

Printed in U.S.A.

www.HarlequinTEEN.com

To Guro Ron, for letting me pick his brain.
And to Nick, for letting me hit him with sticks.

PART 1

CHAPTER ONE
BACK TO "NORMAL"

My name is Ethan Chase.

Just shy of a week ago, I was dragged into Faeryland.

Again.

The first time it happened, I was four. Yeah, four years old, kidnapped by faeries and taken into the Nevernever, home of the fey. Long story short, my older sister rescued me and brought me home, but became a faery queen herself and now rules a part of the Nevernever called the Iron Realm.

Thirteen years later, despite all the precautions I took against the Fair Folk, it happened again. I found myself smack-dab in the middle of the Nevernever, and this time, I wasn't alone. A classmate of mine, a girl named Mackenzie St. James, managed to get pulled in, as well. A lot of weird, screwed-up stuff happened in the next few days, like following a talking cat through the Nevernever, meeting my sister in the Iron Realm, sneaking *out* of the Iron Realm to meet up with the Queen of the Exiles and, oh yeah, discovering that my sister has a son. That's right, I have a nephew. A nephew who is part fey, completely unknown to my parents, and who, by way of screwy faery time, is the same age as me.

There is one other important thing we discovered—the emergence of a new, deadly species of fey called the Forgotten, faeries that almost don't exist anymore because they've been unremembered for so long. Faeries that have to steal the glamour from regular fey to survive, killing them in the process. But for me, the nephew thing sort of stands out. If I thought my family was weird before, it's not even a blip on the weirdness scale now. I thought I'd seen it all. But when I got pulled into the Nevernever, the thing I never saw coming was Keirran.

When Keirran went back into the Nevernever, I knew I hadn't seen the last of him. Still, I had no idea how entangled my life would soon become with his, and how he would be the catalyst...for the end of everything.

Sometimes I wished everyone paid less attention to me. Sometimes I even wished I had faery blood, so that when the really weird things started happening around me, people would forget they'd seen it as soon as I left. That worked for Robin Goodfellow, the most infamous faery in existence. And to a lesser extent, it even worked for my sister. But in the real world, if you're fully human and you vanish into thin air for nearly a week, people tend to notice. If you vanish at the same time as a very rich, popular classmate, they notice even more.

Which was why, I supposed, I was back in the principal's office the Monday after I returned from the Nevernever. Only this time, there were two policemen in the room as well, looming over my chair and looking stern. Kids passing by peered through the door's window and gaped at me before hurrying off with their friends, whispering. Great. I already had a reputation for being a delinquent and a troublemaker; this probably wasn't going to help.

"Do you know why we've brought you here, Mr. Chase?" the principal said, pursing his thin mouth. I shrugged. I'd been in this office on my first day of school and knew the principal thought I was a lost cause. No point in trying to change his mind. Besides, the two officers were far more worrisome.

"We'd like to ask you a few questions about Todd Wyndham," one of the policemen stated, making my stomach twist. "As you may know, he disappeared last Friday, and his mother filed a missing-persons report when he didn't return from school. According to her, the last person to speak to him before he vanished…was you."

I swallowed. Todd Wyndham was a classmate of mine, and I knew exactly what had happened to him that night. But there was no way I was going to tell the police officers that Todd was part fey, a half-breed who had been kidnapped by the Forgotten and drained of his glamour. Problem was, draining his glamour had also robbed him of his memories, his emotions and his sense of self. By the time Kenzie and I had found him, his magic was already gone, leaving him dazed, passive and completely human.

Keeping my voice steady, I faced the officer who had spoken. "Yeah, I saw him at school that day. Everyone did. What's the big deal?"

"The big deal," the officer continued, frowning harder, "is that Todd Wyndham showed up at his home last week completely shell-shocked. He doesn't remember much, but he has told us that he was kidnapped and that there were other kidnap victims. His symptoms are on par with someone who has witnessed a violent crime, and we fear the kidnapper could strike again soon. We're hoping that you can shed some light on Todd's condition."

"Why me?"

The policeman narrowed his eyes. "Because on the day after Todd's disappearance, Mrs. St. James reported her daughter missing, as well. She was last seen at a martial arts tournament, speaking to *you*. Witnesses say that you pulled her out of the building, into the parking lot, and then you both disappeared. Care to tell me what happened, Ethan?"

My heart pounded, but I kept my cool, sticking to the script Kenzie and I had come up with. "Kenzie wanted to see New York City," I said casually. "Her dad didn't want her to go. But she really wanted to see it, you know...before she *died*." They blinked, probably not knowing if I was being serious or overly dramatic. I shrugged again. "She asked me to take her, so I did. She never said her dad didn't know she was leaving."

Kind of a lame excuse, but I couldn't tell them the real reason, of course. That a bunch of murderous Forgotten had found us at the tournament, chased us into the parking lot, and I'd had to send us both into the Nevernever to escape.

The policeman's lips thinned, and I crossed my arms. "If you don't believe me, ask Kenzie," I told him. "She'll tell you the same thing."

"We intend to do that." They straightened and backed away, making gestures to let me know we were done here. "Go on back to class, but we'll be watching you, Ethan. Stay out of trouble, you hear?"

Relieved, I stood and headed for the door. As I left I could feel the principal's glare on my back. He'd probably hoped I'd be arrested and carted off to juvie; one less delinquent for him to deal with. I certainly gave off the image of the sullen, brooding troublemaker: ripped jeans, shirt turned inside out, pierced ears and defiant smirk firmly in place. But whatever. I wasn't here to be a perfect student or win any trophies. I just wanted to get through the year without any major disasters. Any *more* major disasters.

I slipped out of the principal's office with a sigh of relief. Another bullet dodged. I was an expert at lying to cover up the truth no one else could see. That the fey were out there and couldn't seem to leave me alone. To keep the people around me safe, I'd become someone no one wanted to be around. I'd driven away potential friends, isolated myself and basically been a dick to anyone who tried to get close to me. Usually it worked. Once I made it clear that I wanted to be left alone, people did just that. No one wanted to deal with a hostile jerk.

Except one girl.

Dammit, I hope she's okay. Where are you, Kenzie? I hope you didn't get into trouble because of me.

I supposed we were lucky that we'd been gone only a week. In the Nevernever, time flows differently than in the real world. There are stories of those who vanished into Faeryland for a year and when they came home again, a hundred years had gone by and all they'd known before was changed. Losing one week was getting off pretty easy, but to everyone looking for us, we appeared to have vanished into thin air. With one exception, no one had seen or heard any trace of us from the time we left the tournament until the night we came home, several days later.

So Kenzie and I had had to come up with a really good excuse for when we got back.

"Are you sure?" I'd asked, gazing into her chocolate-brown eyes, seeing my worried reflection staring back at me. "That's the story you want to give your dad when we get home? You decided to visit New York, and I agreed to drive you there?"

Kenzie had shrugged, the moonlight shining off her raven hair. Behind her, the great expanse of Central Park was a black-and-silver patchwork quilt, fading into the glimmering towers over the tree line. Her slim arms hung around my waist, her fingers tracing patterns in the small of my back, distracting me. "Can you think of anything better?"

"Not really." I shivered as her fingers slipped under the hem of my shirt and brushed my skin. I resisted the urge to squirm and tried to focus. "But won't he be mad that you just took off without telling him?"

The girl in my arms gave a bitter smile, not looking up. "He has no right to be," she muttered. "He doesn't care what I do. He never checks up on me. As long as I come back with all my fingers and toes, he won't care where I've been. And if he *does* say something, I...I'll tell him that I wanted to see New York City before I died. What is he going to do?"

My gut twisted for a different reason then. I didn't answer, and Kenzie peeked up at me, apologetic. "What about you?" she asked, cocking her head. "What do you want to tell your family when we get home?"

"Don't worry about it," I told her. "My family has dealt with this before." *When we lost Meghan.* "I'll come up with something."

She fell silent, chewing on her lip. Her soft fingers were still tracing patterns beneath my shirt, sending tremors up my spine. "Ethan?" she said finally, her voice strangely hesitant. "Um...I'm going to see you again, when we get back to the real world, right?"

"Yeah," I whispered, knowing exactly what she meant. She wasn't worried that I would fade from sight like one of the fey, but that I would go back to being that mean, hostile jackass who kept everyone at arm's length. "I promise, I'm not going anywhere," I told her, brushing a dark strand of hair from her eyes. "I'll even do normal things like take you to dinner and go to the movies, if you want."

Kenzie grinned. "Can I introduce you as my boyfriend?"

My stomach lurched the other way. "If you think introducing me to anyone is a good idea," I said, shrugging. "I just hope your dad is as lenient on your boyfriends as he is on your whereabouts. You said he's a lawyer, right?" I grimaced. "I can just see how that first meeting is going to go."

Kenzie rose on tiptoe, her hands climbing my chest to my shoulders, and touched her lips to mine. I sucked in a breath and closed my eyes, feeling her soft mouth caress my lips, forgetting everything for a moment.

"Let me handle my dad," she murmured when we drew back.

"Prince Ethan." A short faery with a potato-like nose, wrinkled and stubby, padded up. The gnome was dressed in a long white coat, and one of its arms was mechanical, the fingers made of needles, tweezers, even a scalpel. "You are injured," it stated, gesturing to the rough bandages trussed around my leg and arm where I'd been sliced open by a couple nasty faery knights. My sleeve and half my pant leg were covered in blood. "The Iron Queen has bid me to tend to your wounds. As she said, in her own words, 'I do not want Mom and Luke freaking out the second he comes home.' Please, sit down."

Kenzie let me go, and, suddenly feeling my injuries, I maneuvered painfully into a seated position. "You can stitch me up all you want," I grumbled as the gnome's index finger became a pair of tiny scissors and began cutting away my arm wrap. "They're still going to freak out when they see me half-drenched in blood. I see an emergency room visit in my future."

"Not necessarily," the gnome returned, and waved its regular arm. I felt the tingle of glamour settle over me as the blood on my shirt abruptly…vanished. Holes disappeared, tears stitched themselves together and my clothes looked perfectly normal again. Beside me, Kenzie drew in a sharp breath, even as I recoiled, not wanting any faery glamour put on me, even if it seemed harmless.

"Oh, calm down," the gnome said, taking my arm again. "It's an illusion, nothing more. But it will break the second you remove your clothes, so I suggest you make sure you are alone when you decide to change. As for these—" it plucked at the sleeve of my shirt "—I suggest a nice bonfire."

When I'd gotten home that night, I'd been bracing myself for an interrogation. Thanks to my sister disappearing into Faeryland thirteen years ago, my parents were paranoid and overprotective to the *nth* degree. If I was out five minutes past curfew, Mom would be calling my phone, demanding to know where I was, if I was all right. As I'd slipped through the front door that night, I still hadn't known what I was going to tell them, but when I'd seen them in the living room, waiting for me, I'd realized they already knew.

It seemed they had received a visit from the Iron Queen that very night, and Meghan had told them I was safe. That I had been with her in the Nevernever and I was on my way home. She didn't tell them the whole truth, of course; she'd left out the parts with Keirran, and the Forgotten, and how I'd almost died a few times. I'd thought Mom and Dad would want the rest of the story; even if they couldn't see the bloodstains covering my clothes, or the stitched wounds beneath them, they'd had to know *something* had gone down in Faeryland. But whatever Meghan had told them seemed to be enough. Mom had just hugged the breath out of me, asked if I was all right about four dozen times and left it at that.

Truthfully, I didn't think she wanted to know. Mom was terrified of the fey and thought that if she pretended they didn't exist, they wouldn't harass us. Which kind of sucked for me, because they *did*. But, at least that night, I'd been glad I didn't have to explain myself. It wasn't often that I was let off the hook. I'd just hoped Kenzie's family was as understanding.

Kenzie. I sighed, scrubbing my hand through my hair, worried again. I hadn't seen her since the night she went home, back to her dad and her stepmom. I'd tried calling her over the weekend, but either her phone was still dead or it had been taken away, because my calls went straight to voice mail. Worried and restless, I'd gotten to school early this morning in the hopes of seeing her, finding out how her family had taken her abrupt disappearance, but I'd been pulled into the principal's office before I could catch a glimpse of the girl who was very suddenly my whole world.

Morose, I headed back to class, still scanning the hall for any glimpse of blue-streaked black hair, irrationally hoping to run into Kenzie on her way to the principal's office. I didn't see her, of course, but I did pass a group of girls in the hall, talking and laughing beneath the bathroom sign. They fell silent as I passed, staring at me with wide eyes, and I heard the murmurs erupt as soon as my back was turned.

"Oh, my God, that's him."

"Did you hear he forced Kenzie to run away with him last week? They were on the other side of the country before the police finally caught them."

"So that's why the cops are here. Why isn't he in jail?"

I clenched my jaw and kept walking. Gossip rarely bothered me—I was so used to it by now. And most of the more colorful rumors were so far off it was laughable. But I hated the thought that, just by being around me, Kenzie would be the target of speculation. It was already starting.

She wasn't in any of the classes we shared, which made it difficult to concentrate on anything happening around me. Even so, I caught suspicious glances thrown my way, whispers whenever I slid into my desk, the hard stares of some of the popular kids. Kenzie's friends. I kept my head down and my usual "leave me the hell alone" posture going, until the bell rang for lunch.

Kenzie still hadn't made an appearance. I almost went down

to the cafeteria, just to see if she was there, before catching myself with a grimace. *Geez, what are you doing, Ethan? You've gone completely stupid for this girl. She's not here today. Just accept that already.*

As I hesitated in the corridor, trying to decide which direction to go, my nerves prickled and the hair on the back of my neck stood up, a sure warning that I was being watched—or stalked. Wary, I casually scanned the surging throng of teenagers for anything that might belong to the Invisible World, the world only I could see. The source of my unease wasn't a faery, however. It was worse.

Football star Brian Kingston and three of his friends were pushing their way through the corridor, broad shoulders and thick arms parting the crowd with ease. By their faces and the way they were scanning the halls, it was obvious they were on the warpath. Or at least the quarterback was, with his ruddy face and thick jaw set for a fight. I could just guess who was the target of his wrath.

Great.

I turned and melted into the throng, heading in the opposite direction, hoping to disappear and find someplace I could be alone. Where vengeful football jocks and their cronies couldn't smash my face into lockers, where I didn't have to hear whispers of how I'd kidnapped Kenzie and forced her to go to New York with me.

Once more, maybe by fate, I found myself back in the library, the quiet murmurs and rustle of paper bringing with it a storm of memories. I'd come here during the first week of school, too, in an attempt to avoid Kingston. It was also here that I'd promised to meet Kenzie for one of her infamous interviews. And it was here that I'd held my last lucid conversation with Todd, right before he vanished.

Hiding my lunch under my jacket, I ignored the no-food-

or-drink sign on the front desk and sauntered into the back aisles. I earned a suspicious glare from the librarian, who watched me over her glasses, but at least Kingston and his thugs wouldn't follow me here.

I found a quiet corner and sank down against the wall, engulfed in déjà vu. Dammit, I just wanted to be left alone. Was that too much to ask? I wanted to get through a school day without getting beat up, threatened with expulsion or arrested. And I wanted, for once, to just have a day where I could take my girlfriend out to the movies or to dinner without some faery messing everything up. Something like normal. Was that ever going to happen?

When the last bell rang, I grabbed my books and hurried to the parking lot, hoping to make it out before Kingston or any of Kenzie's friends. No one stopped or followed me in the halls, but when I started toward my beat-up truck, parked at the far end of the lot, my nerves went rigid.

Brian Kingston was sitting on the hood, legs swinging off the edge, smirking at me. Two of his football buddies leaned against the side, blocking the door.

"Where do you think you're going, freak?" Kingston asked, sliding to the ground. His cronies pressed behind him, and I took a deep breath to calm down. At least they hadn't damaged my truck in any obvious way...yet. The tires didn't look slashed, and I didn't see any key marks in the paint, so that was something. "Been wanting to talk to you all afternoon."

I shifted my weight onto the balls of my feet. He didn't want to talk. Everything about him said he was itching for a fight. "Do we really have to do this now?" I asked, keeping a wary eye on all three of them. Dammit, I did *not* need this, but if the choices were "fight" or "get my ass kicked," I wasn't going to get stomped on. I supposed I could have run away like a coward, but the fallout of that might be even worse. These three didn't scare me; I'd faced down goblins, redcaps, a lindwurm and a whole legion of murderous, ghostly fey who sucked the glamour out of their normal kin. I'd fought things that were trying their best to kill me, and I was still here. A trio of unarmed humans, thick-necked and muscle-headed as they were, didn't register very high on my threat meter, but I'd rather not get expelled on my first day back if I could help it.

"This is stupid, Kingston," I snapped, backing away as his cronies tried to flank me. If they lunged, I'd need to get out of the way fast. "What the hell do you want? What do you think I've done now?"

"Like you don't know." Kingston sneered. "Don't play stupid, freak. I told you to stay away from Mackenzie, didn't I? I warned you what would happen, and you didn't listen. Everyone knows you dragged her off to New York last week. I don't know why the cops didn't toss your ass in jail for kidnapping."

"She *asked* me to take her," I argued. "I didn't drag her anywhere. She wanted to see New York, and her dad wouldn't let her go, so she asked me." Lies to cover up more lies. I wondered if there would ever come a point where I didn't have to lie to everyone.

"Yeah, and now look where she is," Kingston shot back. "I don't know what you did to her while you were gone, but you're gonna wish you never came here."

"Wait. What?" I frowned, still trying to keep the jocks in my sights. "What do you mean? Where is Kenzie now?"

Kingston shook his head. "You didn't hear, freak? God, you are a bastard." He stepped forward, eyes narrowing in pure contempt. "Kenzie is in the hospital."

CHAPTER TWO
MACKENZIE'S FATHER

My stomach dropped.

"She's in the hospital?" I repeated as fear and horror spread through my insides. I remembered something Kenzie had told me about herself while we were in Faery, something big and dark and terrifying. "Why?"

"You tell me." Kingston clenched his fists. "You put her there."

Pain exploded through my side; one of the other jocks had lunged in with a punch to my ribs while I was distracted, knocking me to the side. I gasped and staggered away, ducking beneath the other's left hook and raising my fists in a boxing stance as all three came at me.

Kingston swung viciously at my face; I jerked my head back, letting the knuckles graze me, before lunging forward with a body shot that bent him forward with a grunt. At the same time, one of his friends hammered a fist into my unprotected back. I winced, absorbing the blow, then spun around Kingston to use him as a shield. He snarled and threw an elbow back, trying to bash me in the face. I caught his arm, pivoted him around in a circle and threw him into his friend.

As they both toppled and rolled to the concrete, the last jock slammed into me from behind, wrapping me in a bear hug, pinning my arms. I jerked my head back, cracking my skull into his nose, and the jock shrieked a curse. Slipping from his grasp, I whirled behind him, drove my foot into the back of his knee and yanked down on his shoulders. He hit the pavement with a gusty *whoof,* expelling all the air from his lungs, and lay there dazed.

But the other two were climbing to their feet, looking homicidal, and I didn't want to stay any longer. Breaking from the fight, I leaped into my truck and slammed the door. Kingston stepped up and smashed a fist into the window as I pulled out, glaring at me with murder in his eyes. A hairline crack appeared where his ringed knuckle struck the glass, but thankfully nothing more, as I maneuvered the vehicle around the jocks out for my blood and fled the parking lot.

It took a few minutes on my phone to find the hospital closest to Kenzie's house, and I drove there immediately. I was supposed to go straight home from school, and probably should have—my parents still weren't recovered from my trip into the Nevernever—but all I could think about was Mackenzie. And how *I* was the reason she was hospitalized. Maybe not directly, but it was still certainly my fault.

Kenzie had leukemia, an aggressive type of cancer that affected the blood cells. She'd told me as much when we were stuck in the Nevernever, and the prognosis wasn't very hopeful. That was the main reason she'd wanted the Sight, why she wanted to stay in Faery. She didn't know how long she had, and she wanted to see everything she could. Her illness also made her relatively fearless and a lot more daring than she should have been. Even when offered the chance to go back home, she'd refused to abandon me, sticking it out through sword fights, kidnappings and near-death experiences, tromping from one end of the Nevernever to the other while dodging faeries, Forgotten and other things that wanted to eat us.

And now she was in the hospital. It had been too much. Everything had finally caught up with her, and it was all on me. If I'd never brought her into Faery, she would be fine.

I pulled into the crowded parking lot and sat there, gazing at the big square building in the distance. A part of me, the part that had withdrawn from the whole world, the part that kept other people at arm's length to keep them safe from the fey, told me not to go in there. That I had already screwed up Mackenzie's life by dragging her into the hidden world, and the best and safest thing for her would be to stay far, far away from me.

But I couldn't. I'd already promised her I wouldn't disappear, and honestly, I didn't want to. Kenzie had the Sight now, same as me, which meant the fey would be drawn to her. And there was no way I was going to let her face them alone. Besides, she would never let me get away with that.

I crossed the parking lot and entered the hospital, finding a waiting room full of bored, solemn and worried-looking people. Ignoring them, I approached the reception desk, where a frizzy-haired nurse was sitting behind the counter, talking to a policeman.

My heart jumped a little, and I backed up, watching the officer from an inconspicuous corner. There was no need to be twitchy, I told myself as the nurse laughed at something the cop said. I wasn't in trouble. I'd done nothing wrong. But I'd also had my fill of talking to cops for the day, and I wasn't winning any Upright Citizen awards with my appearance. If the officer thought I looked suspicious, all he'd have to do was pull up my file to see a list of crimes staring back at him. It wasn't worth the risk or the hassle.

I hung back in the corner until the policeman finally left, then approached the desk.

"Excuse me," I said as the receptionist lifted her gaze and raked me up and down from behind her glasses. "I'm here to see a friend of mine. Can you tell me which room Kenzie St. James is in?"

The nurse gave me a doubtful look. I could see her stamping the *hooligan* label on my forehead even before she informed me, in a voice of strained politeness, "Visiting hours are almost over. Are you a friend of the family, young man?"

"No," I replied. "Kenzie is a classmate of mine. We go to the same school."

"Mmm-hmm." She gave me another skeptical look, as if questioning that I even went to school, and I bristled.

"Look, I just want to see her for a few minutes. I won't stay long. I just want to make sure she's okay." The nurse wavered, and I forced out a near-desperate "Please."

She pursed her lips. For a second, I thought she would refuse, tell me to get out before she called the policeman back. But then she gave a short nod toward the hall. "Very well. Ms. St. James is in room 301, on your left. Just keep it short."

Relieved, I thanked her and hurried down the hall, checking the number beside each door frame, passing identical rooms full of beds and sick people. As I wove around a janitor's cart, a woman and a young girl, maybe around nine or ten, came out of one of the rooms ahead of me. I stepped aside to let them pass, feeling a jolt of recognition as they walked by without glancing at me. I didn't know the tall blonde woman, but the little girl I'd seen before. She had been in a key-chain photograph with Kenzie, both of them smiling at the camera.

Mackenzie's stepsister. Alec or Alex or something like that. Her dark brown hair was pulled into a ponytail, and she wore a blue-and-white school uniform as she trailed beside her mom, heading back toward the waiting room. I watched until they turned a corner and disappeared, wondering if Kenzie's sister really knew what was happening to her stepsibling. When I was her age, I didn't understand why I never saw my older sister; I only knew she wasn't home, wasn't part of the family, and I missed her. I hoped Kenzie's sibling never had to go through that—the pain of knowing you *had* a sister, and then you suddenly didn't anymore.

The doorway they'd exited shone with a faint blueish glow. Peeking into room 301, I swallowed hard. Against the far wall, Kenzie lay in a white hospital bed surrounded by softly beeping machines. Her black hair was spread across her pillow, and her eyes were closed. A round table overflowing with flowers and get-well-soon balloons hovered next to her.

Guilt stabbed at me, raw and painful, but it was nearly smothered by the worried ache that spread through my chest when I saw her. The Kenzie I knew was never still—she was always bouncing from place to place, smiling and cheerful. To see her like this, pale, fragile and motionless, filled me with dread. Ducking into the room, I crossed the floor to her bedside, gripping the rails to stop myself from touching her. If she was asleep, I didn't want to wake her, but as I approached the bed, she stirred. Dark brown eyes cracked open blearily, confused as they focused on my face.

"Ethan?"

I forced a smile, even as I cringed at the sound of her voice, so faint and breathy. "Hey, you," I said, sounding a little faint myself. "Sorry I couldn't be here sooner. I didn't know you were in the hospital."

Her pale brow furrowed. "Oh, crap. M'fault. Phone was dead when I got back." Her words slurred together, either from exhaustion or whatever drugs they were giving her. "Was gonna call you when it charged, but I got sick."

"Don't worry about it." I dragged a chair from the corner and sat down next to her, reaching through the railing to take her hand. "Are you okay? Is it…?"

I trailed off, but Kenzie shook her head. "This is nothing. I just picked up some nasty virus or something while tromping around 'New York.' My immune system isn't that great, so…" She shrugged, but that didn't stop the guilt that continued to gnaw at me. Kenzie smiled weakly. "I should be out of here in a day or two, at least that's what the doctors say."

Relief swept through me. She would be all right. Kenzie would be home soon, and then we could get back to "normal," or whatever passed for it with me. I wanted to try for normal, give it my best shot at least, and I wanted to do it with her.

I reached out with my other hand and stroked her cheek, feeling her soft skin under my fingers. She closed her eyes, and I asked, "What did your dad say when you came back?"

Her brow furrowed, and she opened her eyes again. "He actually had the gall to be upset that I didn't call him. He said he had the police looking for me for days, and was angry that I never told him where I was. He never took an interest in my life before. Why bother now?"

"Maybe he was worried about you," I offered. "Maybe he realized he made a mistake."

She sniffed, unappeased. "I vanish for a few days and *now* he's interested in being a dad? After ignoring me for years and not caring about anything I did?" She wrinkled her nose, bitterness coloring her voice. "Too little too late, I'm afraid. I don't need him looking out for me."

I didn't answer. It would take a lot of talking, tears and forgiveness for Kenzie and her dad to settle their differences and start to heal old wounds, and I didn't want to be that mediator. Not with my own screwed-up family. As if reading my mind, Kenzie asked, "What did your parents say when you got back? Were they very mad?"

"No." I shrugged. "They...sort of had a visit from the Iron Queen before I got home. She talked to them, told them where I had been, that it wasn't my fault I disappeared."

"Have you talked to Keirran since New York? Or your sister?"

I shook my head, my mood darkening at the thought of Keirran and Meghan. "No. I don't think I'll see either of them for a while."

"I'm worried about him," Kenzie muttered, sounding as if she was fighting sleep. "Him and Annwyl both. Hope they're all right."

A nurse peeked into the room, saw me and frowned, tapping her wrist. I nodded, and she ducked out.

I stood, wishing I didn't have to leave so soon. "I have to go," I told her as she blinked sleepily up at me. Reaching down, I gently brushed the hair from her face. "I'll be back tomorrow, okay?"

Her eyes closed once more and didn't open this time. "Ethan?"

"Yeah?"

"Bring chocolate? The food here sucks."

I laughed quietly, bent down and kissed her. Just a brief, light touch of her lips to mine, and she sank back into the pillows. Already asleep. I watched her for another heartbeat, then turned and left the room, vowing to come back as soon as I could.

As I stepped into the hall, a shadow pushed itself off the wall and moved toward me, blocking my path. I blinked and stumbled to a halt as a tall, dark-haired man loomed over me, cold black eyes regarding me with suspicion. He wore a business suit that probably cost more than my truck, a large

Rolex on one wrist and an air of aggressive superiority. He didn't look distraught. In this corridor of rumpled, haggard-looking people, he was tall and clean shaven with not a hair out of place or a wrinkle in his clothes.

We stared at each other, and I narrowed my eyes. I didn't like the way this guy was looking at me, like I was a stray dog wandering around and he wasn't sure if he should call animal control. I was about to shove past him when his lips twitched into a cold, unamused smile, and he shook his head.

"So." The man's voice wasn't loud or even hostile. It was cool and pragmatic. "You're him, aren't you? The boy that took my very sick daughter away from her family, and her medicine, and her doctors, to go gallivanting up to New York for the week."

Oh, crap. You had to be kidding me. This was Kenzie's father. Kenzie's very rich, very powerful lawyer father. The father who, by Kenzie's own admission, had had the entire police force searching for his missing daughter all week.

I was in trouble.

I didn't answer, and Kenzie's dad continued to regard me without expression. His voice didn't change; it was still perfectly reasonable, though his eyes turned steely as he said, "Explain yourself, please. Tell me why I shouldn't press charges against you for kidnapping."

I swallowed the challenge on the tip of my tongue. The unfairness of it all burned my throat. He wasn't making idle threats. I'd dealt with my share of lawyers, though they were all public defenders, not the same caliber as Kenzie's dad. If he decided to press charges against me, there was little I could do. My word held no weight; if the cops did get involved, who would they believe—the rich lawyer or the teenage thug?

I took a deep breath to cool my anger so when I spoke I wouldn't sound like the delinquent brute he thought I was.

"Kenzie wanted to see New York," I began in the most reasonable voice I could manage. "She asked me to take her. It was a split-second decision and probably not the smartest thing we could have done, but…" I shrugged helplessly. "We should have talked to you about it first, and I'm sorry for that. But it's done now. And you can try to keep me away, have me arrested, whatever. But I'm not abandoning Kenzie."

He raised a skeptical eyebrow, and I wanted to kick myself. *Nice, Ethan. Keep antagonizing Mr. Big Shot lawyer; that's a great way to stay out of jail.* But he was still waiting calmly for me to go on, and the next words out of my mouth were the absolute truth. "I swear, I would never do anything to hurt her. I wouldn't have taken her anywhere if I'd known she'd end up here."

He regarded me with a practiced blank expression, giving no hint of what he was thinking. "Mackenzie speaks very highly of you," he said. "She told me that while you were in Central Park, you fought off a gang of thugs who tried to hurt her. She has never lied to me before, so I have no reason to doubt her words. But I think, in this case, I must ask you to stay away from my daughter."

I blinked, taken aback by his quiet bluntness, unsure of what I'd just heard. "What?"

"You are not to see Mackenzie anywhere outside of school," Mr. St. James continued, still in that cool, unruffled voice. "You are forbidden from calling her. You are not to speak to her if you can help it. If you come around our house, I will call the police. Do you understand, Mr. Chase?"

"You can't be serious." I was torn between laughing and wanting to slug this guy in the jaw. "You can't forbid me from seeing anyone. And good luck getting Kenzie to agree to anything like that."

"Yes," Kenzie's father agreed. "I know my daughter. And

I know I cannot control what she does. But I can make *your* life very unplesant, Mr. Chase. Which is why I am asking you, politely, to stay away from Mackenzie. I think we both know that you're no good for her. I think we both know that she ended up here—" he gestured back to Kenzie's doorway "—because of you."

That hit me like a punch to the gut. I stared at him, unable to find the words to defend myself or disagree. Kenzie's dad regarded me a second longer, then moved aside. "You should go now," he said, a hint of warning below the smooth tone. I glared at him, then shoved past. I was tempted to tell him to go screw himself, just to prove he couldn't order me around, but tempting fate right now seemed like a bad idea. There was nothing to be gained from it tonight.

"Think on what I said, Ethan Chase," St. James added as I stalked down the hallway, silently fuming. "I will protect my daughter at all costs. Do not think you can fight me on this. You will lose, and you will lose badly."

I continued to the parking lot without looking back. I saw the cop standing in the waiting room again, and he might've given me the evil eye as I ducked out. Maybe Kenzie's dad had said something to him before confronting me...I didn't know. I did know one thing—there was no way that A-hole would keep me from seeing Kenzie.

As I climbed into my truck and yanked the door shut behind me, my phone buzzed. Digging it out of my pocket, I checked the number and winced. Mom. Damn, I hadn't called to let her know where I was. Guiltily, I hit the answer button and braced myself for the explosion. "Hey, Mom."

"Where are you?" her frantic voice screeched in my ear. "I told you to call me if you were going to be late!"

"Um, yeah, sorry. I'm...uh, I'm at the hospital."

"What?"

"Visiting a friend," I added, mentally kicking myself. "I'm just visiting a friend."

A long, shaky sigh, the kind that hinted she was holding back tears. "Come home, Ethan. Right now."

"On my way," I answered softly, and she hung up.

I expected a lecture when I got home. Something along the lines of "It's only been three days since you vanished into Faeryland for a week, do you know how worried we were, you're supposed to call if you're going to be late."

You know, the normal issues.

However, when I walked through the front door, bracing myself for scolding or yelling or general parental displeasure, it wasn't Mom who rose from the living room couch to greet me.

It was Meghan.

CHAPTER THREE

THE IRON QUEEN'S WARNING

My stomach flip-flopped. My half sister, the queen of the Iron fey, was standing in my living room, looking as normal as any average, non-faery-related teenager. Almost. She wore her standard jeans and T-shirt, and her long, straight blond hair was pulled up behind her head. Only the slender, pointed ears gave her away; though the glamour concealed her true appearance, making her look perfectly human to mortals, my Sight always let me see through the disguise.

I cast a furtive glance around the room for other fey, well, for *one* faery in particular. For a long black coat and a glowing blue sword, silver eyes appraising and wary. Was he in my house, lurking in some dark corner? He'd never come inside before....

"He's not here," Meghan said quietly. Embarrassed, I flicked my attention back to her, finding her solemn blue eyes on me. She looked...tired. Worried. "I need to talk to you, Ethan," she said. "In private, if we could. I don't want Mom or Luke overhearing us, and there are some things that need...explaining."

"Yeah. There are."

I motioned her down the hall to my room, following her through the frame and closing the door behind us. Meghan perched on my bed while I dropped into my computer chair, facing her.

So many questions. So many secrets she had kept from me, from Mom, from everyone. Where should I even begin? I opted for the largest one.

"Keirran," I said, and she closed her eyes. "When were you going to tell us? Or were you hoping to keep him from us forever?" When she didn't answer right away, I nodded slowly, even though she couldn't see. "That's why you stopped coming around, isn't it?" I muttered. "You never wanted us to meet. You didn't want Keirran to know about his human family." My chest squeezed tight as I thought of all those years, waiting for my sister to come back, just to visit, and she never had. "Are you ashamed of us?"

"Ethan." She sighed, and the pain in her voice made me wish I had never opened my mouth. When she opened her eyes, I caught the sparkle of tears on her lashes and felt like a complete ass. "I'm sorry," Meghan whispered and took a deep breath, composing herself. "I'm sorry," she said again in a stronger voice. "No, I'm not ashamed of you, Ethan. I love you, and Mom, and Luke, more than anything. You'll always be my family, even if I can't be here."

"Then...why the big secret?" I had to swallow the lump in my throat to continue. I remembered, suddenly, Puck's look of concern when he'd seen Keirran and me together; Keirran's own words about secrets being kept from him by everyone. "It's not just you," I said, watching her reaction carefully. "There's something about Keirran that has everyone nervous. What's going on?"

"I...can't tell you."

Stung, I stared at her. Meghan paused, seeming to gather her thoughts, her face suddenly pinched and agonized. "I know I've failed you, Ethan," she said in a shaky voice. "I wanted to protect you from Faery, from everything. I wanted…" She swallowed hard, and her eyes glimmered. "I wanted you to know Keirran. I wanted Mom to meet her grandson, and it killed me that she might never know him."

Meghan sniffed, then composed herself once more. "You don't understand now," she said, "but there are reasons why I chose what I did, why I decided it was best that you and Keirran stay away from each other." She sighed again, but her voice was steady when she continued, "I am sorry, Ethan. I know how hard it's been. The last thing I wanted to do was hurt you and Mom, but I thought this was the best choice."

I wanted to be angry with her. For years I had blamed her for abandoning us, for putting her life as a fey queen before her own family. But…maybe she *couldn't* come back. Maybe it was just as hard for her to stay away. I didn't understand why she was still keeping me in the dark about Keirran, but there was something else going on here.

"Well, I guess Keirran and I sort of screwed that plan up, didn't we?" I said, wanting to ease some of the tension in the room. My attempt at a joke did not have the effect I wanted.

Meghan's brow furrowed. "From the moment you walked into the palace, I knew what was going to happen," she murmured, almost to herself. "I even sent someone to track Keirran down once you arrived, but he pulled one of his vanishing acts before we could find him. Then when I heard he'd helped you and Kenzie sneak out of the palace…" She shook her head. "He has no idea what this means, what it has started. Neither of you realize what could happen now. Ethan…" Her blue eyes met mine, angry and pleading all at once. "Where is he?" she asked. "Please, if you know where he is, tell him to come home."

I gave a start. "Who? Keirran? Why would I know where…" I stopped as the very obvious answer hit me in the face. "He's gone, isn't he?" I guessed. "That's why you're here. Keirran's run off again."

"He disappeared not long after you went home," Meghan replied, her face lined with worry. "No one has seen any sign of him since." She looked around the room, as if hoping to catch him hiding in the closet or something. "I was hoping… he might've come here."

I shook my head. "I haven't seen him." She stared at me, suspicious, and I raised my hands. "I swear, Meghan. I haven't seen him, or Annwyl, or anyone since New York. If Keirran is gone, he hasn't come to me."

In that instant, I wondered if I did know exactly where Keirran was and if I should voice that concern to Meghan. The Iron Prince, as he was called, was in love with a faery of the Summer Court, a love that was forbidden according to ancient faery law. Annwyl was a banished Summer fey who lived with the self-proclaimed Exile Queen, Leanansidhe, in the Between, the Veil between Faery and the real world.

When Annwyl had been kidnapped by the Forgotten, they'd used her to draw Keirran out, forcing him to appear before their queen. But when Kenzie and I had gone to rescue him, as well as Todd, Annwyl and a whole troop of half-breeds robbed of their glamour, Keirran had been shockingly sympathetic to the Forgotten and their cause. I didn't know exactly what had been said between the Iron Prince and the Forgotten Queen, but when we'd left, Keirran had made a promise to return to her, of his own free will, sometime in the future.

Could he be with the Forgotten Queen right now?

Meghan was still watching me, her gaze appraising, almost as if she could see my thoughts. "If he hasn't come to you," she asked slowly, deliberately, "do you know where he might be?"

I looked away. I didn't want to rat Keirran out. We might've had our disagreements in the past, but he was still family.

And after everything that had happened, I did consider him a friend. But Meghan was my sister, and this whole thing with Keirran and the Forgotten couldn't be kept a secret for long. Too much was at stake.

"Yeah," I rasped, still not looking at her. "I have an idea. When we were with the Forgotten, Keirran told their queen he'd come back to see her. He might be with the Forgotten right now."

I saw the change, the subtle shift from my familiar older sister to the immensely powerful Iron Queen, right there on my bed. She didn't move, but her energy filled the room, making the air crackle and the lights flicker.

I swallowed. "Hey, sis? I sort of need my computer not to explode, if that's okay."

Meghan blinked, and the power surging around her died down. "Of course," she murmured and rose off the bed. "Thank you for telling me about the Forgotten, Ethan," she said, back to being normal Meghan. "I know you and Keirran went through a lot, and you don't want to get him in trouble, but you did the right thing. I needed to know what he's capable of."

I felt pretty wretched. Meghan looked smaller now, less a faery queen and more a concerned parent, weighed down by worry, guilt and something much darker. "I have to get back to Mag Tuiredh," she said, walking to the door. "Ethan, if you do see Keirran, will you please tell him to come home? Let him know he isn't in trouble—we just want to talk to him. Whatever it is, whatever he's doing, we can work it out. He isn't alone in this. Will you promise me that much, at least?"

"If I see him," I said, "I'll let him know."

"And…don't tell Mom or Luke. Not yet." She ran a hand over her eyes. "They have to find out about him, but…I want to be the one to explain."

"I won't tell them."

She gave me a sad smile, and I followed her to the front door, where Mom was waiting for us both. Her face was red, her eyes swollen, though she still smiled and hugged Meghan tightly, reminding her that she was always welcome here, that this was always home. Even though we all knew it was not.

Outside, a horse and carriage waited, both invisible to mortal eyes. The horse was a bright copper beast of ticking clockwork, the driver a green-skinned faery in a top hat. He tipped the hat to us and smiled as Meghan pulled away from Mom and embraced me, pulling me close. "Take care of Mom," she whispered, as she always had back when she still visited us. I hugged her back and nodded.

"I will."

And then, as she had so many times before, she left. Glamour shimmered around the Iron Queen as she faded from human vision—though my Sight still allowed me to see her clearly—and walked to the invisible carriage waiting for her on the sidewalk. The driver leaped down, opened the door for the queen to enter and sprang back onto the seat. At the flick of a shiny wire whip, the carriage rolled off down the sidewalk and was quickly lost to the darkness.

I braced myself for the questions as we returned inside; Mom would certainly want to know what Meghan and I had discussed behind closed doors. But all she said was "I don't feel like cooking tonight, Ethan. Would you be all right with ordering pizza?"

"Sure," I said, wondering what Meghan had told her before I came in. She gave me a shaky smile and wandered upstairs, probably to her bedroom. Probably to lock herself in and cry for a little while before returning to act like everything was normal. Like her daughter wasn't an immortal faery queen who hadn't aged in thirteen years and her son wasn't a juvenile thug who attracted trouble at every turn.

I figured it was actually a good thing she didn't yet know that she also had a defiant part-fey grandson who could be anywhere at the moment.

I returned to my room, placed the pizza order online and gazed at the spot where my sister had been moments ago.

So, Keirran was out there now. The Iron Prince had run off again, and no one knew where he was. Not that I was surprised; even in the short time I'd known him, Keirran had never been one to follow the rules. Not that he was spiteful or malicious; my nephew didn't have a mean bone in his body and was unfailingly polite, amiable and soft-spoken. But he was also stubborn, rebellious and in love with a girl from the wrong court. He'd already demonstrated the lengths he would go to keep Annwyl safe; I wondered if she was the reason he had gone AWOL.

What are you doing, Keirran? I thought, trying to shake the ominous feeling creeping over me.

My phone chirped, indicating I had a text message. Curious, I grabbed it and clicked on the screen.

Brrwed nurse's phone, she thought u were cute (me 2). Dont reply just wanted 2 say thanks for coming in 2nite & they decided 2 release me tomorrow, yay! So don't come in cause I won't b here. Miss ya, tough guy. -Kenzie.

A second later, it was followed with:

P.S. Why do all hospitals think green Jell-O is food? *Gag*Dies*

I couldn't help the smile that spread across my face as I clicked the phone off and set it back on the desk. I couldn't worry about Keirran now. I had something else, someone else, to focus on. Kenzie deserved more than I could give her, but I wanted to try to do this boyfriend thing right, despite her father's warning to stay away from his daughter. Obviously, I wasn't going to listen to that, though he was more right than he knew when he said I was no good for her. To say I sucked in the relationship department was a huge understatement; I just hoped Kenzie could be patient with me as I figured it out. And that her dad wouldn't make things *too* unbearable.

And that, for once, *They* would leave us alone and not screw everything up.

Wishful thinking.

CHAPTER FOUR

THE LAST NORMAL EVENING

The next day at school was fairly uneventful. I parked close to the school building, right outside the principal's office window, to prevent further ambushes in the parking lot. I kept my head down in class, only engaging teachers if spoken to first. I ignored the constant whispers and looks thrown my way in the halls. The normal routine.

When lunch rolled around, I was heading to my favorite corner of solitude when my phone vibrated. Another text had come through.

Guess who has her phone back, the new message read. I grinned, hurried outside and called the number on the other end.

"I hope you're at lunch right now," Kenzie said by way of greeting, "and not cutting class just so you can call me."

"Actually, I'm taking a break between car heists," I replied, making her laugh. I smiled at the sound of her voice. "Where are you?"

"Home." She gave a little sigh. "Cleaning my in-box. Being bored. Wishing I was at school right now."

My gut churned. "Where's your dad?"

"Oh, don't worry." Her voice turned defiant. "He got roped into some important out-of-town meeting and won't be back until tomorrow." She snorted. "I can't believe him, telling me I had to stay away from you. Like that's going to happen."

Relief spread through me. "So, what do we do now?"

"Well…" She pondered that, then continued in a strangely hesitant voice. "As luck would have it, Alex has a volleyball game tonight, and my stepmom already promised she would go. No one will be home if you happen to drop by and pick me up. Let's say, sometime between five and six?"

Right. This was the whole boyfriend thing. Picking her up, taking her to dinner. Normal going-out stuff. So why was I suddenly terrified? "I'll pick you up at six," I heard myself say in a voice that sounded perfectly calm, a stark contrast to the twisted mess within. "Is there anyplace you want to go, a movie you want to see?" *Anything to give me a hint of what I'm supposed to do?*

I heard her bitter smile without seeing it. "Anywhere but here."

School the rest of the day was a lost cause. I couldn't concentrate in any of my classes, couldn't think of anything at all except the coming night. I wasn't so distracted that I didn't notice Brian Kingston glaring at me in the halls, however, his two cronies at his back. Thankfully, he didn't attempt a repeat of the day before. I felt a small, vindictive pleasure knowing I'd kicked his ass yesterday and gotten away with it, but it was never a good idea to tempt fate. At least now he knew that I couldn't be abused like some stray dog, but knowing him, the next time I would be facing the entire football team.

I went home, surfed around online, attempted to do my homework and drove myself crazy glancing at my watch every three minutes, cursing it to go faster. When evening rolled around, I showered, changed into my "nicer" clothes—non-ripped jeans and a shirt that didn't scream "I'm a thug"—and flopped onto the living room couch with the TV on to wait out the last few minutes.

"I'm going out," I announced when the clock finally hit five-thirty. Bouncing upright, I turned off the screen, not even remembering what I'd been watching. Mom wasn't in the room, and I raised my voice to shout down the hall. "I'll be back in a few hours. Don't wait up for me."

"Ethan," Mom called as I snatched my jacket from the back of the couch and headed for the door. Her face was suspicious as she came out of the kitchen, eyeing my clothes and the keys in my hand. "It's not karate night, and hospital visiting hours are long past. Where are you going?"

I stifled a sigh. "I have a date," I said simply.

Mom's eyebrows shot up. "A date?" she repeated, like she couldn't quite believe it.

"Yeah. With a real girl and everything."

I expected her to ask where we were going or to at least warn me to be careful. But unexpectedly, a smile broke across her face, almost like she was...relieved. Relieved that I was acting like a normal teen, maybe. Or that—and I cringed at this thought—I was finally "making friends." Whatever the reason, it was nice to see her happy with me for once, even though this wasn't quite as normal as she thought.

"Where did you meet her?" Mom asked excitedly, and I stifled a groan. "At your new school? Do you have classes together? What's her name?"

"Mom, I'm going to be late," I said, backing away. "I'm picking her up now. Back before eleven."

"Ethan."

Impatient, I turned in the door frame. *Now what?*

Mom still wore that faint, relieved smile. "Midnight," she said, shocking me. "Curfew is at midnight."

I blinked, astonished, but I wasn't going to question it. With a quick smile, I nodded and let the screen slam shut behind me.

Tonight was going to be normal, I told myself as I hopped into my truck. A normal evening with my girlfriend, no weirdness or craziness allowed. However, as I was pulling out of the driveway, I caught a hint of movement in my side-view mirror, a shadow moving through the trees behind my house. The silhouette of a tall, impossibly thin man paused in the space between trunks, glowing eyes fastened on me.

I stopped the truck, turning back to look, but there was nothing there anymore.

I muttered a curse. This was nothing new. I'd been seeing things move my whole life: silhouettes in the trees, shadows from the corners of my eyes, brief glimpses of things in mirrors, doorways and reflections. That was the world of the fey, and you either got used to it or you became a neurotic freak. I just wished they'd stop hanging around my house despite all the anti-fey charms I'd placed inside and around the property. And I *really* wished they would quit popping up at the worst possible times.

Whatever. I wasn't going to worry about the fey tonight. They couldn't get into the house, Mom wasn't going anywhere, and Dad wouldn't be home from work until early morning. Tonight, I had a date with Mackenzie St. James, and I wasn't going to miss it. The damned fey could just go bother someone else for once.

Putting my truck into Drive, I shoved all thoughts of invisible pests from my mind and roared off down the street.

I cruised through an older, well-kept neighborhood, massive trees towering over either side of the road, until I found the right address.

"Are you kidding me?" I stared up the circular driveway,

past the glowing fountain shooting plumes of water into the air, to the huge mansion at the top of the steps. I didn't know much about houses, but this thing looked like a Victorian-era castle, with stone columns and a round turret soaring above a perfectly landscaped yard. "Yeah, that's not intimidating at all."

I felt weird parking my old truck behind the silver Audi in the driveway, and even more uncomfortable walking up the lighted path to the double doors looming at the top of the steps. This place probably had a ton of security and cameras, all fixed on me right now. I wondered if a security guard would automatically call the cops if he saw me edging up the walk, a lurking shadow definitely out of place.

The huge doors had a brass lion-head knocker and a doorbell, but I chose to just rap on the polished wood. A great, booming bark echoed from inside, making me wince. I suddenly had a vision of myself tearing across the lawn, two snarling Rottweilers on my heels.

Without so much as a squeak, one of the doors swung open. And there was Kenzie, grinning up at me. She wore tight black jeans, a green sweater, and the neon blue streaks in her hair had returned, brighter than before. She was beautiful, smiling and not lying in a stark hospital bed, pale and fragile. My stomach untwisted, muscles relaxing, as suddenly everything was fine.

Then a massive shaggy head pushed its way past her leg and lunged at me, and I leaped back with a yelp.

"Oh, Tiny. No." Kenzie grabbed the thing's collar, dragging it back inside. "Bad dog. Sit! Stay."

The huge black animal panted and plopped into a sit. Kenzie turned back with a sheepish grin, raking bangs from her eyes. "Sorry 'bout that," she said, maneuvering around the dog to pull the door shut. "He doesn't bite. He's just over-friendly. Most he'll do is slobber on your pants. Newfies are good at that."

"Yeah?" Seeing her like this, bright and bouncy and back to normal, awakened something inside me. This was the Kenzie I knew, the girl who had gone into the Nevernever with me, who'd seen my screwed-up world for what it really was and hadn't left. I had the impulse to pull her into my arms and kiss her until we were both breathless, but I didn't want to do that here, on her doorstep, while any number of cameras could be pointed at us. I wondered if her dad would make good on his threats if he saw me later on the security footage.

"Ready to go?" I asked instead, and she nodded vigorously.

"God, yes. Get me out of here. Between my stepmom's hovering and Alex being extra clingy, I need the air."

We hurried down the driveway. I kept a close eye on the gate, half expecting Kenzie's father to pull in at any moment. For once, luck was on my side and the drive remained empty, though I still wanted to leave as fast as we could.

"Are you sure you're okay with this?" I asked as I slid into the driver's seat. "Not that I'm going to stop seeing you, but I'd really like to avoid going to jail if I can help it. And I don't want *you* to get into trouble with your dad, either."

"He won't do anything." Kenzie slammed the door with a little more force than was necessary, I thought. "Don't let his 'you must not see that hooligan' act fool you. It'll blow over soon. Really, he's just embarrassed that his faultless eldest daughter ran away. Now the image of our 'perfect family' is tarnished, and he's trying to save face with all that posturing. Trust me." She shook her head, looking out the side window. "He doesn't care what I do. Hasn't for a long time now."

I turned the key and didn't say anything. I recognized that anger, the veiled hurt in Kenzie's voice. Thinking that someone you loved had abandoned you, that they didn't care any-more… I knew that feeling all too well.

I took her to a nice restaurant, nothing fancy but not fast food, either, and we sat in a booth and ate and talked about normal, real-world things: school and teachers and classmates, deliberately keeping words like *faeries* and *the Nevernever* out of the conversation. I learned that there was a rumor about me circulating the school, that I had met Brian Kingston in the parking lot and kicked the ever-loving crap out of him. Great. That was going to do wonders for my record, not to mention my reputation. And knowing Kingston, he would take the rumor very personally and be looking to even the score. At least Kenzie seemed amused by it, stating that some of the girls now viewed me as *the* dangerous bad boy to tame. In fact, Chelsea had called her house earlier that day to ask if she would bring me to a party that weekend.

"So I 'beat up' the quarterback, and now people want to go out with me?" I asked in disbelief, watching Kenzie fin-ish the last of the chocolate brownie we'd split for dessert. "What is wrong with girls? *Tame* me? Like I'm some kind of wild horse?"

Kenzie giggled. "Must be that bad-boy allure," she said, putting down her spoon. "You know, they see you as a dan-gerous, broken mystery man. They want to be the one to fix you."

"Yeah, well. My problems are too big for anyone to 'fix.'" I handed the waitress a couple twenties when she dropped off the check. "And any one of those girls would run away scream-ing if they saw what I have to live with every day."

Kenzie nodded sympathetically, and I realized I'd strayed back into "un-normal" territory. Reaching across the table, I took her hands. "Besides, they'll be wasting their time," I said, running my thumb across her fingers. "I'm taken."

And apparently turning into a big sap. But I didn't care. Kenzie's brilliant smile made it all worth it.

We went to the movies, and I sat with Kenzie in the back row, feeling her head on my shoulder and trying desperately to behave myself. I wasn't a prude; I knew what the back-row theater seats were for, but this was also our very first date. Not only that, this was my very first date with someone I actually wanted to be with; I did not want to push too far and screw everything up.

So I forced myself to be content with my arm around her shoulders and her slender hand on my knee, even though it was driving me crazy. When the credits rolled, it was all I could do to stand up and follow the rest of the crowd out of the theater.

In the parking lot, I couldn't take it anymore. When Kenzie walked to her side of the truck, I snagged her around the waist, pulling her against me. She didn't resist, allowing herself to be drawn close, pressing her body to mine. Leaning against the hood, I tangled my fingers in her silky hair, and her arms looped around my neck as she gazed up at me. My heart pounded. I was still finding it hard to believe that this beautiful girl was mine. What could I offer her, really? Tonight was the most normal evening I'd had in a long time, but it couldn't last forever. Sooner or later, They would find me again.

"You look worried, tough guy." Her fingertips brushed the nape of my neck, making me shiver. "You've gone all frowny and serious. What's up? Are you regretting this already?"

I blinked and unfurrowed my brow, gazing down at her. "No," I said, easing the concern in her eyes. "Honestly, if anyone should regret this, it's you." She tilted her head in confusion, and I sighed. "You know that normal isn't…normal for me, right?"

Kenzie grinned. "I'm counting on it."

"Mackenzie, I'm serious."

"I know."

"This isn't a game. As long as you hang around me, your life is going to be really screwed up."

Her cool fingers touched my lips, silencing me. "Do you trust me, Ethan?"

More than anyone. "Yes."

"Then believe that I want to be here, with you. Not because of Them, not because I have the Sight or because I'm sick or anything like that. I'm here because…" She faltered, and I held my breath. "Because you make me feel like nothing in my life is wrong. Because you treat me like a real person, and I need that right now."

I swallowed. "Is that the only reason?"

She colored slightly, but her lips quirked up. "Oh, fine. And because you're pretty cute, too."

Well, what had I been expecting? This was still really new, for both of us. "Cute?" I narrowed my eyes. "Kittens are cute. Baby goats are cute. I'm the dangerous wild beast that needs to be tamed, remember?"

"Good thing I'm up to the challenge, then." Kenzie didn't miss a beat. "I knew those dog-training classes would come in handy for something."

I chuckled, shaking my head in defeat, and pulled her closer. "Kiss me," I told her. And she did, raising herself up on tiptoe to brush her lips to mine. I closed my eyes, forgetting the fey, the Sight, the Nevernever, everything about Them for the moment, and lost myself in her.

"Oh, my God!"

Kenzie pulled back, and we both turned our heads toward the shrill, shocked voice. A group of teenagers stood a few yards away, gaping at us over the pavement. I recognized Kenzie's blonde friend, Regan, another cheerleader whose name escaped me and the Football Gorilla King himself, Brian Kingston. Who looked like he was about to burst a blood vessel. If he'd hated me before, he was homicidal now. Our little scuffle in the parking lot hadn't cooled him off any; he was ready for round two. Another broad-shouldered jock type stood in the crowd behind him, but I'd never seen him before. Still, if Kingston decided to take me out here and now, he would gladly join in.

Hell with it.

I smirked and kept my arms firmly around Kenzie's waist. Kenzie, it seemed, didn't have any intention of moving, either. "Hey," she said, smiling at the group of stunned teens, her arm draped casually around my neck. "What are you guys up to?"

"Kenzie," the other cheerleader stammered, her eyes wide and blinking. "I heard you were out of the hospital, but…" Her gaze flicked to me and away again just as fast, like she was afraid of letting it linger. "You're…with *him* now?"

Kenzie shrugged. "Looks that way."

"The dick that dragged you up to New York without telling anyone about it?" Kingston added, taking a threatening step forward. I tensed as he moved closer, bolstered by his friend and the wide-eyed cheerleader audience. "The piece of shit that put you in the hospital?"

"Hey!" Kenzie turned and stepped out of my arms to face the quarterback, blocking his path to me. He blinked and stumbled to a halt as she glared up at him. "Back off, Brian. This is my decision. And you'd better not give him a hard time at school, or I'm going to be very pissed at you."

Kingston stared at me over her head, his lips curled in a

sneer. "So, you gonna hide behind the girl from now on, freak? Let her fight your battles for you?"

I pushed myself off the hood, making the quarterback stiffen. Anger made my lungs burn, and I breathed slowly to cool off. Kingston stood tall, chest puffed out, daring me to step forward. Knocking his ass to the ground wasn't enough, it seemed. He wanted a real fight, with fists and blows and broken jaws, and I was about ready to oblige him. Let him know that this dangerous reputation of mine wasn't just lip service. I'd taken kali for years. I'd fought things a thousand times nastier than him and his thugs.

I'd *killed* before. Taken my sword and driven it through a faery's chest, watched it writhe away into nothingness. Not the same as killing a human, but I had taken another creature's life, and that sort of thing changes you forever.

It would be so easy; we weren't at school this time, the parking lot was dark and mostly deserted. No one would stop me if I shoved Brian Kingston's face into the pavement and stomped on it. Maybe then he'd finally leave me alone.

But that would just be another black mark on my record. If I put Kingston in the hospital, I could be expelled. My parents would be unhappy, my kali instructor would be unhappy... and Kenzie would be unhappy. And at this moment, her opinion meant more to me than showing some jock the business end of my fists.

"Let's get out of here," I told her instead.

She glared at Brian a moment longer, then nodded. "Yeah," she agreed, backing away. "It's gotten a little stupid here for my taste."

He gave her a wounded look as she walked toward the passenger side of my truck. "Mac, come on. I'm just looking out for you. You can't be serious about this loser."

She slammed the door and rolled down the window as I slid

into the driver's seat. "It's none of your business, Brian," she said as I turned the key and the truck growled to life.

"He's just using you, Mac! You know that, right?"

She glared fiercely as we cruised past. The girls still stared at us wide-eyed, but the quarterback followed the truck for a few steps, and Kenzie poked her head out the window. "Yeah, well, at least he doesn't call me Mac when I ask him not to!" she snapped in return and rolled up the window, ignoring his protests. I stomped on the pedal and squealed out of the parking lot, leaving him standing in a cloud of black smoke and exhaust.

My hands were shaking. I gripped the steering wheel and glared at the road, trying to calm down. I was aware of Kenzie watching me, and humiliation flared up to join the anger. I should've said something, anything. I should've stood up for myself, or at least for my girlfriend. Instead, I'd let the football jock talk to Kenzie like he had and walked away like a wimp.

"You did good, tough guy," Kenzie said softly, surprising me. I glanced at her, and she offered a wry grin. "Don't worry, I know that you're a badass. You don't have to prove anything to me. I do realize you could've punched the teeth out of Brian's stupid head if you wanted to. If he saw even half the things we have, he would pee his pants."

The knot of fury loosened a bit, and I gave her a half smile. "You know they're going to talk about us," I said as her warm hand came to rest on my knee. "This will be all over school tomorrow."

"Let them talk." Kenzie shrugged. "It's not like my life isn't under constant scrutiny as it is." She snorted and gazed out the window, her face darkening. "Everyone thinks they know what's best for me," she muttered. "I wish they'd just let me live my life."

A lump settled in my stomach. I swallowed the last of my

anger and checked my watch. "It's still fairly early," I said, determined to salvage the rest of the evening. "Is there anywhere you want to go?"

"Um, actually…" Kenzie gave me a sideways look, suddenly shy. "I was wondering if we could go to your place for a while."

"My place?" My stomach twisted at the thought of her in my room, but I tried to sound casual. "I guess. It's nothing special, and my mom will be home."

"That's fine." Her fingers drummed my knee. "I just don't want to go home yet, and I'd like to see where you live, if that's okay."

I eyed her warily. We'd pretty much avoided talking about the un-normal parts of my life until now, but Kenzie and I were far from normal, and bringing her into my home would only prove it. "You might see a few of Them hanging around the yard," I warned her, not liking the way her eyes lit up. "There are a couple piskies who come by every so often, and a brownie shows up occasionally, hoping I'll let him into the house. They're not dangerous, but it's better if you don't acknowledge them. Don't give them any attention, or they'll just keep pestering you for more." I paused, running through the list of wards in and around my property, wondering if this was a good idea after all. "Also, if you see something weird, like a bunch of plants tied together in the tree or a line of salt across the windows, don't touch it. They're protective charms to keep out unwanted guests. And don't say anything about Them to my mom. She knows about the fey, but she can't see them like me." I exhaled, gazing out the windshield. "And really, she'd rather pretend they don't exist."

Kenzie nodded, looking sympathetic. "I won't say anything," she promised. "And I won't move any of your anti-faery charms around unless you tell me to. Anything else?"

"One more thing," I said, thinking that I'd probably put the news off long enough. I really didn't want to bring it up, but Keirran was her friend, too, and she deserved to know what had happened to him. "It's about Keirran."

"Keirran?" Her eyes went wide. "Is he all right?"

"Far as I know. But he's missing. Meghan came by last night and said he went AWOL not long after we went home. No one knows where he is."

Kenzie looked grave. "Do you think he's with…her?"

The Forgotten Queen. I shrugged. "I hope not."

She was quiet until we reached the familiar streets of my neighborhood. There were no faeries on the sidewalk in front of my house or hanging in the trees next door. I saw Kenzie looking for them, scanning the trees and branches and the dark shadows of the yard for invisible fey, but she was disappointed. I was relieved. I remembered the fey I'd seen earlier, that brief glimpse of something tall and thin lurking around the yard. Call me paranoid, but that was no harmless piskie. Whatever it was, I did not want to run into it again.

Mom was on the couch watching television when we came in, probably waiting up for me, and seemed completely charmed when I introduced her to Kenzie. Of course, I couldn't imagine any parent not liking Kenzie; she was cute, perky, intelligent and knew how to handle herself around adults. I was the one they'd worry about: the brooding thug, the dangerous hooligan. All I needed was a motorcycle and a cigarette hanging from my mouth to be the Every Parent's Worst Nightmare poster child.

I finally managed to get Kenzie away from Mom's relentless questions, blaming Kenzie's nonexistent curfew, and steered her out of the kitchen and down the hall to my room. "Sorry about that," I muttered once we were in the clear. "This is the first time I've brought someone home. I think Mom was testing to see if you were, in fact, a real person."

"It's okay." Kenzie smiled. "At least your parents actually take an interest in what you do. And your mom seems nice." She stopped at the end of the hall, in front of a plain white door with a nail poking out near the top. "So…this is your room?"

I narrowed my eyes. "Yeah," I muttered, because everything was not how I'd left it. There was supposed to be a twist of Saint-John's-wort hanging on the nail, a final deterrent for faeries wanting into my room. The nail was empty, and both my parents knew better than to take it down. Something else had removed it.

I took Kenzie's wrist, gently pulling her behind me. "Stay back," I warned. "Something's tampered with my door, and it might be in there right now." I wished I had the swords my kali master had given me, the twin short blades I'd used in my last battle with the Forgotten, the ones crafted especially for my hands. But they were stowed away in their case under my bed. Even my wooden practice sticks were on the other side of the door. I'd have to go in weaponless, unless I wanted to grab a knife from the kitchen, which I did *not* want to do with Mom still out there. Fortunately, I could handle myself pretty well empty-handed, too.

Keeping myself between Kenzie and the entrance, I slowly turned the knob until it clicked, then flung the door back.

There was a girl sitting on my bed. A lithe, beautiful girl in a green-and-white dress, long chestnut hair tumbling down her back. The tips of her slender, pointed ears peeked up through the shining waves, and her large moss-green eyes regarded me solemnly.

"Annwyl," I breathed as Kenzie quickly stepped through the door and closed it behind us. Seeing the Summer faery caused a flood of apprehension to surge up with a vengeance. There was only one reason she could be here, one reason she would come. "What are you doing here? What's happened to Keirran?"

CHAPTER FIVE
THE VANISHED PRINCE

At the mention of Keirran's name, Annwyl shivered. I breathed deeply and tried not to let my prejudice of all things fey cloud my reasoning. Annwyl didn't deserve that. Still, sitting in my room, on my bed in the mortal world, the Summer girl was even more obviously fey. Her dress, made of leaves, petals and wispy cloth, left her shoulders and arms bare, and her skin gave off a faint glow as if sunlit, even though it was the middle of the night. Light and warmth seemed to pulse around her, and my room smelled of cut grass and leaves. I also noticed that vines were crawling up my bedposts from the carpet, coiling around the frame like it was a tree. A huge orange moth fluttered by my head, alighting at the top of the post, and I waved a hand to shoo it away.

"Annwyl," Kenzie said, stepping around me. "What's going on? Are you hurt?"

"No," Annwyl replied, looking up at us. "I'm…well, I'm not *fine,* but this isn't about me." She brushed back her hair and sighed. "I apologize, Ethan, Kenzie. I know this is unexpected, and I didn't mean to barge in. But I couldn't think of anywhere else to go. It's…about Keirran."

A chill ran through me. "What's happened to Keirran?"

"I don't know," the Summer girl whispered. She looked

tired, worried and frightened. "I haven't seen him. Not since…
that night."

"How did you even get in here?" I asked, frowning. "The
whole house is warded, not to mention all the deterrents outside. Not that I was trying to keep *you* out, but I make pretty
sure no fey can get in unless I want them to."

Annwyl fidgeted, nervously brushing back her hair. "The
protective charms and wards around your house are quite
good, but they are also very old. I've seen them before, back
when my sisters and I still accompanied the Summer Queen
to the mortal realm. Lady Titania was very good at finding
loopholes in the protective wards. I learned from her."

Well, damn. I was going to have to find some new anti-
fey charms. Something that would deter even the sidhe of the
Summer and Winter courts. Less plants and more iron, maybe.
It made me think, though. Should I be concerned about
Annwyl? She was so unassuming and quiet, easy to overlook.
But she was an ageless Summer sidhe, just like Titania and
the most infamous faery of the Seelie Court, Robin Goodfellow. I knew that if Puck wanted to get into a house, no anti-
faery charm in the world would stop him short of building
the whole place out of iron. And even then, he'd probably
find a way. Annwyl might not be on that same level, but the
fact that she'd gotten around my wards and into my room was
proof that she was more than she appeared.

"I am sorry, Ethan Chase," Annwyl went on, perhaps sensing my unease. "I did not mean to alarm you. I would have
waited for you outside, but—" she shivered "—the Thin Man
was coming, and I had to get somewhere safe."

I jerked up. Annwyl saw my reaction and wrapped her
arms around herself, looking frightened. "I don't know what
he wants, or even what he is," she said. "I think he might
be a Forgotten, but this isn't the first time I've seen him. He

was waiting for me at the trod to Leanansidhe's when I went to find you. I would have come sooner, but when I left the Between, the Thin Man came after me, so I ran back to Leanansidhe's mansion and used another trod to the mortal realm. Perhaps he is also looking for Keirran and hoped I would lead him to the Iron Prince." She frowned and lowered her arms, her voice taking on a faint edge. "He would be disappointed."

Everyone was looking for Keirran, it seemed. And now I had another faery nuisance hanging around my home, waiting for Annwyl. Great. "So, you don't know where he is, either," I said. She shook her head.

"No. But he sent me this." She held out a roll of paper, tied with a blue ribbon. Her hand trembled as I took it and unrolled the note, which was handwritten in neat, simple black lines.

Annwyl,

Forgive me for not giving this news to you in person. But my parents know about us now, and Leanansidhe's mansion would be the first place they would look. If the rulers of Mag Tuiredh come to you asking about me, it's better that you don't know where I am. That would be best for everyone.

I don't care what the courts say; I cannot stand by and watch you Fade from existence, knowing what I do now. One way or another, I will stop this. If I have to search the world over, I won't stop until I find something to keep you here. The price doesn't matter; I'll do whatever it takes. I think you know by now that I love you, and even if we can't be together, I will accept that, if I know you're alive and well. It will kill me, but I can let you go if I know that you're out there somewhere, living, dancing, smiling your beautiful smile.

You're always in my thoughts, Annwyl. Please try to endure until I return.

Your prince,

—Keirran

I lowered the note, handing it to Kenzie, and looked at Annwyl in alarm. "What's Keirran up to?" I asked, studying the faery on my bed. She looked down as tiny yellow flowers began unfurling from the vines coiled around my bedposts. "What's going on, Annwyl?"

"I didn't want him to go," Annwyl said, closing her eyes. "I don't want him making deals, putting himself in danger, for me. It's too late. There's nothing he can do, now that it's started."

"*What* has started?"

Annwyl took a deep breath and opened her eyes to look at me. "I'm Fading, Ethan Chase," she said. "Whatever the Forgotten did to me when I was with them, I think it accelerated the process. I can't remember...a lot of things now." She gestured to the vines on my bed, startling the moth into taking flight. "I can't control this anymore. I'm honestly not trying to turn your room into a forest." Shivering, she closed her eyes. "But worst of all, sometimes I'll blank out, and when I come to, hours will have passed and I can't remember anything. Like I'm not there anymore."

Kenzie looked horrified. "You're dying?" she whispered, but Annwyl shook her head.

"Faeries don't really die," she answered. "We can be killed, but our 'death' is more of a vanishing from existence. Nothing is left behind. For exiles cut off from the Nevernever, we just...fade away."

"And there's nothing you can do?" Kenzie asked.

Annwyl shook her head. "The Between normally slows the

process a great deal, that's why it's a haven for exiles, but it's not working for me anymore. Once the Fade starts, nothing can stop it, except returning to the Nevernever. And that's not an option. Titania herself would have to lift my banishment, and we all know how likely that is."

"So Keirran is trying to find a way to stop it," I mused, and Annwyl nodded. Well, at least we knew what he was doing, even if we didn't know where he was. "But why come here?" I asked. "What do you want me to do?"

"I don't know." The Summer faery covered her face; she seemed on the verge of tears. "I've just...I've tried everything else. Everyone else. I even tried to contact Grimalkin, but he's vanished, too. Or he's not answering me."

"What about Leanansidhe? She has a whole network of minions. If anyone could find him, she could."

"She's been trying. After a visit from the Prince Consort of Mag Tuiredh, she's had her people out looking for him, too, but no one can track him down."

The Prince Consort of Mag Tuiredh meant Ash. Both Ash and Meghan were out looking for Keirran, and they probably had others scouring the Nevernever for him, too. After I told Meghan about Keirran's promise to the Forgotten Queen, it wasn't surprising.

Annwyl swallowed, giving me a pleading look. "Please, Ethan Chase. I'm desperate. You're his friend—I thought you could help. Or at least have an idea of where to find him."

I raked a hand through my hair. "I haven't seen him," I told her. "Meghan showed up last night with the same question, but he hasn't come to me. I have no idea where Keirran could have gotten to or who he's hanging out with." A thought crept into my head, turning my insides cold. "Annwyl, has Leanansidhe lost any more exiles? Has she been keeping track of what the Forgotten are doing?"

"She has." The faery's eyes glittered. "There haven't been any more disappearances, at least not on that scale. The Forgotten are lying low, it seems. And as far as we can tell, Keirran isn't with them."

"Are you sure?"

"Yes." The Summer faery gave a firm nod. "Leanansidhe is keeping a close eye out. There have been glimpses of the Forgotten from time to time, but Keirran is never with them." Annwyl hesitated, picking at my bedspread. "Apparently, Keirran is on the move and never in the same spot for any length of time. There have been rumors of where he's *been,* but by the time anyone gets there, he's long gone."

I relaxed. So, at least he hadn't gone back to the Forgotten Queen just yet. But if that wasn't the case, where the hell was he? What was he doing?

Kenzie hopped onto my bed, sitting beside the Summer faery like that was a perfectly normal thing to do. "Is there anything you know of that can stop this?" she asked gently. "What Keirran might be looking for?"

"No." Annwyl shook her head. "There's nothing. Glamour slows it down. Iron and technology speed it up. That's how it's always been. We've tried to find a way to cure it—exiles and banished fey have struggled against the Fade for centuries. But the only way to stop it completely is to return to the Nevernever."

I took the note from where Kenzie had put it on my desk, scanning it again, searching for any hint of where my hardheaded nephew could be. "The letter says something about 'price,'" I muttered. "That probably means he's looking to either buy something or make some kind of deal." Never a good idea in Faery.

I crossed to my desk and sank down into the chair, thinking. "All right," I muttered, leaning back, "where is he going?

What is he looking for?" I glanced at Annwyl again. "You said he's been seen before he disappears. Where?"

"All over the place," Annwyl replied. "Cairo, New York, the goblin market in Dublin—"

I sat up straighter in the chair. The girls blinked at me as I reached into my desk drawer and pulled out a leather journal, faded and worn with use.

"What is that?" Kenzie wanted to know.

"Research," I muttered, flipping to a certain page with the words *Known market locations* scrawled across the top. Several places had been jotted down in messy rows, rumors and locations I'd picked up over the years. I'd written them down for the sole purpose of knowing when and how to avoid them. "Everything I've learned or have discovered about the fey. Including goblin markets."

"What's a goblin market?" Kenzie asked.

"A place where the fey come together to deal, sell and make bargains," Annwyl replied. "You can find almost anything there, if you know where to look."

"So, a faery black market."

"Pretty much," I said. "They're all over the place, and they sell almost anything for the right price. If I were trying to find something without being asked too many questions, that's where I would go."

"So, we need to find a goblin market?"

"It's not that easy," I told her, still scanning the list. "You can't just walk into one. Most goblin markets move around or are only in a particular spot at a particular time. Even if Keirran is hitting the goblin markets, I don't know where to find..." I trailed off as my gaze rested on one of the market locations. Dammit. Of course this would happen now, just when my life was starting to be normal.

Kenzie frowned. "What is it?"

I sat back in the chair. "New Orleans," I muttered, glaring at the journal, as if it was the cause of my headaches. "One of the biggest goblin markets in the country comes to New Orleans every month, on the night of the full moon."

I felt Annwyl's gaze on me. "Do you think he'll be there?"

"I don't know, Annwyl." I rubbed at my eyes, frustrated. "We could be grasping at straws. All I know is, if Keirran wants to find something expressly forbidden or dangerous, the goblin markets are as good a place as any. No one asks questions, and no one cares who you are."

"The first full moon," Kenzie mused, then jerked upright on the bed. "That's this weekend! That means we only have three days to figure out how we're getting up there without our parents blowing a gasket."

"Whoa, wait a second." I stood quickly, holding up my hands. "Who said we're going anywhere?"

"Ethan." She gave me an exasperated look. "Keirran is my friend and your sister's son. Annwyl came to us for help. Are you really going to stand there and tell me you're not going to do anything?"

"Kenzie…" I paused. If I agreed to this, I would be plunging right back into that world I hated. Chasing down my half-fey nephew, searching for him at a goblin market, lying to my parents again; I didn't want more faery drama. And I didn't want to drag Kenzie into more dangerous situations, not with everything she'd already been through. And not when I was on such thin ice with her father.

But she was right. Keirran was out there. And even though he was part fey, stubborn, infuriating and probably going to get me in a lot of trouble, he was family. More than family, more than my nephew and Meghan's son; he was a friend.

And Annwyl was in danger now, too. The Summer girl might've been part of the Seelie Court, but I didn't want to see her Fade away to nothing. She'd risked a lot by coming here and obviously cared for the Iron Prince as much as he did her. If she disappeared, I didn't know what Keirran would do, but it would probably be fairly drastic.

Her green eyes watched me now, beseeching, and I raked both hands through my hair. "I'll think of something," I told them both, seeing Kenzie smile at me and Annwyl sag with relief. "Right now, though, I need to take Kenzie home. Annwyl, you're welcome to stay here if you like. I can get the sleeping bag down if you need a place to sleep." Though I'd never thought I'd offer to let a faery stay in my room. Again. The last time it'd happened, Todd, the half phouka, and his piskie friend had spent the night, and I hadn't gotten a wink of sleep.

Annwyl nodded solemnly. "I am...grateful, Ethan Chase," Annwyl said. "I would not have come if I did not think you could help."

I nodded, knowing that was the closest the fey got to saying thank-you, as they never spoke the actual words. Leaving the house, I told Mom I was taking Kenzie home, and we walked down the driveway in silence, me scanning the bushes and shadows for this mysterious Thin Man. If he was anywhere nearby, I didn't see him.

I unlocked and opened the truck door for Kenzie, but instead of climbing in, she stepped close and put her arms around me. "Well," she said as mine slipped around her waist, "here we go again."

I sighed, knowing it was useless to argue or try to convince her not to go. Tonight, anyway. "You are way too eager for this," I told her, and she grinned cheekily. "It would be so much easier if you were one of those girls who ran away screaming."

She laughed. "Sorry, tough guy. Looks like you got the abnormal girlfriend who talks to little green men and sees invisible things." Her cool fingers slipped into my hair, and my stomach knotted. "But you know you can vent to me about any of this, right? You don't have to face them all by yourself anymore."

My voice came out kind of husky. "I know. I just… I want you to be safe."

Her smile turned bittersweet. "I don't have that kind of time."

The porch light winked on, Mom's way of letting me know she was still up, and I winced. "Come on," I said, reluctantly drawing back. "I'll take you home."

After dropping Kenzie off at her house—and the stomach-curling good-night kiss in the driveway—I returned home to find Annwyl in the living room, hovering over my mom's potted plants. The wilted houseplants looked better than they ever had under Mom's not-so-green thumb, but having a faery wandering around my home made me nervous, even if it was Annwyl, and I steered her back into my room.

"Where would you like me to sleep?" she asked as I closed the door. Mom had finally gone to bed, but Dad might be home any minute and didn't need to hear me talking to myself in the wee hours of the morning. Annwyl regarded me solemnly. "If you have charms placed around your house, I could go outside. I don't think the Thin Man will come through the wards."

But she sounded frightened, and I shook my head. "No, Annwyl, I'm not going to make you sleep *outside,* especially if something is after you." I scrubbed a hand through my hair, not liking the other alternative but seeing no other choice. "You can stay here. Take the bed, in fact—I have a sleeping bag in the closet."

Her eyes widened. "Oh no, that would be improper," she protested, looking stunned. "Especially since I owe you so much. You are the Iron Queen's brother. I cannot presume to sleep in the prince's bed."

"Annwyl, you're not a servant anymore." I opened the closet and hauled the sleeping bag and pillow from the top shelf. "That changed the second Titania banished you from the Nevernever. And I'm *definitely* not a prince." I turned, tossing the sleeping bag on the floor, unrolling it with my foot. "You're not with Titania or Leanansidhe now. You're a guest here, and you don't owe me anything."

She gazed at me, still unsure, and my heartbeat picked up. I won't lie; Annwyl was beautiful. Big green eyes, shining brown hair, her body soft and graceful beneath her dress. I was a guy, after all, and I wasn't blind. But seeing her didn't make my stomach twist with nerves or the corners of my mouth want to turn up in a smile like they did with Kenzie. Besides, Annwyl was someone else's, someone whose insane protective streak ran even deeper than mine, and she was a *faery* on top of that. So that pretty much killed any tempting thoughts about having a beautiful girl spend the night in my room.

"Take the bed," I told her again, pointing to the mattress. "I know this is a little awkward, but we'll have to get through it until we can find Keirran. Hopefully it won't be too long."

After the Summer faery finally fell asleep on my mattress, I lay awake on the floor, thinking. About Keirran and his whereabouts, what he thought he was doing: hiding from everyone, dragging me into his problems. About Annwyl. She was Fading, dying, really, and the Iron Prince had to be frantic to save her, if there was a way at all. How the hell I would convince my parents that I needed to disappear again.

But mostly, I thought about Mackenzie and how I was going to protect her from the world she insisted on being a part of.

CHAPTER SIX
GURO'S ADVICE

School the next day was…interesting, to say the least.

Word had definitely spread, probably from the moment Kenzie and I had left the theater parking lot. People stared at me in the halls—not that they hadn't before, but it was almost full-blown paparazzi-style now. Whispers and unsubtle glances followed me down the corridors, and I was sure I saw one or two camera phones aimed at me—or it could've been my paranoid imagination. I kept my head down and my usual ignore-everyone stance going until I reached my locker. Only to discover two girls were already there, and none of them was Kenzie.

"Hey, Ethan." The tallest of the pair gave me a hesitant smile, flipping her blond hair over one shoulder. I'd seen this girl in class, though I'd never spoken to her and knew only that she was one of Kenzie's friends. Christy? Chelsea? Something like that.

"Can I help you?" I asked, reaching past her to open my locker.

"Um, well. I…we…wanted to know if you would sit with us this afternoon. We never see you at lunch, and now that you're with Kenzie, the four of us should hang out sometime."

"No, thanks."

A pause, where the duo eyed each other nervously but didn't back off. "Why not?" Christy/Chelsea demanded. "Kenzie always sits at our table. Aren't you going to eat with your girlfriend?"

Well, the short answer was getting me nowhere. Clearly, I was going to have to step my Mean Asshole persona up a bit.

I slammed the locker door, making them both jump, and turned to stare them down. "What part of 'no' don't you understand?" I said, forcing my voice to be hard and cold.

The girls shrank back and would've fled, but a soft hand suddenly traced my back, and Kenzie stepped around me to smile at them.

"Hey, guys." If she felt the obvious tension between me and the other two girls, she didn't comment on it. "I need to talk to Ethan for a second. Wait for me?"

The girls nodded and backed off, giving me dark, unfriendly looks, before hurrying around a corner. I swallowed and turned to face Kenzie, who was watching me with amused exasperation.

"Are you terrorizing my friends, tough guy?"

"They were stalking *me*," I answered, gesturing in the direction the girls had gone. "What do you want me to do?"

My girlfriend shook her head. "You could try being *nice*," she suggested. "I know it's in there somewhere. I've seen it, at least twice."

I lowered my voice, stepping close to her so that the passing crowd couldn't eavesdrop. "You know that's not an option for me. I have to be this way."

"No, you don't." Kenzie's voice was equally low; she reached out and took my hand, squeezing gently. "You can't push the whole world away because of Them, Ethan. That's... that's kind of like letting Them win, you know?" I started to protest, but she overrode me. "They're out there, and They hurt people—I understand that. But are you really going to close your eyes and hope They don't see you? Or are you going to fight back? Let them know that They can't screw around with you or your friends and get away with it."

"It's not that simple."

"No?" Kenzie cocked her head, her brown eyes staring into mine. "It sounds pretty simple to me. They can control your life—what you do, how you act—or you can."

I blinked. I'd never thought of it that way. I thought I was protecting people; if no one got close to me, the fey would leave them alone. But…I guess They were controlling my life in a way. I was so concerned about what They would do to others, I'd let myself become someone I hated. Someone I really didn't want to be.

"Fine." I put my head back in defeat before looking down at Kenzie again. "I'll try to be nicer to your friends. No promises, though. Especially if Kingston decides to put my head through my locker. Then all bets are off."

She grinned as the first bell rang. "You're such a charmer, tough guy. Wanna walk me to my class?"

"Sure."

"Without snarling at Zoe and Chelsea?"

I rolled my eyes. "I'll try not to snarl."

Her friends gaped at us when we found them around the corner, still waiting for Kenzie and probably hoping for gossip. They continued to glance at me as we walked down the hall, and even more so when Kenzie casually laced our fingers together, squeezing my hand while still chatting to all of us. I didn't say much, though I did make an effort not to be gruff when one of the girls asked me a question about New York. It was a weird sensation; it had been years since I'd been in any kind of group, a long while since I'd spoken to a classmate without intending to drive them away. I ignored the stares we were getting from everyone and concentrated on getting Kenzie to class. This whole normal boyfriend thing was going to take some getting used to.

When we got to her classroom, Kenzie turned to me, waving the others through. Stepping close, she murmured, "Meet me in the library at lunch. I want to talk to you about something."

I grinned at her, feeling suddenly evil. Everyone in school knew about me and Kenzie, it seemed. No use fighting it now. "Talk?" I leaned in. "Or *talk?* As in, the very back corner aisle?"

"Behave, you." She wrinkled her nose at me. "Let's not *try* to start more gossip. See you at lunch."

I let her go and sneaked a glance at the wall clock before continuing to my class. Four hours till lunch suddenly seemed like a lifetime.

Wonder of wonders, Kingston actually left me alone, though he continued to shoot me Death Glares all through class and in the halls, hinting at future confrontations. I didn't care, really. Kenzie wasn't bothered by what others thought of her dating me, so I wasn't going to dwell on it, either.

Besides, I had plenty of other problems to dwell on. How to find Keirran. How to keep Annwyl from Fading. How to keep Mackenzie safe, again, while venturing into a goblin market full of taboo items and shady faeries.

And maybe the most pressing, how to convince my parents to let me go tromping off to New Orleans this weekend. I refused to just vanish on them again; not only would Mom have a nervous breakdown, I shuddered to think of the trouble I would be in when I came back. Not only with my parents this time, but with Kenzie's.

And that was yet another problem. I hoped Kenzie had a

good story to feed her dad; from our short meeting at the hospital, he didn't seem like he was going to just "forget about her" again.

All that flew out of my head, though, when I walked into the library and found Kenzie alone in one of the aisles. Her head was bent, an open book in her hands, and I was reminded of our very first meeting, where a certain stubborn journalist had refused to leave me alone despite my attempts to drive her away.

Sliding up behind her, I put my hands on her waist and whispered "Whatcha reading?" in her ear. She jumped.

"Ethan! Geez, stop doing that!" She glared back at me. "I swear, I'm gonna tie a bell around your neck." I chuckled, resting my chin on her shoulder, and wrapped my arms around her as she held up the book. *Guide to New Orleans,* the title read. I raised an eyebrow.

"You seem awfully confident that we're going," I said, resisting the urge to kiss her neck as her fingers slipped into my hair. "I haven't even talked to my parents yet."

"I have. My dad, anyway. That's…what I wanted to talk to you about."

She sounded hesitant, and her body tensed against mine. My nerves prickled, but I kept my voice calm. "What did he say? Did he forbid you to go?"

"Worse." She lowered her arm and slid gently from my grasp, turning to face me in the narrow aisle. Her face crinkled with disgust as she said, "He's coming with me."

"You're kidding."

The disgusted look stayed firmly in place as she continued, "I told him I wanted to visit several places before I graduate," she said. "That New York was just the first, and I had a long bucket list of cities and places I wanted to see before I… well, you know."

A lump of ice settled in my stomach, and I nodded. "Go on," I rasped.

She sighed. "I thought that he would do what he always does—warn me not to get arrested and to call if there's an emergency. Surprise, surprise." She threw up her hands in annoyance. "He was completely into it and thought that it would be a great idea to see New Orleans together, as a family. A 'fun weekend trip.' So now my stepmom and Alex are coming, too."

"Your whole family?" I repeated in disbelief. Kenzie winced.

"Obnoxiously, yes. My disappearing act must've really shocked them. And now Dad won't leave me alone. He thinks this will be a great way to 'connect' again." She shook her head, her expression going dark. "I know what he's trying to do, and it's too late. He doesn't get to be a dad after he's forgotten I exist for so long."

"That's going to make things difficult," I muttered. "Does your dad even know I'm coming?"

"Noooooo," Kenzie said quickly. "He does not, and it's probably better that way. I'd told him I wanted to go to New Orleans with a group of friends, but I think he may have suspected who my 'friends' were. Probably another reason he wants to come along—to make sure we don't run off together and join a gang or something." She shrugged. "Don't worry. I'll meet up with you when we get there. We just can't let him see us."

"And if we have to sneak out in the middle of the night to look for faeries in goblin markets?"

"Then we'll have to do it quietly."

I groaned, dragging both hands over my face. "Your dad is going to throw me in prison and lose the key."

Kenzie's arms slid around my neck as she leaned in, smiling

up at me. "Well, if that happens, I'll just bust you out with my mad ninja skills and we can vanish into the Nevernever."

I was torn between telling her how unlikely that would be and kissing her, but at that moment the librarian strolled by with a cartful of books and we broke apart. "So, have you thought of what you're going to say to your parents?" Kenzie asked, serious again. I shook my head.

"Not a clue. I'm still thinking about it."

"Want me to come over after school to brainstorm?"

I would love nothing more than to have Kenzie in my room again, but... "I can't tonight," I told her. "I have kali."

Kali was the Filipino martial art I'd been taking for over five years. It taught you how to defend yourself with swords, sticks and knives, as well as empty hands, which was the main reason I was drawn to it; I wanted to learn to use weapons when protecting myself from the fey. My Guro—my instructor—believed in the spirit world and hadn't questioned my sanity when I'd told him invisible things were after me. He'd even helped us when we were looking for Todd, when I had nowhere else to go. The double, razor-edged swords he'd gifted me when I went to see him sat in an honorary spot in my room, and I knew Kenzie still wore his protection amulet beneath her shirt.

I hadn't see Guro since I got back home, and I wanted to talk to him, to thank him for his help and to fill him in on everything that had happened. I owed him that.

I thought Kenzie might protest, insist that we come up with a plan together, but she only nodded. "Say hi to Guro for me" was all she said.

I was nervous when I walked onto the mats, wondering what Guro would say when he saw me. The room was full of people; the kempo and jujitsu classes that shared the dojo with us were just wrapping up, students in white *gis* and colored belts shuffling off the floor, laughing and talking with each other. Our class was smaller, just a handful of people in normal workout clothes, a rattan stick in each hand. They had already staked out the far corner of the mats, and I hurried over to join.

Guro spotted me the second I walked into the room. He looked the same as he always did, a small, sinewy man with close-cropped black hair and dark, piercing eyes. He didn't say anything as I approached, just nodded for me to take my place in line. A few of the other students stared at me; either they'd heard the rumors or they'd seen my face on the news, as one of the teens involved in a suspected kidnapping. But Guro started the class as per normal, and soon I was too busy blocking bamboo sticks to the head and dodging rubber knives to think of anything else.

After class, however, he gestured for me to follow, and I trailed him down the hall into the office. Suddenly nervous and tongue-tied, I waited as he closed the door and motioned toward a couple chairs in the corner.

We both sat. I stared at my hands, feeling Guro's eyes appraising me. He didn't speak right away, and I wondered what he was thinking, what he thought of me now.

"How are your parents?" Guro asked at last.

"Fine," I replied, knowing exactly what he meant. "A little freaked-out, but okay otherwise. They took it a lot better than I thought they would."

"Good." Guro nodded, still watching me intently. I waited, knowing this wasn't over yet. Leaning forward, Guro folded his hands and fixed me with a piercing stare. "Now," he continued, in a voice that made my heart start to pound, "you don't have to tell me everything, Ethan, but tell me as much as you can. What happened after you and your friends left my home that morning? Did you find what you were looking for?"

I took a deep breath.

And ended up telling him everything.

I didn't intend to, but as I spoke, words just kept pouring out, and at one point I was horrified to feel my eyes stinging. I told him about Meghan, the Nevernever and how I'd been taken by the fey when I was four. I told him about Kenzie, Todd, Annwyl and the Forgotten; who they were, what had happened to them. I confessed my hatred of the fey, my anger at Meghan for abandoning us, my mom's worry and fear that I might vanish into the Nevernever, too. And I told him about Keirran, his relation to me and what I was planning to do that weekend.

When the words finally stopped, I felt exhausted, drained. But also strangely liberated, as if some huge weight had been taken from me. I'd never told anyone my whole story before, not even Kenzie. It was a relief to finally get it out. To tell someone who understood, who believed.

Through the whole thing, Guro hadn't said much, just quiet encouragements for me to go on when I faltered. He still wore his same calm, serious expression, as if he hadn't just spent an hour listening to a teenager ramble about invisible creatures that only he could see, that he'd been to a magical place called the *Nevernever,* that he was related to a faery queen.

"I know it sounds crazy," I finished, now wondering what had possessed me to spill my guts. "I know I sound like a raving lunatic, but I swear everything I've told you is real. I wish there was a way I could make people see Them without gaining the Sight, but once They know you can see, They'll just torment you forever. So, I guess it's better that way."

"I can see Them," Guro said very softly.

I jerked up, staring at him, my jaw hanging a little slack.

He gave me a tight smile. "Not like you," he went on in a calm voice. "I've never seen Them clearly. It's more a brief glimpse of something in the mirror, a reflection or a shadow on the ground that doesn't match anything visible. But I know They're there. My grandfather had this talent, also," he continued as I still gaped at him. "But he was very in tune with the spirit world and things that no one else could see. Our family has always been sensitive to magic and the creatures no one else believes in. So I understand how difficult it is."

I swallowed hard to clear my throat. "I wish everyone did."

Guro didn't say anything to that. "Have you told your parents?" he asked instead. "About what you plan to do this weekend?"

"No." I shook my head. "I haven't come up with a good enough excuse, and anything I say is going to freak them out, especially Mom. But I have to go." I crossed my arms, frowning. "I just don't know what I'm going to tell them."

"Sometimes, the simplest answers are the hardest to see."

I gave him a puzzled look, before I got it. "You want me to tell them the truth," I said. Just the thought made my stomach tighten.

"That's your call, Ethan." Guro rose, and I stood, too, ready to follow him out. "But let me ask you this. Do you think this is the last time you'll have to deal with Them?"

I slumped. "No," I muttered. "I'll never shake Them. They'll never leave me alone. There will always be something I'm dragged into, especially now."

Guro nodded slowly. "Be careful in New Orleans," he said, opening the office door. "Do you still have the protection amulet I gave you?"

Technically, I'd given it to Kenzie, but... "Yes."

"Keep it close," Guro warned. "Other than your kali skills, that's the best protection I can give you. If you or your friends need anything, magical or otherwise, please come to me. I cannot go with you into the hidden world, but I can make it so it is not quite so dangerous. Remember that, if you are ever in need of help."

"I will, Guro. Thanks."

He nodded solemnly, and I left the gym feeling a little lighter but still dreading what I had to do that night.

When I got home, things were normal. Annwyl was nowhere to be seen. Mom was putting the dinner plates in the dishwasher, and Dad was getting ready for work. I paused in the kitchen, watching Mom over the counter, and took a deep breath, preparing myself for the hardest conversation I would ever have.

CHAPTER SEVEN
THE TRUTH

"Absolutely not."

We were all three in the kitchen, me sitting on one of the bar stools, my parents facing me across the counter. Both of them wore looks of horror, anger and disbelief.

"No," Dad said, as if that was the end of it. "Not after the stunt you pulled last week. You think we're going to let you go to New Orleans alone? No, Ethan. Out of the question."

A stunt? I tried to hold on to my anger, remembering that Dad wasn't sensitive to the faery world. He tended to truly forget about it, like most normal humans did. Unlike me and Mom, who knew it was out there but tried to avoid it. We didn't talk about it.

Well, that ended today. "What do you think I was doing last week?" I asked, startling him and causing Mom to straighten in alarm. "I wasn't in New York to sightsee. It wasn't some stupid ploy to get attention. I got pulled into the Nevernever because of the fey, because it was either disappear into Faery or get torn to shreds in the real world."

Mom flinched. Dad stared at me like I was crazy...until he remembered that faeries were real, and we'd dealt with them before.

"I went into the Nevernever," I went on, determined not

to stop. Finally, all this would come out; it was no use trying to ignore it. I refused to ignore it anymore. "And I met
Meghan. She's the Queen of the Iron Realm and lives in this
huge palace with thousands of faeries. Everything she told us
was true. And now They all know about me." I wanted to
mention Keirran, but I'd promised Meghan I wouldn't, and
besides, this conversation was awkward and stressful enough
without bringing my nephew—their unknown grandchild—
into this.

"Ethan," Mom began, but I cut her off.

"No, Mom, I'm not going to pretend any longer." I gave
her a half angry, half apologetic look. "I've tried ignoring
Them, avoiding Them, trying not to See Them, and it doesn't
work. I'm just as much involved in Their world as Meghan
was, and no matter what I do, that won't change or go away."
Mom bit her lip, looking like she might cry, and I softened
my voice. "I'm not normal, and we both know that. We have
to accept that, every once in a while, They're going to come
for me, and I'm going to have to disappear for a bit. This is
one of those times."

"Why?" she whispered, on the verge of tears now. Dad had
gone quiet, recognizing, I think, the fact that this was out of
his control, that this world was one he had no part in. "Why
can't They leave us alone? I've already lost Meghan...why do
They have to take you, too?"

"They're not taking me anywhere," I assured her. "Never
again. Mom, I promise, I'm coming home. I have no intention of staying in Faery."

"You can't promise me that," she said angrily, pushing away
from the counter. Her eyes snapped at me, furious and terrified. "You can't control what They do, if They want you
to stay...there. What am I supposed to do while you're gone,
Ethan? I waited for Meghan to come home for a *year,* only to

lose her to Them for good! How long am I supposed to wait until I'm sure you're not coming back?"

"I'm not Meghan!" I snapped. "I'm not part faery. I'm not going to fall in love with one of Them, fight Their wars and become Their king. I hate Them and I hate what They've done to us. After all this time, you should know that!" At a sharp look from Dad, I stopped, getting control of myself again. Even if I was discussing faeries and the Nevernever and things he didn't understand, he still wouldn't let me talk to Mom like that. I took a deep breath and continued in a calmer voice. "But I am a part of that world, especially now. Even if I stay on this side of the Veil, They won't ever leave me alone."

"There's a difference between Seeing Them and rushing headlong into Their wars, Ethan. You were doing so well, keeping your head down, not getting involved."

"Yeah, well, I can't do that anymore." I swallowed and hoped that the universe would forgive this one small lie. "Meghan needs my help. This is something I have to do." Mom gave a choked sob and turned away, making my stomach contract, but I kept going. "I'm tired of being afraid, and I'm tired of pretending. I'm not running from Them anymore."

"You're going to get yourself killed," Mom protested, a little desperately now. "Or taken away, just like Meghan. I won't lose another child to Them. I will not watch Them drag you into that world. You can't go, Ethan. I refuse to see that again."

"I'm almost eighteen," I said softly, watching as she stalked to the dishwasher and wrenched it open. "You can't protect me forever."

Mom didn't answer, but Dad finally spoke up, his voice low and controlled. "And if we directly forbid you to go?" he asked. Not challenging or angry, just seeing where I stood. How serious I really was. I took a deep breath.

"Then I'll go anyway and face whatever punishment you give me when I get back."

"That's what I thought," Dad said. He checked his watch and frowned, then glanced at Mom, still standing over the dishwasher but not moving anything from it. "I'm calling in tonight," he announced, backing away from the counter. "Let's continue this talk in the living room, and Ethan can tell us exactly where in New Orleans he's going and what he plans to do while he's there."

"Luke!" Mom whirled around, aghast. I blinked in shock, too. "You can't be serious! He can't go to New Orleans by himself! What if They find him?"

"He's not going alone," Dad said. "I'll drive him up myself."

"Uh." I blinked. "What?"

He gave me a stern look. "You heard me. I realize this is something you have to do, but you're certainly not going to New Orleans alone. At least I can be there if you run into trouble."

"That's not a solution, Luke," Mom broke in. "So, instead of forbidding him to go, you're going to drive him up and deliver him to Their doorstep? How is that better?"

"Melissa." Dad faced Mom wearily. "The boy is going, whether we like it or not. He's been fighting Them since he was a kid. I might not be able to see it, but I'm not blind." He sighed, looking much older now, grizzled and tired. "We've always known it was only a matter of time before something like this happened, before They came for him. I'd rather have him know he can turn to us for help, instead of thinking we're oblivious to what he's getting into."

"But..." Mom blinked back tears. "Meghan..."

"Is gone," Dad said quietly. "And we have to accept that, just like we have to accept the fact that Ethan is involved in her world, too. Or we're just going to be fighting this for the rest of our lives."

Mom stood there, staring at both me and Dad, before she walked stiffly out of the kitchen without looking back. We heard her climb the steps to the upstairs bedroom, and then the door slammed with a crash that rattled the house.

I winced. Dad looked at me, haggard and grave. "When do you want to leave?" he asked in a resigned voice.

"Tomorrow," I replied, hoping my voice wouldn't betray me, let him know what I was thinking. Because there was no way he could come with me. Dad was only trying to help, to keep me safe, but he couldn't find out about Keirran or the very dangerous thing I was planning tomorrow night. "I thought we could get on the road after lunch, if that's okay."

"Is anyone meeting you there?"

Damn. "No," I said, hating that I had to lie, again, but I wouldn't rat Kenzie out and possibly get her in trouble. And I didn't think even Dad would be okay with me meeting my girlfriend in New Orleans, unsupervised. "Just me."

He nodded and glanced to the door of the upstairs bedroom as if steeling himself. I took that to mean the conversation was over and began to slip away to my room.

"Ethan."

I paused in the hall, looking back, as Dad scrubbed a hand across his face. "You'll be careful, right, son?" he asked, sounding uncertain now. "I know I don't understand much about this...other world, but your mother has never been the same since Meg left. You have to promise you won't go the same way. It would kill her."

"I won't," I told him. "I swear."

He went up the stairs, and I continued to my room, shutting the door behind me.

Well, that was about as awful as I'd thought it would be.

Mental note, Ethan: let's not do that again. Except, I could see more conversations like that in the future, explaining to my parents why I had to disappear *this* time, because Faery couldn't seem to leave me alone.

Speaking of faeries, where was Annwyl? I'd left her sitting on my bed that morning, and she'd assured me she had no intention of leaving the room unless it was an emergency. The thought of a full-blooded Summer gentry wandering around my house made me a little nervous, but I trusted Annwyl enough to know that she wouldn't cause trouble or glamour my parents. I hadn't seen her in the rest of the house, and I was pretty sure she wasn't upstairs in my parents' room. So where was she?

"Annwyl?" I called softly as I stepped farther into the room. "Are you here?"

There was no answer.

CHAPTER EIGHT

THE THIN MAN

I frowned at the mattress, wondering where the Summer faery could have gone. When I left her that morning, she had been curled up on my pillow reading, petals and leaves idly sprouting around her from the bed frame. Worried that she might be bored, as bored faeries were a recipe for disaster, I'd gathered a large stack of random books, magazines and novels from around the house, sneaking them into my room for her. Before leaving for school, I'd also offered to let her watch movies on my laptop, but she had shuddered at that idea and refused. Though, when she shyly asked if the strange metal device could play any music, I'd found a classical music station and left it on, turned down so my parents wouldn't come into the room and shut it off.

The bed was empty now, a paperback book sitting forgotten on my pillow. The music station still crooned softly, and I clicked it silent.

"Annwyl," I called again, wondering, absurdly, if I should check the closet or under the bed. "Where are you?"

Still nothing. The subtle warmth and scent of flowers that filled my room when Annwyl was present was also gone. I suddenly remembered the faery's words about Fading away, and a sharp ache gripped my stomach. Had she just…disappeared? Ceased to exist? My gut twisted even harder. What would Keirran have to say about that? What would he do if he found out?

Desperate now to find her, I searched the rest of the house, but she wasn't in the living room, kitchen, bathrooms, basement or study, and I definitely wasn't going to barge into my parents' room right now. Hoping that she hadn't forgotten the danger and wandered outside, I went to the back door to search our small, fenced-in yard for the vanished faery.

I yanked the door open and froze.

A thin, pale figure stood a few yards away, perched atop the wooden privacy fence surrounding the lot, silhouetted against the night sky. He stood in profile so that he faced me from the side, and one large, pale eye peered down at me from a narrow face.

My heart nearly stopped, but as soon as I saw him, the Thin Man *turned,* as if to say something to me, and vanished. I jumped, startled and disbelieving. With the exception of an obnoxious gray cat, I'd never seen any faery just disappear in front of me.

"Oh, blast it all" came a high, clear voice out of nowhere. "I keep forgetting. One moment, Ethan Chase."

The Thin Man turned back, visible again, and I realized he hadn't disappeared at all, only that he was really, *really* thin. Like the edge of a paper thin. So thin he could be viewed only when he turned to the side. I wondered how the hell he could stand up straight, let alone walk, if he was basically the width of a sheet of paper. But he *was* a faery, and things never made sense with the fey.

"Good evening," the Thin Man said, smiling and peering down at me from the corner of his eye. "Lovely night, isn't it?"

I closed the door behind me but did not step into the yard, watching the faery from the top step. The wards might be keeping him at bay for now, but if he somehow broke through them and came after me, I wanted enough time to reach my room and grab my swords.

"What do you want?" I demanded.

"Now, is that any way to greet a guest?" the faery inquired, clasping his pale hands in front of him. "I have come far to find you, Ethan Chase."

The Thin Man took off his hat and turned it in his long, spiderlike fingers. "I have a problem, Ethan Chase," he said, gazing down at his hands. "I was hoping you could fix it for me."

"And what's that?"

"Well, you see..." The faery fiddled with his hat. "Long, long ago, I made a mistake. A very costly mistake, one that is having an impact on both our worlds right now. Are you familiar with the Fade, Ethan Chase? It is what happens to those of us who have either been cut off from the Nevernever or have been unremembered so long, we have forgotten our own names."

"I know what it is."

"Clever boy. I thought you might." The faery smiled, showing a row of thin, sharp teeth. "Then listen well to my story. In the farthest reaches of the Between, the Veil between the mortal realm and the Nevernever, lies a town. And in that town dwell the creatures that the world has forgotten. It is their final resting place, their haven to move peacefully into nonexistence. I was the caretaker, Ethan Chase. The mayor, if you would. It was my duty to see that all those who came to Phaed were comfortable, and to help them ease into oblivion, for however long it took."

"Sounds pretty awful," I commented. The Thin Man ignored me.

"But then, several years ago, something came through my

town that never should have been there, and something left that should have remained there forever. Because I let it go, that ripple awakened a long-sleeping darkness. A darkness that was never meant to stir. And now she is in the world again, and the things that had nearly Faded away are coming back." The Thin Man's gaze sharpened even more. "Even worse, because of my mistake, something was born into Faery that never should have been. A catalyst with the power to change everything."

"So what does that have to do with me?" I asked.

The Thin Man blinked that large, pale eye. "It is the smallest things that are often the most important, Ethan Chase," he said. "The cornerstones that will topple the whole tower. The prophecy cannot come to pass without *him,* and if I take away his reason to fight, the flame that keeps him going will flicker and die. The Forgotten will Fade back into the Deep Wyld once more, and all will be as it should."

Prophecy? I felt cold. Suddenly, Meghan's warnings, Keirran's own words that everyone knew something he didn't, made a lot more sense. "What prophecy?" I rasped, and the Thin Man looked at me in surprise.

"You don't know? Surely the Iron Queen would have told you." He paused then, as if just figuring something out. "Ahhhh," he breathed, nodding. "No, she would not. Of course she would not, not something like this."

"What?" I snapped. "What isn't she telling me? What is she keeping from both of us?"

The faery steepled long fingers together. "I will tell you, Ethan Chase. I can tell you the prophecy, and *your* part in it, for a price."

Dammit. Should've seen this coming. My knee-jerk instinct was to refuse. That was my number one rule: never make a bargain with the fey, under any circumstance.

But this prophecy sounded bad. And a lot bigger than I had imagined. "What price?" I asked warily. The Thin Man smiled.

"A small thing. Simply remove the wards you have put up and allow me to collect what I've come for. I will be on my way after that."

Remove the wards. Let the faery into the house. Why would he want...

Wait. He was talking about Keirran. The catalyst, the power that could change everything, was Keirran. And *Keirran's* reason to fight was... "Annwyl," I guessed, anger and horror spreading through me. "You're here for Annwyl."

"The Summer girl is already Fading," the Thin Man said patiently. "Her end has begun. You cannot stop it. *He* cannot stop it. This mad quest, his determination to halt the Fade, for exiles and Forgotten, must cease. You cannot fight inevitability. Once she is gone, the Iron Prince's spark will die, and he will forget why he wanted to save the exiles in the first place."

"Or you'll piss him off so badly he'll do something *really* stupid."

"That is a chance I am willing to take."

"Well, I'm not." I stepped back, putting a hand on the doorknob. "And I'm sure as hell not turning Annwyl over to you. So go away. You're not getting into my house, and you're not getting anywhere near Annwyl or my family."

The Thin Man gave a heavy sigh. "Foolish boy. Very well. Delay the inevitable awhile longer, if you wish. But the girl *will* Fade, and until that time, I will make sure she never sees the Iron Prince again."

With that, he turned to face me head-on...and disappeared.

Making a mental note to strengthen the hell out of the wards later, I hurried back to my room.

"Annwyl?" I called again, pushing open the door. "Are you here?"

She looked up from the bed, moss-green eyes wide and frightened. Relieved, I shut the door, locking it behind me just in case. "He was here, wasn't he?" she whispered. "The Thin Man. I could feel him, like an emptiness, sucking away at me."

"Where were you?" I asked. "Didn't you hear me looking for you earlier?"

The faery blinked at me, confused. "I...I never left the room," she said. "I was here all day. Or I was, until..."

She glanced at the book, dropped and lying forgotten on the pillow, and her face paled. "I wasn't here," she whispered, horror creeping over her. "I...Faded out for a few minutes."

She might've been fey, and she might've been Keirran's sort-of girlfriend, but at that moment she looked more like a frightened girl than an ancient Summer sidhe. "Look, we'll figure this out," I promised. "One way or another. Once we find Keirran, we'll try to find a cure for this."

She gave me a shaky smile. "No," she whispered, shaking her head. "I'm grateful, Ethan Chase. But there is no cure. No hope. I'm only fighting the inevitable."

Her words had an eerily familiar ring to them, much like the conversation I'd just had with the Thin Man. "You can't just give up," I told her. "Keirran is out there fighting for you. He wouldn't want you to roll over and let it win."

"Keirran..." Annwyl closed her eyes. "This is wrong," she murmured. "He shouldn't be trying to save me. Not after..."

She paused, biting her lip, and I frowned. "Not after what?"

"Not after he's already done so much," she finished, and I knew she was lying. Well, not lying, since technically the fey couldn't tell an outright lie. But there were a thousand ways to bend and dance around the truth, and they were experts in all of them. It was one of the key things that made them so dangerous.

"Why is he doing this?" Annwyl continued. "He knows there's no way to halt the Fade."

"He loves you," I said, shrugging. "Love can make us do stupid things sometimes."

"My existence is nearly done." Annwyl picked up the book and held it in her lap, staring down at the cover. "There's nothing I can do to stop it. But I want to see Keirran before I'm gone. Before I Fade completely, I want to make sure Keirran is safe, that he won't get himself bound to a contract he'll regret forever."

"We'll find him," I told her. "Tomorrow. We'll head up to New Orleans, find out where the goblin market is being held and look for him there. And if he's not there, we'll just keep asking around until we find out where he's hiding." Someone had to know *something* about the whereabouts of the Iron Prince, even if the price for such information would probably be very high.

She gave a faint smile. "It's…easier with you around, Ethan Chase," she murmured, making me frown in confusion. "Your belief in us is very strong. Your emotions are very powerful. I think I can hold out against the Fade, at least until I see Keirran again, if you are with me."

And then what? I wondered. *What are we supposed to do after that—watch you cease to exist? You think you'll be able to convince Keirran to just let you go?*

Collapsing into my computer chair, I jiggled my computer to life and stared blankly at the screen, my mind in several places at once. I tried to focus. Find Keirran. That was the first issue. All the other stuff we'd worry about later. We would figure out this thing with Annwyl, Meghan and the Thin Man after we tracked down the Prince of the Iron Realm.

And I smacked him on the back of the head for all the trouble he put me through.

The prophecy cannot come to pass without him, the Thin Man had said, causing a chill to crawl up my spine. Great, one more thing to drive me crazy. What kind of prophecy? Did it involve me? Annwyl? Kenzie? Was Keirran meant to do something, or were certain events destined to unfold around him? I suddenly felt like Glinda the Good; *is it a good prophecy, or a bad prophecy?* Could it be avoided if I stayed away from him, or would that just make certain it came to pass? Whatever *it* was.

Argh. I scrubbed my hands down my face. This sucked, big-time. Like I needed a reason to be more neurotic. One thing was certain, though: I had even more cause to find Keirran and ask him what the hell was going on. Or at least warn him about this prophecy thing. If it had to do with both of us, maybe we could figure it out together.

"Ethan Chase?"

I glanced back at Annwyl. She sat on the bed with her knees drawn to her chest and her arms wrapped around them, long hair spilling over her shoulders. Her eyes were solemn as they met my gaze.

"If I...disappear...before we find Keirran," she began in a halting voice. "If I vanish forever, will you...will you let him know that I love him? I haven't told him, and I don't want him to think that I don't care for him."

"No, Annwyl," I said gently, and she raised her head, eyes widening. "I'm not going to tell him anything. You're going to tell him yourself. Don't give up before we even get started."

She blinked, her forehead creasing as if she'd never thought of that. Before she could answer, my phone rang, the screen flashing Kenzie's name. I slipped into the hall to answer it.

"Well, we're all set," Kenzie said when I picked up. "The

whole family is ready to go—Dad hired a car to take us and everything."

"Kenzie—"

"Oh, and I have the hotel address where we're staying."

"Kenzie…I don't want you coming with me. To the goblin market."

A long pause on the other end. I swallowed and braced myself.

"Come again, tough guy?" Kenzie's voice was cool, but I could hear the fury beneath it. "Care to say that again? I don't think I heard you the first time. Did you just tell me you don't want me going to New Orleans?"

I bit my lip. *You can retract it, Ethan. She's giving you the chance to take it back. This will not go well for you if you don't. Abort, abort!*

I hardened my feelings. No, this was necessary. The goblin market was dangerous, full of conniving fey that would trick you into giving them your own heart if they could. Not only that, now a faery assassin was skulking around, and I did not want that creepy Forgotten anywhere near my girlfriend. Kenzie had followed me into the Nevernever and ended up in the hospital. She was still gravely ill. This was for the best. Even if she disagreed, even if she hated me for it, I wanted her to be safe.

"No, I don't want you to come."

I heard her take a quick breath, as if holding back a sharp reply. "And all the plans we made?" she asked in an overly quiet voice. "Agreeing to meet in New Orleans? Looking for the market together? Me convincing my dad to take my whole family on vacation, just so I can find you there? That doesn't mean anything to you."

I could feel her anger through the phone line and knew I was on dangerous ground, but still stuck with my convictions. "Kenzie, you're sick. You just got out of the hospital. If we go to the goblin market and something happens to you, your dad will kill me. It's not that I don't want to see you," I went on, trying to be reasonable. "I'm just trying to keep you out of all this craziness. If you get hurt again, I'll never forgive myself." I paused, then added the final nail to my coffin. "I don't want you following me this time. Stay with your family."

"Please tell me you're not doing this." Her voice cracked a little, making me wince. "After everything I confessed, about borrowed time and my mom and wanting to live my life, please tell me you're not going to ignore that like everyone else."

"I'm sorry."

"Fine." Her words were stiff, cold and sent a fiery lance through my stomach. "If you don't want me there, Ethan, fine." A tiny sniffle echoed over the receiver, worse than if she had screamed or yelled or cussed me out. "I guess I was wrong about you. You are just like everyone else."

"Kenzie…"

She hung up.

I lowered my arm, not knowing exactly what I felt, apart from pretty lousy right then. Wandering back to my room, I saw that Annwyl had fallen asleep on my bed, her hair spilling in waves over my pillow. Unable to relax, I sat in my computer chair and opened my laptop, but I didn't do anything with it. I just sat there and stared vacantly at the screen, replaying Kenzie's last words over and over, and wondering if I had just sabotaged what I had with her beyond repair.

CHAPTER NINE
THE SHADOW FORGOTTEN

Early the next morning, I woke up two minutes before 5:00 a.m. and instantly turned off the alarm set to buzz at the top of the hour. Stifling a groan, I threw back the cover and sat up, already dressed, stretching my stiff limbs. I'd gotten maybe a couple hours of sleep on the floor of my room, lying in my old sleeping bag, and my neck ached as I stood and looked around for Annwyl.

She was awake and standing at my window, gazing out into the early-morning dark. The brightness around her, that faint sunlit glow that was present even in the darkness, had faded a bit, and she looked small and fragile as she drew back from the glass with a shudder.

"He's still out there," she whispered.

"He'll have to get past me," I replied, reaching for my duffel bag, already packed and ready to go. Atop the bag lay my twin swords in their slightly curved leather sheaths, the hilts glimmering in the dim light. I picked up both and slipped them through my belt, letting the kali blades rest against either hip. Looping the bag over my shoulder, I glanced at the Summer faery, waiting by the bed. "Ready to go?"

She nodded.

"You're certain you can make the drive up to New Orleans?" I gave the faery a serious look. "It's not going to be very pleasant, Annwyl. We'll be in my truck the whole way, nearly two hours."

"I know." Annwyl looked like someone getting ready to march out to the gallows. "But we have to do this. I don't know of any local trods to New Orleans, and I don't dare go back to Leanansidhe's. I can endure two hours of iron sickness if it gets us closer to Keirran."

The desperate hope in her voice made my stomach tighten. Turning away, I opened the bedroom door a crack and peered into the hallway. The rest of the house was dark; both parents were still sleeping. Guilt and fear raised goose bumps on my skin; I didn't want to do this, but I didn't have much of a choice. I couldn't let Dad drive me to New Orleans. He didn't understand the fey, and I refused to drag my family into the hidden world. This was something I had to do myself.

I glanced over my shoulder at Annwyl. "Stay close," I warned in a whisper. "It'll be most dangerous when we go outside. Creepy Thin Man shouldn't be able to get past the wards, and once we're in the truck, we should be safe. Still, let's do this quickly and quietly."

"I'm ready," Annwyl whispered, and we stepped into the hall.

Tiptoeing through the silent house, I paused in the kitchen just long enough to grab a soda and leave a quick note on the counter.

Mom, Dad, I've gone ahead to New Orleans. I'm sorry, but I have to do this alone. Will call you this afternoon from the hotel. Please don't worry about me, I'll be fine. Back in a couple days.
—Ethan

They would be pissed at me for certain, and I'd probably get an angry phone call from Mom as soon as she found the note, but I couldn't wait. Annwyl needed help, and I didn't trust Creepy Thin Man to stay on the other side of the wards. Even if he did, I certainly didn't want him hanging around my house, watching us, waiting for someone to step outside.

Outside.

The front door creaked softly as I eased it open, peering around the front lawn and my old truck parked in the driveway. Annwyl pressed close behind me, her warmth and the smell of new leaves at my back.

"I don't see him," she whispered.

I didn't, either, but that didn't mean he wasn't watching us. "Hurry," I growled and slipped onto the steps, jogging lightly down the walk toward the driveway. Annwyl followed, making absolutely no sound, as graceful as a deer bounding through the trees.

And then he was there at the end of the driveway, *turning* suddenly into existence, pale eye gleaming with wicked intent. Annwyl gasped, and I snarled a curse, drawing my sword in one smooth motion. He didn't step forward, couldn't cross the driveway, but his mouth opened impossibly wide, like a snake unhinging its jaws, revealing a gaping black hole within. I felt a faint pull in the air, a cold, sluggish feeling in my limbs, and my heart shrank with fear. Not for me; I'd felt this before and knew it couldn't hurt mortals. But Annwyl stumbled like she was fighting a sudden typhoon, falling to her knees on the pavement. She flickered, nearly blinking out of existence, as the thin Forgotten sucked away her glamour, magic and everything she was.

Snarling, I leaped across the driveway and slashed at the Thin Man, stabbing my blade toward his wizened chest. He darted backward shockingly fast and *turned* again, vanishing from sight.

Panting, I raised my sword and glanced around. I'd always been able to see the fey; that this sneaky bastard could get around my Sight made me nervous and a little angry.

"Ethan!" cried Annwyl somewhere behind me, "to your left!"

I spun, lashing out with my blade, just as a long arm appeared out of nothing, reaching for me. I felt fingers catch my duffel bag with a tearing sound and slashed the empty air beneath the arm, feeling the very tip of my blade strike something solid. A pale ribbon of blood coiled through the air like mist, followed by a thin wail.

I ran back to Annwyl, pulling her upright as a light came on in my parent's bedroom. Biting down curses, I half carried the Summer faery over to my truck, wrenched the door open and pushed her into the cab. Slamming the door, I turned to see the Thin Man in the center of the road, silvery blood writhing into the air from a gash in his side. He was no longer smiling.

"You cannot hide from me, Ethan Chase," he called as I hurried to the driver's side of the truck. "No matter where you take the Summer girl, no matter how far you run, I will find you both."

I ignored him as I tossed my bag onto the floor and leaped behind the wheel, slamming the door behind me. Annwyl was hunched on the seat with her eyes closed, leaning away from the door, but I couldn't worry about her now. Jamming the key into the ignition, I cranked the truck to life as another light gleamed in the windows of my house—the kitchen this time. Throwing the truck into Reverse, I backed out of the driveway, hoping to hit Creepy Thin Man with a few tons of iron and steel as I did. Sadly, that didn't happen, but nothing attacked us as I yanked the shaft into Drive, hit the gas pedal and sped off down the street.

★ ★ ★

"Well," Annwyl said after a moment of letting our heart-beats return to normal, "that was…exciting."

I glanced at her. She sat as far as she could get from the door of the cab, arms around her stomach, leaning forward. Her jaw was set, her moss-green eyes slightly glazed. She looked like she was experiencing the world's worst hangover and was about to hurl all over the floor of my truck.

"Annwyl," I said urgently. "Can you do this? Will you be all right?"

The Summer faery gave a tight, painful nod. "It's been a long time since I've experienced the iron sickness," she murmured, not looking up. "I'd forgotten…how unpleasant it is." She sat up carefully, as if checking to see whether she was all there. "I'm all right," she breathed, as though trying to convince herself. "I'm not gone yet."

Two minutes later, my phone rang. I dug it out of my pocket, checking the number, and my stomach dropped.

"You're in big trouble, young man" was Dad's greeting when I answered. I winced.

"Yeah, I figured."

"Care to tell me what was so important that you had to lie to me last night?"

I sneaked another glance at Annwyl. She gazed back apologetically, as if she knew who was on the line and what we were talking about. I thought of the Thin Man, skulking around the yard, and how Mom would react if I told her what had happened. "No," I said, feeling Dad's disapproval all the way from the house. "But I'll explain everything when I get home."

"Ethan!" Mom's voice crackled in my ear; it sounded like she had been crying. "Come home, do you hear me? Come back right now."

A lump caught in my throat. "I can't," I whispered. "I'm sorry. I'll be back in a couple days, I promise."

No answer, just a muffled sob, and then Dad took over again. "Call us as soon as you get to New Orleans," he ordered, his voice stern and controlled, trying to mask his anger. "And every few hours after that, do you understand?"

"Yes, sir."

"You be careful out there, Ethan." Almost a warning. I swallowed hard.

"I will."

I pressed End Call and lowered the phone, wishing it didn't have to be this way. I almost regretted telling them the truth, but no, it was better that they finally realize what I had to deal with. At least this way they would know what had happened to me...if I never came home.

The drive to New Orleans was mostly silent. Annwyl huddled in the passenger seat and gazed out the side window, her eyes glassy with discomfort and pain. I flipped on the radio and searched until I found a classical music station, trying to make the ride more bearable for her. Every so often, she would flicker and blur from the corner of my eye, making my skin crawl and my head snap over to make sure she was still there.

We took a break at a rest stop, and I followed her to a stand of trees, watching in concern as she pressed her forehead to the trunk, breathing hard.

"You gonna be okay?" I asked again, just to get her talking, to hear her voice. The farther we went, the more it felt like I was sitting next to a ghost, slowing dissolving in the sunlight.

Annwyl nodded. "Yes," she whispered, looking back with a brave smile. "I can make it. I'll be all right. How far is it to...to..." Her forehead creased. "Where are we going again?"

I ignored the stab of fear. "New Orleans," I replied. "The goblin market."

"That's right." Annwyl leaned a shoulder against the tree, where strands of bright green ivy were slowly creeping up toward the branches, rustling softly as they coiled around the trunk. I swallowed and hoped no one would look this way. "Keirran," Annwyl mused, her quiet voice colored with longing. "Will he be there?"

"I don't know," I admitted. "I hope so. We're really just grasping at straws, and I still have to find where this month's goblin market is being held." Luckily, I had a pretty good idea of who to ask for that information. The local dryads of City Park were rumored to be some of the oldest faeries in New Orleans and knew almost all there was to know about the city's secret life. I just hoped the price for that information wasn't too high.

"The full moon is tonight," I went on as Annwyl absently brushed a dead branch. It came to life again beneath her fingers. "Once we find out where the market is, we'll head over and have a look around. Even if Keirran doesn't show up, there has to be someone there who might know where he is and where he'll be."

Annwyl nodded again. "I hope so," she whispered. "I don't know how long I have left."

The sense of foreboding grew. "Come on," I said, starting back toward my truck. "I'll tell you the whole story on the road. But we should get going." *And let's hope that when we find Keirran, Annwyl will still know who he is and why she wants to see him.*

It was still morning when we cruised past the New Orleans city limits and into the urban sprawl of one of the most heavily populated faery cities in the human world. New Orleans was a place of voodoo and magic, mystery and superstition, and it drew countless fey to its haunted corners and near-mythical streets. I'd never been to New Orleans before; it was in the top five of my Places to Avoid Due to Faeries list. Of course the irony that, not only was I here, I was here looking for the biggest goblin market in the country, a place where thousands of fey would converge to bargain and make deals, wasn't lost on me.

The highway went right through City Park, and I had Annwyl read me the directions I'd copied from MapQuest, until we finally pulled into a near-empty lot at the edge of the lawn. It was quiet when I got out of the truck, the serene stillness of early morning, and almost no one else was out. As we entered the park, a woman and a frizzy terrier jogged past us down the sidewalk, and the dog took a moment to yap hysterically at Annwyl, much to the woman's embarrassment. Apologizing to me and scolding the dog at the same time, she pulled it away around a bend, and then we were alone.

"I like it here," Annwyl mused, gazing around the park in quiet awe. Since leaving the truck, she looked better, not quite as pale and insubstantial. "I can breathe more easily—my mind doesn't feel like it's in a fog. Magic is still strong here."

"Yeah." I couldn't feel the magic and glamour in the air, not like she could, but I could certainly See the evidence all around us. A piskie buzzed by my head like a mutant wasp, leaving high-pitched laughter in its wake. An undine, pale blue and piranha-toothed, glanced up from the edge of a pond before sliding noiselessly into the water. A huge black dog glided through a patch of mist between trees, looking like someone's pet that had slipped its collar—until you saw its eyes glowing with blue fire and noticed that it walked *on top* of the grass instead of crushing the blades beneath its paws. It blinked solemnly and trotted into the mist again, leaving behind no evidence that it had been there at all.

I suddenly wished I hadn't left my kali blades under the seat of my truck, hidden and locked away. Wandering around a public park with a pair of swords was risky and could get me into real trouble, but if we were jumped by a redcap motley or a hungry Nevernever beast, I would almost rather take the chance.

Thankfully, the park fey seemed indifferent to us as we made our way toward a cluster of massive oak trees in the center of the lawn. Huge and gnarled and draped in Spanish moss, the ancient trees were home to several dryads who inhabited the park. At one point, the park had also been home to the Elder Dryad, a very old tree spirit who had helped Meghan defeat the Iron King more than thirteen years ago. Over the years, I'd heard enough snippets of this very popular legend among the fey to piece together what had happened. When I was kidnapped by the Iron fey and taken into the Nevernever, Meghan had come here to ask for help in defeating the supposedly invincible Iron King. The Elder Dryad had given my sister something called a Witchwood arrow, a splinter of pure Summer magic that was like kryptonite to the Iron fey. But the Witchwood was also the heart of the Elder Dryad's oak, and giving it to Meghan essentially killed the tree and the dryad it was attached to.

I sobered, thinking of Meghan as we stepped into the shade beneath the enormous boughs. She had risked so much for me, all those years ago. Left home, gone into the Nevernever, made bargains with faeries and endangered her life, all to rescue me. Why couldn't she be here, right now, when I needed her most? Why was she keeping secrets when so much was at stake?

"Ethan?" Annwyl's quiet voice broke me out of my dark thoughts. The Summer faery cocked her head at me, green eyes inquiring. "Are you all right? Has something upset you?"

Only the same person for the past thirteen years. "No." I shrugged. "Why?"

"Your glamour aura changed just then," Annwyl said solemnly. "It became very dark and...sad. Confused." She blinked, and I suddenly felt exposed, like all my secrets had been dragged into the open. I'd forgotten that the fey could sense strong emotion. Fear, anger, grief—they could read it like a rain cloud over someone's head. Some theorized that was what made humans so fascinating to the Good Neighbors, that the fey had no true emotions, so they experienced them through human contact. I didn't know if that was true, but Annwyl didn't need to know my family problems and, being fey, wouldn't understand them if she did.

"It's nothing," I said, waving it off. "I was just...thinking of someone, that's all." She blinked, puzzled, and I turned away. "It's a human thing—you wouldn't understand."

"You were thinking about your sister," Annwyl said and offered a faint smile when I turned on her, frowning. "I have been around a long time, Ethan Chase," she said, and her voice wasn't smug or proud or unkind; it was just a statement. "I may not be human, but I have observed them throughout the years. I have seen them born, and I have watched them live, and love, and die. It does not matter the age or the time or the season—human emotions have remained ever the same. And in the past, your particular glamour aura only shifts that way when you have spoken about the Iron Queen." She blinked again, tilting her head, looking genuinely puzzled now. "You...miss her, then?"

I wanted to snap that it was none of her business but caught myself. It wasn't Annwyl's fault that I was so transparent, though she had surprised me again with how insightful she really was. It was hard to see slight, beautiful Annwyl as some ancient, all-knowing sidhe, though with the fey, looks were forever deceiving. For all I knew, she could be as old as Titania.

She was still watching me, her head cocked like she was trying to understand. "Don't worry about it, Annwyl," I said, not wanting to talk about Meghan, especially not with a faery. "We're not here for me."

She nodded and let the subject drop, which surprised me a bit. Maybe I'd been around Kenzie too long; I was used to her not letting anything go. But we'd reached the center of a cluster of huge oak trees, swathes of Spanish moss dangling from the branches like lace, and I could suddenly feel eyes on me. A blanket of mist hung in the air and pooled between tree roots, and the air beneath the canopy was damp and still.

Movement caught my attention. From the corner of my eye, I glimpsed a face, young and solemn, watching me from the center of one of the gnarled trunks, but when I turned my head, it was gone.

"Annwyl," I whispered, knowing we were being watched from every angle. "Dryads are part of the Summer Court, right? How do you get them to talk to you?"

Annwyl gave me a puzzled look, as if the question was ridiculous. "It isn't difficult," she replied, perfectly at ease in the center of the tree stand. "You just ask."

"Politely, if possible," said a new voice, as a slender, bark-covered figure melted halfway out of the trunk, regarding me with dark, beady eyes. "We're usually very reasonable, Ethan Chase."

"Oh, great," I remarked as two more dryads slipped from the oaks to stare at me. They were very tall, their limbs long and graceful, with hair like the ribbons of Spanish moss hanging from the trees. "You already know who I am."

"The wind told us you were coming, mortal," said the dryad who had first spoken. "Years ago, your sister came to the Elder Dryad for help. To rescue you and to save the Never-never from the Iron King. We will do the same for any of her kin, and we will ask for no price in return."

"Oh," I said, surprised. First time for everything, I guess. "That's...good, then."

The dyrads continued as if I hadn't spoken. "We have heard whispers of your plight against the Fading Ones," the second dryad said. "Rumors circling the wind. Of you, and the Iron Prince, and the shadows creeping ever closer. The wind is full of dark tidings these days."

I gave a start at the mention of the Iron Prince, and An-nwyl gasped.

"Keirran?" I asked, stepping forward. "Have you seen him? Do you know where he is?"

"No." The dryad shook her head, and a large green beetle buzzed out of her hair, landing on the trunk. "There have been...snatches of where he is, where he's been," the faery continued. "Brief glimpses. Then he is simply not there any-more. And not even the wind knows where he has gone."

Annwyl's shoulders drooped, and I gave her a reassuring glance. "But he's out there," I told her. "He's still out there, Annwyl. We'll catch up to him eventually." She nodded, and I turned back to the dryad. "Speaking of Keirran," I went on, "we think he might show up at this month's goblin market. Do you know where it's being held?"

The dryad inclined her head. "I do," she replied, and I sti-fled a sigh of relief. "The goblin market will be where it has always been, on Bourbon Street."

"Really?" I raised a disbelieving eyebrow. "Bourbon Street. The most famous street in New Orleans. I find that a little hard to picture, what with all the tourists and cars and drunk people wandering around. Are you sure that's where it is?"

"Yes." The dryad's expression didn't change. "The entrance

to the market is hidden to mortals, but the Summer girl will be able to get you through. After midnight, go to a place called Lafitte's Blacksmith Shop. Enter the building through the door on the left, close your eyes and turn thrice widdershins. Exit through the door on the right, and you will find yourself in the goblin market. Where you go from there is up to you."

"Sounds easy enough." I glanced at Annwyl. "You'll be able to get us through, right?"

She nodded. "Yes. If you can remember how to enter the market for me, I'll do the rest."

A sudden wind rattled the branches of the oaks, making the dryads jerk their heads up. Glaring around, I noticed the mist had thickened and was coiling like a blanket of white around the trunks, muffling the rest of the world. The space between the oaks and the faint light filtering through the branches dimmed rapidly, plunging the grove into shadow. I tensed, and the dryads drew back, melting into their trees.

"Hey!" I called, turning to the one who had spoken to me. She was halfway into the trunk now, just her face and one arm showing through the bark, glittering black eyes fixed on me. "Wait a second. You can't just disappear on us now. What's going on?"

"They are coming," the dryad whispered as her arm and shoulder vanished, sucked back into the tree. Now only her face showed through the bark. "Run, Ethan Chase." And she was gone, leaving me staring at a faceless tree trunk. The mist surrounding us coiled tighter, shutting out the rest of the light.

"Ethan," Annwyl whispered in a choked voice, gazing wide-eyed at something behind me. I spun…

…and came face-to-face with an eyeless hag, floating at the edge of the mist.

My stomach dropped. I leaped back, but the ragged figure with thinning hair and no eyes in its withered face lurched toward me like a puppet whose strings were being yanked. One thin, shriveled hand stretched out to me, long talons flashing like steel as it snagged the front of my shirt, tearing through the cloth. I yelled and grabbed its wrist, trying to pry it loose, but the withered hag was stronger than she looked, because I couldn't budge her an inch. Her face leaned close to mine, smelling of dust and cobwebs and things in the attic that hadn't seen the sun in decades. I jerked back, struggling to free myself as her slit of a mouth opened and cold, dead air rushed against my face.

"No time!" The words were a rasp, and her other hand clamped my shoulder, claws digging into my skin. "No time, Ethan Chase! They are coming. But you must understand. You must see this!"

"Get off me!" I snaked my arm beneath the bony elbow and shoved with all my might, and the creepy hag fell back, tearing a hole in my shirt and a few in my skin, as well. She hissed, reaching out again, and I hastily backed up, keeping Annwyl behind me.

"No," the eyeless thing moaned, sounding despondent. I didn't care; she was not going to grab me again. "Ethan Chase, wait! You do not understand. I must show you something, before it is too late."

"Stay right there," I told it and snatched a stick from the ground, holding it in front of me like I would my swords. "If you have something to tell me, you can say it from there."

"Ethan," Annwyl whispered behind me, sounding faint. "It's the Oracle."

"What? *The* Oracle?" The ancient seer of Faery, who'd helped Meghan when she first came to the Nevernever looking for me, who could see the future, or glimpses of it? That Oracle?

I didn't get a chance to ask. The mist roiled, and suddenly, dark *things* erupted from the wall of white, rushing toward us from all sides. They looked like shadows, black silhouettes with no defining features except for a pair of glowing yellow eyes. They weren't human shadows, either; their arms were too long, ending in curved talons, and they moved like huge insects, skittering over the ground. Tendrils of shadow streamed from their heads and backs like inky ribbons, writhing into the air as they closed in, silent as the mist they came out of.

I yelped as one shadow-thing bounded toward me, swiping at it with the branch. It ducked, or rather, it *flowed* beneath the blow, moving like a spill of ink and coming up on the other side. For an instant, it was right in front of me, bulging yellow eyes inches from my face. But then, before I could even register that I was in trouble, it was gone, leaping away.

Toward the dusty hag floating in the center of the grove. In fact, the whole swarm seemed to be converging on her like a flood of dark water. She hissed, rags billowing as she slashed the air around her, talons flashing. Several of the shadow creatures jerked, then seemed to come apart, fraying into ribbons of darkness that seeped into the ground and disappeared.

But even more of the shadow things got through and piled on the Oracle, clinging to her dusty form like splashes of ink. They didn't attack; from what I could see, they just grabbed her and hung on. But the shrieks and wails coming from beneath that dark mass made my hair stand on end.

"Ethan," Annwyl cried, grabbing the back of my shirt. "It's the Oracle! Please, help her!"

"Are you crazy?" I said, tearing my shirt from her grasp. She gazed back at me, wide-eyed and pleading, and I groaned. "Fine. I don't know why I'm doing this, but...do you think you can distract them long enough for me to get her away?"

The Summer girl nodded. I sighed, turned to the indistinguishable blot of darkness in the center of the grove and raised my stick. "Right. Rescuing creepy faeries who tried to kill me, again. Why not?"

As I lunged toward the fight, the trees above me groaned. Ancient oak branches swept down, sweeping away dark creatures like a broom, flinging them back. Vines erupted from the ground, coiling around the creatures' legs and arms, pulling them away. The mass of darkness was peeled aside, and I could see a pile of dirty rags crumpled on the ground.

Darting in, I slammed into a cloud of frigid cold that nearly took my breath away. My skin prickled, and my breath billowed in front of me as I reached down and grabbed a limp, shriveled arm among the pile of rags.

"No!" The arm came to life, bony fingers clamping on to my wrist, startling me. I jerked, failing to free my arm, and looked down. The Oracle's withered, eyeless face peered up at me from the ground, mouth gaping open. Around us, the shadow beings fought the vines holding them back, slithering through the coils like snakes, their chill coating everything with frost.

"Dammit, let go!" I tried wrenching my arm back, tried to drag her out, away from the shadows closing in on all sides. "Will you stop? I'm trying to help you!"

"No," she whispered again, her voice faint. "Listen. It is too late for me, Ethan Chase. The darkness has come, as I foresaw it would. This is my fate—you cannot stop it. But you must…see…this…."

The shadow creatures had almost freed themselves; several pressed forward, grabbing the Oracle again, covering her like ratty blankets. I snarled and hit at them with the branch, but they either slithered aside or accepted the blows, making no sound as they piled on the Oracle again. None of them retaliated against me, though the air grew painfully cold. In horror, I saw a corner of the Oracle's rags, fluttering as though caught in a breeze, tear away and vanish into one of the shadow creatures. Right *into* it, like it had been sucked down a black hole. And then I felt that faint, sluggish pulling sensation coming from all around us, and I knew what these creatures were.

Forgotten. Of a kind I'd never seen before, but there was no mistaking what they were doing. Sucking away her magic and glamour, just like the rest of their kind. Draining away her life and her essence, and if I didn't get her out of here now, she would be sapped away to nothing.

I yanked backward, trying to drag the Oracle away, but somehow her other hand reached through the swirling mass of darkness and touched the side of my head.

There was a stab of pain, like she had sunk those steely talons right into my mind, and a flash of something white across my vision. And for just a moment, I saw him.

Keirran. Covered in blood, staring down at something on the ground, his face full of grief and horror. Another flash, and I saw what he was staring at.

No. My mind went blank with shock. *No.*

The grip on my arm was released. Reeling, I fell backward, and the Oracle vanished beneath the pile of strange Forgotten. Scrambling upright, I lunged forward, yelling, kicking, beating them with my stick, until the dark mass of Forgotten finally drew back. Panting, pushing the last of the creatures away, I gazed down at the spot where the old faery had been.

A few dusty rags lay in the grass at my feet, fluttering like paper. The Oracle, whoever she had been, was gone.

Behind me, Annwyl made a strangled noise and sank to her knees. I backed toward her, glaring at the Forgotten, who surrounded us in a dark ring, their eyes glowing yellow in the gloom. But they didn't attack. Silently, they drew away into the mist and faded from view. The fog broke apart, sunlight streamed into the grove, and everything was normal again.

My arms were shaking, and it was questionable whether my legs would continue to hold me up. I dropped the stick and leaned against a trunk, uncaring that it might be a dryad's tree. That vision, that split-second flash the Oracle had shown me—it couldn't be true. I refused to believe it. Of course, if it *was* true, then it certainly would explain some of the reactions I was getting from Meghan, the courts, the Thin Man, everyone. I understood Meghan's fear now. I understood a lot more than I wanted to.

"I can't believe the Oracle is...gone," Annwyl whispered after a moment.

I didn't reply. Truthfully, I wasn't thinking of the Oracle. I was still reeling from the load of bricks she'd dropped on my head, unable to stop seeing it. The vision. Keirran covered in blood, staring at something on the ground at his feet. His face a mask of grief, despair and horror. And in the grass...a body, blood pooling from its chest, gazing sightlessly up at him.

Me.

PART II

CHAPTER TEN
THE FADE

I was going to die.

That was what Meghan was so afraid of. She knew. She knew something was going to kill me, and Keirran would be there when it happened. Was this the prophecy everyone was so worried about? How would it happen? Would Keirran and I end up fighting something too strong for us, something vicious and powerful, and it would end up killing me? Or had he just found me lying there in the grass? I hadn't gotten more than a glimpse of him in the vision, but I did remember the blood streaking his face and arms, though I wasn't sure if it was his or an enemy's. We might have been in a fight; in that brief flash, I couldn't remember if he had his sword out. Come to think of it, I couldn't remember if I had *my* swords out.

I didn't know, and at that moment, I didn't really care *how* that vision had come to pass, only that it had. Would. I had just seen my own death. I was going to die, and Keirran would be there when it happened.

"Ethan?"

Annwyl rose and came hesitantly forward, her green eyes concerned. "You're white as a sheet," she remarked. "And you're shaking. What did the Oracle show you?"

Damn, I *was* shaking. Clenching my fists, I pushed myself off the trunk, taking a deep breath to slow my pounding heart. "Nothing," I told her, forcing myself to be calm. "I'm fine. It's nothing, Annwyl, just adrenaline from the fight."

And seeing my own death, of course. That's always an eye-opener. Dammit, I'd never get that vision out of my head; it was imprinted on my mind like a brand, and would be there forever. Myself sprawled at Keirran's feet, bloody, limp and most assuredly dead, Keirran looking down in horror. I started to shake again, but stopped myself. *No. There's no way I'm going to let that happen. If the Oracle wanted me to see that, there must be a way to avoid it. Otherwise, why would she show me at all?* Resolved, I shoved back the fear spreading through me, determined not to turn into a basket case. *Whatever. It hasn't happened yet, and like Kenzie said once: I don't believe in Fate. I am* not *going to die, not like that.*

"Those creatures." Annwyl shivered, rubbing her arms as if cold. "They were Forgotten, weren't they? Why didn't they attack us?"

"I don't know," I muttered, gazing down at the limp pile of rags, all that was left of the Oracle. I found myself thinking that we had just witnessed something huge and terrible, and I wondered if the death of the ancient faery was an ominous sign for everyone. "I guess…they were just after her."

We hurried out of the park, wary now for any shadowlike Forgotten as we fled back to my truck. This time, Annwyl scrambled inside without hesitation, and I fished my swords out from under the seat, laying them beside me on the cab. That was it—I was not going anywhere without them again.

I found a hotel fairly close to Bourbon Street—not *on* it, because the places located down that famous strip would probably be mega expensive—and paid for a room with cash. Even then, it cost way more than I wanted it to, and I tried not to cringe as I handed over the wad of money. I would definitely have to get another job this summer, as it appeared this trip was going to suck my limited funds dry.

Dammit, Keirran. You'd better be worth it.

At least the well-dressed man behind the desk didn't ask any questions, such as why a seventeen-year-old with no parents in sight needed a room, alone, and handed me a key without hesitation. With Annwyl trailing invisibly behind me, I walked down the narrow orange-and-gold hallway until I found the right door, then pushed my way inside.

The room was small, but at least it was clean, and I tossed my pack on the bed. "Well, we're here," I announced, glancing at Annwyl, who was looking around the room curiously. "I guess we'll just have to hang tight until tonight, unless there's anything else you want to do."

I suddenly wondered what Kenzie was doing, if she and her family were already here, walking around, soaking up the local history. All the things you were supposed to do on a family vacation. I wished I could've done that with her. This wasn't a vacation or a pleasure trip for me, not by a long shot, but it would've been nice to take my girlfriend to New Orleans. We could go to restaurants, listen to jazz music, visit a museum or take a sightseeing tour; all the normal stuff that I'd probably never get to do.

Annwyl was giving me that appraising look that hinted that she knew what I was thinking or feeling. Maybe my glamour aura was giving me away again. "You miss Kenzie," she said, confirming my suspicions. I shrugged, and she tilted her head. "Why don't you call her?" she suggested. "You can do that, can you not? With your...telephones?"

I smiled at the faery's confusion with the mortal world. She had been in the Nevernever so long, tech and modern conveniences like phones and computers were completely foreign to her. Just as quickly, though, the smile faded. "I can't," I said, scrubbing a hand through my hair. "She's pretty mad at me. I don't think she's going to want to talk."

"Why?"

"Because I don't want her going into the goblin market. Not with that creepy thin faery stalking us, and especially not now, with those shadow Forgotten out there. It's too dangerous." I remembered Kenzie lying in the hospital room, pale and weak, and my stomach turned. "She's sick, Annwyl," I said in a near whisper, at the same time wondering why I was telling this to a faery. "I can't put her at risk. Not like that."

Annwyl gave me a very strange, unreadable look, and I frowned. "What?" I challenged, crossing my arms. "What's that look for?"

"I'm sorry," Annwyl whispered, and the peculiar stare turned to frustration. "I know you but, I...seem to have forgotten your name. Where...are we?"

And before my horrified gaze, she started to disappear.

"No!" I lunged for her, grabbing a slender wrist before it became transparent. "Annwyl, look at me," I demanded, shaking her. She blinked and stared at me with glazed green eyes. "What's my name?" I asked, holding her tightly. She felt so...fragile. I could see the dresser right through her head and gave her another little shake. "Annwyl, focus! Answer me. What's my name?"

"I...I don't know." Her voice was barely a whisper, her eyes the only spots of color left. Everything else was becoming transparent and pale. "I can't...remember...anything."

"Dammit," I growled. "Don't do this. Not now." My fingers slipped through her wrist, and I could only watch helplessly as she grew fainter and fainter. I was losing her. If she Faded out, I didn't know if she would return. Annwyl stared through me, her expression blank, nearly gone. Desperately, I played my last card. "Keirran!" I burst out. "Do you remember *him?* The one we're looking for, who's out there fighting for you right now. Do you remember Keirran?"

A spark of recognition finally flashed over Annwyl's face, and she jerked her head up. "Keirran," she choked out, her eyes filling with horror. "Ethan Chase. Yes, I…remember…"

She shivered, and color returned, washing out the ghostliness, turning her solid again. I slumped in relief. Annwyl turned away, covering her face with her hands, trembling.

I let her be, not knowing what else to do. *So this is what Keirran is fighting against,* I thought, suddenly understanding him a lot more. *Not just for Annwyl, either. For all of them.* I remembered his words when we were leaving the Forgotten Queen's chamber that night. *You don't know how horrible it is for exiles, for all of them, to face nothingness. Losing pieces of yourself every day, until you cease to exist.*

Well, I'd seen that firsthand now, and it was pretty horrible. A couple months ago, I wouldn't have cared about the fate of exiled fey. If they disappeared from the world forever, good. Fewer faeries to torment me.

It was different now.

"I'm sorry," Annwyl finally whispered, lowering her arms. "I let my guard down. I stopped trying to remember who Kenzie was, who you were, why we're here. I'm so tired. I want to let go, to stop fighting this." She sank onto the mattress and bowed her head, long chestnut-colored hair sliding forward to cover her face. "I just want to see Keirran one more time."

I sat next to her, not touching, but letting her know I was there. "We'll find him," I said, hoping I wasn't making empty promises. "Just hang on a little longer. And who knows? Maybe he's found something to stop it."

But Annwyl shuddered. "I hope not," she murmured. "The

price would be so high. And so dangerous. Cheating death, even if it's not your own..." She shook her head. "Even our kind avoids making that type of bargain at all costs." She shivered again. "We have to find him, Ethan. Stop him from whatever he's planning to do. Before he promises something he can't ever take back."

"Yeah," I rasped, standing up. "That's why we're here." Grabbing my backpack, I set it on the bed and rifled through it to make sure I had everything I needed. Besides a change of clothes, my laptop and my toothbrush, I also brought a small canister of salt, several bottles of honey and my old leather journal containing all my research on the fey. Digging it out, I flipped it open to a blank page and scribbled: *Laffite's Black-smith Shop—entrance to goblin market. Go in left door, turn widder-shins 3 times, leave thru right door.* I paused a moment, tapping my pen on the paper, then also wrote down: *Dryads of City Park—3 oaks near edge of pond; be polite.*

And under that: *Who was the Oracle? What is the prophecy?*

My pen wavered as the Oracle's vision crept up again: me dead on the ground at Keirran's feet. Keirran covered in blood but looking unharmed. And Annwyl's comments about the fey's price for cheating death cast a sudden, dark thought into my mind.

What if Keirran *was the one to...*

I shook my head, snapping the journal shut. No, I wouldn't think about that. That vision could be anything. Even if it *was* true, what was I going to do? Leave? Refuse to help him and Annwyl? Abandon Keirran to whatever crazy, dangerous thing he might be doing out there? I couldn't. He was family. I owed it to him, and Annwyl, and even Meghan, to help.

Stuffing the journal into the pack again, I turned to Annwyl, still sitting on the bed. "Come on," I told her, making her look up in surprise. "I'm starving. Before I go looking for a market full of bloodthirsty goblins, I at least want breakfast."

My phone didn't ring all afternoon. Except one time at the coffee shop, when I got an irate call from Dad because I hadn't let them know I made it to New Orleans. I debated whether or not to call Kenzie, but each time decided against it. She was probably still pissed at me. Besides, she was likely with her family now, touring the streets of New Orleans. She didn't need me hanging around.

Still, I found myself gazing out the window of the small coffee shop, looking for a girl with blue streaks in her hair. Even now, hours away from walking into a street teeming with dangerous fey and forbidden items, I couldn't stop thinking of her. I wondered if she would even want me around after this. I'd screwed this boyfriend thing up big-time, but if it meant keeping her safe, I would deal with the terrible wrath I knew was coming. Maybe she wouldn't be able to get past this. She might dump me, and the saddest thing was, that was probably for the best.

I brooded into my coffee. Across the table, Annwyl curled her fingers around a cup of tea, gazing blankly out the window. I peeked up at her and frowned. I didn't like how the sunlight seemed to be shining right through her, making her almost transparent. On the tile floor, I could see the shadow of myself, hunched over my cup, but nothing in the seat across from me.

"Hey," I said quietly, so as not to alert the people around us. "Annwyl. Talk to me."

She blinked out of her trance. "Hmm?"

I had to keep her talking, keep her remembering, about anything. If she started Fading right here in the coffee shop, I'd look like a nutcase when I leaped up and started yelling at nothing. At worst, someone would call the cops. "Tell me something about yourself," I said, and she gave me a puzzled look. "What did you do in the Summer Court?"

Her brow furrowed. It looked like recalling the past was difficult. "The Summer Court," she began in a slow, halting voice. "I don't...remember much now. Trees and sunlight. Music. I was happy there, I think."

Her voice became wistful and very sad on the last sentence, and I switched tactics. "So, how did Keirran ever get you to talk to him?" I went on. "Didn't he tell me you sicced a pack of undines on him when he was visiting Arcadia one day?"

"Undines," Annwyl repeated. Suddenly, her eyes darkened, a shadow falling over her face as she stared into her cup. "I remember that day," she murmured, sounding very unlike herself, solemn and grim, and choked with guilt. "Keirran was only trying to talk to me and...I almost had him drowned."

"What happened?"

She fiddled with the edge of her cup, a very human gesture of embarrassment. "One afternoon, I was beside the river that separates Arcadia from the wyldwood when I looked up and saw him on the other bank. I knew he was there for me—he'd been trying to get me alone ever since that night at Elysium when I danced for the court. Back then, I was afraid of him. He was the son of the Iron Queen, and there were all sorts of rumors about the horrible things he did to regular fey. So when I saw him at the river that day, I didn't know what he wanted, and I think I panicked a little." Annwyl winced. "I asked the undines to stop him from crossing to the other side. He was walking over the bridge, and they just...yanked him right in."

I snorted a laugh into my coffee, managing to turn it into a cough. It was hard to picture the calm, refined Iron Prince getting dragged into a river by a school of water faeries. Sort of like Batman falling off his batcycle; it simply didn't happen. "Was he mad?" I chuckled. Annwyl grimaced.

"He nearly died," she admitted, making me sober quickly. "I didn't tell the undines *how* to stop him, so naturally they tried to stop him *permanently*. I could see them in the center of the river, the whole school, all trying to drag him to the bottom to drown. But the strangest thing was, Keirran didn't fight back. Not lethally. I've seen him fight—I know he could have drawn his sword and sliced them all to pieces, but he didn't."

"How'd he get out?"

"He froze the whole river," Annwyl whispered, and I raised my eyebrows. "The water turned frigid, and the surface iced over as far as I could see. Everything around it became covered in frost."

"Geez," I muttered.

"Undines are Summer fey, so they can't stand cold water," Annwyl went on. "I don't know what exactly happened between them and Keirran once the surface iced over—they were all underwater when it happened. I do remember standing at the edge of the bank, looking at the frozen river and waiting for Keirran to surface. I thought I really might have killed him, and I was terrified."

"I assume he finally surfaced."

The Summer girl smiled faintly. "No," she said. "I never saw him break out. I kept waiting for him, when suddenly, I heard a quiet 'Excuse me,' at my back. I turned, and he was right there, dripping wet and smiling."

I snorted. "Show-off."

Annwyl's smile grew wider, though more wistful. "He wasn't even angry," she murmured. "I think I started falling for him that very afternoon. Though I didn't know it until later, and even then, I thought it could never work between us. The courts would never allow it." She gazed into her cup, her eyes far away. "We had…a few nights. When he would sneak out of Mag Tuiredh and come visit me, first in Arcadia and then at Leanansidhe's. I wish we'd had more time. But it doesn't matter now." Her gaze darkened again, and she closed her eyes. "I'll be gone soon enough. And Keirran will move on. It's better that way."

I started to reply, when there was a dark shimmer outside the window, like an ink blot moving through water, and my skin prickled.

Not far from where we sat, perched on the railing of a balcony across the street, a shadowy thing watched us with glowing yellow eyes. Annwyl followed my gaze, and her face tightened with fear.

I drained the last of my coffee and rose. Without speaking, Annwyl and I hurried back to the hotel room, where I dug a sprig of Saint-John's-wort out of my backpack and taped it to the door. I also poured a line of salt across the windowsills, not caring what the cleaning ladies would think when they came in. Small precautions. Not perfect, but better than nothing.

"Get some rest," I told Annwyl, flopping down on one of the beds. "Looks like we're stuck here until tonight. Might as well sleep while we can." Not that I thought I could relax enough to sleep; I'd likely stay up with my swords close by, just in case any shadowy figures slipped under the door and into the room. But Annwyl looked tired and still frighteningly pale.

Better than she had in the truck, and much better than that awful moment when she'd started to Fade from existence, but she still didn't look great.

The Summer girl didn't argue. Settling wearily atop the other bed, she curled into herself and closed her eyes. I waited a few minutes, then quietly eased off my bed, grabbed my laptop and swords, and settled in the armchair in the corner.

"Ethan?" came Annwyl's soft voice after a few minutes of silence. I'd thought she had fallen asleep, and glanced up in surprise.

"Yeah?"

The Summer faery hesitated, her back still to me. "I wish I could express how grateful I am," she murmured. "My kind doesn't say...those words...but you've done so much for me and Keirran. I just want to say..."

"It's fine, Annwyl." I spoke quickly to reassure her. "You don't have to say it. I know what you mean." She relaxed, her shoulders slumping in relief. "You're welcome, but we haven't found Keirran yet. Just concentrate on not Fading away until we do."

I saw her nod, and a few minutes later, she seemed truly asleep. In the silence, the urge to call Kenzie returned, stronger than ever. I missed her. I hated the thought that she was angry with me now. But I didn't regret my decision. In a few hours, Annwyl and I would head into the dangerous, unpredictable goblin market, and it was better that Kenzie stay far away from the madness.

If I was being honest with myself, she'd be better off staying away from me, too.

The hours dragged and yet went more quickly than I would've liked, every minute bringing us closer to midnight. Annwyl slept most of the afternoon; maybe she'd never really gotten to sleep until now, or maybe her condition made her tired and sluggish, sort of like having the flu. I didn't know, but she politely declined leaving the room when I headed out to get food. Fearful of having her disappear, I grabbed a couple candy bars from the vending machine outside and hurried back to find she had fallen asleep again. Restless, I watched TV and Netflix and envied the faery, still curled up on the bed. She did wake up later that evening when I forced her to go to McDonald's with me because I was starving after nothing but chocolate bars for lunch. But she remained quiet and nervous, not speaking much. Truthfully, I was more than a little nervous, too.

At eleven-thirty, I grabbed my backpack, stuffed my swords inside, out of sight of the public eye, and turned to Annwyl.

"Ready?"

"Yes," she replied, with a determination that reminded me of someone on the way to the gallows. Terrified but resolved to show no fear. "Let's go find Keirran."

Bourbon Street wasn't far, and New Orleans glowed an eerie green and orange under the light of the full moon. It was almost surreal. We walked the couple blocks to the famous street, passing neon signs and lampposts shining feebly in the artificial haze. People wandered by, not paying any attention to either me or the faery at my side. A goblin peered at us from a narrow alley, picking his teeth with a fragment of bone, but didn't make any move to follow.

Laffite's Blacksmith Shop was a tiny building on the corner of St. Philip and Bourbon Street. From the outside, it looked deliberately run-down, white plaster peeling away to reveal spots of red brick. Wooden shutters and doors stood open to the night, and an old-fashioned lantern hung beside the entrance, flickering orange.

I gazed behind us to the road, watching cars cruise down Bourbon Street and people drift over the sidewalks. With the orange lights, full moon and faint strands of jazz music playing from one of the open bars, New Orleans did have a magical quality to it. I knew why this place was such a haven for the fey, and I knew they were out there, skulking between buildings and slipping invisibly through crowds. Still, I couldn't imagine the whole street teeming with faeries, an entire marketplace of them. I hoped that dryad knew what she was talking about.

Annwyl and I crossed the street and ducked through the leftmost door of Laffite's bar to find ourselves in a dim, old-fashioned room. Round wooden tables were scattered about a stone floor, and the bar stood against the back wall, most of the stools occupied. The only lights came from the candles set on the tables and hanging from the walls, and the flames in the huge stone fireplace in the center of the room.

Someone pushed past me from behind, jostling me with barely a grunt of apology. I stepped farther into the bar and glanced back for Annwyl, nearly lost in the shadows.

"All right," I muttered, stepping up to the fireplace and turning to face the doors. Annwyl followed silently. "So, according to the dryads, we just have to turn widdershins three times and walk out the door on the right—left now, since we came inside—and we'll be in the market." I checked my watch to make sure it was 12:00 a.m. Six minutes past midnight. "On three?"

She nodded, and on my signal, we closed our eyes and spun counterclockwise in place three times, me feeling slightly ridiculous and hoping no one was watching.

On the first two circles, nothing happened. But when we completed the third, I opened my eyes to find the inside of the bar had…changed. It wasn't full of fey. The lights and tables and patrons sat where they had always been; really nothing had moved. But everything around us was slightly out of focus. Conversations were muted, and everything seemed to be going in slow motion.

Except us. And the door a few yards away. It stood out sharply against the blurred, hazy backdrop, the opening shimmering like heat waves. That was it. Our entrance to the goblin market.

I nudged Annwyl, and together we walked across the floor, past indistinct shadows and nearly frozen candle flames, and ducked through the opening.

CHAPTER ELEVEN

SECRETS FOR SECRETS

Toto, we're not in Kansas anymore was the cheesy first thought that went through my head as we stepped out into the street.

Noise surrounded us—not the muffled sounds of cars and street traffic at night, but the louder, garbled sounds of a huge crowd. "Normal" Bourbon Street had disappeared; though I could see it was still the same stretch of pavement, the same buildings lining the sidewalks, it was definitely not the same world. Streetlamps had been replaced with torches and faery fire, orbs of blue-white flame floating overhead. There were no cars, but horse-drawn carriages glided down the road— only the horses' hooves never touched the ground, and their eyes glowed blue in the shadows. The buildings, though they looked the same at first, appeared old and run-down on closer inspection, covered in vines and moss, as if we had stepped back in time a hundred years.

And of course, there were the fey.

They were everywhere, milling about the road in huge numbers, faeries of every shape, size and description. Short, warty goblins with beady eyes and huge ears. Hulking ogres, their thick knuckles dragging along the ground as they lumbered by. Redcaps flashing their shark-toothed grins at everyone. Rail-thin bogeys hiding in the shadows and narrow crevices. And faeries I didn't have a name for, all wandering down Bourbon Street, looking like the world's largest freak convention.

Oh, this was going to suck.

Shrugging off my backpack, I pulled out my swords and slipped them onto my belt. No way I was going out there unarmed. Taking out my jacket, I shrugged into it and pulled up the hood, hoping it would shield me from any curious looks. And if my luck held, hide the fact that I was human long enough to find Keirran and get out of here without trouble.

Glancing at Annwyl, who looked slightly overwhelmed as well, I grimaced. "Ready for this?"

"No," she replied, her eyes wide. "But...lead the way."

We slipped onto the crowded road, moving more slowly than I would've liked. Faeries weren't the only thing making the street difficult to navigate. Booths and wooden tables were arranged in narrow aisles down the pavement, displaying the weirdest merchandise you'd ever see in your life: weeping fish and glass eyes and jewelry made of bones and teeth. Bird skeletons, crystal balls, shriveled hands and hats that whispered to you as you passed. A yellow-eyed woman in gypsy robes caught my eye and grinned, beckoning me toward her booth, waving a deck of cards in her long fingers. A kimono-clad girl with fox ears peeking from her hair gave me a coy smile, fluttering a fan and pointing to her table of rice cakes. I ignored them all and hurried on.

After several minutes of wandering the aisles and dodging requests by persistent vendors to take a look at their goods, it became pretty apparent that the chances of just stumbling into Keirran were slim to none. This place was massive; I could walk right past the Iron Prince and never know. Luckily, that hadn't been my only plan. I had hoped it wouldn't come to this, though, because it meant I was going to have to do something I hated and tried to avoid at all costs.

Bargain with the fey.

I searched the market until I found a booth that sold "potions for all ills," run by a well-dressed, ancient-looking gnome. He stood on a stool beside a counter full of different-size vials and bottles. *Vial of Forgetfulness,* one read, next to a large display of *Minor Love Potions* and *Jars of Friendship.* The gnome blinked as we came up, raising an eyebrow that looked like a fuzzy gray caterpillar.

"Human?" His voice squeaked like a centuries-old mouse. "Unusual. How did you find your way into the market?"

"Does it matter?" I asked him, keeping my head down and my voice low.

The gnome sniffed, and his voice turned wheedling. "No, I suppose not. But while you're here, how 'bout you buy one of my wares? I have a lovely selection of love potions. Guaranteed to work, you know. You have that pining aura all around you, boy." He grinned, showing crooked yellow teeth. "Or perhaps there is a rival? This lovely vial right here will turn your enemy into a cockroach."

"No," I said, repressing a shiver. "I'm just looking for someone, a friend of mine. Part human, silver hair, my age." I didn't say exactly who he was; the gnome definitely would've recognized him, but I didn't want word spreading that we were looking for the Iron Prince. If the vendor had seen him, he'd know who I was talking about. "Have you seen him? And if you haven't, do you know of anyone who might have?"

As I was talking, I swung my bag off my shoulders, unzipped it and reached into the side pocket. The gnome gave me a sly grin, but before he could say anything about cost, I pulled out a full bottle of honey and plunked it on the table.

He blinked. "What's this?"

"Payment," I replied flatly. "For information."

"Hmm." The gnome regarded it appraisingly, trying not to look eager, though I saw it anyway. "I do use honey in a lot of my potions, but I don't know if that will be enough of a trade..."

I snatched the bottle off the counter and turned. "Fine. We'll just find someone else."

"Wait! Wait." The gnome threw out his hand, scowling. "Very well." He sniffed. "You drive a hard bargain, human. Give that to me, and I'll tell you what I know."

Still wary, I handed it over, placing it within reach this time. The vendor snatched it up, sniffed the cap deeply and smiled. Tossing it behind the table, he turned back to me with a grin.

"Sorry, human. Haven't seen him."

I breathed deeply to stop myself from punching this faery in his smirking head. "That's not what I asked."

"You wanted me to tell you if I've seen your friend." The gnome sounded smug. "And I answered. I haven't seen anyone like that around here. I gave you the information we agreed on, human. This bargain is done."

Dammit, this was why I hated faeries. I didn't have many bargaining chips left, and we still didn't know where Keirran could be. At least we hadn't been negotiating for something important, like my voice or my future kid. I'd have to word any requests very carefully next time.

But before I could say or do anything else, Annwyl spoke up, startling us both.

"No," she said, coming around to stand beside me. Her voice was firm, shockingly different than the shy, quiet girl I'd known so far. "Not everything. You're 'forgetting' the second part of the question. Do you know of anyone who might have seen our friend? This market has an information broker, does it not? Where can we find it?"

"Ahhh." The gnome shuffled his feet, not meeting Annwyl's fierce glare. I was still staring at her in shock and also kicking myself for not catching that myself. "Well, like I said," he muttered, "I haven't seen your friend. But there *is* an information broker around here, I believe."

"Where?" Annwyl asked, her tone hard.

"She has a tent two blocks down," the gnome said, pointing with a crooked finger. "Not very obvious—you'll have to be looking for it to see it. Just keep an eye out for the crows." He glared at me. "And you'll have to have something better than a jar of honey to get the information you're looking for. She ain't nearly as nice as I am."

Oh, goody. More bargains. Wonder what this *faery will want. If it even mentions my firstborn kid, I swear I'm going to punch something.*

Without another word, Annwyl turned and headed back into the market. Giving the gnome one last glare, I followed.

"I thought you didn't remember anything about goblin markets," I said as we dodged around a booth to avoid a troll stalking by, sharp tusks curling from his jaw. "Not that I'm complaining, of course. I was just surprised. Are you starting to remember?"

"No," Annwyl said, back to being quiet and shy, not looking at me. "But I've made a few bargains in my lifetime, and I know my way around the tricks and loopholes." Her voice hardened. "I wasn't going to let that gnome get away with not telling us about Keirran."

"Well." I exhaled, suddenly very glad that she was there. "You'll have to help me out with this information broker, then. I've avoided making deals with the fey my entire life, so I'm a little rusty." I glanced around the market, with all its crazy, surreal merchandise and vendors, and repressed a shiver.

"I swore I'd never do this," I groaned. "So, just poke me if I'm about to bargain away my voice or something."

Annwyl nodded solemnly, and we continued deeper into the goblin market.

The market thinned out a couple blocks down. Booths and tables still lined the sidewalks, but not as many, though there were still crowds of fey milling between them. I kept my head down and my hood up as I skirted the edges of the booths, searching for anything that might be our mysterious information broker. *Keep an eye out for the crows,* the gnome vendor had said. What was that supposed to mean?

"Any idea what we're looking for?" Annwyl murmured at my shoulder.

I was about to reply when I caught a split-second glance of a figure gliding through the crowds of fey. A girl...with long raven hair streaked with blue. My heart gave a violent lurch and I turned quickly, running into someone in my haste.

"Excuse me."

The faery I'd bumped into turned, a tall Winter sidhe with a furry white cloak draped over her shoulders, the head of a fox peering sightlessly down at me. Her tone was as icy as her eyes and hair. "What's this?" she said, glaring down her nose at me and Annwyl. "A dirty little human and a Summer harlot. Did you *touch* me, human?" Her blue lips curled with distaste. "I will never get the stench out of my cloak."

"Sorry," I said hastily, backing away. "I didn't mean to."

"Oh, but you did, all the same." The Winter faery's voice was cruel, and she snapped her fingers. Three trolls stepped out of the crowd, boxing us in. They were bigger than the normal variety, their skin pale blue instead of green, their lank hair white. They growled, baring curved tusks, flexing long black claws. The Winter faery's lips curved in a slow smile. "I believe compensation is in order," she purred as my hands twitched for my swords. "Or I will have my pets take it out of your hide."

"Milady, please," Annwyl began.

"Silence, Summer filth," the Winter lady snapped, giving Annwyl a look of pure hatred. "You're lucky the mortal was the one to transgress. I would have ripped out your weak Summer heart and fed it as a treat to my pets. Dare to speak to me again, and I *will*."

"Don't even think about it," I snapped, pulling my weapons. "Unless you want to take home three less pets than you started out with." The trolls surrounding us snarled, but the sidhe woman laughed. I bristled at that laugh but tried to keep my voice reasonable. I did not want to fight three scary-ass trolls in the middle of a goblin market. But I also did not want to bargain with a Winter gentry, not now. "I don't want any trouble," I told the faery, who offered a patronizing smile in return. "Just let us go, and we can get on with our lives."

"I don't think so, little human." Her eyes narrowed to blue slits, though that sadistic smile didn't waver. "And I don't think you're in any position to tell me what to do. So, what's it to be, mortal?" She edged closer, looming over us. "What do you have to offer for your pathetic blunder?"

"Nothing," I snarled, raising my swords. "I don't have anything."

"What he means to say," interrupted a new voice, making my heart stop, "is that he has to wait for me to make any bargains on his behalf."

The faery turned, the trolls grunted and I stared...as Kenzie pushed her way into the circle and stood in front of me, facing down the sidhe. Annwyl gasped, but I couldn't move or even make a sound.

"Another human," the gentry mused. "The market is practically infested with them tonight. Well, go on, then, mortal." She waved an airy hand at the girl. "Tell me who you are, before I have my pets rip off the boy's head and turn his skin into a new cloak for me."

"You don't need to know my name," Kenzie said in a clear, unwavering voice. "All you need to know is that I can pay for whatever *he*—" she jerked her head back, though she didn't look at me "—owes you."

"No!" I started toward her, but one of the trolls moved. Lightning fast, it lashed out with a huge fist, slamming me in the stomach. Pain exploded through my gut, and all the air left my lungs. Gasping, I dropped to my knees on the pavement, feeling the world spin around me and trying not to hurl.

Annwyl sank down, trying to help me up as the trolls closed in, growling. Kenzie spared me a brief, frightened look, then turned back to the Winter faery, holding something out to her. From my angle on the ground, I couldn't see what it was.

"Here!" Kenzie said as I struggled to get up, to stop her. "You can have this. Take it and leave us alone."

The sidhe's thin eyebrows rose. "A Token?" she mused, unable to mask her surprise. "Well, how very *generous,* little mortal." She reached out, plucking something bright from Kenzie's hand, and snapped her fingers. The trolls backed off, still growling, but retreated until they stood behind the Winter faery. "I suppose this will do," she said, and her gaze strayed to me, still on the ground. "You're very fortunate, boy. Next time, I will have your lovely eyes on a string. Run on home, before you get in real trouble, mortals. You don't belong here."

She glided off, her trolls stumping along behind her, and the small crowd that had been watching dispersed.

I rose, breathing slowly, carefully, to make sure none of my ribs were broken. "I'm all right," I rasped, to ease the concern on both Annwyl's and Kenzie's faces. But while Annwyl hovered anxiously, her green eyes solemn and worried, Kenzie remained where she was, watching me with a mixture of concern, wariness and anger.

My shock hadn't faded. I didn't know what to feel; my insides were such a chaotic, churning mess of emotion, I didn't know what to settle on. Relief that she was here. Anger that she was here and not safe with her family. Astonishment that she had found us. A horrible, gnawing guilt that I had ditched her, left her behind while I went looking for the fey.

And of course, there was that knowledge that she had just saved us. Again. I remembered Kenzie's quick thinking in the Nevernever, when I'd been in trouble and she'd managed to turn it around. The odds hadn't looked good for me a few seconds ago, either. Those trolls probably would've torn my arms off.

Why didn't you want her to come, again?

Oh yeah. Because she was gravely ill. Because there was a creepy faery assassin following me around. And because, no matter what she said, the world of Faery and everything in it was dangerous.

And I couldn't lose her to Faery the way I'd lost Meghan.

"Kenzie, what are you doing here?" I snapped, which didn't come out as strong as I wanted as my lungs were still a bit flattened. "How did you even find us?" Her eyes flashed and shifted all the way to anger.

"I asked around," she replied, glaring at me. "You're not the only one who can see the fey anymore, remember? When we got here, I kept my eyes open and found a faery living in the hotel we're staying at. A brownie, I think. He was all too happy to tell me how to find and get to the goblin market."

"Dammit, Kenzie," I growled, glaring back at her. "What did you give him for that information?"

She raised her chin. "I brought a whole suitcase full of gifts and bribes, tough guy. It's amazing how far costume jewelry will get you."

Relief spread through me. At least she hadn't come unprepared, though, really, what had I expected from her? It wasn't even that much of a shock that she had found her way with little to no information. Kenzie would always find a way, whether it was a good idea or not.

"You shouldn't have come," I insisted, and her expression darkened.

"Yeah, well, I'm here now," Kenzie shot back. "So unless you're going to throw me over your shoulder like a caveman and cart me out, I'm not going anywhere."

I clenched my fists, wondering how badly she would hurt me if I did just that. But Annwyl moved up beside me and touched my arm.

"Ethan, look," she murmured, nodding to something across the street.

Tearing my attention from Kenzie, I followed Annwyl's gaze. On the other side of the road, I caught sight of a line of birds perched along a telephone wire, black and nearly invisible against the darkness. Below them sat a plain, nondescript tent, also nearly invisible against the carnival-like backdrop of the market.

Kenzie glanced at the line of birds and the tent beneath it. A puzzled frown creased her forehead. "Crows," she stated matter-of-factly. "Am I missing something? I thought we were here for Keirran. Do we think he's in there?"

I slumped. "No," I muttered, picking up my dropped swords and sheathing them at my waist. No use in standing around arguing. Kenzie was here, and she wasn't leaving. I was certain she'd lay into me about it later, but right now, we needed to find what we were looking for and get out. "But it's a place where someone might know where he is. Just...we have to be careful. I don't think honey and fake jewelry are going to work here."

Kenzie still looked pissed but gave a stiff nod. Still, something nagged at me, and I caught up to her as we crossed the road, heading for the tent. "Wait, what did you give that Winter faery?" I asked in a low voice as we passed under the telephone wires, hearing soft, garbled *caws* overhead. "She said it was a Token." A Token, in faery terms, was an item that had been so loved, hated or cherished in real life, it had actually developed a life of its own. The item, whatever it was, became the embodiment of that emotion and was like a lump of pure glamour to the fey. "That wasn't costume jewelry, was it?" I asked, and Kenzie swallowed.

"No," she whispered, not looking at me. "It was...my mom's ring. I was saving it, in case I needed something really valuable to offer for trade."

I stopped, looking at her in horror. "Kenzie..."

"It's fine, Ethan." But she still didn't meet my gaze. "I don't regret it. And it was the only thing I could think of."

The guilt I'd felt before was nothing compared to the bonecrushing weight I felt now, squeezing the air from my lungs. I didn't know whether to apologize or yell at her for doing something so stupid, giving up something so precious, for me. But Kenzie walked doggedly forward, head and back straight, and ducked through the tent flaps at the edge of the sidewalk. Annwyl and I had no choice but to follow.

The inside of the tent was dark, musty and warm. Orange candle glow flickered around us, on tables and hanging lanterns, and the air smelled of bark, dust and animal droppings, making me stifle a cough.

Near the back of the tent, a ragged, hooded figure sat in the center of what looked like a huge nest. Twigs, string, grass stalks and branches were woven into each other, surrounding the hunched form in the middle of the nest. A pair of crows perched on the edge, regarding us with shiny black eyes.

The figure in the center of the nest stirred, cocking its head like it was listening for us. "Visitors," it rasped, its voice low and harsh. "Step forward."

We eased up to the tangle of sticks and branches, where one of the crows cawed and aimed a sharp peck at the side of my face, making me flinch. The robed figure burbled a laugh.

"Watch your eyes," it warned. "They like shiny things."

I eyed the crow warily, then noticed something else. The bottom of the nest was covered with feathers, string and bird droppings, but beads of brilliant color glinted among the offal. Rings, keys, earrings, buttons and other shiny objects were scattered about as well, but even they seemed dull compared to the glowing orbs of color lying among feathers and bird crap. Eyes shining with fascination, Kenzie reached out to touch the closest one, but the hooded figure swatted her arm with a folded paper fan, and she pulled back with a yelp.

"No, no," the figure rasped and raised its head. Beady eyes glinted under the cloth as I stared into the face of a huge raven, beak snapping in irritation. A scaly black talon reached out and plucked the bead that Kenzie had been reaching for, drawing it into its chest. "Secret is not for you. Not without a price." The bird-thing rolled the glowing green marble back and forth in its claws and watched us, unblinking. "You seek information," it said, its gaze settling on Annwyl. "All who come here seek information, secrets, hidden things." It closed its talons, and the bead vanished. "Perhaps I have what you seek, yes? Ask. Ask."

"What is the price?" Annwyl asked instead, echoing what I was thinking. "You spoke of a cost. What do you want for the information we seek?"

"Depends" was the croaked answer. "Depends on the secret, how well hidden it is, how hard it was to discover. Don't know until you ask." It clicked its beak with a grinding sound. "Ask," it demanded again. "Ask. Then see if the price is too high to pay."

Annwyl looked at me. I nodded. We wouldn't get anywhere standing around doing nothing, much as I wasn't enjoying this. "We're looking for someone," the Summer faery said, turning back to the bird-thing. "Prince Keirran of the Iron Court. We need to know where he is, where we can find him, please."

"Iron Prince?" The bird faery didn't seem surprised or distressed. "When do you wish to find him?"

"As soon as possible."

"Hmm." The bird faery thought a moment, then plucked a marble out of the debris, holding it up. It pulsed with a soft blue light.

"Large secret," it rasped. "Not difficult to get, per se, but demand makes it expensive. The Iron Prince is well hidden. His location is one that many would like to know. But I know where he is." It chuckled, a low sound in the back of its throat, and I clenched my fists. The answer to Keirran's whereabouts, not three feet away. If I just grabbed it and ran, would a mob of angry crows run me down and peck me to death? Not that I had any intention of doing something so stupid, especially with Kenzie and Annwyl around, but I wished we could get it without all this ridiculous, dangerous bargaining.

Annwyl's voice remained calm. "What do you want for it?"

The faery's eyes glittered as it looked at all three of us. "For secrets to be revealed," it rasped, closing its talons over the marble, "secrets must be shared. One piece of information for another. If you want to know the location of the Iron Prince, you must give me a secret in return. Something you have never shared with anyone. And I will decide if the combined weight of your secrets is enough to share this one with you."

"Really?" Kenzie asked, sounding puzzled. "That's all? Just one secret from each of us?" She blinked, then frowned slightly. "What's the catch?"

"The catch," Annwyl said quietly, startling me again, "is that our secrets become brokered merchandise that anyone can pay for. Something that can be traded away to whoever wants it, if their offer is high enough."

"Yes," the crow faery agreed, not bothering to deny it. "Secrets for secrets, one whisper for another. Information is very powerful. Some would die for it. Some would kill for it. How much are you willing to pay, little wingless ones? How badly do you want to find the prince?"

"I'll agree to your price," Annwyl said without hesitation. "If this is the only way to find him. But Ethan and Kenzie don't have to do this." She spared us a quick glance. "This isn't their burden."

"No." The faery shook its head, dislodging a feather that floated lazily to the side of the nest. "You are all looking for the Iron Prince. You all want the information. You all must pay the price." It snapped its beak with a sharp clicking sound. "Secrets from all, or secrets from none. That is how it works. And do not attempt to tell me falsehoods, humans." It fastened a beady black eye on me. "I will know if what you speak is truth or lies. So." It cocked its head, regarding us all. "What is it to be, wingless ones? Do we have a deal?"

Dammit, I didn't want to do this. And I sure as hell didn't want Kenzie to do this. Trading honey, jewelry or material things wasn't bad; I could easily replace them. It was *this* kind of thing that scared the crap out of me. Bargaining away something personal, something that was a part of me, that I could never get back.

But if it was the only way to find Keirran…

I sighed. "All right," I murmured, and Annwyl looked at me in surprise. "I'll agree to it, too. Kenzie?"

She didn't look at me, and her voice came out stiff. "You already know I'm gonna say yes."

"Excellent," rasped the bird faery as the two crows flapped their wings and hopped to its hunched shoulders. One scaly talon rose to beckon to us. "Step forward, then. Come around to this side and whisper your secret into my ear. But remember—trivial secrets are of little use to me. Deep, dark secrets carry power and are the only thing that will pay for the information you desire. Do not waste my time, wingless ones. Step forward."

I swallowed hard as Annwyl walked around the nest, coming to stand at the faery's side. The crow on the ragged shoulder eyed her, unblinking, as she bent down, bringing her mouth close to the hooded cowl. Her lips moved, and I averted my gaze, feeling I shouldn't watch her spill her darkest secret to the hunched form in the nest.

The crow on the faery's shoulder suddenly lunged at her, driving its sharp beak into her ear. Annwyl gasped, jerking away, as the bird pulled back, holding a glowing green orb the size of a marble.

Ruffling its feathers, the crow hopped onto the bird faery's arm and dropped the glowing ball into its open palm. The faery's claws curled around it instantly, and Annwyl's secret vanished from sight.

The Summer girl shivered.

"Yes," the faery hissed, sounding pleased. "Good, very good. We are off to an excellent start." It clacked its beak and looked at Kenzie. "Now, are the human's secrets as interesting?"

Kenzie's eyes met mine, and something in her solemn gaze caused chills to creep up my back. More secrets. I thought she'd already told me her biggest secret, the one she shared when we were alone and trapped in the Forgotten cave. The thought that she was hiding more from me made my insides hurt.

Kenzie walked around the side of the nest, bent down and whispered something into the faery's ear. This time, though I felt rotten doing it, I watched her carefully, trying to catch a hint of what she was saying. My heart stilled when, for just a moment, I thought I saw my name on her lips, but I couldn't be certain. Kenzie flinched when the crow's beak darted into her ear, emerging with a shining orb of blue, and it disappeared into the faery's claws like the other one.

Then it was my turn.

My heart pounded as I made my way around the nest. Secrets. What could I say? Kenzie already knew my biggest one. The regret I'd never told anyone before, that day with Samantha and the black pony, when I'd watched a faery hurt my friend, ruin her life and couldn't do anything to stop it. She already knew. And the bird faery wanted something I'd never told anyone before. A secret that could be bought. That could be used against me.

I still didn't know what I was going to say as I bent down, nervously eyeing the crow's sharp beak, so close to my eyes. But I took a deep breath, my lips parted, and without even thinking about it, I breathed:

"It's Keirran's fault Meghan never comes around. She would still be part of this family if he was never born."

Whoa. Where had *that* come from?

CHAPTER TWELVE

MR. DUST

I barely felt the crow stab its beak into my ear, still reeling from what I'd just told the faery. I... Did I blame Keirran for Meghan's absence? It sure sounded like I did, which made me an irrational jackass. Okay, so I'd already known I was a jackass, but an even bigger one.

The bird faery cackled, tucking the secret into the folds of its robe. "Interesting," it said, giving me a sideways look with one beady eye. "Sometimes the biggest secrets are the ones we keep from ourselves, eh, human?"

I crossed my arms, vowing to deal with this newest personality wrinkle later. Right now, we had to find the prince. "You got your secrets," I told the faery, stepping back to join Kenzie and Annwyl, ignoring their worried looks. "Now, tell us where we can find Keirran."

The bird faery clacked its beak. Reaching into a tattered sleeve, it withdrew the bright blue marble and held it up, letting it glimmer in the dim light.

"Secrets for secrets," it rasped and tossed it at me.

I caught it instinctively, and the second the globe touched my skin, there was a flash behind my eyes, and I was somewhere else.

Or maybe some*one* else. I stood in the same room, facing

the lanterns and the crows and the hunched old bird faery in the center of the nest. But I wasn't *me*. I don't know how I knew this; maybe because I couldn't move or even speak. It was like I was a passenger in someone else's head.

"And you're certain this person can help me?"

The voice echoed inside my head, low and familiar. Across from me, the bird faery shook itself. "Secrets for secrets," it rasped, nodding. "You have what you came for, boy. Leave now."

I, or rather, the person whose head I was inhabiting, turned, slipped out of the tent and began walking.

I kept my eyes open, though I didn't have much of a choice, and tried to pay attention to where I was going. Past the goblin market and the vendors haggling their unearthly merchandise, I ducked down a side alley that took me away from the main stretch. Across a deserted street, a wall of old, crumbling apartments sat at the edge of the pavement. I scanned the line of doors until I found the one I was looking for. Simple, unmarked, painted black.

Walking up the three steps to the stoop, I knocked twice, and the door swung back, revealing a shark-toothed redcap in the frame. The faery's dull yellow eyes widened at the sight of me, but it didn't move.

"Yeah?" it growled, baring crooked fangs. "Whaddya want?"

"I'm here to see Mr. Dust."

Mr. who? I wondered, but the redcap blinked slowly and nodded, stepping aside. As I crossed the threshold, I felt a pushing sensation, as if I was being shoved back. A tall figure in a hooded cloak, the head I'd been hijacking, I guessed, stepped away from me, walking through the frame and leaving me behind. I tried to follow, but I couldn't move without my host body, and the redcap slammed the door in my face.

I jerked, opening my eyes, to find Kenzie and Annwyl staring at me anxiously. The bird faery, too, peered at me from beneath its hood, silent and waiting. I rubbed my eyes, trying to shake the creepy feeling of being in someone else's head.

"You okay?" Kenzie asked, and there was a note of real concern in her voice, not just a courtesy offered to a friend. I nodded.

"Yeah. I'm fine." Turning around, I stared at the tent flaps, remembering the way they'd parted for the figure, his path through the goblin market and the unmarked black door at the top of the steps. "Better yet, I know where to find Keirran."

"Well, that's just all kinds of ominous," Kenzie remarked as we stood at the bottom of the steps, gazing up at the black door. "Didn't I see this once in *American Horror Story?*"

"This place feels wrong." Annwyl gave the buildings and especially the door a suspicious glare and shook her head. "Why would Keirran come here?"

"Let's go ask him." I double-checked to make sure my swords were still in place, then walked up the steps and knocked twice on the wood.

It creaked open to reveal the same redcap on the other side, who gave me an astonished look as he peered through the frame. "Well, well," it mused as the shock faded and was replaced by eager hunger. "What do we have here? You lost, human? You can obviously See me, so you should've known not to come here."

"I'm looking for Mr. Dust," I said, and the redcap snorted.

"How do you know that name? And why would a human need to see Mr. Dust? He ain't got nothing for the likes of you." The redcap bared its fangs. "Beat it, mortal. Don't waste his time."

"Not an option."

"I'm warning you, boy. Get lost, before I bite your tasty little head off."

I drew my sword. "My head isn't the one in danger here."

"Hold."

A soft hand touched my elbow, making me pause. I blinked in surprise as Annwyl joined me at the top of the steps and faced the redcap calmly.

"I am Annwyl, former handmaiden to Queen Titania herself," Annwyl stated in an even, almost regal voice as the redcap eyed her curiously. "And I wish to see Mr. Dust. The mortals are of no consequence—they are here to accompany me. The boy is only doing what he has been trained to do. Let us pass."

"Ah." The redcap smirked and gave me a disgusted look. "Why didn't you say so in the first place?" he growled, opening the door and stepping back for Annwyl. She nodded and swept by without looking at him. I swallowed my astonishment and followed with Kenzie as the redcap's guttural voice trailed us down the hall. "Keep your pets under control next time, lady. I might've eaten your little guard dog on principle."

"I apologize," Annwyl said quietly as we walked down the long, narrow hallway on the other side of the door. "I thought that it would be better to try to get through without bloodshed."

"No arguments here," I told her. "In fact, I think you should act like that more often. I mean, I don't want you to go snooty aristocratic faery on me, but you were part of Titania's circle. You were kind of important."

"Once," Annwyl said with a faint smile. "Not anymore."

The hallway ended at another unmarked black door, and when I opened it, an even longer, thinner alleyway wound off into the darkness.

"Seriously?" Kenzie muttered. "Good thing I'm not claus-

trophobic. Somehow, I don't think Keirran is here to buy uni-
corns and rainbow dust."

The corridor was just wide enough for us to walk through
single file. I drew one of my swords, just in case anything
came at us, and motioned the girls forward. Kenzie stepped
behind me, taking the back of my jacket like she was afraid
we'd get separated, and Annwyl brought up the rear. Carefully, we ventured into the darkness.

The alleyway grew even more winding and narrow, until
it seemed we were weaving our way through a crack between
buildings. Cold, hard stone scraped my chest and back, as if
the walls were slowly drawing together, crushing me until I
popped like a grape between them. My heart pounded against
my ribs, and I imagined it was getting harder and harder to
breathe. And just as I was beginning to think we should turn
around before we all got stuck, I finally spotted a thin black
door at the end of the crazy, twisted passage and hurried toward it.

Spitefully, the door retreated, or at least it seemed that way,
drawing farther back even as we rushed forward, keeping the
same amount of distance between us. Finally, after chasing
the door for several minutes, I lunged forward, and my hand
finally latched on to the glimmering brass knob.

Panting, I looked over my shoulder to see if Kenzie and Annwyl were still with me. They were; Kenzie still had a tight
hold of my jacket, and Annwyl pressed close behind her, gazing up at the door in fear.

"I can feel the glamour through the walls," she murmured,
drawing back slightly, both hands going to her chest. "This
whole place is pulsing with it. But…it's wrong, somehow.
Dark." She shivered, rubbing her arms. "There is something
evil through that door."

Goose bumps crawled up my arms. Annwyl wasn't kidding.

Even though I wasn't sensitive to magic, I could still feel the wrongness of this place. It slithered from the walls, closing in on either side. It seeped from the door in front of me, leaving an oily taint on my skin, making me feel dirty. I gripped my sword with one hand and the knob with the other.

"Stay close," I whispered to the girls behind me and turned the handle.

The door creaked inward. Beyond the frame, darkness hovered like a ragged curtain, broken only by tiny yellow orbs that looked vaguely familiar. As I stepped cautiously into the room, I saw why.

Forgotten. The lights were the eyes of those strange, shadowy Forgotten that had appeared in City Park this morning. The ones who had killed the Oracle. I could barely make them out in the choking darkness, but there were dozens of twin glowing eyes, perched on shelves, crouched in the corners of the room. And all were suddenly fixed on us.

Behind us, the door slammed shut with a bang.

I raised my sword and put myself between the girls and the Forgotten, hoping the strange, shadowy fey wouldn't swarm us like ants. But the Forgotten didn't move, though I saw their glowing eyes shift focus to Annwyl, standing between me and Kenzie. I remembered what the Forgotten had done to her before; drained nearly all her glamour when she was held prisoner by their queen, and I tensed to slice them down if they tried anything like that again. But they stayed where they were, and I took a quick glance around the room.

My eyes weren't adjusting to the clinging darkness like they should be. Even though I saw torches flickering at the corners and in brackets on posts around the room, everything remained choked in shadow, hidden and unseen. I could make out vague impressions of sofas, shelves, a desk in the corner, but the darkness seemed almost a living thing, smothering something as soon as I focused on it, hiding it from view.

"What is this place?" Kenzie whispered beside me.

Somewhere in the blackness, a door creaked open, and footsteps thumped over the ground toward us. Two redcaps, their fangs glimmering in the gloom, stalked around a corner and stopped short when they saw us.

"What the—" Beady yellow eyes peered at me, mean and challenging. "Humans? How the hell did you tidbits find this place? Ain't nothing here for you."

Before I could answer, the other one tapped him on the shoulder and pointed a stubby finger at Annwyl. "There's your answer. That one's a Fader—I'd bet my hat on it." To me, he said, "If you're here to see Mr. Dust, he's busy with a customer. We'll tell him you're here, so stay put till then. The rest of you blighters—" he glared around at the group of silent Forgotten and bared his fangs "—stop thinking you can sneak around back and we won't notice. You're real enough that the arms pop right out of the sockets if we pull, so remember that. You'll get your fix when Mr. Dust gives it to you, not before."

The Forgotten shifted restlessly but didn't answer. The redcap snorted and turned away, while his friend paused to eye me hungrily, running a black tongue over his teeth. I met his gaze, narrowing my eyes, daring him to try. He sneered, spat on the floor and followed the other redcap into the darkness.

"Come on," Kenzie whispered and stepped around me, pulling Annwyl in the direction the redcaps had vanished. "There has to be a door back here somewhere."

"Wait!" I hissed, but they weren't listening.

Gripping my swords, I followed the faint glow of Annwyl's hair, past the staring eyes of the Forgotten, until we came to a small black door in the corner. Kenzie carefully turned the knob and cracked it open to peer through.

"What do you see?" Annwyl asked, hovering behind her, while I glared back at the room, looking for any Forgotten coming after us. "Is Keirran in there?"

"I don't see anything," Kenzie replied and eased the door open. "Come on, before someone finds us."

They slipped through the frame, and I had no choice but to follow.

This room was better lit, but I almost wished that it wasn't. Directly in front of us was an enormous shelf full of things you'd find in a horror film. Knives and wooden baseball bats, hockey masks, clown wigs, eerie dolls, skulls and bones. A scythe leaned against the side of the shelf, huge blade glimmering in the torchlight, and a shriveled, shrunken head dangled by its hair, spinning lazily to face us. Huge, hairy spiders crawled freely over the macabre bric-a-brac, and a large snake lay coiled around a skull on the middle shelf, watching us with beady eyes.

Kenzie pressed a hand to her mouth and shrank back, trembling, but I caught the murmur of voices from the front of the room. Carefully, I eased up to the shelf, trying to ignore the awful contents, and peeked through.

A desk sat against the far wall, a pair of redcaps standing on either side. Seated in the chair was a tall, spindly man with pale skin and dark hair that writhed atop his head like shadows. His ears were pointed, his eyes completely black, and he steepled his fingers under his sharp chin, appraising the cloaked, hooded figure standing across from him.

"I apologize for the delay," the man said, his voice a slithering whisper that reminded me of snakes and insects and other unpleasant things. "Business has been quite busy of late. I normally do not get such esteemed visitors to my humble shop.

My clients are usually exiles or, more recently, the scores of fey you saw outside. I cannot imagine you would need what I offer."

"It's not for me," said a quiet, instantly familiar voice, and my heart leaped to my throat. Annwyl stifled a gasp, and I put a warning hand on her arm. I almost lunged forward to grab the hooded figure myself, but something made me pause. Something about him was different. Even though it was the same calm, polite tone I recognized from before, his voice was cold, and the two redcaps near the desk were eyeing him in fear.

The man behind the desk blinked slowly. "And are you certain I have what your...friend...needs?" he asked. "I normally do not deal with middlemen—if the client has need of my merchandise, they come get it themselves. The price depends on many things—how long they have been exiled, how close to the Fade they are, how soon they need it. All of this affects price, as I need to know how potent a mixture they should have. Your friend should really be here."

"Well, she's not," the hooded figure said, his voice hard. "And you'll deal with me, because there's no time left. The Fade has already begun."

"Already begun?" The man straightened, suddenly intrigued. "Well, if that is the case, she'll need the strongest mix possible. Of course..." He eyed the figure, a slow smile spreading over his face. "That means the price will be...quite high."

"That's fine" was the immediate answer. "Price doesn't matter. Whatever it takes, as long as it's from me."

"No!"

Annwyl couldn't contain herself any longer. Breaking away, she rushed around the shelf into the room. "Keirran, no!"

Cursing, I scrambled out of hiding, Kenzie right behind me, as the hooded figure spun, his cloak swirling around him. My stomach lurched as our gazes met. Cold ice-blue eyes stabbed at me from beneath the hood, and bright silver hair fell around his face, the only spots of color to be seen. Beneath the cloak, he was dressed in black: black shirt, pants, boots, even gloves. I remembered the smiling, easygoing faery from just a week ago. The hard-eyed creature dressed all in black, staring at me in this den of shadow and fear, seemed like a stranger.

But then his gaze slid to Annwyl, and the cold stranger disappeared as shock replaced the impassiveness in his eyes. Keirran stepped forward, his voice an awed whisper. "Annwyl?"

She rushed forward, and the prince's arms opened as the Summer girl threw herself into him. Keirran hugged her close, closing his eyes. "Annwyl," he murmured again, sounding relieved and almost desperate. His hood had fallen back, and the torchlight glimmered over his loose silver hair as he buried his face in her neck. Kenzie smiled, watching them, while I glared at the man and the lurking redcaps, making sure they didn't try anything.

Keirran pulled back but didn't release the Summer faery, pressing a palm to her cheek, his face intense, worried. "Annwyl, what are you doing here? Why aren't you with Leanansidhe? Ethan…" His icy gaze flicked to me, but it was just puzzled now, looking like the prince I remembered. "Why are you and Kenzie here?"

"I asked them to come," Annwyl replied, drawing Keirran's attention back to her. "I needed to find you. They agreed to help."

"Excuse me," said the man behind the desk, standing up. His redcap guards had drawn forward, but he held up a hand, waving them back. "Not to interrupt, but we do have a business transaction to complete." His stark black eyes fixed on Annwyl, and he cocked his head. "I assume this is the friend in question?"

Keirran sobered. "Yes," he replied, keeping a tight hold of Annwyl's hand as he stepped forward. "It is. Can you help her? I'll pay any price."

"No!" Annwyl tugged at his sleeve, and he gave her a puzzled frown. She drew him away from the desk, back toward the corner. Kenzie and I followed, myself keeping a wary eye on the man and his redcap guards.

Back near the shelf with its awful contents, Annwyl faced Keirran again, taking both his hands. "Keirran, please," she whispered, gazing into his eyes. "You can't do this. I don't want you bargaining your life away, not for me. The price is always too high. You don't—"

He kissed her, stopping her arguments. Kenzie blinked, and I looked away, my face heating. Keirran didn't seem to notice or care. Pulling back, he gazed down at Annwyl, his face angry, defiant and tender all at once.

"I love you," he said, without a trace of embarrassment or hesitation. "Please, let me do this. I finally found a way to halt the Fade. Mr. Dust has something that can stop it. No price is too high for that."

"A way to stop the Fade?" Annwyl looked stunned, and Keirran smiled at her.

"Yes," he replied, brushing her hair back. "There is something that can halt it, Annwyl. If it will keep you here, if it will stop you from Fading, I will gladly pay the cost, whatever it might be."

I didn't like where this was going at all. Another cardinal rule of Faery: if something seemed too good to be true, it was. "What is it?" I asked, and Keirran's gaze flicked to me. "This miracle cure that can stop the Fade," I continued. "If it's so wonderful, why don't more of the fey know about it? Why is this place so difficult to find?"

He hesitated this time, and I narrowed my eyes. Kenzie,

it appeared, had caught it, too. "Truth, Keirran," she added, making him wince. "You owe it to Annwyl, before either of you agree to anything. She should know what's going on. What's the catch?"

"There is no catch," Keirran said in a soft voice. Annwyl gazed up at him, and he turned back to her, lowering his head. "Mr. Dust offers a special kind of potent glamour that can temporarily halt the Fade," he began. "He has several clients that are exiles, those banished from the Nevernever, but he has also started working with the Forgotten, now that they can no longer drain the magic of exiled fey. It's distilled from the glamour of mortals, and taken in small, consistent amounts, it will provide the user with enough magic to live in the mortal world. However, the way he acquires it is... upsetting for some."

"How?" I asked, not liking the sound of that at all. "What does he use to 'acquire' this glamour?"

"Fear" was the quiet response. "Fear is very powerful, and the stronger the fear, the more potent the glamour acquired from it. Most mortals don't believe in the fey—they can't see them, and they've stopped believing in monsters." He swallowed. "Except one very select group."

I felt ill and had to fight a very real urge to drive my fist into Keirran's jaw. "You mean children," I growled, remembering my own days as a toddler, seeing my closet door creak open, eyes peering at me from the darkness. "Little kids, before they grow up and forget about the monsters in their room. That's where this 'cure' comes from, doesn't it?"

He met my gaze, unrepentant. "I know. I know it's horrible. But mortal children have been frightened by the fey and the things in the dark since time began. It's nothing new. Why shouldn't someone take advantage of that? Especially if it can save lives?" He turned from me then, drawing Annwyl close, his voice pleading. "I would do anything to save you," he whispered. "If there was another way, someone else I could go to, I wouldn't be here. But this is the only solution I could find, and I've searched the world over, looking for magic spells, scrolls, amulets, anything that would help. Nothing was powerful enough to stop the Fade."

Amulet. Something clicked in my head then. Kenzie wore an amulet, one that contained some pretty potent magic. Magic that had saved her life once. What had Guro told me that night, right before I left for New Orleans?

If you or your friends need anything, magic or otherwise, please come to me. I cannot go with you into the hidden world, but I can make it so it is not quite so dangerous. Remember that, if you are ever in need of help.

It was a long shot for certain. I didn't know what kind of magic Guro could do, if he could even help a faery. But he knew about the hidden world, and I'd seen his magic with my own eyes. And given the choices, I'd rather take my chances with Guro than a creepy faery drug dealer whose "payment" would likely be something horrible.

Of course, we still had to convince my stubborn nephew not to go through with this.

"I've exhausted all other options," Keirran went on earnestly, unaware of my sudden revelation. "There's nothing left. I have to bargain with Mr. Dust."

"At what cost, Keirran?" Annwyl shook her head. "Am I to take this glamour forever? Will you continue to pay for my life? What will happen if he asks for something unforgivable, something you cannot give?" Keirran closed his eyes, pressing his forehead to hers, and Annwyl stroked his cheek. "Even if this could keep me here awhile longer, I couldn't bear the price. I couldn't live with the knowledge that you are taking my place."

"If it's the only way—"

"It's not," I said, interrupting him. "Dammit, Keirran, just listen to me for a second. There might be another way."

Ice-blue eyes turned to me, surprised and wary. Kenzie and Annwyl glanced my way as well, their expressions puzzled. But at that moment, it seemed Mr. Dust had had enough. "Humans," he rasped, a note of irritation in his voice. "This is a place of business, not a place to stand around and chat. If you are quite finished, I believe the boy and I have a contract to fulfill."

He reached into his pocket and withdrew a small leather pouch, pulling it open with long, bony fingers. Reaching into the bag, he pulled out a handful of black dust, letting it slip through his fingers into the bag again. The grains sparkled in the torchlight, like powdered black diamond, and I felt a chill slide up my back. "This is what you came for, is it not?" he whispered, staring at Keirran, who straightened at the sight of it.

"Keirran," I warned, desperate to stop him, knowing he had only to speak one word to complete this bargain. "Do *not* say yes. You don't have to do this. I'm telling you, there's another way. You just have to trust me."

"Keirran, please listen to him," Annwyl said, taking his arm.

The prince finally turned to me, his expression intense. "Can you promise me your way will work?" he asked, his voice fervent. "Can you swear that if I agree to this, Annwyl will be saved?"

"I…" I hesitated, stabbing a hand through my hair. "I can't…make that promise," I admitted, watching his eyes narrow. "I just know someone who might be able to help." Frustration colored my voice, and I jerked a thumb at the faeries watching us. "But it's gotta be better than drugging your girlfriend with whatever crack this sicko is dealing."

"But you don't know." Keirran's tone was frustrated, too. "You don't know if your way will stop the Fade. I can't risk it, Ethan. Not now."

"Boy." Mr. Dust's voice was no longer soothing or cajoling. "You are trying my patience," he warned, and I noticed several more redcaps and an ogre had crept out of the shadows to join him. All the faeries looked pretty unfriendly, watching us with glowing eyes, a string of drool hanging from the ogre's tusk. "And I have other clients waiting up front, so I'll need an answer, boy. What's it to be?"

Keirran took a breath to speak, but Kenzie beat him to it.

"These other clients," she said, making us all stare at her, "they're Forgotten, aren't they?"

Mr. Dust blinked at her, then shrugged. "Yes," he said. "As I said before, many of my clients are exiles, but the Forgotten Queen and I have worked out a deal. I provide them with the glamour they need to live, since they cannot get it anywhere else, and in turn they perform...certain tasks for me. A fair bargain for all."

"Yeah?" Kenzie's expression was hard, angry. "Fair bargain, huh? Then answer me this. The Forgotten didn't always look like that, all dark and shadowy. Did they get that way from taking your black dust or from something else?"

The faery sniffed. "The Forgotten are a special case," he said, and I heard him trying to dance around the question. "My dust is very potent, and it seems they have no glamour of their own to temper it. Very recently, a few of them have begun...changing, taking on the darker aspects that went into its making. They're starting to personify fear. Fear of the unknown, of the shadowy terrors that lurk in the darkness and under beds. Fear of the dark and all that it hides."

"So, you're turning them into nightmares? Is that what's happening?"

"Of course not." Mr. Dust bared flat, even teeth in a very unhuman grimace. "I don't see why I must explain this to you, mortal, but…think of a painting of a sunset. Everyone knows what a sunset looks like. If someone told you to paint a sunset, you would at least know where to start, yes?" He didn't wait for her to answer, but continued in the same slightly irritated voice. "Now, mortal, picture a blank canvas. Imagine that you'd never seen a sunset, didn't even know what one looked like, and someone asked you to paint one. Not only that, the only colors you were allowed were black and gray. Do you think your sunset would look anything like the real thing?

"The Forgotten are a blank canvas," Mr. Dust went on as Kenzie frowned in confusion. "No one knows what they are, no one remembers what they looked like. The Forgotten themselves barely remember anything. Who they were, how they lived—it's all a blank to them. And so, they can be altered, if the only 'colors' they are provided are shades of black and gray. They can change…they can be molded into something completely different than their original form. So you saw with the crowd outside. Soon, that will be all they know.

"But you need not worry your pretty head about that, mortal." Mr. Dust waved a thin, airy hand. "Only the Forgotten are susceptible to that little…side effect. Your friend was part of the Seelie Court once, yes?" He smiled at Annwyl, who shivered. "She will not be affected like them.

"Now." Mr. Dust turned back to Keirran, clasping his hands together. "We keep getting interrupted, my boy," he stated, a dangerous edge creeping into his sibilant voice. "And I am losing patience. I need an answer. This instant. And if your friends attempt to stop us, I will have the redcaps rip out their throats." The pouch appeared again, dangling from a long, bony finger. "Do we have a deal?"

"You still haven't told me the price," Keirran said before I could interrupt. "What do you want for it?"

"Dammit, Keirran—"

"I've come all this way," the Iron Prince said coolly, still not looking at me or any of us. "I can't leave empty-handed. Not if it means saving her life." His gaze met the faery dealer's, cold and rational. "What's the cost for the dust tonight?"

Mr. Dust smiled.

"A very special bargain," he crooned, his sharp gaze flicking to Kenzie and me. "A onetime offer. The price for the dust will be…the two mortals. Give them to me, and I will provide your girl with a lifetime supply of glamour. You will never have to make another payment after tonight."

"What?" My skin crawled, and the walls of the room seemed to close in on us. I glared at the faery dealer, my hands dropping to my swords. "Not that I have any intention of letting that happen, but why the hell do you want us?"

"They have the Sight," Mr. Dust continued, speaking to Keirran and ignoring me. "If they can See us, they can fear us, and that is worth more than the nightmares of a dozen children. Give me the two humans, Prince, and I will provide you with all the glamour you need, for as long as they are alive. Be warned, however. If you refuse, the price will become much higher. That is my offer, boy. What say you? Do we have a deal?"

I met Keirran's gaze. He stared back, eyes glittering, reminding me of that night in the Lady's throne room. When the Queen of the Forgotten asked Keirran if he would return, if he would promise to come back to her of his own free will, and he agreed. I'd tried to stop him then, too. But once Keirran's mind was set, there was no talking him down. I didn't think Keirran would stoop so low as to stab us in the back, but I couldn't get that night, the night he'd almost betrayed me, out of my head.

Don't you dare sell us out, Keirran, I thought, holding his stare. *I will never forgive you, and if we have to fight our way out of this, you'll be the first one I'm going through.*

"Keirran," Annwyl whispered, taking his arm, "please... don't."

Keirran closed his eyes and turned to face Mr. Dust.

"No," he said firmly, and my insides uncoiled with relief. "No deal. That's the one thing I can't give you. This bargain is off." His icy glare stabbed into me for the briefest of seconds before he turned back to the fey dealer. "I'm sorry we've wasted your time. We'll show ourselves out."

"That," Mr. Dust said, withdrawing the leather pouch, "is very unfortunate. But I'm afraid you're not going anywhere."

The redcaps and ogre pressed forward, grinning eagerly. Keirran instantly drew his sword, about the same instant as I pulled my mine. The screech of weapons echoed through the small room as we stepped in front of the girls. The redcaps hooted, baring their fangs, and the ogre rumbled a challenge.

Keirran looked around calmly. "You don't want to do this," he warned.

Mr. Dust clasped his hands in front of him again, seemingly unconcerned. "When I said the price would jump substantially if you refused, I was not making idle threats," he hissed. "The price has just gotten much higher. Now we bargain for something new. Your lives."

"Yeah, I think I've reached my shopping limit for the day," I said, backing toward the exit, keeping myself between Annwyl, Kenzie and the advancing redcaps. The door behind us banged open, and several more of the evil fey spilled into the room, trapping us between them. I cursed and spared a glance at the prince beside me, feeling the air chill around him. "Great. Tell me you saw this coming, Prince."

Keirran gave a small, humorless smile. "From a mile away," he said and raised his free arm.

Glamour swirled around him, invisible, but I could feel the icy cold radiating from the prince, the magic of Winter and the Unseelie Court. It tossed his silver hair, making his eyes glow blue-white. I shivered as frost crept over the walls and floor, making my breath hang in front of my face. The redcaps paused, and Keirran turned a deadly cold glare on Mr. Dust.

"Tell your minions to back off, or none of them will see another day."

His voice was soft but as lethal as the icicles forming on the ceiling, making sharp, crinkling sounds as they grew into wicked points. Mr. Dust gave a soft hiss, staring at Keirran with new eyes.

"Let us go." Keirran didn't move, but the temperature in the room was getting colder. The redcaps looked uncomfortable, and the ribbons of drool hanging from the ogre's tusks had frozen solid. I resisted the urge to rub my arms, keeping my swords raised and myself close to Kenzie and Annwyl. "Let us walk away," Keirran insisted in an icy voice, "or everyone in this room will die, including you."

"You don't want to do that, boy," Mr. Dust whispered, his voice soothing again. "If I am gone, there will be no more dust, no way to stop the Fading of exiles and Forgotten. You don't want to be responsible for that, now, do you?" When Keirran hesitated, the faery smiled. "All you have to do is leave me the two mortals, and we can avoid this unpleasantness. You will have your dust, and the Summer girl will be saved. Surely you can see the wisdom in this? What are two humans to the Iron Prince? The world is crawling with them. Just promise me these two, and our bargain will be complete."

I didn't know what to expect, but it wasn't Keirran's laughter, quiet and mocking, as he shook his head at the faery dealer. "That's quite an offer," he said, lowering his arm. "But I think you're forgetting something."

"Oh? And what is that, boy?"

Keirran dropped to one knee, driving his fist into the wooden floor. There was a blinding flash of blue-white, and I flinched, turning away, as roars and screams erupted around us. But a second later, they cut out as if someone had flipped a switch. My skin burned with cold, and I opened my eyes with a gasp.

The room now resembled the interior of an icebox. Everything was frozen, buried under several inches of solid ice. The redcaps and the lone ogre stood in the same spots, arms thrown up and mouths gaping, encased in a layer of frozen crystal.

In the center of the room, Mr. Dust blinked at us, unharmed. Keirran rose, panting, and gave the faery dealer a hard smile.

"I don't sell out my family."

I was pretty sure my mouth was hanging open as Keirran calmly turned to me and jerked his head at the door. "Come on," he said, sounding tired. "Let's get out of here."

No one argued, and no one tried to stop us. We walked past the frozen ogre and redcaps, trying not to look at the once-living fey, following Keirran as he strode across the room and pushed open the door...

...to face a horde of Forgotten on the other side.

I tensed, gripping my swords. Great, out of the frying pan, into the fire. And here I'd thought we were home free. But the Forgotten didn't move, watching us with glowing yellow eyes, and Keirran, standing in the doorway, gazed calmly back.

And then the crowd of Forgotten parted, bowing their heads and moving aside. Keirran took Annwyl's hand and stepped through the door, moving steadily across the room. Warily, the rest of us followed, and the horde of Forgotten watched us leave, standing to either side like an army of shadows, silent and unmoving.

It gave me the creeps.

Keirran didn't stop until we were out the door, through the twisted alleyway that was far shorter than I remembered and across the street. Pulling Annwyl into the dark space between two buildings, he turned on me with a bright, desperate look in his eyes.

"All right," he began, staring me down, "I did what you asked. I refused the deal that would suppress the Fade, and I think I've burned all bridges with Mr. Dust. Please tell me you have something else, Ethan. Something that will stop this."

I swallowed. "I do. Or, at least, my Guro does. You met him before, remember?" Keirran nodded, and I went on. "He's a *tuhon,* a faith healer of his people, and he's also skilled in the magic arts. He said if we were to find you, to come to him. He might be able to help."

"Might?" Keirran asked and shook his head. "What if he can't? What will happen then?" He glanced at Annwyl, his expression tormented. "If this doesn't work, what am I supposed to do?"

The Summer faery's eyes were gentle as she touched the side of his face. "You could let me go, my prince. Sometimes, that is the only choice."

Keirran's gaze turned defiant, but before he could reply, another voice pierced the darkness above us.

"Master!"

A spindly, bat-eared creature with huge green eyes scuttled down the wall like a huge spider and leaped at Keirran, landing on his chest. "Master!" the gremlin cried again, tugging on his shirt. "Master, he is coming! He is coming!" His head swiveled around then, catching sight of Kenzie, and he flung himself at her with a joyful cry. "Pretty girl! Pretty girl is here!"

"Hey, Razor." Kenzie grinned as she caught him. The gremlin buzzed and scrambled to her shoulders, flashing his blue-white smile. "I was wondering where you were."

"Who is coming?" Keirran asked, and the gremlin's ears pressed flat to his skull.

"Dark elf," he almost whispered. "Dark elf coming. Now."

Dark elf? *Oh no.* That could only mean one person. And by the way Keirran went pale, he was thinking the same thing.

Cautiously, we edged up to the wall and peeked around the corner.

A silhouette was striding down the center of the road, heading for the alley we'd just vacated. Lean, tall, a long black coat rippling behind him, he was instantly recognizable. Even from this distance, I could see the glow of his sword, blue-black and deadly, and the glint of a cold silver eye.

Keirran lunged back from the edge.

"This way!" he whispered and grabbed Annwyl's hand. "Hurry, before he sees us!"

"Keirran, wait!" I hurried after them, Kenzie right behind us, still holding Razor. "Why are you hiding from your parents?" I demanded as we ducked out of the alley into the goblin market, Keirran looking around wildly. "Are you in trouble? What have you done?"

"I haven't done anything," Keirran replied and seemed to pick a direction, jogging toward it with us hurrying to catch up.

"Right. That's why we're running away from the freaking Prince Consort of the Iron Court!"

"Keirran!"

The deep, booming voice made me wince. I glanced over

my shoulder…to see Ash on the rooftops across the street, the full moon at his back, staring right at us.

Keirran took off, weaving through the groups of fey, dodging unearthly vendors and shoppers and trying to melt into the crowd. The rest of us scrambled after him, and I didn't dare to look back to see how close Ash was.

"This way!" Keirran urged, ducking into a small, deserted side street. No fey walked the sidewalks, and the road seemed eerily abandoned. Worse, a tall fence stood at the end of the street, preventing us from going any farther.

I panted and glared at Keirran. "Dead end. Looks like we'll have to face him after all."

"No, we won't." Keirran ran his fingers along the wall, his gaze narrowed. "Where is it?" he murmured. "The Veil is thin here. I can feel it. Where…"

A tall silhouette appeared at the end of the street, just as Keirran pushed his hand *into* the wall and moved it aside, parting it like a curtain. Beyond the sudden crack was darkness and mist, and the prince gestured to us impatiently. "Hurry! Through here!"

Annwyl and Kenzie vanished through the tear, Razor jabbering on Kenzie's shoulder. Keirran glanced at me and jerked his head as Ash came steadily closer. "Come on, Ethan!"

I muttered a curse, ducked my head and plunged into the once-solid brick wall, feeling like I was passing through a film of cobwebs. Keirran was right behind me, dropping the curtain as he did, giving me a split-second glance of the street through the gap. Then the opening swooshed shut, closing the tear between realities, and the real world vanished behind us.

CHAPTER THIRTEEN
THE BETWEEN

"Where are we?"

My voice echoed in the vast emptiness surrounding us. I gazed around in shock; when we'd gone through the gash, I'd fully expected to appear in the Nevernever. Probably in some lonely corner of the wyldwood. But upon reflection, I realized how unlikely that was. Only the fey rulers—the kings and queens of Faery—could create trods between the Nevernever and the real world. I knew Keirran was strong and all, but he didn't have that kind of power. At least, I didn't *think* he did. Maybe I was wrong. But more important, Annwyl had been banished from Faery, so she couldn't go back to the Nevernever; the trods had been sealed off to her by Titania. And yet, here she was, standing beside Keirran and gazing around in awe like the rest of us.

So, logical conclusion: we weren't in the Nevernever.

Where *were* we?

The ground under my feet was hard, though I couldn't see what I stood on due to the thick gray mist coiling around my legs. In fact, I couldn't see anything except mist and fog, swirling around us in eerie patterns. There were no lights, no shadows, no glimpses of trees or buildings or anything through the writhing blanket of gray. There was no sound, either. Except for the four of us and one gremlin perched on Kenzie's shoulder, there didn't seem to be anything alive out there at all. I felt like I'd been dropped into a vacuum.

I looked to Keirran for an answer, and he sighed.

"This," he stated, his voice echoing weirdly in the gloom, "is the Between."

I stared at him. "Care to say that again? The Between? We're between Faery and the real world right now. How is that possible?"

"It's not difficult," Keirran said quietly. "The knowledge of going Between has been lost over centuries, but...the Forgotten know how to do it. Leanansidhe, too, though she keeps to her mansion most of the time." He rubbed an arm, looking embarrassed. "I...sort of picked it up when I was with the Lady."

I nodded. "That's why no one has been able to find you," I guessed. "Because you haven't been in the Nevernever or the real world. You've been here, in the Between."

"Please don't tell anyone," Keirran said, holding my gaze. "When this is all over, when Annwyl is safe, I'll explain everything. I'll go back to Mag Tuiredh and face whatever punishment the courts want to throw at me. But I can't stop now. And I can't let anyone else know where I am or what I've been doing. Promise you won't tell my parents, Ethan. Not now."

"Why?" I asked, genuinely curious. "I've spoken to Meghan— she just wants to talk to you. You're not in trouble, unless you've done something we don't know about."

"It's not that." Keirran raked a hand through his silver hair. "My parents are the rulers of the Iron Court, and what I'm trying to do now is forbidden. The other courts would only see me and Annwyl breaking the ancient law, and they'd call for my exile or something similar. I don't want to put my parents through that, even if they wanted to help. This has to be all on me." He looked away. "Besides, by the time they could figure something out, it would be too late. Annwyl would be gone."

"I am standing right here, Keirran," Annwyl said, sounding angrier than I'd ever heard before. Her green eyes flashed as she stared the prince down. "And I did not ask you to save me if it meant bargaining at the goblin market, making deals that could get you killed and running away from the Prince Consort of Mag Tuiredh. You did not ask me what I felt about this plan—you just disappeared without telling anyone."

"Kind of like another jackass I know," Kenzie added, making me start.

"What? Hey, this isn't about me," I protested, holding up my hands. Kenzie, however, wasn't listening. Her arms were crossed, and even Razor, watching me from her shoulder, looked peeved. My heart sank. In all the excitement and running for our lives, I'd forgotten that Kenzie and I were fighting. It appeared she had not.

"You're no better than Keirran, you know that, Ethan?" Kenzie stated, causing the prince to blink at her, too. "Taking off with Annwyl, leaving me behind? And after we made all those plans to do this together. Did you think I'd be okay with that?"

"Kenzie, you were sick!" I argued. "You just got out of the *hospital*. There was something after us and…" I trailed off. By the look on Kenzie's face, she was seriously unimpressed. "I just wanted you to be safe," I finished quietly.

"*You* don't get to decide that, Ethan," Kenzie said. "God, you sound just like my parents, my teachers, my doctors, everyone! What have I been saying all this time? If I'm going to die, I want to do it on my terms. I don't want people constantly protecting me, telling me what I can and cannot do, 'for my own good.'" Her eyes narrowed. "I trusted you. I thought that *you,* at least, would get me." She swiped a hand across her eyes. "You promised me you'd stay, that you wouldn't leave just because They were out there. What happened to that?"

A noise, somewhere out in the mist, interrupted us.

Everyone stopped talking and became very, very still. Even Razor, buzzing in distress on Kenzie's shoulder, froze, his huge ears pricked and alert.

The noise came again, a soft crying sound, accompanied by a faint slither that raised the hairs on the back of my neck. Keirran motioned us to stay silent, and we listened as the thing, whatever it was, dragged itself over the ground, crying and babbling in a low, raspy voice. I never saw it through the mist and coiling fog, and I really didn't want to. After countless seconds, the thing moved on, its voice growing fainter and fainter, until the fog swallowed both the creature and the noises, and we were alone once more.

I took a deep, steadying breath, realizing my hands were shaking, and glared at Keirran. "What the hell was that?" I whispered.

"Someone, or something, who's become lost in the Between," Keirran replied in an equally low voice as Razor gave a weak, garbled buzz and leaped to his shoulders. "Time and space don't really exist here, and sometimes fey or humans become stuck between the worlds and can't find their way out again. So...they wander. For eternity."

I shuddered. "Then maybe we should get out of here."

He nodded. "Follow me."

The eerie landscape continued, an endless plateau of mist and fog, shrouding everything in gray. It never let up enough to see the surroundings, but one time I nearly walked into a stone archway that loomed out of the mist. Frowning, I peered around and could just make out the ruins of some strange castle, crumbling and ancient. It seemed out of place, surrounded by complete nothingness. I mentioned this to Keirran.

"It's an anchor," he replied, glancing back at the towers as they vanished from sight behind curtains of fog. "Abandoned, by the looks of it, but was once tied to the mortal realm. The Between is constantly shifting, but if you have a tie to the real world, something that exists in both places, you can shape the spaces Between into whatever you want."

"Like Leanansidhe's mansion," I guessed. Keirran nodded.

"Or you can use the Between to slip between the mortal realm and the Nevernever, without a trod. No one does it, because they don't know how to part the Veil, and because if they become lost for even a moment, they'll wander the empty spaces forever."

"How do you know all this?" Kenzie asked, surprising us. She'd been unusually quiet up until now, barely looking at me. I figured she was still furious at my abandonment but was trying to focus on the larger problem at hand. Keirran hesitated, then said in a quiet voice:

"The Lady told me."

Annwyl flinched and drew away from him. Razor hissed, and I glared at the back of his neck. Keirran noticed all our reactions and sighed, looking out into the mist.

"I know," he murmured. "And I know what you're thinking. You have every right to be angry. That night in the throne room…" He closed his eyes. "Ethan, I never apologized to you. My actions that night were inexcusable. I don't know why you'd even come for me, after what I did."

Annwyl frowned, looking at him strangely, and he shrank even further. "What happened when you were with the Lady?" she asked. "What did you do, Keirran?"

"Nothing." I broke in before he could reply. "It was a misunderstanding. I barged into the throne room, the Lady's guards attacked and I got kicked around a bit. Keirran stepped in right before they would've killed me."

That wasn't the whole truth, of course. I left out the part where, when the four heavily armored knights had attacked, I'd yelled at Keirran to help me out, and...he hadn't. He'd just stood there beside the Forgotten Queen, watching me get my ass kicked. Watching as they almost killed me. I remembered the look on his face as I'd fought for my life—cold, blank, impassive—and it made me very nervous. I'd seen that same look tonight, in Mr. Dust's back room. That dark, icy stranger hadn't gone away; he was still here.

I didn't know why I was defending him now.

But the look Keirran gave me was neither cold nor impassive; it was just relieved. Suddenly, he paused, gazing thoughtfully at a portion of mist that looked identical to everything else in this place. "The Veil is thin here," he announced, running a hand through the air, like he could push it aside. "And I don't sense my father anymore. I think we're safe."

He lifted a curtain of mist away, and I could abruptly see the real world through the gash: a New Orleans street and a familiar building on the corner, orange lamplight flickering beside the doorway. Lafitte's Blacksmith Shop.

The sidewalk was deserted as we stepped out of the Between into the real world again, the streets empty and still. I checked my watch, frozen at 12:12 a.m., waiting as the numbers flickered and reappeared as 3:48 a.m. Better than I could've hoped. With the screwy time differences between Faery and the real world, we were lucky this whole crazy adventure happened in the same night.

"Where to now?" Keirran asked, looking at me. I rubbed tired eyes and tried to get my brain to function.

"Home," I said. "Back to my town. Guro is the one who can help us."

"The human we met before," Keirran said. "Your master. Are you certain he can help?"

"He said he'd be willing to try. And he's the only one I can think of."

The Iron Prince nodded, looking weary. "I'll try anything. I hope you know what you're doing, Ethan. All right…" He glanced at the spot where we'd walked out of thin air, then raised a hand again. "Let's go."

I blinked. "Through the Between?"

"Of course." Keirran looked back, confused. "How did you think we would get there?"

"Uh, with my truck?"

"It's much faster to go through the Between," Keirran explained. "Just like Faery and the trods, it doesn't conform to normal space. You can walk from one end of the country to the other in a few minutes, if you know where you're going and if you can find a place where the Veil is almost transparent." A faintly horrified look crossed his face then. "You didn't…*drive* Annwyl up, did you? In a car?"

"How did you expect us to get here?"

Keirran shuddered, then slipped his hand into the air again and parted reality like a pair of drapes. I shivered, too. Call it what you wanted, that was just creepy. "Fine," I muttered, bracing myself for more shadowy Between and coiling nothingness. "I hope you know what you're doing."

"Wait," Kenzie said.

We all turned to her. "Before we go anywhere," she began, gazing especially at me and Keirran, "I have to go back to my dad. I want to tell him where I'll be this time—not that he cares, but I don't want to worry Alex or my stepmom." She gestured to the buildings around us. "I can't just vanish in a strange city, with them having no idea where I am. Even Dad will freak out." She pushed back her hair, suddenly nervous. "So, can we make one quick stop at my hotel before we head out? It won't take long, I promise."

I held my tongue. I knew, by the stiff set of Kenzie's shoulders, the tension lining her jaw, that she was waiting for me to protest, to tell her to stay behind. She was gearing up for a fight, and I…had no desire to argue with her anymore. I still wanted to keep her safe, but her last accusation had shaken me up pretty bad. Kenzie had gotten the Sight knowing exactly what it meant. She wasn't afraid, though she knew the dangers just as well as I did. And I had shut her out, trying to keep her safe. As if I hadn't heard everything she'd told me about wanting to live, and people treating her differently, and not having time to be safe. She'd told me all that before; I just hadn't listened.

God, I was a jackass.

I looked at Keirran, nodded, and he sighed. "All right," he agreed, and Kenzie relaxed. "One more stop, but then we really should go. Ethan, what about your family? Do you need to tell them what's going on?"

I shook my head. "They already know. Well, they know I'm here and that I won't be back for a couple days." I just hoped we could figure this thing out quickly, that Guro would be able to help and that we could avoid crossing the Veil into Faery. I couldn't keep this part of my life from my parents anymore. And if I had to vanish into the Nevernever again, I was *not* looking forward to that conversation.

Not surprisingly, Kenzie had been staying at one of the nicer hotels close to Bourbon Street, a luxurious old building so far out of my price range, I felt scruffy just walking through the front doors. The receptionist behind the desk eyed me suspiciously as I followed Kenzie into the lobby, not seeing the two fey at our back. Keirran had glamoured himself invisible, and Annwyl seemed more spirit than flesh now, so no one even looked at them. Or Razor, jabbering nervously from Keirran's shoulder, his teeth flashing blue-white in the dimly lit room.

Me, however—a teenage thug stalking into a nice hotel in the dead of night—they definitely noticed. Kenzie gave the receptionist a bright smile and received a nod in return, but I continued to get the evil eye all the way down the hall.

At the elevators, I sneaked a glance at Kenzie, knowing that if I had to do this—explain to her father what was going on—I would be far less calm. "Do you want us to wait here?" I asked, making her frown. I continued quickly, wanting her to understand I wasn't abandoning her this time. "It might not be a great idea if you show up at four in morning with... me, and have to explain that I'm driving you home." I was going to say *your boyfriend,* but I wasn't certain where I stood with her now. "We could wait outside, if you need to talk to them alone."

"No," Kenzie said quietly, facing the elevator doors. "I want you there. Dad needs to understand why I'm doing this, even if I can't tell him the whole truth." She flicked a glance at me, and maybe she caught the apprehension on my face, because she added, "But you don't have to come, Ethan. I understand if you want to stay here. It's not a big deal. I can talk to him by myself."

Right then, I would've liked nothing more than to wait in the lobby. I could just see Kenzie's father glaring at me as his daughter told him she was taking off with the guy who'd just recently dragged her off to New York for a week. If he didn't ground Kenzie for life, he would definitely blame me, maybe have me arrested and thrown in juvie for real this time. Even if that didn't happen, I couldn't imagine he'd be very fond of me after this, and Kenzie's father was someone I really didn't want to piss off.

But I caught the underlying fear in Kenzie's voice and realized she was just as nervous, though she would never show it. And now that she was here, I wasn't going to let her do anything alone. Even if it meant facing her dad, I would suck it up and share the responsibility. It was my fault she had come, after all.

"No, I'm coming with you," I told her softly. "But you know your dad is going to hate me after this, right?"

"He'll get over it," Kenzie said, though her voice had gone soft and bitter, and she stared at the elevator doors as if she could will them open. "Don't worry. If he's going to find fault with anyone, it'll be me. He's blamed me for everything else. Why would this be any different?"

I wondered what she meant by that, but a second later, the elevator doors dinged open, and Kenzie stepped into the box. I followed, glancing back at the two fey. Annwyl watched me, looking a little dazed, as if she didn't quite know where she was. I was about to say something, but she blinked and glided over the threshold, standing in the very center of the box with her arms around herself, as if trying to keep from falling apart. Keirran eased behind her, looking worried, but didn't say anything.

Kenzie pressed a button, the doors shut, and the elevator began to move. Toward Kenzie's room, and her dad.

It occurred to me then, in a strange, surreal moment, that I was pissing everyone's parents off these days. Not only Kenzie's rich lawyer father, but Keirran's extremely powerful, immortal faery dad was after us, too. I shivered. If Ash knew Keirran and I were together, he'd probably go straight to my house, or he'd send someone there to wait for us. That meant I couldn't go home now, not until this thing with Annwyl was finished. Keirran wouldn't give up until she was safe.

Speaking of Keirran and Annwyl…

The Summer faery had been standing in the very center of the box, her arms wrapped around herself and her eyes closed.

She looked pretty miserable, and just as I was about to ask if she was all right, she flickered, making alarm shoot through me.

"Keirran," Annwyl whispered in a strange, strangled voice and collapsed into his arms. My insides shivered as I saw Keirran's arm through the faery's transparent body, as the prince knelt with Annwyl in his lap, her hair spilling over the metal floor. Razor buzzed in distress, his voice echoing shrilly inside the box.

"Annwyl!" Keirran grabbed her hand. The Summer faery gazed up at him, her expression resigned but calm.

"It's happening," she whispered as Keirran looked stricken. "The Fade is taking me. I'm sorry, Keirran. I don't think I can stop it this time."

"No." Keirran's voice was choked. He clutched her to him, his gaze bright and intense. One hand pressed to her cheek. "Annwyl, stay with me," he whispered desperately. "Fight it." She closed her eyes, and Keirran gave a quiet sob, pulling her close. "Please."

Kenzie suddenly slammed her thumb into the elevator panel, and the box lurched to a halt. The doors opened, and Kenzie spun on the prince. "Keirran, go! Get her out of here now!"

The prince didn't hesitate. Scooping up the vanishing faery, he lunged out of the elevator, dropping to his knees several yards away in the hall. I sprinted up behind him, gazing over his shoulder at the dying faery. Annwyl was almost completely transparent now, a Fading shadow, though she was still hanging on, her eyes squeezed shut.

"Nooo!" Razor cried, bouncing frantically on Keirran's shoulder. "No leave, pretty elf girl! Stay, stay!"

"Keirran," I said urgently, dropping beside them both. "Keep her talking. Make her remember something, anything."

He swallowed and looked down at the Summer faery, gently

cupping her cheek and turning her face to his. "Annwyl," he murmured, his voice suddenly calm, "listen to me. Do you remember the first night you agreed to meet with me outside the court?" Her eyes opened—colorless and blank—and shifted to him, and he forced a smile. "It was high summer, and I had to sneak out of Mag Tuiredh by train because Glitch was using all the gliders to practice aerial maneuvers. But we agreed to meet in the wyldwood, beside that waterfall. Do you remember?"

I think I caught a tiny nod from Annwyl, and heard Kenzie's footsteps just before she knelt down opposite me, her expression grim and horrified. I met her gaze, wishing there was something I could do, something more than watch Annwyl Fade to nothing in Keirran's arms.

"You were beautiful that day," Keirran went on, his eyes never leaving the Summer faery. "You were standing in that meadow with the flowers in full bloom, surrounded by deer, and I remember thinking you were the most captivating sight in the entire Nevernever. If Glitch had caught me right then, I wouldn't have cared, because I had already seen you."

Listening to Keirran's soft voice, I noticed with relief that Annwyl had stopped Fading and that color was beginning to creep back into her. If Keirran saw, he didn't give any indication and continued speaking in that same quiet tone.

"You were so nervous that night," he went on, smoothing a strand of hair from her eyes, which were slowly turning green again. "Worried that someone would catch us, that we would be exiled for meeting in secret. Do you remember what I told you? What I promised?"

Annwyl blinked, and a shiver went through her. "That you…would wait," she whispered in a shaky voice, and I let out the breath I'd been holding. "For as long…as it took. You would wait."

This time, Keirran's smile was real as Annwyl finally came into focus, becoming solid once more. "That hasn't changed," he told her softly. "And I'm not giving up. We'll find a way to stop this, Annwyl, I swear it. So you can't Fade away on us." He closed his eyes, resting his forehead to hers. "I love you too much to let you go."

I saw the glimmer in Kenzie's eyes before she put a hand on Keirran's shoulder and rose, looking down the hall. I knelt there a moment longer, making sure the danger was truly past, then stood as well, intending to give them a little space.

"Ethan." Keirran's voice stopped me. I looked back down to find the Iron Prince watching me, still holding Annwyl close. "Thank you."

I blinked, surprised at both the words, which never came out of a normal faery's mouth, and the genuine gratitude on his face. "I didn't do anything."

"You did," Keirran insisted. "Just by being here. Your Sight, your belief, was strong enough to keep her from Fading completely. Yours and Kenzie's both." He rose, carrying Annwyl easily, her head resting on his chest. "I won't forget it."

I shrugged, but Kenzie walked to the end of the hall and shoved open the fire door, peering up the stairwell. "Come on," she told us. "We can take the stairs the rest of the way."

We walked up two more flights, Keirran trailing behind us, still carrying Annwyl. The Summer faery appeared solid enough, but still slumped weakly in Keirran's arms, her eyes half-closed. I could hear Keirran murmuring to her as we climbed the steps, keeping her talking, and knew with a cold certainty that Annwyl didn't have much time left. That the next time she started to Fade out, she wasn't coming back.

Walking down the red-carpeted hallway lined with doors, I began to hear voices. Angry, frantic, desperate voices. As we neared the door to her hotel room, those voices grew louder, and my heart sank. Kenzie looked pale, hesitating at the door, where a man's furious voice could be heard beyond the wood. I reached out and touched her arm, leaning close.

"I'm right here," I whispered, and she looked at me gratefully. "I'll be right beside you."

Taking a deep breath, Kenzie slid her key card through the slot and pushed the door open.

The voices ceased instantly. Through the frame, I saw a large hotel room with a single king-size bed and glass doors that led onto a balcony. Three people stood in that room: Kenzie's father, looking a bit more rumpled and unshaven than he had at that first meeting, wrapped in a bathrobe at four in the morning; her stepmother, who was standing at the end table, phone in hand; and a small girl of about ten, clutching her knees as she stared at her parents from the corner chair.

"Kenzie!" Her stepmom dropped the phone and rushed forward, but Kenzie's father held up a hand, holding her back. Kenzie eased into the room and I followed, seeing her dad's eyes harden as they fixed on me. From the corner of my gaze, I saw Keirran slip through the door before it shut, setting Annwyl on her feet as he came through. The faery still leaned against him weakly, though, and he kept his arms around her waist.

Then Kenzie's dad came around the bed, standing before us, and all my attention shifted to him.

"Mackenzie." Though obviously furious, Mr. St. James's voice was calm, probably the "lawyer voice" he used in the courtroom. "I would ask you to explain yourself. But it appears the explanation is clear." His cold black eyes shifted to me and hardened. "So is this why you wanted to see New Orleans."

"Dad," Kenzie began, "it isn't what you think."

"No?" Her father's expression didn't change. "So, you *didn't* want to go to New Orleans solely to meet up with this boy, I *didn't* ruin your plans by insisting the whole family come as well, and you *didn't* sneak out last night to go running around New Orleans doing God knows what." Kenzie swallowed, and her dad's gaze narrowed, cutting into me. "I think it's best you go, Mr. Chase," he said in a tone that left no room for argument. "This is the second time you have dragged my daughter away from her family, and it will be the last. You will leave, and you will not see my daughter again after today, do you understand?"

I ignored my churning stomach and said very carefully, "I'm sorry, sir. But I'm not going anywhere."

"Very well." Her father didn't even blink in surprise. "Christine, call the front desk. Tell them to send security up to room 623."

"Don't!" Kenzie took a step forward, eyes flashing. "Dad, this was my idea. I told Ethan to meet me here. He hasn't done anything wrong!"

"Mackenzie—"

"No, you're going to listen to me for once!" Kenzie clenched her fists and stared her father down. "One time, that's all I'm asking. You've always pushed me aside when I wanted any-thing before this, then I go up to New York with Ethan and suddenly you want to be Dad again? It doesn't work that way!"

"You don't know what you're talking about, young lady." Mr. St. James turned on his daughter, jaw tightening. "Who set up those appointments? Who drove you all over creation looking for second opinions? I got you the best doctors in the country, and you endanger all that to go running off with this…boy, and land yourself in the hospital."

"Yeah, and you were never there with me!" Kenzie shot back. "You never visited…you never came into my room. You sent Christine and Alex to check on me but you never showed up yourself." Kenzie blinked rapidly and swiped at her eyes.

"You couldn't stand to look at me, even then. Because after all this time, you still blame me for Mom's death."

I blinked, staring at Kenzie and her dad, suddenly understanding a lot more. Kenzie's eyes glimmered, and she stood with her back straight, daring her father to say something. Mr. St. James did nothing. He stood there, blank and unresponsive, his face giving nothing away.

Say something, I wanted to shout at him. *Tell her she's wrong.* He didn't, though there was something in his dark eyes that might've been a flicker of regret. But I might have imagined it; his poker face was flawless. If he felt anything, Kenzie would never guess. No wonder she thought he didn't care.

"Kenzie, Ethan." Keirran's soft, desperate voice drifted up from behind us, though we couldn't look at him. "We're running out of time. Please, hurry."

Kenzie sniffled and drew in a quiet breath. "Ethan and I...are going home, now," she said, trying to keep her voice steady. "We have a friend who needs us, and I can't stay here any longer. You guys stay, finish your trip. This was never a vacation for me."

"Kenzie, no." It was her stepmom who spoke this time. The blonde woman came around the bed to stand beside her father. "You're not running off with that boy alone. Michael, tell her she can't go."

"You can't stop me." Kenzie took a step back, brushing my arm. "Why should you even care what I do? But our friend is in trouble, and we're just going home. I'll see you guys when you get back."

Her dad shook his head, as if coming out of a trance. "Mackenzie, if you walk out of this room, I'll have that boy arrested." She spun on him furiously, and my heart stalled. "I'm still your father," Mr. St. James continued in a stony voice. "I don't care what you think of me, what stories you've told yourself to make this all right. But I am not letting you go anywhere with him. You will stay here, with your family, and he will walk away before security drags him out."

"You can't do that!"

"You are sixteen!" Kenzie's father exploded, making us both jump. "You are sixteen, you are sick, and I am not going to lose you like I did Emily. You are not going anywhere!"

"Enough!"

Keirran's voice rang out behind us, and the sudden icy desperation in it caused a chill to run up my spine. Kenzie and I spun to see the Iron Prince staring past us, one arm still around Annwyl, his face hard and determined. Eyes narrowed, he raised a hand toward Kenzie's father, and the room filled with glamour.

I couldn't see it, and it wasn't the cold, lethal glamour released in Mr. Dust's back room. But I could still feel the air turn heavy, dense, like stepping into a sauna without the heat. My eyelids drooped, and I struggled to stay on my feet, leaning against the wall to hold myself up. Kenzie swayed, and I pulled her to me before she could collapse.

Keirran's clear, quiet voice seemed to echo all around me, coming from everywhere, slipping into my head. "Mackenzie St. James is fine," it promised, like a lullaby soothing me to sleep. "You sent her away to live with a relative, and she won't be back for a long while. She is perfectly safe, happy and content, so you don't need to worry about her anymore."

No, I thought, though I didn't know exactly why. I struggled to think, to break free of the fog clouding my brain. *This...isn't right.*

The sluggishness faded. I shook myself and looked down at Kenzie, leaning against my chest, blinking in confusion. I looked to her parents. Her dad still stood where he was, but his face was slack, his eyes blank and unseeing. Her stepmom had sunk onto the bed with the same glazed expression, and in the chair, Alex had fallen asleep.

"Come on," I heard a voice say, Keirran's I think, sounding flat and tired. "Let's go, before they wake up."

Shock and horror flooded in, burning away the last of the cobwebs. I turned on Keirran, but Kenzie was already shoving away from me, stalking out the door after the prince.

Keirran waited for us in the hall, the Summer faery in his arms again. His gaze was resigned as Kenzie marched up to him, fury lining every inch of her.

"Keirran, what the hell?" she hissed, keeping her voice low as it was still five in the morning, and we didn't want other guests poking their heads out to glare at us. "Tell me you did *not* just do what I think you did to my parents!"

"I'm sorry," Keirran replied, bowing his head. "I didn't want to, but they left me little choice. Your father would not have let you go, Mackenzie. He would've had Ethan arrested. And we are running out of time."

"That's still not an excuse! You had no right—"

"I did what was necessary." The prince's voice was calm. "I made a choice, and you don't have to agree with it. But can we please talk about this later? When Annwyl is safe, I promise you can yell at me all you want. But we should go, now. Ethan..." He looked at me apologetically, as if he knew I was furious with him, too. "I don't quite remember the way to Guro's home. If I can get us to that little park a couple blocks from your house, will you take us the rest of the way?"

I glared at him, wanting to argue, wanting to shout at him for both Kenzie's sake and mine. *What is wrong with you, Prince? You don't just put the faery mind-whammy on someone like that, especially in front of her own family members! What the hell happened to you?* But Keirran looked so anxious, and yelling at him would get me nowhere right then. Besides, like it or not, the damage was done. It sucked, but at least we wouldn't have to worry about Kenzie's dad anymore. Her whole family thought she was off visiting a relative and wouldn't even think of her until she came back or the faery glamour wore off. Was I a rotten human being if I said I was the tiniest bit relieved?

Probably.

"Yeah," I growled at him, ignoring his grateful look. "I can get us there."

CHAPTER FOURTEEN
THE RITUAL

I called Guro before I showed up on his doorstep that morning with two gentry and a gremlin, not needing a repeat of the last time we visited. Guro had a little girl and two dogs who apparently did not like gremlins, and I wanted to keep the faery madness to a minimum this time. When I explained what was happening, I still half expected him to hang up at any moment, but he calmly instructed me to come as soon as I could.

We went Between again, following Keirran through a bleak landscape of mist, fog and nothing else. My truck, sadly, would have to stay in the hotel's parking lot in New Orleans. I hated leaving it behind, but what else could I do? I just hoped it wouldn't be towed, impounded or stolen by the time I could go back for it.

The last part of the trip was made by taxi, with Keirran holding Annwyl in his lap and constantly murmuring to her. The mood in the cab was somber; even Razor was quiet, crouched on Kenzie's shoulder, peeking out of her hair. The Summer faery didn't look good, curled up in Keirran's arms, occasionally going transparent and see-through. Keirran's voice was low and soothing as he whispered to her, and I would catch snippets of stories, memories of summer nights and lonely meeting places, of dances under the stars and some truly crazy stunts he had pulled just to see her. Sometimes, Annwyl's quiet, lilting voice would drift up weakly, showing she was still fighting, still hanging on. But these were the last hours of her life now, and everyone knew it.

We finally pulled up at Guro's familiar brick house. As I paid the driver and we all piled out of the cab, the front door opened, and Guro stepped out, waiting for us. I looked at Keirran, still invisible to mortal eyes, and the Fading Summer faery in his arms.

"How is she?" I asked as we started up the driveway. Keirran shook his head. His eyes were grim.

"I can barely feel her anymore." His outline shimmered as he unglamoured himself, materializing into view. In his arms, Annwyl stirred and whispered something I couldn't hear. Keirran closed his eyes. "She doesn't have enough glamour to make herself visible. I hope your Guro can help something he can't even see."

I hoped so, too.

Guro nodded to us solemnly as we met him on the porch, his gaze lingering on Keirran. "Come in," he said, opening the screen door. "The dogs are out back, and I sent Maria and Sadie to their grandmother's for the day, so it is just us." We followed him into the living room, where just last week he had given me the swords now hidden in my backpack. Geez, had it really been that short a time? I felt like I'd been doing this crazy faery thing forever.

"Ethan has told me about you," Guro said, sitting in the armchair across from us. Kenzie and I took the couch, and Keirran perched on the edge, still holding Annwyl. I wondered what Guro could see when he looked at the Iron Prince, if he could see anything at all. "He told me you are family and that you have a friend who is…Fading away?"

Kenzie blinked in surprise, but Keirran nodded, looking hopeful. "Yes. Please, can you help her?"

Guro pondered this for a moment. "I do not know," he said at last, and Keirran's shoulders sank. "My charms—the protection amulets I create—they are for humans only. I have never done anything for…your kind. I do not know if they would have an impact."

"Would you try?" Keirran asked, a hint of desperation in his voice. Guro regarded him thoughtfully.

"First, tell me what is wrong with your friend. If I am to help her, I need to know what she requires protection from."

Briefly, Keirran and I explained as best we could. How faeries lived on through the dreams and glamour of mortals, how faeries banished from the Nevernever began to Fade, how, as the memories and magic that sustained them slowly disappeared, they did, as well.

Guro was silent a few moments after we finished, and the soft buzzing from Razor was the only sound that filled the room.

"Can you help us?" Keirran finally asked. Guro sighed heavily, drawing his brows together.

"I am sorry," he said, and my stomach dropped. "But I am afraid I cannot save your friend."

Keirran made a choked sound and bowed his head, bending over Annwyl. Razor gave a distressed wail, and Kenzie asked, "There's nothing you can do? At all?"

"My amulets provide protection from outside harm," Guro replied, his expression grave and mournful. "They cannot sustain a soul that is dying. There is nothing in the light arts that will help with this. I am very sorry."

That's it, then, I thought numbly. *Annwyl will die. She'll be gone before tonight. And Keirran…what will he do?* I sneaked a glance at the Iron Prince; he was curled over the Summer faery in his lap, shoulders trembling.

As if echoing my thoughts, Keirran raised his head. His eyes and voice sent chills up my spine as he asked, "What about the dark arts?"

I gave a start. "Keirran…"

"You said there is nothing in the light arts that will help," Keirran went on, ignoring me. His icy gaze was fixed on Guro, whose expression darkened. "What about the other arts, then? Cost doesn't matter to me. I'll pay whatever is necessary." Guro hesitated, and Keirran's voice became desperate. "Is there *something* that can save her? I'll do anything."

"You don't know what you are asking."

"I can't lose her," Keirran whispered. "If you can't help us tonight, she'll die. And I can't let her go, not yet. No cost is too high—I would sell my soul to save her."

"You might have to," Guro said quietly. "Black magic is not to be tampered with. When I became a *tuhon,* I swore I would not perform the dark arts unless it was absolutely nessecary."

"It is necessary," Keirran argued. "There is no other way." Guro continued to stare at him, his expression blank, and Keirran closed his eyes.

"I love her," he whispered, and Guro's shoulders slumped, just the tiniest bit. If you didn't know him well, you wouldn't have seen it. Opening his eyes, Keirran gave him a desperate, pleading look, his voice earnest. "Please, I'm *begging* you. Help us. There's nowhere else we can go, and Annwyl is out of time."

Abruptly, Guro rose. For a moment, he stared down at us, his dark gaze lingering on me, appraising. Then he took a deep breath.

"There is a ceremony," he began in a voice that raised the hairs on my neck. "A ritual that will steal the strength, memories and magic from one person and store it in an amulet for another to draw upon. But the ritual will weaken the target of the spell and will continue to weaken him until he is but a shell of his former self. It might corrupt him in ways he cannot see and it will eventually kill him, because he is essentially losing part of his soul. It is a very dark, black piece of magic, and it is something I swore I would never use." He faced Keirran solemnly, and the Iron Prince stared back. "If I do this, I cannot predict what will happen to you. At best, it will buy her time, perhaps enough for you to find a permanent solution. At worst, you will both die. Be absolutely certain this is something you are willing to sacrifice."

Keirran didn't hesitate. "Yes," he said, holding Guro's gaze. "I'm willing. What do you need me to do?"

"Keirran," I said in a shaky voice, still reeling from the fact that my master, my mentor, could perform black magic, "you could *die* from this. What would Meghan say? What if we can't find another solution after this?"

"There's no time left," Keirran whispered. "I'll do whatever it takes."

"There is more," Guro said slowly. He glanced at me, and my heart lurched. "For the ritual to work, Ethan will need to take part in it, too. We can only proceed if *he* is willing, as well."

"Me?" My insides shrank a little. "Why?"

"It is best if I do not explain," Guro said. "But know this— you will not be tied to the ritual in any way when it is done. I simply need your assistance to create the *ating-ating,* the amulet that will steal your friend's magic and drain his strength."

That sounded pretty awful. Guro wasn't pulling any punches; he was being straight with me, even in this. And he was giving both of us the chance to refuse. Hoping we would refuse. But Keirran looked at me, silently pleading, and I swallowed the dryness in my throat. Well, we'd come this far, and Keirran would never forgive me if I said no. I didn't like the idea of being part of this dark ritual, but I trusted Guro. He wouldn't ask me to participate if it was too dangerous.

At least, I hoped not.

"Sure," I rasped out. "I'll do it."

Guro exhaled. "I need some time to prepare," he said, sounding weary all of a sudden. "Ethan, do you have your swords?"

The question threw me, but I bobbed my head. "Yes, Guro."

"And you." He glanced at Keirran and the sword across his back. "You carry a weapon, as well. Do you know how to use it?"

"Yes. My father taught me."

"Good. Let me gather a few things, then I will take you to the ritual spot."

"Ritual spot?" I blinked. "Where is it?"

"Not here," Guro answered simply. "But not far. Ethan," he continued, beckoning me to follow him out of the room, "may I speak to you for a moment?"

Silently, I trailed Guro into the kitchen. He laid both hands on the counter and closed his eyes, before looking up.

"Are you certain you are willing to do this?" he asked. "I have never performed this ritual before, but I know it will get very dark by the end. It is not something I do lightly, and to be honest, I would never consider it had your friend not asked. But I want *you* to be certain, Ethan." He glanced back at the living room, where I could just hear Razor buzzing away on Kenzie's shoulder. "Your friend walks a dangerous line," Guro mused, his worried voice making my skin prickle. "He tampers with forces unseen, and he does not see the darkness rising up inside him. This ritual may bring that all to the surface."

I paused a moment, considering. "Keirran is family," I said

as Guro turned back to me. "And...he's my friend. Even if he isn't thinking straight, I can't let him do this alone."

"Your loyalty is commendable, Ethan," Guro said, smiling faintly. "Just make sure you give it to those worthy of having it." He opened a drawer, took out a box of matches and stepped away. "I will need to prepare a few things before we leave. It should not take long. Wait here, and when I am ready, I will call for you."

Keirran didn't leave Annwyl's side the whole time.

"How're they doing?" I asked Kenzie, who came out of the living room alone, looking tired. Razor had abandoned her, it seemed, as he was no longer crouched on her shoulder, probably in the room with Keirran. She filched a soda from the fridge and slid onto one of the breakfast stools, opening the can with a hiss.

"The same," she murmured, not looking at me. "Annwyl doesn't look like she's getting any worse, but Keirran isn't going to take any chances. He's not letting her out of his sight."

She looked tired. Exhausted, really. Her eyes were dull, and circles crouched under them, sullen and dark. I reminded myself that we'd basically been up all night and had been running from crazy faeries nonstop ever since the goblin market.

I moved beside her, resting my elbows on the granite counter. She didn't look at me, gazing down at the aluminum between her hands. I could feel the gulf between us, the simmering hurt and anger, and swallowed the last of my damn pride.

"I'm sorry," I offered quietly. "For everything. I'm sorry I took off without you, and left you behind, and didn't tell you where we were going. It was a shitty thing to do and... I'm sorry."

She took a deep breath, exhaled slowly. "I know why you did it," she replied, still not looking at me. "But...you really hurt me, Ethan. After everything I told you about my dad and my sickness, and wishing people would let me live my life the way I wanted. I thought you trusted me. Haven't I proven that I can handle the faery world just as well as you?"

"Better than me," I said truthfully.

"Then why—"

"Because I don't want to lose you to Them like I lost Meghan!" My outburst made her blink. It startled me, too. I bowed my head and ran both hands through my hair.

"I know that's a selfish reason," I muttered, staring at the counter. "But when Meghan left...it screwed me up pretty bad. I practically worshipped her, you know, when I was little." The words felt strange, coming from my mouth. I'd never told anyone this before. "For a long time, I believed she would come back. That whenever she finished what she had to do in Faery, she would come home. But she never did, not to stay. And then when Samantha got hurt...I lost her, too. She was my only friend, and..."

I trailed off, embarrassed. Kenzie was quiet, though I could feel her watching me. "That's not an excuse," I admitted. "I know that. But this scares me, Kenzie. Having you so close to this world, when all it's done is rip things away from me..." I sighed, studying my hands so I didn't have to look at her. "I panicked. I thought it would be better to keep you away from Them, even if it meant leaving you behind."

Kenzie's soft fingers on my arm surprised me, and I glanced up into her serious brown eyes. "I don't want you to protect me, Ethan," she said, squeezing my wrist. "I want to stand beside you when you face whatever Faery has to offer. And I want you to know that you're not alone, that you don't have to shoulder this all by yourself anymore. I know I'm sick, but that doesn't mean I'm going to roll over and die. I just wish you would trust me enough to share some of that burden."

I swallowed hard. "I promise," I said, holding her gaze. "From now on, I won't ever try to keep you away. I'll still probably be insanely paranoid and overprotective, but if you want to march into the Nevernever and wave a stick at a dragon, I won't try to stop you."

She raised a disbelieving eyebrow, a faint smile crossing her face. "Really? You won't try to stop me at all."

"Nope. I'll just be sure to stand in front of the dragon with a shield when it tries to cook you."

The smile broke through. "I think you have the roles backward, tough guy. Of the two of us, who's more likely to go waving their sticks at a dragon?"

"Hey, I have swords now. If I'm going to be picking a fight with a dragon, you can be sure it's not going to be with a stick."

"Ethan?"

"Yeah?"

"Shut up and kiss me."

The tightness in my chest deflated, and I straightened. Stepping forward, I drew her into my arms, stool and all, and brought my lips down to hers. She tilted her head up, her hands climbing my chest to the side of my face, burying her fingers in my hair. I groaned, clutching her tighter, feeling relief spread through me, and something else. Dammit, I couldn't stop her from following me into danger, but I sure as hell was going to protect her while she was here. I would throw myself in front of the dragon if it came down to that.

My heart pounded, and I kissed her deeper, my stomach twisting as she parted her lips, letting me in. Her tongue teased mine, and everything that had brought us here—Keirran, Annwyl, the Fade—rushed out of my head. I'd never felt anything like this before: these crazy, swirling emotions, all centered around the girl in my arms. Kenzie scared me, infuriated me, challenged me, and faeries or no, I couldn't imagine a world without this girl. I loved her more than anything else in my life.

My heart turned over, and the air caught in my throat. I pulled back, breathless with the realization.

I...was in love. With Kenzie.

The first sensation that rushed through me after that insight was terror. I'd never meant to fall in love; the fey hurt everyone I truly cared for. I'd resolved never to be so vulnerable, never to open myself up to that again. Everyone I loved became victims and targets....

Stop it, Ethan. You've had this argument a thousand times. It doesn't work with Kenzie, remember?

Okay, yeah. I knew that much. Kenzie wouldn't go for that excuse and wouldn't let me get away with it, either. So, now what?

"Uh-oh." Kenzie's voice brought my attention back to her. She peered up at me with a half smile, her fingers gently stroking the nape of my neck, making my stomach dance. "I know that look. What's going through your head, tough guy?"

I love you, Mackenzie. And it's freaking me out a little. I swallowed. "Nothing," I said, kissing her lightly on the mouth. She gave me a dubious look, and I smiled, running a strand of hair through my fingers. "Are we okay?" I asked instead. "Am I forgiven?"

I expected a smart-ass response, but Kenzie just nodded, leaning into me and laying her head on my chest. A little alarmed, my arms tightened around her. "You all right?"

"Just tired," she murmured, which did not ease the alarm. The last time I'd pulled her into this craziness, she'd ended up in the hospital. I didn't think the stress of running around fighting evil faeries and having her whole family mind-scrambled was helping her condition. "Why don't you try to get some sleep?" I told her, feeling her relax against me. "It's been a long night."

But she shook her head, leaning back. "No, I'm okay. I just need a Red Bull or something. Besides, I can't sleep until I know what will happen to Annwyl."

Or Keirran, I thought.

Footsteps, and then Guro entered the kitchen, looking tired but firm. He had dressed all in black, and for some reason, he looked a little frightening. Which was weird; I never thought of him like that. His sharp black eyes flickered to me, and he nodded gravely.

"It's time."

We trailed Guro out to his SUV, and though Keirran didn't look happy at the thought of riding in a car again with Annwyl, he climbed in without question. Guro was right; the drive wasn't far, just a few blocks down the street until it the road dead-ended at the edge of an overgrown lot. A small dirt path cut through the weeds toward a clump of trees in the distance.

Guro pulled a five-gallon bucket from the back and handed it to me. It was full of lighter fluid, firewood, charcoal briquettes and a rolled-up blanket. Taking out a portable stereo and a small cooler, Guro motioned for us to follow.

We walked single file down a narrow trail that cut through trees and swampland, beneath huge oaks dripping with Spanish moss, until we reached a small clearing at the water's edge. Trees surrounded us, branches dangling close together, lacy curtains of moss waving in the breeze. Guro walked to the perimeter of the glen and laid the quilt over the dusty ground.

"Put your friend right here," he said, indicating the blanket. "She will need to be well out of the way for what we must do tonight."

Keirran obeyed, kneeling and gently depositing the Summer fey on the blanket. For a moment, he stayed there, holding her hand, the Summer faery limp and transparent. His face was anguished as he bent down, gently kissing her. "Hold on, Annwyl," I heard him whisper, pulling away. "Please, hold on, just a little longer."

Kenzie moved to the blanket, putting a hand on Keirran's shoulder. "I'll keep an eye on her," she told him, and he smiled at her gratefully. Sitting cross-legged at the edge, she took Annwyl's slender, transparent hand in her own, and Keirran walked slowly over to me and Guro.

Guro had already built a stone fire pit and was filling it with coal, wood and kindling. Beside it, the bucket of lighter fluid, a box of matches and...

I swallowed. An amulet. The kind Guro had given me and I'd passed on to Kenzie. A small metal disk on a leather cord, sitting there so innocently on the ground. My apprehension grew. It seemed too small and ordinary for what it was supposed to do: stop a faery from Fading into nothingness.

But I trusted that Guro knew what he was doing.

"Ethan, Keirran." Guro turned to us. "I warn you both again, this could get very dark before it is done. You might discover things about each other, and yourselves, that you did not know and do not like. I issue this one final warning before we begin—this is black magic that we are dealing with, and it must not be taken lightly. Do you understand?"

"Yes, Guro," I said, and Keirran nodded gravely.

"Very well." He knelt in front of the bowl and began pouring in liberal amounts of lighter fluid. "This is what I need you to do," he went on, not looking up from his task. "You both know how to fight, yes? When I give the signal, I want you to shadow spar each other around the fire using your blades. Look at your opponent and what they are doing—

block, counter and attack them in the air, but do not touch each other. Understood?"

"Yes," I replied, recognizing this exercise from my kali class. We would stand several feet from each other and spar without touching our opponent or their weapon, trying to block and counter their moves in the air. Though we usually used wooden rattan sticks, not live blades.

Keirran frowned slightly, probably having never done this before, but nodded. "I'll follow your lead," he told me. "Just tell me when."

"One more thing." Guro stood and beckoned to Keirran, who stepped forward instantly. I jumped when Guro pulled out a knife, but Keirran didn't move as the weapon was held up.

"Your blood," Guro said, staring at the faery prince. "You need to spill a few drops onto the amulet so it starts to hunger for you."

My heart pounded. I didn't like where this was going at all, but Keirran took the knife without hesitation. Guro held the amulet faceup, and the fey prince immediately sliced the blade across his palm. Thick red blood pooled from Keirran's hand and dripped onto the polished bronze surface. When the amulet's face was covered in red, Guro turned away and set it on the ground again.

"Ethan, stand over there," Guro said, pointing to one side of the pit. I did, and Keirran took his place on the opposite side. Guro turned and clicked on the stereo behind him, turning up the volume. Dark, eerie drumming began to play, making my skin prickle, and Guro lit the kindling in the fire pit. The flames sprang up, tongues of orange and red, bathing the glade in a ghostly light. They flickered and snapped, clawing at the air, throwing weird dancing shadows over the trees and Guro's face.

"Go," Guro ordered, his voice low and intense, and started chanting.

I met Keirran's gaze over the fire and began to move.

At first, I kept my eyes on my "opponent," my movements smooth and deliberate, so he could see what I was doing. I would swing, he would block. He would counterattack, I would defend. At first, I thought I'd have an advantage with my two swords to his one, but I was wrong. Keirran not only kept up with me, I had to work not to let any of his "imaginary" blows get through. As our sparring got faster and the dance more serious, Keirran began to disappear, until I was only aware of our swords, flashing in the orange light, and my opponent's next move.

Around us, the drums beat a frantic rhythm, primal and dark, and someone's voice rose above it all, chanting words I didn't understand. They didn't matter. Nothing mattered except my swords and the darting blade across from me. Anger flared as all my strikes were blocked, all my blows were deflected. The drums swirled around me, goading and furious. I would not lose to him. I would not—

The clang of metal and the jolt up my arm shocked me back to reality. Somehow, Keirran and I had moved closer to the fire and were now just a few feet apart, glaring at each other over the flames. I blinked and shook myself, ready to draw back.

The cold, icy stranger met my gaze over the fire and swung his blade at my head.

I blocked, stepping to the side and meeting the sword with my own. The metal screeched, raising the hair on my neck, and shock shifted into fury.

I responded in kind, whipping my second blade at his face. He dodged, the edge barely missing him, and slashed up with his own weapon. The clang and screech of metal filled the air, mixing with the roar of drums and the frenzied chanting.

As I slashed at my opponent's chest, a sudden stab of pain went up my arm. It flared red-hot for a moment, surprising me more than anything, and I staggered back. A quick glance revealed what I already knew; I'd been hit, and blood was starting to ooze down my forearm.

My vision went red. The drums, the chanting, they screamed at me, filling my senses. Fury bubbled up from a deep, dark well, consuming me, making me sick with hate. I *knew* him. I saw what he was now. He was the reason I'd lost my sister, the reason she never visited anymore. She had wanted to keep Keirran and me apart, make sure we never met, and in doing so had isolated herself, as well.

I snarled at my enemy, hating him, and lunged forward with a yell.

He met me in the center of the glade, sword flashing, his face frozen in an icy mask. It reminded me of that night in the Lady's throne room, the night he betrayed me, and my rage soared higher. I lashed out viciously, knocking his sword away and stabbing forward with my second blade. The tip pierced his side, right below his rib cage, and his lips tightened with pain.

Setting his jaw, he raised his hand. I realized what was coming a second later and dived aside, as a blast of icicle-laced air tore into the trees behind me, the lethal ice darts shredding leaves and sticking into trunks. Snarling, I whipped around as the prince came at me, his weapon scything down, and brought both blades stabbing toward his heart.

"Ethan! Keirran!"

Kenzie's voice slammed into me, piercing the maelstrom of drums, chanting, fury and hate. I blinked and pulled up just as Keirran did the same, coming to a halt maybe a foot away. I could suddenly feel the cool edge of his sword against my throat, the tips of my own weapons resting on his chest, right over his heart.

I was shaking, anger and violence still singing through my veins. I glared at the opponent across from me, still feeling his betrayal, all the anger I normally kept locked away still raging below the surface. I wanted to hurt him. I wanted him to feel the pain he had caused just by existing, tearing our family apart. Thirteen years of abandonment, of missing my sister, of living in hell, all because he'd been born.

Then Keirran took a deep, shaky breath, and the terrible light went out of his eyes. "Ethan," he whispered, and the blade at my throat trembled. "What...are we doing?"

Horror sliced through me. Dropping my swords, I lurched away, staring at him. What *was* I doing? What was *wrong* with me? Keirran lowered his blade, too, looking dazed and just as horrified. And at that moment, the chanting, the drums, the fire, everything, flared up with a roar.

I staggered, my stomach turning inside out. I could *feel* the dark energy around us now, the anger, rage and hate generated by Keirran and I, swirling around the glade. The fire blazed and snapped in the pit, and I saw Guro on his feet with the knife in hand, still chanting at the bloody disk on the ground.

The amulet was glowing, pulsing red and black, almost like it was panting and alive. Guro shouted something at it, pointing at Keirran with the knife, and I swear I saw the thing try to leap off the ground toward the prince.

Keirran gasped, his sword dropping from his hand and hitting the dirt with a thump. Clutching his chest, his legs buckled, and he fell to his hands and knees, bowing his head. The darkness around us swirled, then, as if it was being forced down a drain, flowed toward the small metal disk on the ground and was sucked into it.

The wind tossing the branches died. The fire flickered

and burned low. Keirran still knelt on the ground, panting, eyes closed. On the blanket, Kenzie met my gaze with a look that clearly said *Go help him.* Still fighting the last vestiges of anger and the now-overwhelming sense of guilt, I sheathed my swords and hurried over to him.

"Keirran."

"I'm...okay," the prince gasped. Shuddering, he sat back on his heels, and I noticed the dark, wet stain marring one side of his shirt. *Shit, that was me. I did that. Why?* I was angry, I guessed. Angry enough to actually land a blow, to deliberately hurt him. Why had I been so furious? I couldn't remember now.

My arm throbbed, and I looked down to see my entire right hand and forearm streaked with blood, running in streams down my skin. Keirran saw where I was looking and winced.

"Ethan, I—"

"Forget it," I said gruffly. "Let's not think about it, okay? Guro said this was dark magic we were dealing with. I'll put this behind me if you'll do the same."

He nodded, looking relieved. I held out my uninjured hand, which he took without hesitation, and I pulled him to his feet.

Guro waited for us by the fire, his expression grave and weary. He didn't say anything about our injuries or the way our "shadow sparring" had devolved into an actual fight. I was too ashamed to say anything, feeling as if I'd just failed an important test, but Keirran stepped forward, his face anxious.

"Did...did it work?"

Guro regarded him solemnly, then held out his hand.

The amulet sat in his palm, glittering copper in the dying firelight. But it wasn't the same. Sure, it looked the same, a small metal disk with a simple leather cord, but it practically glowed with malevolence now. Call me crazy, but I felt like I was staring at a living, breathing, angry thing. All my thoughts about its normality and insignificance disappeared, and I was almost afraid to step close for fear it would leap up and bite me.

"Be careful," Guro told Keirran, who had shivered and drawn back a step when the amulet was uncovered. "The *ating-ating* is connected to you now, but not in a good way. It hungers for your life force, for your strength and magic and everything that makes you who you are. It will bestow that power upon its wearer, but you need to be aware that it will continue to draw from you until your strength fails and your magic is gone. I can destroy the *ating-ating*," he added, perhaps seeing the look on my face, "but it will have to be done soon. The longer you wait, the stronger it grows and the more damage it can do. If it goes too long, that damage will be permanent."

I looked at Keirran. He stared at the amulet like it was a venomous snake, curled in Guro's palm, before taking a deep breath and shaking his head. "No. If this is what it takes to save her, I'll gladly risk it."

"It is not forever," Guro warned. "It will sustain her only as long as you live. How long that will be depends on your own strength, but eventually, you will both perish."

My blood went cold, but Keirran nodded calmly. "I understand. We're just buying her time, buying us all time, until we can find a permanent solution."

And how are we going to do that? I thought. *You've already been all over the goblin markets, looking for a cure. The only other thing we've found is a drug made from the nightmares of children. Annwyl certainly won't agree to that. What other permanent solution is there?*

Guro nodded and held out the disk. Keirran hesitated as if reluctant to touch it, then reached out and deliberately grasped it by the metal face. I saw his jaw tighten, but then he bowed to Guro, turned and walked toward the Summer faery on the blanket.

Kenzie rose and moved aside, watching somberly as the prince knelt beside Annwyl and gently slipped the amulet around her neck, laying the disk over her chest. The blood from his wound spread over the back of his shirt, but he didn't seem to notice, his gaze only for the Summer girl in front of him. Quietly, I walked up to join Kenzie, hoping this would work, that the dark, bloody ritual we'd just participated in wasn't for nothing. I could see the outline of the blanket through the faery's body, the flickering amulet on her chest far more real than the fey it was attached to.

Annwyl's eyes fluttered, then opened—a bright, piercing green—and Keirran smiled.

"Keirran?"

"I'm here," the prince whispered, his voice slightly choked with emotion, with relief. Taking her hand, he held it in both of his, as Annwyl flickered, becoming solid again. "Welcome back."

My stomach uncoiled. Kenzie grinned at me, and I smiled, too. For now, at least, things were all right.

But then my arm gave a sharp flare of pain, making me wince. Turning away, I gingerly prodded my wound, judging the severity. It was hard to see with all the blood, but it appeared to be a fairly deep gash right above my elbow.

Kenzie saw what I was doing and gave a sharp gasp. "Oh, Ethan," she whispered, sounding appalled. "I thought Keirran had hit you, but I didn't know it was that bad." Her eyes flashed, and she glared at the prince, as if ready to stalk up and demand what he was thinking. I put a hand out to stop her.

"It's fine," I said. "It's not that bad, and besides…" I hesitated, wondering what she would think of me now. "The one I gave him is worse."

"What?" She looked at me strangely, then back at Keirran, her eyes widening as she finally saw the blood against his dark shirt. "Ethan, what the hell? What happened out there?"

"Ethan." Guro's voice stopped me from answering, which was good because I had no clue how to reply. I walked up, and without a word, he handed me a first-aid kit. Not the tiny, plastic kind, either. This was pretty heavy-duty. Kenzie padded up behind me, took the kit from my hands and knelt to open it. After a moment of rifling through the contents, she pointed to the ground beside her. I sat obediently.

"What will you do now?" Guro asked, watching us as Kenzie tended to my wounded arm. I let her hold out my elbow and push back the sleeve, wiping the blood away. After everything we'd gone through, she had done this so often it was almost routine.

"I don't know," I admitted, clenching my jaw as Kenzie dabbed at the cut itself with what felt like a peroxide square. That or a strip of acid. "I guess we'll be searching for that 'permanent solution' Keirran was talking about." I sucked in a breath as peroxide seeped into the gash, making my whole arm burn. Kenzie murmured an apology. "Though I really have no idea where we can find one," I breathed. "There's no way to really stop it unless she goes back home."

Guro didn't reply, but Kenzie piped up, as if it was obvious. "So send her home."

"She can't go home," I told her. "Titania banished her from the Nevernever, for being 'too pretty.' That's why she's in exile."

"But exile isn't permanent, right?" Kenzie said, picking up a roll of gauze and unwinding it deftly. "If Titania lifted her banishment, couldn't she go back?"

"Yeah, but..." I trailed off as I thought about it. There was no real reason Annwyl couldn't return to the Nevernever, none, except for Titania. The Queen of the Summer Court was as vain and fickle as she was powerful and dangerous, but Annwyl hadn't exactly done anything wrong. Her banishment was likely done on a whim, and if it had been a whim, then maybe if we reasoned with the Summer Queen…

I groaned. "I'm not going to like what we're going to do next, am I?"

"Nope," Kenzie said cheerfully, winding gauze around my arm. "You're going to hate it. And we'll probably have to hear you whine about how much you hate it the entire trip."

I frowned at her. "I don't whine !"

She raised an eyebrow at me, and I snorted. Guro sighed.

"I don't like this, Ethan," he said, making me cringe. "But I understand that this is something you must do, whatever it is. Just one warning." His eyes narrowed, and he glanced behind us at Keirran. "Be careful around that one," he said in a lower voice. "You saw what happened tonight. It was not only your darkness rising to the surface. And anger is not the only emotion that can force us to consider terrible things. There is only so much a soul can take before it is broken."

The image of my body lying on the ground, Keirran standing over it with a bloody sword, flickered to mind, and I shoved it back. "I'll be careful, Guro," I promised. "Thank you for everything."

I helped him load the stuff back in his car, carrying things one-handed as my arm still hurt like hell. I hoped I hadn't hurt Keirran too badly with that stab to the ribs. True, he'd drawn first blood, but I shouldn't have let it get that far. I'd known what I'd been doing every second of that fight, and it wasn't a case of me just trying to defend myself; I'd really wanted to hurt him.

"Call me if you need anything," Guro said, opening the front door of his SUV. "Anytime, day or night. And Ethan…?"

"Yes, Guro?"

His dark gaze met mine. "You can't save everyone," he said in a gentle voice. "Sometimes, you have to make the decision to let them go."

I watched as he drove away, waited until the vehicle turned a corner and vanished from sight, then hurried back to the group.

His words haunted me with every step.

Kenzie met me at the edge of the glade, alone.

"Where are the other two?" I asked, looking past her to the clearing, quite empty of faeries and half fey. She rolled her eyes.

"They went off to do their own thing," she said, putting emphasis and air quotes on the word *thing.* "Keirran got Annwyl on her feet, but then she noticed he was hurt, so off they went to 'patch him up,' as she put it." She turned and pointed with a finger. "They're in that clump of trees over there, but I wouldn't recommend checking on them just yet."

"Believe me, I have no intention at all."

She grinned, then slipped her arms around my waist, snuggling close with a sigh. My heart jumped, and I wrapped my arms around her as she laid her head on my chest.

"You freaked me out a little back there, tough guy," Kenzie admitted as her fingers began their maddening circles in the small of my back. "For a second, I really thought you and Keirran would end up killing each other."

"Yeah," I muttered, resting my chin atop her head, not knowing what to say. I could blame Guro's magic, but those feelings of anger and betrayal toward Keirran were already there, just buried deep. I wondered what Keirran had been feeling when he attacked, when his sword had cut into my arm and drawn blood. "I don't know what happened."

Kenzie suddenly coughed, hiding her face in her arm, her

body shaking violently against mine. Alarm flickered. She felt so breakable all of a sudden, her bones pressing sharply against her skin, the shadow of a bruise I hadn't noticed before marring the back of her arm.

"Sorry," she whispered when the fit passed. "Leftover ick from the hospital, I guess. I'll try not to cough all over you."

She tried drawing away, but I locked my fingers together and pulled her back.

Kenzie looked up at me, brown eyes widening, and my heart stuttered. Yep, it was official. I was definitely in love. I was in love with a girl who threw herself into danger, bargained with faeries and wouldn't take no for an answer. Who was stubborn and cheerful and relentless, and could probably beat any opponent…except the thing inside her.

I was in love with a girl who was dying.

You can't save everyone, Guro's voice whispered in my head, making my insides cold. *Sometimes, you have to make that decision to let them go.*

Kenzie blinked slowly, still gazing up at me. "Ethan?"

"Yeah?"

"Don't do that."

I frowned, startled. "What?"

"You look at me like I'm already gone. The way my doctors, or my teachers, or even my family does. All sad and resigned and grim. Like they're staring at a ghost." Her hand rose, brushing my hair. "I'm still here, tough guy. I'm not done yet."

A lump caught in my throat, and I swallowed it. Lowering my head, I kissed her, and her arms slid around my neck, pulling us close. I couldn't promise her forever, but I'd give her everything I had in the time she was here.

"Just promise me one thing," I whispered as we drew back a little. "When we do see Titania, do not, under any circumstances, make any kind of a bargain with her." Kenzie raised a teasing eyebrow, but I stayed serious. "I'm not kidding, Mackenzie. Promise me you won't say anything when we meet Titania. She can't screw you over in a faery word game if you don't say anything to her."

Her eyes flashed. "You make it sound like I've never bargained with faeries before. I seem to recall doing just fine."

"I know." I tightened my grip on her. "I know I'm being overbearing and overprotective again. But just this once, for my sanity, promise you won't talk to her. Please."

"Oh, fine," Kenzie huffed, rolling her eyes. "Just this once, then. I promise I won't say anything. But is she really that awful?"

"You have no idea," I muttered. "Leanansidhe was bad enough, but the Queen of the Seelie Court? She's the epitome of everything I hate about the fey. She'll trick you into becoming a deer or a rosebush, just because she can. Because she thinks it's amusing."

"He's right, unfortunately."

We broke apart as Keirran stepped out of the trees several yards away, Annwyl close behind him. The Summer faery looked almost normal now, bright and solid with no hint of the transparency that had nearly killed her. The amulet pulsed at her throat, causing a chill to creep up my spine when I looked at it. Keirran, I noted, moved a bit stiffly, favoring his right side, but other than that, he seemed fine.

"So," he said, looking at each of us, "we *are* going to see Titania." He winced, and on his shoulder, Razor gave a worried buzz. "That's going to be…interesting. At least if Oberon is there, he'll be able to rein her in somewhat. But I think we're still going to have to deal with Titania herself." He glanced at me, frowning. "Are you sure you're okay with this, Ethan?"

"Trust me, I think getting a root canal would rank higher

on my list of things to do," I muttered. "But I think Kenzie is right. The only way to permanently stop the Fade is if Annwyl goes home. And the only way she can go home is if Titania raises the exile."

"You won't get her to change her mind," Annwyl said softly. "Not for free. Not without making some kind of bargain, if she decides to change it at all."

"We won't know unless we try," Keirran said, sounding determined. "And we're out of options. Titania *will* let you come back. I can be very persistent."

"I have a better idea," whispered a cold, familiar voice, and a figure *turned* out of nowhere, smiling at us across the glade. "Why don't you let the girl come with me, and we can return to Phaed together?"

CHAPTER FIFTEEN

RETURN TO THE NEVERNEVER

"Who are you?"

Keirran's voice had changed again. Soft and lethal, it raised the hair on my arms as the prince drew his sword and stepped in front of Annwyl, his cold gaze on the faery across from us.

"That is unimportant," the Thin Man said, smiling at us from profile. One pale eye fastened on me. "I have been waiting for you to return, Ethan Chase. I was hoping the Summer girl would have disappeared by now, but it seems you have found something that has temporarily halted the Fade. And now she lingers on in the world. A grievous mistake, I'm afraid."

Keirran shot me a glance. "Ethan? You know this faery?"

"We've met," I growled, pulling my own swords. "Right before he tried to kill me and kidnap Annwyl."

"Not true, not true," the Forgotten said, holding up an impossibly thin finger. "I wish to return things to the natural order. You have seen the state of the Forgotten, yes? How they are being twisted and used for dark purposes. It is *his* fault," the Thin Man continued, pointing at Keirran, who straightened, "for forcing their Lady to seek alternate methods of survival. They are no longer allowed to drain the magic of normal fey, so they must turn to new sources of glamour."

"That was necessary," Keirran argued, though he sounded a little shaken. "I couldn't allow any more exiles to be killed. I know the Forgotten are only trying to survive, but taking the lives of others wasn't the way."

"The Forgotten are not supposed to be in this world at all!" the Thin Man snapped, narrowing his pale eye at the Iron Prince. "They were forgotten for a reason and must accept that their fate is to Fade from existence. Whether or not this is fair, they are not supposed to be here, to exist, on this side of the Veil. You have disturbed the balance, Iron Prince. Just as your father did, years ago."

What? I stared at Keirran, shocked. Was he talking about *Ash?* How? I'd never heard Meghan mention that before. But the Iron Prince nodded grimly, his expression dark.

"I know," he whispered. "The Lady told me."

"Then you should know," the Thin Man went on, "that I am only trying to fix things. To put right the chaos your father began when he and his companions came tromping merrily through my town. I knew I should never have let them go. I shall alter that mistake right now."

I shook myself out of my shock and gripped my weapons. "I hate to break it to you, pal, but if you think you're going to take Annwyl, you've got another think coming."

The Thin Man looked at me sadly.

"No, Ethan Chase. It is far too late for that. Her life has become irreversibly tangled with yours and that of the Iron Prince. I can no longer simply cut her string without severing all the threads around her." He held up one hand, gripping a thin silver blade. Like its owner, I couldn't even see it except from the side. Razor hissed, baring his teeth, and the Thin Man smiled. "I am afraid I must remove you *all* from the tapestry."

Keirran and I didn't wait. As if on cue, we both lunged forward, slashing at the Thin Man with our blades. Just before we reached him, however, he vanished, turning to disappear from sight. Keirran and I spun together, weapons raised, looking around for our hair-thin attacker.

"Annwyl, Kenzie!" Keirran called as we turned in a wary circle. "Get back! Put something behind you—"

A flash of silver, almost too quick to be seen, stabbed between us, and Keirran's warning melted into a cry of pain. Blood misted on the air, and the prince staggered back, clutching his arm. I whirled, slashing the air beside him, but the blade whooshed through empty space, striking nothing.

"Not there, Ethan Chase," sang a voice, and something whapped my bare arm. I yelped, flinching back, seeing the razor edge of the Thin Man vanish into invisibility again. Razor buzzed furiously.

"Bad man!" he cried as Keirran pressed close, protecting my side. "Bad man cheats! Cheater, cheater!"

My arm stung. I spared it a quick glance, seeing a thin line of red slashed across my forearm but no blood. The faery must've hit me with the flat of the blade instead of the cutting edge, which meant he was toying with us. I swore under my breath and turned, weapons ready for the next attack.

It came from behind me, slashing across my back, leaving a blazing streak of fire down my shoulders. I roared a curse and spun, lashing out wildly, hitting empty air, of course. Keirran turned, too, and the point of the silver blade sank deep into his shoulder, making him gasp.

"No!"

The cry came from Annwyl. The Summer faery stepped away from the tree, eyes flashing. A rush of wind surrounded us, tossing leaves, twigs, dust and grass, spinning it into a miniature cyclone. Squinting through the wind, I saw a twig bounce off something in midair, saw several leaves and blades of grass sticking to an invisible wall, and lashed out wildly.

I felt the tip bite into something solid, and a howl of pain rang out as the whirlwind flickered and died. The Thin Man appeared briefly, holding his wrist. He wasn't looking at me.

"I was wondering what that thing around your neck did, my dear," he said, gazing at Annwyl. "You've become quite the little Forgotten yourself, haven't you? Draining the magic of others to live. And you don't even realize who it is you're killing."

"What?" Annwyl paled and looked at Keirran. The prince had fallen to one knee, the brightness of his hair faded. Annwyl gasped, and the Thin Man smiled, before he vanished again.

"Annwyl, stay back!" Keirran called, pushing himself to his feet as I stepped up to protect his open side, glaring around the clearing. The glade appeared empty, but I knew the Thin Man was out there, waiting to strike. Dammit, where was the sneaky bastard?

"I don't see him," Keirran muttered at my back. "This isn't working, Ethan. We can't keep this up forever. He's just toying with us."

"I know."

"Ethan, Keirran!" Kenzie's voice rang over the glade. "Don't stand together. Spread out a little! You're both looking at him from the same angle, which is exactly what he wants. If he faces you straight on, you can't see him! Move around! Catch him from the side!"

"Clever girl," hissed the Thin Man, appearing right in front of Kenzie, blade drawn back, and my heart gave a violent lurch. "Perhaps too clever. Be silent, now."

My world froze as the faery stabbed toward Kenzie, who flinched away.

A ripple of darkness flashed between them, that same shadow I'd seen once before when Kenzie was in danger, springing up to deflect the killing blow. It knocked the Thin Man's blade aside, and the faery drew back in astonishment. I was halfway across the glen, sword raised to cut the spindly fey in half, when he vanished once more.

"Dammit!" Reaching Kenzie, I grabbed her arm, my heart still pounding. "Are you all right?"

She pushed at me. "Don't stand here, Ethan! Spread out. The more we're clumped together, the harder it is to see him." She looked at the Summer faery and pointed. "Annwyl, go to the other side of the clearing. Keirran, you and Ethan keep moving around. We have to come at him from all angles."

I nodded and headed back toward Keirran, circling around instead of taking the direct path. As I did, the spindly form of the Thin Man appeared behind him, sword raised high, though it was obvious the prince couldn't see him. "Keirran, behind you! Twelve o'clock!"

He spun, blocking with his sword, and the faery's blade screeched off the metal. With a hiss, the Thin Man turned toward me and vanished. I cursed and backed away, raising my weapons. "I can't see him! Where is he?"

"Coming right at you, Ethan," Annwyl called from the side. "High left...now!"

I swung blindly and felt my blade connect. At the same time, Keirran lunged in from another angle and drove his sword into the air in front of me. There was a thin, painful wail, and several silvery drops spattered to the ground.

Panting, the Thin Man reappeared at the edge of the glade, visible to all of us. A shimmery, wet stain marred one shoulder, and his face was twisted with pain and fury. "This is not over," he warned, raising a thin, bloody finger. "You cannot hide from me. I will find you, and I will put an end to this madness once and for all." His pale gaze shifted to me. "Time is running out, Ethan Chase. For all of us."

He disappeared again, but this time, we knew he wouldn't be back.

For now.

"Ouch," Keirran said several minutes later, seated on a log while being fussed over by Annwyl. She gave him an exasperated look and went back to binding his shoulder. The stab wound looked pretty deep, but the prince hadn't seemed to notice until Annwyl forcibly sat him down, ordered Razor onto a tree branch and pulled up his sleeve. Kenzie had already examined the throbbing red welts on my arm and back, which were extremely painful but not very deep. I was going to need a new shirt soon, though, as this one was getting pretty shredded.

My mind was awhirl with questions, the thing with the amulet being front and center. When Annwyl had used her glamour, Keirran's life was drained. Of course, I'd known about the consequences; Guro had made very certain we all understood. But seeing it happen right in front of me made it much more real.

Then there was Kenzie and that weird shadow-thing that had appeared again to protect her. By now, I had figured out that it came from Guro's protection amulet, which only cast more questions on my mentor. Who was Guro Javier, this man who could see spirits and create powerful magical artifacts, both positive and extremely malevolent? Why hadn't I ever known this side of him?

And of course, looming over me like a black cloud, the knowledge of where we had to go next. Back into the Nevernever, to the Seelie Court, to find an infamous faery queen and convince her to let Annwyl return home.

"Ouch," Keirran said again, pulling away as Annwyl did something to his shoulder. Razor buzzed worriedly and peered down from the branch. "Annwyl," the prince said, "not that I'm complaining, but what are you doing?"

The Summer faery didn't look up from her task. "This was your answer, Keirran?" she asked, a quiet anger beneath the soft tone. "Killing yourself to keep me alive? Did you think I would be happy with that choice?"

"Annwyl…"

She didn't look at him. "This…thing around my neck…it feels wrong. Hateful. I can feel it clawing at you. Sucking out your magic. Just like they did to me." She shivered, tugging the last of the bandages tight before stepping away. "I don't want this, Keirran," she whispered, closing her eyes. "I don't want you to die for me."

"I'm not going to die." Keirran pushed himself to his feet and reached for her. She didn't move, but she didn't raise her head as he gently took her arms, pulling her forward. "Annwyl, look at me. Please.

"This is just a temporary solution," he promised, when Annwyl finally glanced up at him. "I had to find something to halt the Fade, just long enough for us to find Titania. Now we have a real course of action. We'll go speak to the Summer Queen, get your exile lifted, and then we can destroy that thing and not look back. And you can go home." One hand rose, and he brushed her cheek with his knuckles. "I know you've wanted to go back to Arcadia for a long time now. Let me try to make this right."

Annwyl took his hand, holding it to her face. "If I return to the Summer Court, Keirran, we can't be together. The law still stands, and a relationship between courts is still forbidden. I wouldn't be able to see you again."

"I know," he said. "But to know you're alive…that's more

important." He swallowed and continued in a pained voice, "I told you before—I can let you go if I know you're all right. That somewhere in the Seelie Court, you're still out there, dancing with your sisters, singing with the wood nymphs, directing undines to attack hapless princes." Annwyl blushed, and Keirran smiled, dropping his head to hers. "I love you, Annwyl," he murmured as the Summer girl gave a muffled sob and leaned into him. "I will do anything to see you safe. Even if it means letting you go."

My face was burning, but the two faeries seemed to have forgotten I existed. Without a word, Kenzie took my hand and pulled me away, giving them some privacy. Except for Razor, chattering at Keirran from the branch.

"I hope things work out for them," Kenzie said, leaning back against me and resting her head on my chest. I snaked my arms around her waist and held her to me, enjoying the feel of her body against mine. "It must suck, knowing you can't be together just because the faery courts say so. Why are they like that, anyway? Why do they even care?"

"From what I understand," I said, "they believe that cross-court relationships will have disastrous results for Faery later on. That the consequences of such forbidden love will be dire, for everyone."

"Lame," Kenzie stated, unimpressed. "What about your sister?" she asked, and my insides jumped at the mention of Meghan. "Keirran said his own parents defied those laws, right? It seemed to have worked out for them. No disastrous consequences there."

"I don't know," I said softly as a cold, terrible thought entered my mind. I looked toward the place Keirran and Annwyl stood, seeing Keirran's bright form through the trees, and shivered. "Maybe there were."

★ ★ ★

We had to say goodbye to Annwyl before we crossed into the Nevernever. Keirran was reluctant, of course, but there was nothing else to be done. She couldn't return to Faery unless her exile was raised, which was the reason we were going there in the first place. She decided to return to Leanansidhe's, stating that the Exile Queen's mansion was the safest place for her now. Keirran insisted we escort her to the trod that would take her back to Leanansidhe's home in the Between, which meant we had to return to the little park a few blocks from my house, clear across town. But with Keirran's new-found talent, we slipped back into the Between, and only a few minutes passed before he parted the misty curtain of the Veil and we stepped through the gap into the park.

The old slide sat next to the peeling monkey bars, bent and unremarkable. As we approached, Razor sniffled from Keirran's shoulder, mumbling "no leave, no leave" to himself sadly. The prince raised his arm, and the gremlin hopped to the monkey bars, looking despondent.

Keirran drew Annwyl close, stroking her hair. "Be safe," he whispered. "We'll get to Arcadia and speak to the queen as soon as we can. When you see me again, hopefully it will be in the Summer Court."

Annwyl smiled up at him sadly. "I love you, Keirran," she murmured, making his breath catch. "If this is the last time we can see each other without fear and laws and threats of punishment, I want you to know. From the day you pulled yourself out of that frozen river, I have been completely yours. Even if I return to Summer, and the courts dictate that we never meet again, know that I will always love you, and you will always be in my thoughts."

He kissed her. Fiercely, passionately, as if this might truly be their last time. Maybe it was. Faery law was rigid and uncompromising, unchanged for centuries. Meghan had struggled with it, as had Ash, before they finally found the one loophole that allowed them to be together. If anyone else could get around those laws, find the loophole that allowed him to be with the one he loved, I was pretty sure it would be Keirran. Like father, like son.

The only question was, at what cost? How far would he really go?

Annwyl drew away, her eyes glassy. Breaking from Keirran's embrace, she backed to the old slide, pausing in the space between the steps and the frame, her gaze only on the prince.

"Goodbye, Prince Keirran," the Summer faery said as Razor buzzed and waved frantically from the monkey bars. Keirran remained where he was, watching her sadly as her gaze shifted to me. "Ethan, Kenzie, I am forever grateful for your help. Please, watch out for each other in the Nevernever. I truly hope we will meet again someday."

"Noooo," Razor buzzed, bouncing on the monkey bars, huge ears flapping. "No leave, pretty elf girl. No leave!"

She smiled at him. "Razor, I hope to see you again, too. Take care of Keirran, all right?"

"Annwyl," Keirran called as she turned away. "Promise me you'll wait," he said softly as she looked back. "No matter what happens, no matter what that amulet is telling you, promise you'll wait until I return. I swear, as long as I have the breath to keep going, I'm going to find a way for you to live. So, please," he finished, locking eyes with her. "Will you wait for me?"

Annwyl bowed her head. "Always," she whispered and disappeared, slipping through the trod that would take her back to the Exile Queen.

Keirran sighed, gazing at the spot where the Summer faery had disappeared. Then, abruptly, he drew his sword. Marching over to the slide, he brought his weapon down in a vicious arc, smashing it into the top and tearing sideways. The blade sheared through poles, steps and slide with a deafening screech, making my teeth hurt and causing sparks to fly everywhere. The slide shuddered, then collapsed into a pile of twisted pipes and aluminum, and Razor howled with glee atop the monkey bars.

Kenzie and I gaped at the prince. "What the hell was that about?" I demanded as Keirran sheathed his weapon, looking grim.

"I destroyed the trod to Leanansidhe's," he said, as if that was obvious. "Now nothing can follow her back from here. Just in case our thin friend is lurking around."

"That's a little extreme, don't you think?" I asked, looking down at the mangled pile of metal that was once a slide. "You couldn't have asked Annwyl to tell Leanansidhe to close the trod on her end?"

"Maybe." Keirran shrugged, sounding unrepentant. "But I'm not taking any chances. Let's go."

"Where are we going now?" I asked, following him out of the park and down the familiar streets of my own neighborhood, keeping a wary eye out for an old blue Dodge Ram, my dad's truck. If one happened to come cruising toward us down the road, that was my cue to jump into the bushes or behind a tree. Keirran didn't look back.

"To the Summer Court," he answered, as Razor swatted at a bug that zipped over his head. "That was the plan, right? We're going to see Titania."

"Yeah, but first we'll need a trod to the Nevernever," I replied. "I assume you just happen to know of one close by?"

"Actually—" Keirran grinned, looking back at us "—I do."

"Close by" was a relative statement, and it was several streets and neighborhoods later when Keirran stopped us at an old, grass-strewn lot, a chain-link fence around the perimeter and a no-trespassing sign at the gate.

"Oh, sure," I said from the edge of the lot, gazing over the weeds. "A condemned, abandoned house. That's the first place I would look for a trod to Faeryland."

Keirran sighed. "I would take you through the trod in the occult shop," he said. "But it's too far away and the hag that owns it doesn't like gremlins." Razor hissed, almost sounding offended. "This one will get us into the Nevernever just as easily. The house is rumored to be haunted, though, so be careful."

"Why?" Kenzie asked as we slipped through the gap in the fence, squeezing under the rusty chains wrapped around the gate. "Don't tell me it really is haunted." Her tone was excited as she followed us up the walk. "Are there real ghosts inside?"

"No," Keirran said, looking back with a smile. "But there are a couple bogeys living here, and they make certain that all the neighborhood kids know the house is haunted. All that glamour, all that fear and suspicion, is what keeps the trod alive. So, if you see a spoon or a flowerpot or anything floating around, don't panic. They've gotten really good at playing poltergeist."

"Great," I muttered, easing up the steps. Yellow tape had been stretched across the entrance, and the front windows were broken and jagged. I nudged the door with one of my blades; it creaked and swung open with an appropriate, hair-raising groan, and the room beyond was dark, musty and full of shadows. "I swear," I muttered, hoping the resident "ghosts" were listening, "if anything jumps out and grabs me, it's going to be stab first, ask questions later."

Kenzie giggled. "I bet you're fun at Halloween parties," she mused as Keirran ducked beneath the yellow tape and stepped into the house. Giving her a dark look, I raised my swords and followed.

Inside, the rooms smelled of dust, mold and ancient plaster, and the floorboards groaned ominously beneath my shoes. Keirran moved across the dilapidated entryway as lightly as a cat, then beckoned us toward a big wooden staircase at the back of the room. The steps, ascending into the darkness, were old and rotten and didn't look very stable.

"The trod to the Nevernever is upstairs," he murmured, his voice unnaturally loud in the gloom. On his shoulder, Razor's huge green eyes and neon blue teeth cast eerie shadows on the walls as the gremlin growled and buzzed warily, looking around. "Be careful, though. The bogeys don't really like people venturing upstairs. Not many get this far."

"Kenzie," I called, holding a hand to her, "you go after Keirran. I'll be right behind you." That way, if something nasty waited for us up top, Keirran would deal with it, and I'd take care of anything wanting to jump us from behind.

Carefully, we started up the stairs, which groaned and creaked under my weight and felt rotten as hell under my feet. I kept my steps as light as I could and hoped the whole thing wouldn't collapse beneath us.

In the center of the staircase, however, Keirran stopped. Kenzie pulled up behind him, and I nearly walked into her, catching myself on the railing. "Hey!" I whispered, peering up at the head of our little train. "Keirran, what are you... Oh."

Something crouched at the top of the steps, nearly invisible in the darkness. Something wispy and black, as dark as the shadows themselves. But its huge yellow eyes peered down at us, easily visible in the gloom.

I looked behind me and saw three more of the creatures crowding the foot of the stairs, gazing up at us. Forgotten, inky and black, melting into the shadows and gloom surrounding us. They didn't press forward, though. Just watched silently from the bottom of the steps, like the time in Mr. Dust's office. Waiting.

"What do you want?" Keirran asked, his voice stony but calm, facing the single Forgotten at the top of the stairs. "What did you do to the fey who lived here? By order of your Lady, you aren't supposed to harm any more exiles."

"We have not," whispered the thing crouched before the prince. I couldn't even see a mouth on it, just flat, empty darkness and shadow. "The bogeys fled at the sight of us. They are no longer here. We did not drain their glamour. We have not killed a single exile or half-breed since the time you left the Lady's presence."

"Good," Keirran replied in that same flat, cold voice. "But what do you want with us?"

"The Lady wishes to see you, Iron Prince. Now."

"Now is not a good time."

The Forgotten made a hissing noise. "You swore, Iron Prince," it reminded him. "You swore to return to her if she called for you. That was the bargain for the exiles' lives. We have upheld our end of the deal, at great cost. You must honor your word and return to the Lady."

"I will," Keirran replied. "But I also said I would return to her of my own free will. As a guest, not as a prisoner. If you're here to drag me back, I'm afraid I cannot go with you." His voice remained polite, but the air around him chilled and frost crept over the railing, making the Forgotten draw back. "I have something important to take care of first," Keirran went on. "Tell the Lady that when it's done, I'll come to her. Not before."

The Forgotten wasn't pleased, but after a moment, it bowed its shadowy head. "As you wish, Prince Keirran," it rasped, and the Forgotten below us slipped away into the darkness.

"We will inform the Lady, but do not keep her waiting long. We will be waiting for you."

It backed away, then glided along the wall and became one with the shadows before it disappeared.

"You're not really thinking of going to see the Forgotten Queen, are you?" I asked as we continued up the steps. Keirran didn't answer, and I scowled. "Hey, I know you can hear me, Prince."

"I have to" was his quiet reply as we eased into a bedroom. An old bed stood in the corner next to a dresser, both rotting to pieces under a film of dust. Once-colorful wallpaper lined the room, moldy and peeling away. "I gave my word," Keirran went on, picking his way over the floor and the broken remains of toys and picture books scattered around us. "I may be part human, but I don't break my promises. If she wants to speak with me, I'll listen. I didn't promise anything more than that." He stopped at the closet, putting his hand on the tarnished handle. "But it's the least I can do. Especially since it's our fault the Forgotten are here."

"Wait," Kenzie said before he could open the door. "I'm curious about that. The Thin Man said something to that effect, too. What did the Lady tell you? How is your family connected to all of this?"

Keirran's gaze darkened. "That's a long story," he said softly. "And we don't have time to discuss it now. When Annwyl is safe, I'll tell you the whole thing, I promise."

He opened the door and stepped through without looking back.

I took Kenzie's hand. "Back into the Nevernever," I groaned, and she squeezed my fingers in sympathy. "Are you ready for this?"

"Don't worry about me, tough guy." Kenzie grinned, her eyes sparkling. "I've been waiting for this ever since we got back. Oh, and if you see a dragon, be sure to point it out so I can go poke it with a stick."

"You know, that would be funny if I wasn't terrified you'd actually do it."

She rolled her eyes, pulling me forward. "Come on, Ethan. We've already fought some of the nastiest things Faery has to offer. What's the worst that could happen?"

Never say things like that, I thought as we crossed the threshold and slipped into the closet. The darkness surrounding us cleared, and we stumbled between a pair of gnarled trunks, into the familiar twilight of Faery.

PART III

CHAPTER SIXTEEN
BENEATH THE WATERFALL

We followed Keirran through the wyldwood for several hours, walking beneath huge dark trees that shut out the light, passing shocking flashes of color in an otherwise gray world. The Nevernever was just as strange, murky and dangerous as I remembered from my last trip. Which was only last week, I reminded myself. I wondered what my parents were doing, if I had really crossed the line with this last stunt. I was going to have to talk to them—again—when I got home. I couldn't rely on Meghan to show up and give me a free pass whenever I went off into Faery. And by the looks of things, that was bound to happen more and more now. My days of hiding from the fey, of hoping they wouldn't notice me, were over.

Strangely, that didn't bother me as much as it should have.

I kept my swords out, scanning the trees constantly, ready to act against any nasty fey that tried to ambush us. Amazingly, our hike through the wyldwood was uneventful; except for a will-o'-the-wisp and a curious wood sprite that kept appearing in the branches overhead, I didn't see any fey.

Night was beginning to fall, the eternal twilight of the wyldwood shifting into darkness, when Keirran led us down a twisty narrow path, beneath a silvery waterfall and into a small cave. The floor was covered in pale sand, and the ceiling glittered with millions of tiny lights, resembling the night sky.

"We'll stop here for the night," Keirran said as Razor hopped from his shoulder to roll about in the sand, buzzing. "I'd continue on, but pressing through the wyldwood in the dark is asking for trouble."

"How far to the Summer Court?" I asked, finally sheathing my weapons. The cave was small and appeared uninhabited, no bones or blood spatters on the wall, at least. I guessed that was as safe as you could get in the Nevernever.

"Not far," Keirran said. "We should reach it tomorrow. Provided we don't run into any unforeseen problems."

Unforeseen problems. Yeah, that still wasn't likely. I was amazed we'd gotten this far without trouble. And when we did reach the Seelie Court, we would have to deal with our biggest challenge yet: convincing the infamously fickle Queen of the Summer Court to lift Annwyl's exile and let her come home. I didn't know how we were going to manage that. Frankly, Titania scared me. I knew the stories. I knew that one wrong word or action could get you turned into a rabbit, or a rosebush, or trapped in the Summer Court forever, dancing for the queen's amusement. You did not screw around with the queens of Faery. In fact, the only other person I was less enthused about meeting in the entire Nevernever was Mab, the ruler of Winter. I only hoped Keirran had a convincing plan in mind.

Speaking of Keirran, he hadn't said much through the entire hike. I knew he was concerned about Annwyl, and the amulet sucking away at his glamour was probably on his mind, too, but the flat, blank look in his eyes worried me. He stood at the entrance of the cave now, his back to us, gazing through the falling water.

"Hey," I said, walking up to him. He turned, looking very

tired, and I tapped his shoulder in encouragement. "She'll be fine," I said. "We're almost to the Seelie Court. You'll just have to convince Titania that it's in her best interests to raise Annwyl's exile. I'm sure you can agree on something, right?"

Keirran gave a faint smile. "Titania…doesn't like me very much," he admitted. "Well, at all, really. She's always hated Mom and barely tolerates me when I visit Arcadia. I'm sure the queen will be ecstatic when I come begging her for a favor. She'll finally have me right where she wants—not even Oberon will be able to help." He winced, then gave me a grave look. "Ethan, the price Titania will demand of me is going to be very high. You don't have to come. I don't want to drag you and Kenzie into this. You can go home if you want…. I won't hold it against you."

I snorted as Kenzie joined us, Razor buzzing worriedly from her shoulder. "Wow, is that how I sounded all this time?" I asked the girl, who nodded fervently. "Why didn't you smack me earlier? Keirran, we're not leaving. Annwyl is our friend, too, but more important—"

"—we're not letting you do this alone," Kenzie finished, giving the prince a fierce look. Maybe it was my imagination, but she sounded rather breathless, as if the walk had taken a lot out of her. Though she continued without hesitation. "And if I have to tell you this as much as I told Ethan, I will. We're not leaving until this is done, one way or another."

"Kenzie." Keirran bowed his head. "I'm sorry for what I did to your family," he said in a low voice. "Please forgive me. I don't deserve your friendship, but I'm glad you're here." He flicked a glance at me. "Both of you. And I swear, I'll make everything right when this is all over."

Kenzie gave him a small smile and started to reply, but suddenly winced and fell, her legs giving out beneath her. Alarmed, I started forward as Keirran caught the girl, steadying her as she sagged against him. Razor buzzed and leaped to the prince's back, peering down anxiously as I crowded in.

"Kenzie!"

"I'm okay" was the gasping reply. But she didn't look okay, clinging to the prince, barely able to stand. Keirran gently drew her upright, then stepped back to let me take over. I looped her arm around my neck and lifted her off her feet, ignoring her protests.

Carrying her over to the far wall, I gently sat her down and knelt beside her, watching her face. She was pale, breathing hard, and dark circles crouched under her eyes, making my heart twist. Keirran hovered nearby, his expression concerned, Razor whimpering from his shoulder.

"Kenzie? What happened?"

"It's all right, Ethan," she murmured, sounding extremely tired. "I'm fine. Don't worry about me. I guess I'm not fully recovered from the hospital."

"I'll go find some food," Keirran announced, stepping back. "We haven't eaten all day, and she'll need to keep up her strength. I'll be all right," he added as I looked up at him sharply. "I've hunted the wyldwood countless times. I know what I'm doing. Trust me."

I didn't like us splitting up, but Keirran was probably right. The wyldwood was practically his backyard. "Be careful," I warned, and the prince nodded once, turned and slipped out of the cave with Razor. His bright form glimmered briefly through the curtain of water, the gremlin's eyes flashing as he looked back, and they were gone.

Kenzie shivered, wrapping her arms around herself as if she was cold. I sat beside her and pulled her into my lap, tucking her close to my body. She sniffed and curled into me, and I held her tight. "Déjà vu, huh?" she whispered, reminding me of another cave with a sandy floor, and Kenzie in my lap, pressed close for comfort. Our first kiss… "Sorry," she went on, dropping her head. "I didn't want you worrying about me when we got here."

I sighed. "Kenzie, I'll always worry about you whenever we go into the Nevernever," I told her, running a hand down her hair. "Or when you follow me into a goblin market. Or when you make a bargain with a faery. I'm always going to worry, and I'm always going to try to protect you. It's just something you'll have to accept about me.

"But," I continued, "when I said I wouldn't try to stop you anymore, I meant it. I'll still be insanely overprotective, and you'll probably want to punch me sometimes, but…I want you here, with me. However long we have—" I slipped my fingers under her chin and gently turned her face to mine "—I want to spend it with you."

Her eyes prickled as I kissed her. Softly at first, wanting to be gentle. But Kenzie responded with shocking urgency. Her hands fisted in my hair, and her tongue pressed against my lips, demanding entry. And then I stopped being aware of anything but her lips, her scent, her hands on my chest, slipping under my shirt. I groaned against her mouth as soft fingers traced my stomach, making my skin dance and my blood sizzle. My face dropped to her neck, trailing kisses down her shoulder, and she gasped and arched her head back, whispering my name.

Hooking her fingers behind my neck, she leaned back, easing us both to the sandy floor. I shifted so I wasn't crushing her, gazing down at the girl beneath me, my elbows straddling her head. She was beautiful, an angel who had reached down and yanked me out of my miserable, lonely existence, and dammit if that wasn't the sappiest thing I'd ever thought but it was completely true. Kenzie smiled up at me, sad and tender and a little scared, and my heart began pounding in my chest.

"Ethan?" She chewed her lip in an uncharacteristic display of nervousness. "Do you want to know the secret I told the bird faery at the goblin market?"

I looked at her, puzzled. Strange that she'd bring that up now. "I guess so," I said, shrugging. "But only if you want to tell me."

"I do," Kenzie said quickly and looked away. "Well, not really, but…um…it's…it's something you should know, I think. I mean…" She winced. "Crap."

Normally, I would've found the idea of Mackenzie stuttering cute, as infrequent as it was, and would've called her on it. But right now, the last thing I wanted to do was tease and lose whatever was happening between us, whatever this was. I brushed my thumb across her cheek, making her close her eyes, and murmured, "You can tell me."

"It was that, well…I just…" She sighed and continued in a whisper, "I've never…been with anyone before. You know, really *been* with anyone. And I was afraid I would die before I ever found someone to…you know." She bit her lip again, brow furrowing. "That's the secret I traded away. The secret the bird faery knows about me."

She colored fiercely and averted her gaze. I was having trouble breathing. "I don't know why I wanted to tell you now," she went on softly, still not looking at me. "I certainly don't expect to rectify that *here,* but…I guess I wanted you to know. In case…" She trailed off again, but I knew what she meant. Everything was borrowed time with Kenzie. Being afraid she would never get the chance to do everything she wanted.

Very gently, I kissed her, just the slightest touch of her lips to mine. "I'll wait," I told her softly. "You don't have to worry about that. Not with me." A tear slipped from the corner of her eye, and I caught it before it hit the sand. "Whenever you're ready, just let me know. I'm not going anywhere, I promise."

★ ★ ★

When Keirran returned, Kenzie was nearly asleep, drifting off against my chest. She woke up long enough to eat a couple wild pears Keirran had found—after he swore to me about a dozen times they were safe—before curling into me again. I held her quietly, watching as Keirran started a fire, piling wood into a sandy pit before holding his palm over the kindling. Glamour shimmered, and a small flame sprang up to consume the wood, throwing back the shadows. The Iron Prince sat down in front of the fire, drawing a knee to his chest, and brooded into the flames.

Kenzie shifted in my arms, murmuring something about "Alex" in her sleep. I wondered what her family was doing now, what *my* family was doing now.

By the fire, Keirran's gaze was dark. Was he thinking of Meghan or Ash? Did he miss his family, or were all his thoughts on Annwyl and the thing connecting them both? The amulet that was slowly killing him.

"You can go to sleep if you want," he announced without looking up. "I'll take first watch."

I smirked and shook my head, speaking quietly so as not to wake Kenzie. "I couldn't if I wanted to. My irrational paranoia of goblins eating my face while I sleep sort of makes that impossible."

"That's probably wise." Keirran rested his chin on his knee. Razor hopped off his shoulder to poke a twig at the fire. "I didn't realize Kenzie was so ill," Keirran said after a moment. "She mentioned being sick, but I just didn't put it together. I swear, Ethan, I wouldn't have asked her to come if I knew."

I snorted. "You wouldn't have been able to stop her. Trust me, I made that mistake once. It doesn't work." I looked down at the sleeping girl in my arms, holding her tighter. "She made her choice," I said softly. "All I can do now is protect her."

"Do you ever…?" Keirran paused as if worried he might offend me, then continued. "Do you ever think that there's something you can do, a deal or bargain you can make, to help her get better? I mean, magic exists everywhere in the Nevernever. If you just accepted the cost—"

"No." My voice came out slightly choked. "No faery magic, no bargains, no deals. I refuse to gamble for Kenzie's health. Some prices are too high."

"Even if it meant saving her life?" Keirran glanced at me, the flames casting weird, flickering shadows over his hunched form.

"Leave it alone, Keirran."

"I don't like it, either, but…aren't some prices worth paying for the one you love?"

"I said leave it alone," I snapped, and Kenzie stirred against me. Wincing, I adjusted my arms around her and buried my face in her hair. *I wish I could,* I thought, closing my eyes. *I wish there was some way, some bargain or deal or contract, to make you well again, but I know the rules. Nothing is free. Magic and power always come with a price. And maybe that's selfish and paranoid, but I'm not willing to pay that price, or have* you *pay that price. Not yet. Not when there's still a chance you could be okay without it.*

Keirran fell silent, and when I looked up again, he had gone back to staring into the fire. Razor was curled up in the sand by the pit, buzzing and twitching in his dreams.

"I envy you sometimes, you know," Keirran said quietly after a moment. He glanced my way, a faint, bitter smile crossing his face. "Sometimes I wonder what it's like, being completely human. Not having to deal with the courts and the crazy politics that come with them. Not having to give up the one you love because the ancient law says you can't be together." He hunched forward again, staring into the flames. "I know I can't have her," he said, his face pinched and tight.

"I know when she goes back to Arcadia, we'll be forced apart. Even if I'm willing to face exile, I can't do that to her." He blew out a breath, raking both hands through his silver hair. "I just...I wish there was something, some way to get around this stupid law. My parents did it. Dad went all the way to the End of the World to be with Mom. He even woke up an ancient queen in the process, but they still found a way."

"So, Ash did wake up the Lady, just like the Thin Man said."

"Yes," Keirran sighed, hanging his head. "At least, that's what she told me. She had been sleeping for centuries, forgotten by everyone in Faery and the mortal world. And then, one day, there was a change in the air. Something broke through her slumber, a glamour so powerful it woke her up and brought her back from the edge of oblivion. When she finally grew strong enough to emerge from the darkness, Faery as she knew it had changed, and there were many others like her, confused and forgotten. But they were no longer content to sit back and wait for the Fade to take them—they wanted to live. So, she gathered like-minded Forgotten to her side, and eventually they made their way to the mortal world. The ironic part is, she wouldn't have awoken if my father hadn't gone on that quest to be with Mom. So you see," he finished, tossing a stick into the fire, "it's sort of our fault the Forgotten are here."

"That might be true," I said as Kenzie mumbled and shifted against me, making it hard to concentrate. "But that doesn't mean you're responsible for them, Keirran. It doesn't mean you have to help them find a way to live."

"Doesn't it?" Keirran looked at me, blue eyes gleaming. "If not me, then who? The other courts won't help.... They'll want the Forgotten destroyed. My parents are responsible for bringing their queen into the world again. And...and it's because of me that they've turned to Mr. Dust for the glamour to exist. Because I told the Lady to find another way." He sighed, resting his chin on his knees. "I've made a huge mess of everything, Ethan," he murmured, narrowing his eyes. "I have to find a way to fix it, but Annwyl comes first. Once she's safe, I'll talk to my parents and the other courts about the Forgotten, and we'll try to find a solution together. But not before I make sure that Annwyl goes home."

He winced, clenching his fists as his brightness flicked and dimmed a little, before returning to normal. Alarm coursed through me. "It's the amulet, isn't it? Does it hurt?"

"I knew what I was agreeing to," Keirran murmured. "I'll gladly pay the price, if it means she will live."

His words stung, even though they weren't directed at me. I glanced down at Kenzie, sleeping peacefully in my arms, and wondered if there wasn't something I could do. Some contract or deal that would make her well. But it was so risky, taking that chance, making a bargain with the fey. Annwyl's own words came back to me: *The price would be so high. Cheating death, even if it's not your own… Even our kind avoids making that type of bargain at all costs.*

And though I didn't want to remember, Guro's words slipped into my head, haunting me, the memory of his grim, final warning.

You can't save everyone. Sometimes, you have to make that decision to let them go.

It was those words, more than the fear of goblins chewing on my extremities, that kept me awake the rest of the night.

I didn't exactly sleep, but sometime near dawn I must've dozed, because when I opened my eyes, Kenzie was peering down at me. The sight of her lovely face, filling my vision first thing in the morning, coaxed a tiny smile from me. "Hey,"

I murmured, reaching up to smooth her hair back. "Did you sleep all right?"

She nodded. "You?"

"Not a chance." I wrapped my arms around her waist, drawing her closer. "But I could definitely get used to waking up like this."

She actually blushed. I glanced past her at the empty cave with the smoldering fire pit, and frowned. "Where's Keirran?"

"Hunting, I think. He took Razor and left a few minutes ago, but he said that he would be back soon. I didn't want to wake you, so I didn't say anything."

"So, it's just us again, huh?" Gazing into her eyes, I found myself unable to look away. Here we were in the Nevernever again, about to pay a visit to the very dangerous Queen of the Seelie Court. A queen who had the power to turn us both into tulips if she thought it would be amusing. Who hated Meghan's family and anyone associated with them. I had a crapload of things I should be worried about—faeries, bargains, soul-sucking amulets—but when Kenzie was this close, everything around me sort of faded to insignificant white noise, and all I was aware of was her.

A very dangerous issue, and one I would have to work on… later. Right now, no one was around, we were fairly safe and I could afford to let down my guard. "Can you think of anything we could be doing," I asked, unable to keep the grin from my face, "now that we're alone? In the few seconds before Razor comes in and interrupts, that is?"

Kenzie smiled. Putting her hands on my shoulders, she leaned down and kissed me, and I closed my eyes.

It didn't last long. A buzzing laugh echoed overhead, making me wince. "Kissy!" cried an obnoxious, high-pitched voice, gratingly loud in the silence. "Kissy kissy, funny boy! Ha!"

"Go away, Razor," I called, still holding Kenzie close. She

giggled and pulled back, and I released her just as Keirran stepped through the waterfall into the cave. The curtain of water didn't actually touch him, I noticed; it drew aside, just like the mist of the Between, to let him through unsplashed. Seeing us, he offered a small smile, though it was tinged with longing. I knew he was thinking of himself and Annwyl, and how, even if he saved her life, he would likely never see her again.

"I'm glad you're feeling better," he said to Kenzie, holding a branch that had several tiny berries hanging among the leaves. They glittered like strange green jewels as he sat down, raising the branch like a peace offering. "The Summer Court isn't far—will you be able to make it?"

She nodded, plucking one of the small fruits and staring at it curiously. "Yeah, I'll be fine. Sorry about last night. I think I just needed a few hours' sleep. And food. Food is always good. We really need to put together a travel kit for the Nevernever or something." She tossed a berry into her mouth, then offered a clump to me. I took it warily.

"Are you sure—" I began.

"Yes, Ethan, they're safe for humans." Keirran gave me a slightly exasperated look. "I know the wyldwood like the back of my hand, including what will and will not turn humans into rabbits. I learned from the best, so relax."

Kenzie offered a fruit to Razor, but the gremlin wrinkled his nose, bared his teeth and scampered to Keirran's shoulder. The prince sighed. "However, there is another thing I wanted to discuss with you," he said, sounding reluctant. "I talked to a local dryad about the state of the Summer Court, and she gave me some potentially bad news. Oberon isn't there at the moment. He's off hunting with his knights, somewhere in the Deep Wyld. No one knows when he'll return."

Kenzie looked confused, but I groaned. "That means it's just Titania holding court now."

"Yes." Keirran raked a hand through his hair with a grimace. "Which will make things challenging. I was hoping to send a request to Oberon—he usually allows me to visit Arcadia without much trouble. But now that he's gone, I'm either going to have to sneak us past the border and risk punishment for trespassing or send the request to Titania, who will probably deny it out of spite." His eyes narrowed to cold blue slits. "And I can't afford that. We don't have time to spare."

"So, how hard is it to sneak into the Summer Court?" Kenzie asked.

"Not difficult" came a familiar, bored voice near the entrance of the cave. We spun, Razor hissing furiously, as two golden eyes blinked into existence, regarding us lazily. "Provided you know where to look. And do not blunder into any guards. But I suppose that is too much to hope for."

We leaped to our feet, and Grimalkin yawned, raising a hind foot to scratch an ear. "Hello again, humans," the cat purred, as Razor screeched a loud "Bad kitty!" that made Keirran wince. "Still getting into trouble, I see."

CHAPTER SEVENTEEN

APPLE ORCHARD OF DOOM

"Bad kitty!" Razor buzzed again from Keirran's shoulder. His huge ears flapped as he bounced up and down. "Evil, bad kitty! Shave off fur! Throw kitty off mountain! Burn, burn!"

The prince sighed.

"What do you want, Grimalkin?" Keirran asked, putting a hand over Razor's head, muffling his snarls, hisses and death threats. "Did my parents send you to find me?"

"Please." Now that he had everyone's attention, Grimalkin closed his eyes and began washing his paw. "Do you think I have nothing better to do than scurry about like a clueless mortal, searching for another clueless mortal? No, human. The Iron Queen and Prince Consort do not know I am here. They are both busy looking for *you*." His yellow gaze slid to me. "Both of you."

Keirran and I shared a glance. Something didn't seem right. That Grimalkin had found us wasn't unusual, but why would he come looking in the first place if Meghan hadn't sent him? The cat never did anything for free. I remembered something Annwyl'd said earlier that week—that she hadn't been able to find Grimalkin, he was either unreachable or ignoring her inquiries. Where had he been? Why was he here now?

"How did you find us?" I asked, frowning at the cat. "And

if you knew we were going to be here, why didn't you let Meghan know?"

The cat yawned. "Must you be so tedious?" He sighed. "I am not a dog, to come to every ruler's beck and call. And chasing down the Iron Prince as he goes gallivanting across the mortal world seems very tiresome. I knew you would come here, eventually."

"How?"

"You ask a wearisome amount of questions." Grimalkin stood and stretched, curling his tail over his back. "Honestly, I do not know how mortals came up with that ridiculous phrase 'curiosity killed the cat.' Certainly they have never been around the lot of you." Straightening, he gazed up at me, waving his tail. "Come, now. Time is of the essence. Do you wish to get into the Summer Court or not?"

"What?" I blinked at him. "How did…?" The cat stared at me, and I raised my hands. "You know what, I don't care anymore. You're here to take us to Titania, right? Fine. Lead the way."

"Finally." The cat sniffed and gave me a look of triumph. "I never thought I would see the day when a human said something sensible."

It was obvious when we crossed the border from the wyldwood into Arcadia. The dark, murky twilight of the wyldwood fell away, and the sun blazed down on us, hot and bright. The forest was suddenly full of color, the leaves were extra green, the flowers screamingly bright, almost to the point of ridiculousness. Birds chirped overhead, bees and other insects spiraled through the air, some monstrously big. When an orange-and-black bird landed on Kenzie's shoulder, I jumped, only to realize it was a huge butterfly with wings the size of dinner plates.

"This way," Grimalkin said, slipping through the rails of

a wooden fence, the kind that kept in cows or horses. "The mound and the entrance to the Summer Court are on the other side of this field. We are not far, but I will issue this warning only once. Do not, under any circumstances, steal, pick up or take anything from this property. I would suggest you hold your breath for the duration of the passing if I did not know humans are quite incapable of not breathing. Such an inconvenience, but we shall have to deal with it. Let us go."

"Wait, I know where we are," Keirran said, looking reluctant as we slipped over the fence into the pasture. "Puck took me here once. Father was furious. This isn't a good idea, Grimalkin."

"Mmm." The cat seemed unconcerned, leaping onto an old log to face us. "This is the quickest way to the Summer Court, and all the other entrances will be guarded," he stated. "We can find a way around, but it will take time. I thought you wanted to reach the court as quickly as possible."

"I do. I just…" Keirran gave a helpless shrug. "Fine. We'll just have to be careful. Lead on, then."

"What is this place?" I asked as we continued across the field. Bees and butterflies floated everywhere among the flowers, sparkling like living jewels, and I could feel the sun's warmth beating down on us. Everything looked peaceful, but I knew what a horrible lie that was in Faery. If everything appeared this tranquil, there was probably something stupidly dangerous lurking nearby. "If you visited this spot with Puck, that means you weren't really supposed to be here, right? And you probably got into trouble with whatever lives here."

"It's sad that everyone knows him so well."

"That's just great." I sighed, looking back for Kenzie. She walked quietly behind me, looking at everything. I dropped back a pace and took her hand, wanting to be close in case a dragon or other nasty creature burst out of the flowers and attacked. "Just let me know when I should be running," I called to Keirran.

He glanced back with a humorless smile. "Oh, you'll know," he said ominously and gestured to something ahead.

I blinked. Rolling fields spread out before us, teeming with flowers and thick grass, but rising out of the dirt, planted in rigidly straight lines marching to the horizon, were hundreds upon hundreds of apple trees. I knew they were apple trees because the nearest one, a huge gnarled giant, had bright red clusters hanging everywhere. The branches were bent under the weight, and the grass around the trunk was scattered with red, bulbous fruit. And the smell... The breeze shifted, and the heady, powerful smell nearly knocked me down and made my mouth water. I didn't even like apples that much, but I was suddenly filled with the desire to stuff my face with them.

"Oh, wow," I heard Kenzie breathe, and her hand tightened on mine. "Does anyone else have a craving for pie?"

My stomach growled. Annoyed, I turned to Keirran. "Okay, hundreds of apple trees, all begging me to pick up an apple and eat it. What's the catch here? Will I turn into something? Fall asleep for a century? Or will I just keep stuffing my face and be unable to stop eating until I burst?"

"No," Keirran said solemnly. "They're just regular apples. They don't do anything special."

"But...?" Kenzie prodded.

"But look at the ground beneath them. The branches. Do you see anything else eating them? Birds, deer, even insects?"

"No," I muttered, casting another glance toward the lines of fruit trees. He was right; the apples hung full and untouched on the branches or rotting on the ground. The orchard was still, with no birds pecking at the fruit, no signs of deer, raccoons, rodents or anything. Except for the bees hovering around the flowers, nothing moved out here except us.

"The trees are guarded," Keirran said, confirming my suspicions. "Nothing is allowed to eat the fruit here. The owners chase off anything that comes through the orchard. If they catch someone poaching their apples, they grind their bones—"

"To make their bread?" Kenzie joked. I snorted a laugh despite myself. Keirran rolled his eyes.

"To fertilize the trees," he finished. "The point is, we don't want to let them catch us trespassing, and we really don't want to steal their fruit. They're quite protective of it. Puck and I found that out the hard way."

"Humans." Grimalkin's furry head poked out of the grass, tail twitching in annoyance. "Are you coming? Or are you going to stand there and talk until the guardians return and crush your bones to powder? And at the expense of repeating myself—do not touch any of the apples as we are making our way through the orchard. Do not even look at them. Please attempt to have some semblance of self-control, as small as it might be."

Razor made a disgusted noise on Keirran's shoulder as we followed after the cat. "Yuck," he stated, curling his lip. "Nasty apples. Bleh!"

Well, at least we didn't have to worry about the gremlin.

The rows of trees seemed to stretch on forever, marching up and down the lazy hills like soldiers in a line. They were all massive, ancient things, with thick trunks and gnarled branches overly full of bright red fruit. Plump apples dangled enticingly from the limbs or were scattered everywhere in the grass, not even a nibble taken from the skin. The scent was intoxicating, and I breathed as shallowly as I could to avoid being tempted by the sight and smells of the orchard.

"These guardians seem awfully greedy," Kenzie remarked

when we were deep between rows of trees. "I mean, they obviously have far too many to eat. What's a few apples to them?"

"It's the nature of the fey, sadly," Keirran said. "We're not really known for sharing." On his shoulder, Razor had buried his face in his shirt and hadn't come up since we'd entered the orchard. Kenzie gave the prince a puzzled look.

"You say 'we,'" she observed, "but you don't think of yourself as fey, do you?"

Keirran paused. "It's hard to explain," he said at last. "Would it be confusing if I told you I've been raised to be both? Human and faery, I mean. Dad taught me everything I know about fighting and magic and the Nevernever, and how to work the politics of the courts. But Mom...the queen...she made certain I understood that I was human, too. That I didn't get so caught up in magic and glamour and faery politics that I forgot I wasn't one of them."

"Was it hard?" Kenzie asked, looking sympathetic. "Growing up human, being the only non-faery in the Nevernever besides your parents?"

"Not as bad as you might think." Keirran smiled. "My parents were always there for me, no matter what happened, so I can't complain about that. And growing up with gremlins and hacker elves and gliders, well, let's just say I drove Glitch and the guard pretty crazy. But yes..." His smile faded, and he looked away, over the hills. "Sometimes, it did get...kind of lonely."

As they talked, I continued to scan the orchard, trying to keep an eye out for these mysterious guardians and not to stare at the apples at the same time. From what Keirran had said, I guessed they were giants of some sort, but unless they were hiding behind a tree, I couldn't see them.

A raven cawed somewhere overhead.

Normally, this wouldn't have caught my attention. Except

that the orchard was so very quiet that the sound of a bird's call in the absolute stillness made me jerk my head up, searching the branches.

A dark shadow swooped overhead and alighted on a branch, making my stomach jump. Bright green eyes peered down from the raven's dark, intelligent face as it ruffled its feathers and gave a chiding caw.

"Oh, great," Keirran said as the raven shook itself once more…and exploded in a cloud of black feathers and dust. I blinked, taking my eyes off the bird for a split second, watching the feathers spiral to the ground. When I looked back, a figure stood on the branch with his arms crossed, smirking down at us. The sunlight streaming through the leaves caught in his red hair, making it glow like an ember.

"Hey, kiddies," Robin Goodfellow greeted with his usual nonchalant flair. "We meet yet again. What are the odds?"

What the hell. First Grimalkin, now Puck? Did *everyone* know we'd entered the Nevernever? I wondered if Meghan realized we were here and had sent Puck after us. I wondered how long it would be before Ash showed up. That wasn't a pleasant thought.

As if reading my mind, Puck grinned at me. "Don't worry, kid. Your sister didn't send me to drag you home by the ear. I was just in the area and heard the rumors drifting through Arcadia. Can't keep dryads from gossiping, I'm afraid." His gaze slid to Keirran, and he shook his head. "Princeling, you are in *soooooo* much trouble," he announced. "Your dad has been looking everywhere for you."

Keirran's gaze narrowed, and Razor flattened his ears at Puck and hissed. "You're not going to tell him, are you?"

"Well, that depends." The Summer jester leaned back against the trunk, regarding us with a smirk. "What are you three planning now? I seem to remember the *last* time we met, you told me you wouldn't get into trouble. And then you did. So, you tell me." He shrugged, though his gaze never left me and Keirran. "I could go find ice-boy and point him in your direction, and trust me when I say he is *not* happy at the moment, or you can tell me what you're doing right now. But hey, it's your call."

"We're going to see Titania," Keirran answered. "We came to Arcadia to seek an audience with the Summer Queen, to request a favor. I would use the regular channels, but Oberon isn't at court right now and…"

"And our lovely Summer monarch might deny you entrance to the court," Puck finished, nodding thoughtfully. "So, you're planning to sneak in, I take it. That's why Furball is here."

Grimalkin looked up from washing his paws on a nearby rock, where nothing had been a moment before. "Please. As if they could have found a way in themselves."

Puck rolled his eyes, then turned a serious gaze on Keirran. "Why do you want to see Titania?" he asked, his tone suspicious beneath the cheerful demeanor. "No offense, princeling, but the only other person she dislikes more than you is… well, me. And maybe Mab. If you're going to be requesting any kind of favor, it's not going to go well for you."

"I know," Keirran replied.

"And you'd be putting the queen's brother in danger," Puck went on relentlessly. "Meghan's not going to be happy if Scowly over there gets turned into a gerbil."

"I'm right here," I announced, tired of being ignored, "listening to everything you say. You can talk to me like I'm a real person, you know."

Puck's amused gaze flicked to me, though I still saw the shadow of concern in his eyes. "Why are you here, Ethan Chase?" he asked, his emerald stare suddenly piercing. "You should go home—there's no need for you to be tromping all over the Nevernever with the princeling. I can take him to Arcadia from here."

My skin prickled. That secret again. The one about me and Keirran. The reason Meghan had disappeared, cut herself off from our family and never told us she had a son. The vision of me dead on the ground, a horrified Keirran standing over my body, came back in a rush, and I shivered. Everyone in Faery had known, it seemed. Everyone…except Keirran and me.

Kenzie spoke up before I could answer, putting her hands on her hips and frowning up at the Summer prankster. "Why are you so eager to ship us home?" she demanded, and Puck's eyebrows rose. "We're fine. We're here to help Keirran and we're not going back until it's finished. So everyone can stop telling us to stay out of it."

Puck grinned at her. "Wow, don't you remind me of someone I know," he exclaimed, and Kenzie blinked. "Okay, fine. You're not going back to the safe, boring mortal world where you belong. Point taken. That doesn't really answer my question, princeling." He eyed Keirran again. "Why are you trying to get an audience with the Harpy Queen? You might as well tear out your heart and offer it to her on a silver platter. With sprinkles."

"It's for Annwyl," Keirran said firmly. "She's Fading, and the only way to stop it is if she returns to the Summer Court. I want to ask Titania to raise her exile. It wasn't fair, how she was banished. I just want to be able to send her home."

"Ah." Puck sighed, shaking his head. "I was afraid it was something like that. Well, then." He straightened on the branch, briskly rubbing his hands together. "I guess I'll just have to come with you."

Startled, I gave him a wary look. "What? You're not going to tell Ash or Meghan where we are?"

"What can I say?" Puck shrugged and walked along the

branch, balanced perfectly on the slender limb. "I'm a sucker for forbidden love. Besides, you'll need someone watching your back when you're talking with our lovely Summer Queen. Spread the loathing around a little bit... Whoa."

At that moment, the ground vibrated, making the limbs of the trees rustle and shake. Puck jerked, catching himself on the branch as a single apple fell from a cluster above him, bounced off his head and dropped with a thump to the grass.

"Uh-oh," Razor commented, and Grimalkin vanished.

The ground shook again, this time accompanied by an angry rumble that seemed to echo through the orchard. Puck grimaced and raised his hands.

"Oh, come on! I wasn't even trying this time."

The rumble turned into a roar as a few yards away, one of the trees shook violently, shedding apples everywhere, then began to rise from the ground. Dirt and apples tumbled away as a huge gnarled face pushed itself up from the grass, glaring at us with glowing yellow eyes. With a creaking and groaning of massive limbs, the creature stood up, towering forty feet in the air: a tangled giant of roots, moss and tree branches, its arms dangling past its stumpy legs to brush the ground. The apple tree was perched on its head, still shedding fruit that bounced off its massive body, and it would've been comical if it wasn't completely terrifying.

Puck groaned and leaped from the branch, pulling two daggers as he landed beside us. "You know, you guys have got to learn to share!" he called up to the monster looming over us. "I bet it would really cut down on those ugly stress wrinkles!"

The giant roared. Stepping forward, it smashed down with a huge, bristling fist, and we all dived aside. The limb struck the earth like a wrecking ball, sending dirt and apples flying and making the ground shake.

Scrambling for shelter, I pulled Kenzie around a tree and

pressed back into the rough bark, panting. She squeezed close, hands clutched in my shirt, shaking. "What now?" she whispered.

"I don't know." I drew one of my swords, though I wasn't sure what I could do with it. Hack at the giant's ankles, maybe? It would be like trying to cut down an oak with a pocketknife. If the oak was dancing around. And trying to step on you.

The giant rumbled and stepped closer. We sidled around the trunk, watching as the creature moved between the tree aisles, crouching and peering over the branches as it searched for us. At one point, it passed right by the trunk we were hiding behind, making the ground shake as it stepped close. Kenzie hid her face in my shirt, and I wrapped my arms around her, feeling her heart pound until the giant moved away.

"Ethan! Kenzie!"

Keirran's hiss caught our attention. The prince crouched behind another tree, sword drawn, beckoning to us. With a quick glance at the giant to make sure its back was turned, we bolted from our hiding place, crossed the open aisle and dived behind the trunk with Keirran.

The giant spun, creaking and groaning, as if it sensed we were close. With heavy, laborious steps, it began trudging toward us.

"I hope you have a plan," I growled at Keirran, feeling the earth tremble as the thing behind us got closer. "Right now, 'run like hell' is looking pretty appealing."

Keirran nodded. "On my signal," he said, his blue eyes hard as he watched the giant's progress. "Puck will provide the distraction. When it comes, run as fast as you can and don't look back. And let's hope it hasn't called its friend."

"Oh, great. There are more of them."

A massive foot smashed down a few yards from the trunk,

and the tree rustled and hissed, dropping apples everywhere, as the giant parted the branches overhead and spotted us.

It roared in triumph. But at that moment, a screaming flock of ravens erupted from the branches, flying in the giant's face. With a bellow, the monster lurched back, swatting at the birds, which swooped around him, pecking and cawing. Keirran leaped to his feet.

"Go!" he yelled, and we didn't need encouragement. Bolting from our hiding place, we tore across the field, hearing the giant's angry bellows grow fainter as we ran.

Of course, nothing was ever that easy.

About two hundred yards or so from the first giant, I was just thinking of slowing my all-out run to a jog, when we went up a little hill and the enormous bulk of a second giant rose up out of nowhere, howling as it saw us.

Dammit.

We changed direction and kept running, but instead of lashing out at us, the giant plunged its thorny claws into the ground as we passed. The ground shook, and gnarled roots erupted from the earth, curved and wickedly barbed like the giant's fingers. They shot out of the grass in a shower of dirt, trapping Kenzie between them, a cage of spiky wood and thorns. She screamed as the fingers began to close around her, like a fist crushing an egg.

"Kenzie!" I whirled, swords flashing, sinking one blade into the tough wood. The edge bit deep, but didn't cut through, and I yanked it out to hack at it again. Kenzie had fallen to her knees as the roots closed around her, thorny talons stabbing in, ready to crush the life from her. I could barely see her through the cage of branches now, and desperation flared up to suffocate me.

"No!" I screamed, and at that moment, the claws stopped moving. They trembled, shaking and groaning, as if straining against a force that held them back. I didn't pause to wonder about it. Raising my arm, I slashed down with all my strength, shearing through one of the talons, snapping it off. A few more hacks, and there was a space just large enough for Kenzie to squeeze through. I could see her, lying on the ground, curled up to escape the wicked points of death stabbing in from all sides.

"Kenzie," I gasped, dropping to my knees and reaching an arm through the space. The cage shuddered, the talons moving a few inches, as if ready to crush the barrier holding it back. She crawled forward, wincing as the thorns snagged her hair and clothes, then reached out and grabbed my wrist.

I yanked her to me, through the space, as the cage gave a tremendous groan and curled in on itself, crushing anything that might've been inside. Gasping, we scrambled away from it as the fist sank into the earth again and disappeared, leaving a giant hole behind.

Keirran, standing a few yards away, collapsed to the ground.

Panting, we crawled over to him. He was still breathing, his chest rising and falling in shallow waves, and his blue eyes were closed. His skin was pale, his hair damp with sweat as if he'd run several miles. The color had faded out of him once more, the silver in his hair leached to white, an ominous gray pallor settling over the rest of him. Razor buzzed in alarm and bounced on his chest, tugging at his shirt.

"Master!" the gremlin howled, sounding distressed. "Master, wake up!"

"Keirran." Shooing off the gremlin, Kenzie took his hand, and his eyes fluttered open. For a moment, the pupils were colorless, but he blinked, and they returned to their normal piercing blue once more.

"Kenzie, you're all right." Keirran's voice was faint, but he offered a relieved smile, struggling into a sit. "Thank goodness. I tried to hold the roots back, but the giant was strong. I'm glad Ethan was able to get you out in time."

"So that was you." I remembered the way the fist had stopped moving, straining to close. It had been Keirran's Summer glamour holding it back. "Dammit, Keirran. You can't keep using glamour like that. You're going to kill yourself."

"Would you rather I'd let Kenzie be crushed to death?"

An angry roar jerked us upright. The giant had apparently opened his fist and found it empty, instead of the broken body it was expecting.

"Humans." Grimalkin appeared in the long grass, tail lashing, glaring at us in exasperation. "Stop your infernal talking and run."

A raven swooped overhead with an impatient caw, seeming to agree with the cat. Scrambling to our feet, we did.

Zigzagging between trees, we ran until we reached the other side of the field, marked by the inconspicuous wooden fence. With the giants still bellowing behind us, I flung myself over the railings, tumbling to the other side in the grass. Kenzie and Keirran were right behind me, and we staggered a safe distance away from the fence as the giants glowered menacingly from inside the field, before turning away and lumbering back over the hill.

I collapsed to the grass, panting, while Keirran stood with his hands on his knees, breathing hard, and Razor gibbered and bounced on his back, throwing insults at the retreating giants. Kenzie plopped down beside me, and I pulled her into my arms, listening to her heartbeat as our breath caught up to us. She leaned back against my chest, closing her eyes and wrapping one arm around my neck.

"I don't think…I'll look at apples the same way…ever again," she panted.

"Oh, come on. You can't be tired now." Puck appeared

from the long grass, shaking feathers from his hair. Tossing an apple in one hand, he crunched into it with a grin and winked at us. "The party's just getting started."

CHAPTER EIGHTEEN

BESEECHING THE SUMMER QUEEN

"Well, there's the Summer Court," Puck remarked sometime later, nodding to a gap between the trees. In the distance, rising above a ring of brambles and thorns, an enormous grassy hill could be seen through the trunks. A pair of figures on horses trotted out of the bramble wall, which parted for them like a huge, thorny gate, and cantered away into the forest. "Home sweet home," Puck said.

"All the entrances will be well guarded," Keirran said, narrowed blue eyes sweeping over the landscape and the huge mound in the center. "And Titania isn't expecting me. Even if you're with us, Puck, they're not going to just let us walk into court."

"Walk in?" Puck snorted, giving Keirran a smirk. "Please. What fun would *that* be?"

"This way." Grimalkin sighed, turning deeper into the woods. "Follow me. I will get you into the Summer Court without the trouble we are certain to run into if you follow Goodfellow."

"Trouble? Me?" Puck gave him a wide-eyed, innocent look as we started after the cat. "I'm hurt, Furball. It's like you don't trust me or something."

"Imagine that," I muttered, and Keirran choked back a

laugh. Puck frowned at us both as we trailed Grimalkin deeper into the forest.

"Here," Grimalkin said a few minutes later, stopping at the bottom of a hillock. I blinked and stared down where the cat was sitting. A tiny burrow, just big enough for a rabbit or fox—or cat—to squeeze through snaked into the darkness. "This will take you where you wish to go."

Kenzie crouched down to peer into the narrow hole, then looked back at me. "Um...so we're all going to turn into weasels to get through this, I guess?"

"I could turn you into a mouse if you want," Puck offered. "Don't really know when you'd turn back, but hey, it would be an experience, right? I'd watch out for Furball, though. He might think he's smarter than anyone else, but like he says, he's still a cat."

"Do not be ridiculous, Goodfellow," Grimalkin said with an offended air. "There is no question that I am smarter than all of you." And he slipped into the dark hole without a backward glance or any hint of how we were supposed to fit down a freaking rabbit hole after him.

In desperation, I looked at Keirran, who gave me an encouraging smile. "It's all right," he reassured me, nodding to the hole. "Don't think that you won't fit. You will. It's much bigger than it looks. Try it."

Dubiously, I looked down at the hole. I would've said something about the impossibility of it all, but I reminded myself that we were in Faery, and nothing ever made sense here. Slowly, I bent down, peering cautiously into the darkness in case something with large teeth came lunging out at my face. Weirdly enough, the closer I got to the hole, the bigger it seemed. When I was just a foot or so away from the embankment, crouched all the way on my hands and knees, the burrow seemed just wide enough for my head to fit through.

Trying not to think of how stupid I'd look if my head got stuck while my ass poked out the end, I inched forward and leaned into the opening.

My head did not get stuck. In fact, I discovered I could wiggle my shoulders through and slide all the way into the tunnel. Cold dirt pressed against my jeans, and feathery roots tickled the back of my neck as I crawled in farther. The tunnel stank of mud, leaves and some kind of potent animal musk, making me wrinkle my nose. I hoped we wouldn't run into the owner of this burrow on our way to the Seelie Court. I didn't think I'd have a great advantage waving my swords around in such a tight space. Hopefully, nothing would come up on us from behind, either, because there was no way I could turn around.

I could still hear Keirran and Kenzie at the mouth of the burrow, and glanced back to see that the hole looked the same size as it did before, tiny and rabbit-size. Kenzie's face abruptly peered through the opening, eyes wide, and I wondered if I had shrunk while trying to wiggle into the burrow. Or did the tunnel somehow conform to my presence, expanding to allow me to slip inside? Or was this all some kind of illusion?

Ugh, stop thinking about that, Ethan. Logic doesn't apply here and you're going to make your brain explode.

"Human." Grimalkin's disembodied voice drifted out of the dark. A pair of glowing yellow eyes floated ahead in the shadows, though I couldn't see the rest of the cat. "Are you going to move, or are you going to sit there like a lump and block the opening of the tunnel?"

Oh, right. I crawled forward, giving Kenzie and Keirran room to slide in behind me. It was weird; I watched them both crawl into the tunnel, but for the life of me I couldn't tell if they shrank or if the hole got bigger or if I was going completely batty or what. It just happened, and a few seconds later, they were behind me, Razor's neon blue grin lightening the walls of the burrow.

"Funny!" He cackled, and I had to agree. Not the funny-ha-ha kind, though.

"Oof," Puck muttered as he joined us, bringing up the rear. "Oh yeah, I forgot about this," he mused, peering up the burrow. "Been a while since I've used this shortcut, though. Hey, Furball, where does this lead, again?"

The floating eyes ignored that question. "This way," Grimalkin said and turned away, padding down the tunnel. "And do try to keep up."

It wasn't a straight shot, we discovered. Almost immediately, the tunnel branched out in several directions, twisting off into the unknown. I concentrated on the bobbing yellow eyes as we navigated this labyrinth on our hands and knees, feeling my skin crawl every time we passed another dark tunnel. Except for the blueish glow of Razor's teeth, it was pitch-black down here, and the earthen walls seemed to press in on me the farther we went. I tried not to imagine the tunnel collapsing around us, or Grimalkin vanishing without a trace, leaving us behind in the dark. If there was ever a time to be thankful I wasn't claustrophobic, this would be it.

Finally, after a much longer time than I thought it would take, I followed the eyes around a corner and found a door sitting at the end of the tunnel. Not a regular, full-size door; this one was short and square, looking like the entrance to a cupboard or cabinet. It was halfway open, and a sliver of yellow light peeked through the crack.

Crawling forward, I pushed it open and looked down.

Yep, I was in a cupboard, apparently. Right below me was a stone sink, and next to that, a long counter with piles of chopped vegetables and bloody bits of meat and bone. Were we in…a kitchen of some sort? The thought made me very nervous; of all the places to end up in the world of Faery, kitchens were not at the top of my list. All those stories about people getting stuffed into ovens or baked into pies? They didn't happen in the living room.

"Are you ever going to come down?" Grimalkin wondered, now sitting across the room on top of a shelf. "Or are you going to sit there and gape until the cook opens the door and finds you?"

I carefully eased out of the cupboard, using the sink to balance myself until I could step down. Kenzie followed me and I helped her to the stone floor, where she looked around eagerly.

"Are we in a kitchen?" she asked, voicing my own question earlier. Looking up at the cabinet, where Keirran slid out and hopped gracefully to the floor, she frowned. "And…did we just crawl through a cupboard to get here? How…?"

"Don't ask," I said. "Trust me, it's better if you don't wonder about it."

Puck joined us, dropping to the ground, dusting off his hands as he rose. Taking a swift glance at our surroundings, his eyebrows arched.

"Uh-oh."

"Uh-oh?" Keirran gave him a weary look as Razor buzzed with alarm. "We're not going to like what you're going to tell us next, are we?"

"Well…" Puck scratched the side of his neck. "I just remembered why I stopped using that shortcut—"

Footsteps echoed outside the hall. Loud, ponderous footsteps, made by something large and heavy. Atop the shelf, Grimalkin disappeared.

Puck grimaced. "Maybe you should hide now."

We scrambled for a nearby closet, crowding in among brooms, mops and bags of potatoes. As Keirran pulled the door mostly shut, leaving a crack to peer through, a shadow darkened the door, and a massive green troll filled the frame. It—she?—wore a once-white apron, now stained with red, and carried a meat cleaver in one thick claw. A brown braid was tossed over a shoulder, and two long tusks curled up from her jaw as she stared at Puck, her lips curling back in revulsion.

"Robin Goodfellow?" the troll bellowed as Puck gave her a cheeky wave. "You are not supposed to be here—you were banned from this kitchen for life!"

"Aw, come on, Sarah," Puck answered as the troll stalked into the room. "You've missed me. Admit it."

"Out!" roared the troll, swinging her knife, which he instantly dodged. "Get out, you miserable thief! I'll have no more pies stolen by the likes of you! Out, out!"

Laughing, Puck ducked, rolled and finally scrambled out the door, the troll stomping after him waving her meat cleaver. Keirran shook his head as Razor cackled with glee and bounced on his shoulder.

Grimalkin was waiting on the top shelf as we emerged from the closet, looking as though nothing had happened. "Are we quite finished?" he asked, as if a giant troll storming into the room and chasing after Puck was *our* fault, somehow. "Are you ready to go find the queen?"

"What about Puck?" Kenzie asked.

"I am sure Goodfellow will rejoin us when he is done playing with the cook," the cat said, leaping to the floor. "Now, shall we move on before anything else can happen?"

Following Grimalkin, we left the kitchens, opened a large wooden door and found ourselves in a brambly tunnel. Once the door was shut and we were a good distance away, no longer able to hear the furious bellows still echoing through the branches, the cat paused and turned to face us.

"That is the way to the throne room, where Titania is holding court," he said, nodding to where another bramble tunnel twisted off into the thorns. "I assume you can find your way from here, Prince?"

"Yes," Keirran said as Razor hissed at the cat from beneath his hair. "I take it you're not coming with us to see the queen?"

"I have no business with the court." Grimalkin yawned. "I brought you into the Seelie Court, as I said I would, and though it would be amusing to see how you fare with the queen, I have other things to do. Fear not, humans." He turned and trotted off, tail held up like a flag behind him. "I am certain we will meet again soon."

Slipping beneath the thick hedge, he vanished.

The walk to the end of the tunnel wasn't far. Several dozen steps down the brambly corridor, around a bend, and then it opened into a large clearing, thorny walls still surrounding it on every side.

A pair of thrones sat in the center of the glade, shafts of sunlight streaming down on them from above. They seemed to have grown right out of the forest floor, as they were covered in vines and blooming flowers, with birds perched on the arms and back and insects floating around them. The throne on the left was empty and probably Oberon's, the absent Summer King. But sitting in the chair on the right...

"Oh boy," Keirran whispered, and Razor hid beneath his hair.

Titania, Queen of the Summer Court, lounged on her throne like a lazy cat, a tiny, amused smile on her full lips as she observed her subjects. She was tall and slender with golden hair cascading down her shoulders, her face that of a goddess, perfect and frightening. I was beginning to reach a point where the inhuman beauty of the gentry didn't affect me as much anymore, but still, the Seelie Queen took my breath away.

I swallowed and reminded myself that this was the second-most powerful faery in the Summer Court, that one wrong move or word on our part could get us turned into rabbits or harts or mice, or whatever struck the faery queen's fancy. And judging by the pack of whip-thin moss-green hounds roaming about the clearing, being turned into any sort of small animal would end very badly for us.

"Razor, wait here," Keirran said, putting the gremlin on a branch. Razor buzzed and shook his head in protest, and Keirran frowned. "Titania hates Iron fey. I can't have you with me when I'm bargaining with her. It will be too much of a distraction."

"No!" Razor buzzed, looking desperate. "No leave Razor! No!"

"Here, Razor," Kenzie said and held out her arm. "You can stay with me if you're quiet. I won't be talking to the queen, either." She shot me a quick glance, letting me know she hadn't forgotten her promise. "We'll be quiet together."

The gremlin let out a happy cackle and leaped to her shoulder. She shushed him, and he bobbed his head earnestly. Burrowing into her hair, the spindly fey vanished except for his glowing green eyes, peering out from behind the dark curtain.

"Kenzie," Keirran murmured as the gremlin muttered nonsense beneath Kenzie's hair, "I'm grateful for your support, but you don't have to do this. You can still leave, or wait here while I talk with the queen. You and Ethan both."

"Oh, shut up," I whispered back and took a determined step toward the throne. "Come on. Let's get this over with."

Fey stared at us as we crossed the clearing, Summer gentry in ridiculous finery that defied the laws of nature. Cloaks of leaves, gowns of petals still in bloom, a cape made of thousands of butterflies, gently fanning their wings in the sun. The gentry eyed us with cold amusement, curiosity and alarm, especially as their gazes fell on Keirran and they realized exactly who had crashed their little party. Whispers and muttering trailed us through the meadow. The lyrical music ground to an inelegant halt, and someone in the crowd gasped.

Keirran kept walking, not looking at any of the Summer fey as we strode forward, his gaze only for the queen. On her throne, Titania straightened, her crystal-blue eyes narrowing to dangerous slits as they fell on us.

"Prince Keirran," Titania said as we reached the foot of the throne. Keirran bowed, and Kenzie and I followed his example, though the queen barely flicked a glance at us. The Summer Queen's voice, though as smooth as honey over velvet, was not pleasant. "I don't recall giving you permission to be in Arcadia."

"Please forgive this intrusion, Queen Titania," Keirran said, his tone polite but unwavering. "We would have gone through the proper channels, but I'm afraid an audience with the Summer Court could not wait."

"Is that so?" The queen smiled, beautiful and terrifying. "Then tell me, Iron Prince. What is so dire that you would dare break the rules of my court to speak with me? You do realize I could punish you where you stand for trespassing, but I find that I am in a curious mood today. What brings the elusive Iron Prince out of hiding?" Her gaze slid to me, and one elegant eyebrow rose. "And with the Iron Queen's brother in tow. How very amusing. There are rumors about you circulating the courts, Prince—your disappearing acts have not gone unnoticed, and many people are looking for you. Have you come for Sanctuary, then?" Her smile grew even more evil. "The Iron Prince seeking refuge from his own kind? How delicious. Well, if you want to stay here, Prince Keirran, you're more than welcome, of course. Provided you can meet the requirements."

"I didn't come for refuge, Queen Titania," Keirran said before the Summer monarch could go any further. "I'm well aware that the Iron Court is searching for me. I will return to Mag Tuiredh soon. Your generous offer of Sanctuary is not needed at this time. But I did come…to ask a favor."

Titania's eyes gleamed, and the hairs on the back of my neck rose.

"A favor, Iron Prince? Do go on."

"You had a maiden named Annwyl in your court once," Keirran continued, oblivious or uncaring of the glee in the queen's eyes. "Do you remember her?"

"Annwyl." Titania wrinkled her nose, appearing deep in thought. "The name does sound familiar," she continued in a vague manner, though it was fairly obvious she was being coy. "Wasn't she one of my servants? A simple, plain girl if I remember. It's so hard to keep track of the help. They all begin to look the same after a while."

Keirran didn't show any outward signs of offense, but Kenzie stiffened beside me, eyes narrowing angrily. Hidden in her hair, Razor growled and mumbled under his breath. I hoped neither of them would lose it in front of Titania; that would play right into her game.

"Annwyl was exiled from the Summer Court and the Nevernever," Keirran continued, his voice as coolly polite as before. If you didn't see the stiff set of his shoulders, you wouldn't know he was angry or upset. "She was banished, but she didn't break any laws. I am officially requesting that you lift her exile and allow her to return to Arcadia, in the same manner and with the same expectations as before her banishment." He hesitated a moment, then added, "Please."

"Lift her exile?" Titania sniffed and sat back on her throne, regarding us with amusement. "Why in the world would I want to do that? If I banished the Summer girl, I'm certain I had good reason for it."

You didn't, I thought angrily, and by the thinning of Kenzie's mouth, I knew she was thinking the same. Titania must've caught something in our expressions, though, for her piercing, slightly feral gaze zeroed in on me.

"You're being awfully quiet, Ethan Chase." Titania's smile sent a chill through my stomach. "Your disdain for our kind is well-known. You have never bothered to venture into the Nevernever before, not even to visit your sister. Why the change of heart?"

I swallowed the dryness in my throat and tried to keep my voice light, uncaring. "I'm just helping out a family member," I said, shrugging. "When this is done, I'm going home, and you'll never see me again."

"How very noble of you," Titania replied. "But being in my court means you are subject to my rules, and you are just as guilty of breaking the law as the prince. Therefore, you will share his fate should I decide to punish him. You *and* your little friend there."

Panic flared as the Summer Queen's cruel gaze fastened on Kenzie. *Calm down,* I ordered myself. *Don't jump to her defense; that's what Titania wants. If she suspects how much you care for Kenzie, she'll use that as a weakness against you. Don't give her anything.*

"Queen Titania," Keirran began, but she raised a hand, silencing him.

"I will be with you in a moment, Prince Keirran," she said without looking his way. "Right now, I am very curious as to what the mortals are doing here."

Kenzie remained silent, though I could see it was a struggle. I was amazed, and sort of proud, that Kenzie was keeping her head, not giving the queen anything that could be used against her. But Titania wasn't done yet. "You are adorable, aren't you?" the Summer Queen went on, regarding Kenzie with a lazy smile. Kenzie met the queen's stare, quiet but unafraid, and Titania chuckled. "And quite fearless. You'd make a lovely rosebush, I think. Or perhaps a hart?"

Kenzie bit her lip. I could see she was trying not to say anything, and the queen turned a purely sadistic smile on me. "What do you think, Ethan Chase? Perhaps I will have *you* choose the girl's form. Do you think she would make a better rosebush or hart?"

The panic in my chest grew, making it hard to breathe. *Dammit, I have to get her attention off Kenzie, but how?* A heartbeat, and then I knew. *I have to make her think I don't care. If she believes nothing she'd do to Kenzie would upset me, maybe she'll leave her alone.* Taking a furtive breath, I shrugged again and said in my most flippant, jackass-y voice, "She's been following us around for days and she never shuts up. Turn her into whatever you want—maybe I'll finally get some peace and quiet."

My stomach twisted even as I finished those words, but I pushed down my fear and concentrated on not showing any emotion in front of Titania. Like sharks or wolves or rabid dogs, faeries could sense fear a mile away.

"Harsh words, Ethan Chase," the queen mused at last, and I could see her scrutinizing me, maybe searching my glamour aura for the truth. "Do you not have any compassion for your fellow humans?"

I searched for that cold, hostile loner I was before I met Kenzie, and threw him up again, even managing a faint smirk as I stared at the fey queen. "Not when my fellow humans are annoying, pushy and won't leave me alone. Maybe a couple weeks as a rosebush will teach her not to follow me into Faeryland. So, by all means…" I shrugged again. "I can't stop you, so do whatever you want. It makes no difference to me."

All the while, I could feel Kenzie's eyes on me, and I hoped we would be around long enough for me to apologize.

Don't say anything, I begged her. *Don't draw attention to yourself and maybe we'll all get out of this without any major catastrophes.*

Titania stared at us, while I forced myself to breathe normally, to give her the impression that I really was the cold-hearted jackass who didn't care if she changed one of his friends into a plant. The queen blinked and seemed about to lose interest, when Razor suddenly poked his head out of Kenzie's hair, baring his teeth at the Summer monarch.

"Bad queen!" he hissed, flattening his ears. "Not hurt pretty girl!"

Titania recoiled. "Ugh! What is that...thing?" she spat, and the rest of the nobles drew away with gasps and cries of alarm. Rising, the queen towered over Kenzie, pointing at her with a slender white hand. "How dare you bring that abomination into my court, mortal? Out! Both of you—get out of my sight!"

Razor hissed and ducked back into Kenzie's hair, and Keirran quickly stepped forward.

"Apologies, Queen Titania," he soothed as the queen's furious glare turned on him. My heart pounded, but at least she wasn't staring at Kenzie anymore. "The gremlin is mine, so it's my fault that he's here."

"You try my patience, Prince," Titania said, narrowing her eyes. "I am quickly becoming annoyed with you and your little mortal friends, so perhaps you should all be on your way."

"Of course. We'll leave, as soon as we have your consent to let Annwyl back into Arcadia."

"I do not bow to the requests of you, Prince Keirran." Titania sneered. "This is my court, and you have no power here, even if you are the Iron Queen's son." She straightened, fixing us with a cold glare. "If you want me to raise this girl's exile, you will do something for me in return."

Okay, now we came to the heart of the matter. When asking a favor of any faery, always be ready to bargain for something in return. Keirran was prepared for it and simply nodded.

"What would you have of me?" he asked in a calm voice. Titania smiled again. Settling back on her throne, she regarded us all with a smug, pleased expression, making us wait.

"There is a place in Tir Na Nog," the Summer Queen began, and my heart sank at the mention of the Winter Court, "in the region they call the Frozen Wood. It sits just beyond the Ice Maw, the chasm that separates the wyldwood from Mab's territory. Do you know of it?"

"I've heard of it," Keirran said cautiously.

Titania preened, looking like a cat with a mouse in its claws. "Deep below the wood lies an ancient creature," she continued in a grand voice, and my heart sank even further as I suspected where this was going. "It has been sleeping for centuries, but its very presence keeps the land above it eternally frozen. The Cold it generates is a living thing itself, stealing into the wood, snuffing the life from all who venture there. Nothing can live in the wood for long—creatures that wander or get caught out in the open become trapped in ice, forever." The queen gave a disdainful sniff. "Barbaric, don't you think? And all because of this creature. Something should be done."

I sighed. "You want us to kill it."

The Summer Queen blinked. "Why, Ethan Chase, what a horrid idea. Certainly I would not risk offending Mab by suggesting you slay the beast. However, if the creature does meet some untimely demise, well, nothing can live forever, can it?"

Keirran looked grim. "If we do this," he began, "you'll raise Annwyl's banishment and allow her to return to the Summer Court?"

"You make this sound like a contract, Prince Keirran," Titania said, looking surprised. "Such an idea might spark a war between Summer and Winter. No, this is just a friendly conversation. Do what you wish, but if the creature does perish in some unfortunate event, it would please me greatly, and I will consider raising the girl's exile. Provided you don't perish on the way to the beast's lair. That would be a tragedy. Now..." She leaned back, waving a hand. "I've become bored with this. Remove yourselves from my court, before I turn you all into rabbits and call in the hounds for entertainment."

I shared a glance with Keirran, and he nodded. Silently, we bowed once more and left the queen's presence, slipping back into the bramble tunnel and moving well out of earshot of the court before we stopped.

"Well, that went better than I expected," I muttered, only now realizing my hands were shaking. "At least she didn't turn us into marmosets or anything."

Razor emerged from Kenzie's hair, buzzing and hissing like a furious cat. "Bad queen," he stated and leaped to Keirran's shoulder, clinging like a leech and glaring back toward the court. "Not turn Master into rabbit. Bad."

Kenzie was unusually quiet. In the shadows of the bramble tunnel, she looked pale, and her eyes were dull. "You okay?" I asked, knowing I was probably annoying her by asking about her health so often, but I couldn't help it. Falling in love had apparently kicked my overbearing tendencies into overdrive.

She nodded without looking at me, and I moved closer. "You did good back there," I said, half teasing, wanting her to argue, to see some kind of reaction. "I was sure you'd jump in and tell Titania what she could turn herself into."

"I wanted to," Kenzie replied. "But you and Keirran seemed to be doing fine on your own, and I didn't want to make it harder. I do try to keep my promises, Ethan. Even though I poke my nose where it doesn't belong, tag along when I'm not wanted and talk too much."

"Hey," I said quietly, taking her arm. "You know I didn't mean any of that. I was just trying to throw Titania off."

"I know," Kenzie said and rubbed her eyes. "Sorry, I'm just tired. It's hard hearing your shortcomings listed off in such an obvious manner. I know I can be pushy, and stubborn, and overbearing." She turned away, not meeting my gaze. "I'll try not to whine at you anymore."

"Come here," I muttered and pulled her to me, wrapping my arms around her. She leaned against me and closed her eyes, and I pressed my lips to the top of her head. "I'm sorry if I hurt you," I whispered into her hair. "And for the record, I don't want you to change, ever. I'm glad you were pushy and stubborn and wouldn't leave me alone. I wouldn't be here now if you weren't."

Kenzie sniffled. "So, what you're saying is you *want* me to boss you around."

"Me, Keirran, Razor, everyone," I answered, making Keirran snort. "The kings and queens of Faery, too, if they would ever stop turning people into rodents every five minutes."

She squeezed my waist. "Well, now I regret not telling Titania where she could stick her rosebushes."

Keirran smiled. "I'm sure you'll get the chance later," he said as we drew apart. "After all, we have to return to the Summer Court when we've finished this task for Titania."

"So we're still planning to do it," I said, glaring at him. "Head into Mab's territory, cross this Frozen Wood, find this ancient power or whatever is sleeping beneath it and somehow manage to kill it." Keirran nodded solemnly, and I half laughed. "Normal day in the Nevernever."

"What's normal?" said a voice behind us, and Puck poked his head out from behind a cluster of branches. "Sorry I had to split," he apologized, grinning as he came into the open, dusting himself off. "Man, trolls can sure hold a grudge. You'd think she'd be flattered I think so highly of her food. Anyway." He crossed his arms and gave us an appraising look. "Did you say you were going into Tir Na Nog? Lemme guess— you met with our lovely queen, she threatened to turn you into lemurs or something ridiculous and then she told you to go complete some ludicrously impossible task for her. Am I right?" When we nodded, he shook his head. "I thought so. Well, you know what this means, don't you?"

"Yes." Keirran's eyes were hard as he faced Puck, his expression one of grim determination. "We have to find a way into Winter."

CHAPTER NINETEEN

THE WAY TO WINTER

"Finding" the way to Winter wasn't difficult. Puck bragged he had been there countless times, obviously to cause trouble, so he knew several paths to Queen Mab's territory. Of course, if we wanted to remain in Faery, we could tromp back through the wyldwood until we reached the border of Tir Na Nog. But that would take time, Puck said, and the chances of getting through the wyldwood without running into trouble were slim. The quicker way to the Frozen Wood, he explained, was back through the mortal world.

"Why are you helping us?" Keirran asked as we followed Puck down the sidewalk of some unknown city. It was snowing lightly, and the gutters were full of slush. Beside me, Kenzie hugged herself and shivered, and I found myself wishing for a jacket, too. I didn't know what we were going to do when we got to Winter, where it was probably far colder.

Keirran frowned at Puck, his expression both puzzled and wary, though the Summer fey seemed oblivious. "You know what Titania wants us to do," he said. "Shouldn't you be searching for my father or at least letting the Iron Queen know where I am?"

"Hey, I'm just looking out for my best friend's kid," Puck

replied airily. "And her kid brother. But let me ask you this. If I wasn't here, would you still be trying to get into Tir Na Nog?"

"Yes."

"And if I told you not to go, would you stop?"

"No."

"So, there ya go." Puck shrugged. "Better that I'm here to bail you out of trouble than let you face whatever it is you're going to face on your own. Besides, I never turn down the chance to annoy the Winter Court. I haven't been to Tir Na Nog in a while. I'm sure they've missed me terribly."

Kenzie sneezed then, rubbing her arms. I wished I could offer her a coat or something, though I was freezing myself. "Quick question," she said through chattering teeth. "This is the *Winter* Court, right? Not that I'm complaining, but I assume it's going to be very, very cold. And from what Titania said, this Frozen Wood doesn't sound very nice. How are we going to keep from freezing to death?"

"Ah, worry not," Puck stated and ushered us down an alley. "I've already got that figured out."

A door stood at the end of the alley, narrow, unmarked and black. I stared at it uneasily as we approached. It reminded me of the entrance to Mr. Dust's, but this door had a rectangular eye slit near the top and what looked like a pet door near the bottom. Weird. Maybe Grimalkin used this door sometimes?

Puck strode up without hesitation and rapped on the wood three times.

The small rectangular slit near the top snapped open, and two bloodshot eyes peered out, wary and guarded. "Who's there? Go away. We're closed!"

"Mortimer," Puck said, all smiles. "Is that any way to treat an old friend?"

The beady eyes widened as they saw Puck. "Robin Good-fellow?" the voice rasped, and it was difficult to see, but I think the skin around the eyes paled a bit. "Why are you here? I have nothing for you. Go away!"

The slit door slammed, but not before Puck had shoved his hand inside, stopping it from closing. "Ow. Hey, Mort, you realize you still owe me a favor, right? That time I saved you from those redcaps? Remember that?"

"No!" howled the voice on the other side, futilely trying to shut the eye slit. "I cannot let you into Tir Na Nog this time! Queen Mab would skin me alive if she knew."

"Life debt, Morty," Puck reminded him. "If it wasn't for me, Mab would have to find a new trod gatekeeper. All we want is passage to Tir Na Nog. This wasn't even my idea."

I stood behind Kenzie, rubbing her cold arms and watching this little scene in wary amusement. I had no doubt Puck would get us into Tir Na Nog; when and how was the question. The trod keeper shouted a protest and tried shutting the door again, but Puck wasn't going anywhere. I moved closer to Kenzie, protecting her from the wind, and sighed. This might take a while.

Suddenly, Keirran stepped forward, striding up to the door and bringing his face close to the opening. The bloodshot, beady eyes flickered to the prince as he leaned in.

"Do you know me?" Keirran's voice was hard, the cold stranger that had reared its head on occasion. "Do you know who I am?"

Puck blinked, a dangerous look crossing his face as he stared at the prince, but Keirran wasn't paying attention to him. The face peering through the crack nodded.

"I know who you are, Iron Prince."

"Let us through," Keirran ordered, sounding very much like his father. "Or there won't *be* a trod to Tir Na Nog here any longer, or a gatekeeper."

The bloodshot eyes narrowed sharply. "Is that a threat, Iron Prince?"

Keirran didn't answer, but the air around us began to chill. My breath writhed out in front of me, and frost spread over the door and brick walls of the alley. Kenzie shivered and pressed back into me, but the gatekeeper on the other side gave a harsh laugh.

"Winter magic, Iron Prince? I am the gatekeeper of the Frozen Wood. I do not fear the cold—"

A flash, and the acrid odor of smoke and metal. Keirran didn't move, but the wooden door suddenly erupted with long spikes tipped with metal at the ends. Puck yelped and leaped back, barely missing being impaled, and the gatekeeper inside gave a piercing scream. Smoke began billowing out of the eye slit, along with the sudden stench of burned hair.

"Let us pass," Keirran continued in that cold, lethally calm voice, "or I will infect your entire trod with Iron glamour, and then we'll see how well it fares."

"All right!" The eyes appeared again, wide and frantic. "Enough! Stop! I will give you passage to Tir Na Nog, but you'll say nothing of how I let you into Winter. If the queen finds out, she'll have all our heads." A groan, and the eyes drew back a little. "One moment. I will prepare the trod to the Frozen Wood. It will take but a moment."

"Be quick about it," Keirran said, and the eye slit snapped shut.

Puck glared at the prince. "You didn't have to do that, princeling," he said in an annoyed voice. "I had it under control."

"You probably did." Keirran's soft, cold tone hadn't changed. The icy stranger stared unwaveringly at the door, frost continuing to spread over the pavement around him. "But he was in our way. I don't have time to play with trod keepers, not with Annwyl's life on the line."

"Maybe," I agreed, frowning at the prince over Kenzie's head. "But that was kind of a dick move, Keirran."

Keirran didn't answer, and a moment later the slat opened again, the eyes peering out sullenly. "The trod is prepared," the raspy voice announced. "And the door is unlocked. When you are ready, just open it, and the way to Winter will be revealed."

"Not so fast," Puck said, rapping the door as the eyes started to pull away. "We're going into the Frozen Wood, and we have two humans in the party. Aren't you forgetting something?"

The gatekeeper glared at the Summer fey, but a second later, the flap at the bottom swung up, and a bowl of strange orange fruits was shoved out. They were the shape of a pear but the size of a strawberry, and the air around them shimmered with heat. Then the eye slit slammed shut once more, and I knew it wouldn't open again.

Puck sighed. "Well, better grab a few of those things," he said, nodding to the fruit in front of the door. "You'll need it where we're going."

Kenzie immediately stepped forward and snatched one, lifting it up curiously. The skin had an odd rippling effect, like the air around a fire. "What is it?"

"Flamefruit," Keirran answered, sounding back to his normal self, though his voice was slightly weary. "It'll keep you from freezing to death in Tir Na Nog. Don't eat too many, though. It's pretty potent for humans. Not as bad as summerpod, but still…be careful."

"Ah, summerpod." Puck sighed, sounding wistful. "Lots of fun with that little fruit. Good times, good times. Well…" He glanced at me and Kenzie with a grin. "Are you two ready for this party?"

Kenzie handed me a trio of the small orange fruit, and I took them reluctantly. "Ready as we'll ever be, I suppose."

"One more thing," Keirran warned as Puck marched up to the door. "The Cold in the Frozen Wood is a living thing. The flamefruit will protect you from freezing, but if you get sleepy or want to close your eyes for a moment, don't give in to the compulsion. Creatures that fall asleep in the wood never wake up again."

A chill not related to temperature skittered up my back. With a grand gesture, Puck flung back the door, and a blast of icy cold whooshed into the alley, making me shiver. Kenzie stepped forward, her eyes bright as she gazed through the opening. Beyond the frame, a pristine, snowy forest stretched out before us, sparkling in the afternoon sun. Leafless trees grew close together, the sunlight peeking through their branches to dapple the snow, and every tree, trunk, twig and branch was coated in ice. Not just a little ice, either. Entire trees were encased in crystal, though you could still see every detail through the frozen shell. Huge icicles hung from everything, and the air swirling through the open door was so cold it hurt to breathe.

"Brr." Kenzie shivered and quickly popped a fruit into her mouth before I could stop her. Instantly, a flush darkened her cheeks, her skin losing its paleness and regaining some color. "Oh, wow. That little thing works fast." She looked at Puck and grinned. "You'll have to get me some seeds one day. Think of the money we could make if we bottle that stuff."

Puck laughed. "Oh, believe me, I've thought about it," he said as we went through the door. My feet sank into about a foot of snow, and the air burned my nose and lungs when I inhaled, it was so cold. Shivering, I gritted my teeth and marched doggedly forward as Puck and Kenzie continued talking like they were on a forest stroll. "Sadly, there are two reasons that could put a damper on that plan," Puck went on, holding up a finger. "One—flamefruit only grows beside pools of molten lava, so unless you want to move next to a volcano, it might be difficult to harvest. Second—eat too many, too fast, and you might...uh...spontaneously combust. Though that might make for some interesting conversations."

"Can we please stay on target?" Keirran asked in an exasperated voice. "We have to find the creature that lives beneath the woods, and I haven't any idea how to do that, do you?"

An icy wind cut through the forest, rattling icicles and making my skin shrink with cold. I'd wanted to hold off eating the faery fruit for as long as I could, but my willpower was rapidly disintegrating with all my body warmth, and I shoved a fruit into my mouth, swallowing quickly.

Instantly, I felt warmer, like I'd just taken a huge swallow of hot tea or coffee, except the sensation didn't fade, and it spread to all parts of my body. Now that I could actually feel my face again, I concentrated on what Puck was telling Keirran.

"There's a series of caves several miles north of here," Puck said, nodding to where the snowcapped tops of a mountain range peeked over the forest of ice. "Stumbled onto them a few times with ice-boy, but we never went all the way to the bottom. Dunno what could be living down there, but that's probably where you'll find your beastie."

Kenzie drifted closer and took my hand, holding it tightly as we made our way through the forest, the only sounds being the crunch of our feet in the snow. "I'm worried about Keirran," she told me in a whisper, watching the Iron Prince stride purposefully through the snow ahead. "He's been acting really weird lately, not himself. I think whatever the amulet is doing has started to affect him."

"I know," I muttered. I was worried about him, too. "But there's nothing we can do right now except get this stupid task done as quickly as possible. Then Annwyl can go back to Summer, and we can destroy that amulet."

As we passed a clump of trees, a large shape between the trunks caught my eye and made me jump, hand going to my sword. It was an elk, shaggy and massive, with huge antlers branching out from its skull. It knelt in the snow between two trees with its head up and its eyes closed.

And it was completely encased in ice.

Kenzie blinked and stepped toward it, even as I hastily backed up. "Kenzie," I warned as she put out a hand to touch its frozen muzzle. The stag was perfectly still, a motionless statue, but I had visions of it surging up with a roar and lunging at us. It was just too still, like the "corpses" in horror movies that you *know* will leap up and take a swat at the hero the second he gets close. "Don't mess with it," I told her. "We don't know what it will do."

Kenzie, of course, ignored me. Her eyes were wide as she ran a finger along its snout, shivering. "It's so cold," she whispered. "How long has it been like this, I wonder?"

"Kenzie…"

A shout boomed from behind me, and something grabbed my arms. I yelped and spun, drawing my swords and slashing wildly at whatever had sneaked up on me from behind.

Puck—of course it was Puck—staggered away, gasping with laughter, having already dodged my swords. I relaxed, lowering my weapons as annoyance swiftly replaced alarm.

"Hilarious." I sheathed my blades and glared at him. He cackled, and I stifled the urge to march up and punch him in his grinning mouth. "I could've cut your head off, you know."

"You're way too uptight, kid," Puck said, giving me a friendly wink. "Man, you're just like your sister when she first came to the Nevernever, jumping at everything like a startled rabbit. And *no,* you couldn't have. I spent decades tormenting ice-boy, who has far better reflexes than you. I'm afraid you're no *touch-me-and-I'll-kill-you* Unseelie prince, human."

A few yards away, Razor cackled with glee on Keirran's shoulder, bouncing up and down and shouting "Funny, funny!" in a high-pitched voice, but the prince looked far less amused. "We should keep moving," he said, sounding like he was trying to hide his impatience. "Kenzie, Ethan, you'll probably see several more frozen animals, or even people, before we reach the caves. It's best to leave them in peace."

Kenzie stroked the elk's furry neck. "Will it ever wake up?"

"It's dead," Keirran told her gently, and she pulled her arm back in horror. "The Cold took it when it lay down to sleep. And if we stand in one place for too long, it will try to take us, too. Come on, let's keep going."

We kept marching, our steps muffled by snow, barely making any sound as we forged ahead. The forest around us remained eerily silent and still, except for brief flashes of color from once-living creatures trapped in ice. A fox sleeping in a hollow log, its bushy tail curled around itself. Another stag, its antlers entangled in the branches of a low tree, now immobilized for all time. Countless birds frozen to the twigs they perched on, feathers puffed out against the cold, looking like fuzzy golf balls. Even a gray wolf, its fur bristling with icicles, lay curled in a ball at the base of a tree. Solemn and beautiful, in a morbid kind of way. Kenzie and I ate another flamefruit as evening approached and the effects slowly wore off. But our supply was dwindling, and I hoped we could do whatever we had to do here quickly and return to Arcadia before we ran out and froze to death.

As darkness began to fall and the sky overhead turned navy blue, the temperature dropped sharply. Even through the warm haze of the flamefruit, I could feel the chill prickling my skin.

Puck glanced nervously at the sky and made a comment about picking up the pace.

"Why?" Kenzie asked, briskly rubbing her arms. "Does something happen at night?"

"Oh, nothing serious," Puck said cheerfully. "It's just the frost wraiths come out at night, and we probably want to avoid running into any. Nasty buggers, no sense of humor at all. Will suck the warmth right out of you, and all the flamefruit in the world won't save you from them."

I felt a weird sensation along my own forearms and looked down to see frost creeping over my skin. Shivering, I followed Kenzie's example and quickly scrubbed it away.

"The caves aren't far," Keirran said, looking up at the mountain peaks. Razor peeked out of his collar, his huge ears and eyes the only things visible. "If we hurry, we should be there in a few..."

An unearthly wailing rose from the trees around us, making Puck wince and everyone else jump. Razor buzzed with alarm and hid down Keirran's shirt.

"Well, I told you so," Puck said and drew his daggers. "Better get ready. Here they come!"

Figures floated through the trees, blurred and indistinguishable. As they drifted closer, I saw they looked like gray wisps of tattered cloth, fluttering over the ground. Glowing blue eyes stared out at us as bony hands slipped from within the layers of rags and reached out, clawing and grasping.

I shoved Kenzie behind me and met the first two that flapped toward us, pale fingers reaching for my face. My first slice hit one right in the center of the floating rags and it frayed apart with a wail, the cloth fluttering to the ground. The second one tried sliding around me and going for Kenzie. Snarling, I whirled, slashing viciously at the wraith as it passed, cutting it from the air. It flopped limply to the snow, an empty pile of rags, before the wind blew it away. More ragged figures floated toward me from the darkness. I glimpsed Puck and Keirran a few yards away, slashing and dancing around their own attackers, blades whirling. Kenzie stood protected in the center of the triangle, and I intended to keep it that way. Raising my swords, I faced the next three swooping down from the branches of the trees.

Two wraiths came shrieking at my face, skeletal arms outstretched. I jerked back as one clawed at me, lashed out and sliced through its neck. The next attacker flung itself at me, right onto the tip of my sword as I stabbed upward, impaling itself on the blade.

The last dodged my swing and swooped low, darting beneath the second blade like a jerky puppet. Before I could move, it latched on to my leg, wrapped itself around my jeans and sank needle-sharp teeth into my calf.

The cold that lanced through me from the thing's bite was a physical pain, sharp and burning. It was like I'd plunged my leg into a vat of ice water. My leg nearly buckled, and my howl of pain came out as a strangled rasp because my jaw was clenched so hard.

With shaking fingers, I put my weapon between my leg and the thing clinging to it and shoved hard, hoping I wouldn't cut myself by mistake. By this time, my arms were shaking violently as well, but I managed to pry the wraith off and hurl it away. It darted back at my face with a shriek, and I slashed wildly, cutting it in two by sheer dumb luck.

That was the last of the wraiths, but I was shaking so hard now I thought I might throw up. I couldn't keep ahold of my swords; they dropped from my numb fingers into the snow, and I didn't think I had the muscle coordination to pick them up again. My teeth chattered, and breathing had suddenly become a painful chore.

"Oh, God, Ethan." Kenzie put a hand on my arm; it felt like a hot coal, searing and wonderful. "Your skin is like ice. Here. This is my last one."

She pressed something to my lips—one of the flamefruit pods, which was good, because my hands were shaking too hard to hold anything. I swallowed and felt the little fruit burn a path down to my stomach, easing some of the pain. Just a little, but it was enough for me to be able to move again.

Keirran and Puck walked up, both looking grim. "One of 'em got you, huh?" Puck muttered, peering at my face. "Nasty. Good thing you managed to get a flamefruit into your system before everything shut down. Even so, you probably won't be able to get completely warm for about a week. But hey, better cold than dead, right?"

A sarcastic retort came to mind, but I couldn't force it past my chattering teeth. Keirran swept up, shrugging out of his black cloak, and wordlessly handed it to Kenzie. She smiled at him gratefully and turned back to me, wrapping the dark fabric around my shoulders. I was beginning to feel a little embarrassed with their concern; I was just cold, not bleeding to death. But I couldn't think of an argument right now, and besides, another layer of cloth between the air and my bare skin felt pretty good.

"Let's get out of the open," Keirran muttered as an icy breeze tossed his hair and made my teeth clack together painfully. "The caves aren't far now."

We finally reached the cliffs, following Puck through a gorge with huge sharp crystals spiking out of the ground and walls. I was still freezing, shivering badly even with the flamefruit and Keirran's cloak, and moving around didn't seem to be helping. So when we stumbled upon a large black hole in the cliff wall, surrounded by jagged blue crystals that looked sharp enough to impale yourself on, I was relieved to get out of the wind, at least.

Inside the cave, the walls and floor glittered with more jagged crystals that glowed with a faint blue light and threw weird toothy shadows over the cave. I glanced up and saw that the ceiling was covered in dangling icicles, insanely long and sharp enough to worry me if I wasn't so freaking cold.

Farther back, the cave continued into the darkness. Keirran walked to where the shadows hovered at the edge of the glow and stared into the black.

"There's a tunnel," he murmured. "It looks like it goes down, below us."

Puck shot me a glance and shook his head. "Yeah, well, we're not going anywhere tonight. Not until Popsicle Boy thaws out a little." He gave an exaggerated shiver, rubbing his arms. "Geez, it's cold! I hate winter. Don't see how ice-boy can stand— Oy, princeling, where do you think you're going?"

Keirran had taken a few steps into the tunnel, but paused and turned to stare at us. In the looming darkness, his eyes glowed an eerie blue-white.

"I can feel it," he said, his voice cold and lethal again. "It's down there, waiting for us."

"Yeah, well, like I said, we're not going anywhere for a while." Puck glanced at me. "Fire first, then when this one can hold a sword again, we'll see about marching down and taking on the big nasty. So you're just gonna have to sit tight and cool your heels until we're ready, princeling."

Shaking his head, Puck moved to an open spot on the floor, kneeling down to start a fire. How he was going to do that with no wood and everything covered in ice was beyond me, but that was where magic came in, I guessed. After a moment, Keirran went to help, leaving me shivering in the middle of the room, wishing I could help but grateful not to move right then.

Kenzie came up beside me, peering into my face. "Your lips are blue," she stated, her brow creased with worry. I tried managing a shrug and a smirk, but I couldn't quite feel my face.

"I'm okay," I gritted out, clenching my jaw to keep my teeth from chattering. "Once the fire is going, I'll be better."

Kenzie's frown deepened. Stepping close, she pried my arms away from my body and slid beneath the cloak with me. I winced at the rush of cold air, but then Kenzie wrapped her arms around my waist and pressed into me, and the warmth of her small body against mine almost made me groan with relief.

She shivered. "God, Ethan, you're freezing," she whispered. Reaching up, she placed a warm hand against the side of my face, and I closed my eyes, leaning into it. I felt her gaze on me, imagined her faint smile. "You've got to stop throwing yourself in front of dragons for me, tough guy," she murmured. "I know you want to do the whole knight-in-shining-armor thing, but I don't want you to get killed because of it."

"Can't help it," I murmured, still keeping my eyes closed, basking in the warmth of her palm on my skin. "I already told you that. Not negotiable, sorry."

"There you go again." She shifted against me, but instead of withdrawing, her fingers traced the side of my cheek, softly stroking with her thumb. "Being stubborn and all." I opened my eyes and stared down at her.

"Wait, was that actually *you* calling *me* stubborn? Me? This from the girl who practically stalked me until she was dragged into Faery? Who bargained with a faery queen even though I begged her not to? Who tracked me into a goblin market because she didn't want to be left behind?"

Kenzie looked like she was trying not to grin. "What's your point?"

Hell with it. I dropped my head and kissed her, the touch of her lips sending tendrils of heat curling through me. I forgot about the cold. I forgot why we were here. I was just aware of Kenzie, her warmth, her soft fingers on my skin. The emotion burning me from the inside.

Don't stop. Don't ever leave. Stay with me, Kenzie. The Nevernever, the Between or the real world, I don't want to face anything without you.

I snorted quietly to myself. Man, I was going soft. Next thing you knew, I'd be writing song lyrics and spouting poetry.

"Kissy," said a new voice, and I felt a tug on my jeans, like something was climbing my pant leg. I jerked and looked down to see that Razor had wedged himself between us and the cloak and was using me as a ladder.

"Ow!" I yelped as his sharp little claws poked my ribs. "Razor, get out of here!"

"Cold," he replied, curling up in the space between us. "No like. Too cold."

"Go bother Keirran, then," I said, glancing to where Puck and Keirran had a cheerful fire crackling on the rocks. "I'm sure it's warmer where he is." Razor shook his head and curled tighter into himself.

"Master cold," he whimpered.

I frowned in confusion. Keirran was part Winter faery; subzero temperatures didn't faze him at all. "Master cold," Razor insisted, sounding sad and a little frightened. "Master scary now, feels cold all the time."

Oh. Damn, now even the gremlin was starting to notice Keirran's slow change. I wasn't sure whether it was the amulet or his worry for Annwyl that was driving it, but we had to finish this task and destroy that thing before Keirran was sucked away to nothing. Or became that cold stranger permanently.

"Come on," Kenzie whispered, tugging me and Razor toward the fire, cloak and all. "Let's get both of you warm."

Puck grinned at us from where he leaned back against a rock, hands behind his head. But Keirran, brooding into the fire on the far side, didn't look up at all. Carefully, I shrugged out of the long cloak, gritting my teeth as the frigid air hit my skin, sending goose bumps crawling along my arms. But I was feeling slightly warmer now, standing close to the flames. At least, I didn't feel like my veins were full of ice water. As I removed the cloak, Razor whimpered, crawling beneath Kenzie's hair and burrowing into her neck. I held the garment out to Keirran.

"Thanks," I muttered. He eyed me without expression, then smiled.

"Anytime," he replied, reaching out to take it. "You're my friend, and I'm just grateful that you're here."

"Well," Puck said, rising to his feet and stretching long limbs. "It's been an exciting day. Why don't you three get some sleep if you can? Don't worry—it's safe enough here. The Cold won't come into the cave, especially if there's a fire, and being nearly frozen to death tends to be fairly exhausting." He wrinkled his nose. "Trust me, I know. So get some rest. You'll need it for the big nasty beastie we'll be facing tomorrow. I'll take watch."

He wandered off toward the mouth of the cave. I sat as close to the fire as I could, brooding into the flames and trying not to think about what came next.

Kenzie stepped between my knees and sat down, wedging herself in front of me like she was always meant to be there. I was startled, but I wasn't complaining. Sliding my arms around her, I lay my chin on her shoulder, ignoring the gremlin who buzzed "Kissy, kissy" in my ear, and soaked up the heat.

"So," she murmured after moments of contented silence.

"I guess tomorrow we go fight a big ice monster or some-thing, huh?"

"Mmm," I grunted, not wanting to think about it.

"Do we have any plan for how we're going to do that?"

"Mmm-mmm," I mumbled, in an "I dunno" tone. I was sleepy all of a sudden, and the heat felt good against my skin, as did the girl in my arms. My eyes closed, and my head dropped lower onto her shoulder. I didn't want to think about anything right now. Kenzie sighed, and I felt her shift to get more comfortable, her breaths becoming slow and deep, as if she, too, was drifting off.

Wait. This wasn't like me. Wasn't I way too paranoid to fall asleep in Faery? Something was wrong. I struggled to open my eyes, but they felt stupidly heavy, almost sealed together. I finally managed to crack them open, to see Keirran on his feet, the cold, eerie glow of his eyes trained on me.

"I'm sorry, Ethan," he murmured, and though his voice was full of regret, his face was resolved. "It's better this way. I've dragged you both through enough." Swirling the cloak around himself, he drew up the hood, becoming hidden in shadow. "Take care of Kenzie. And Razor." He paused, a flicker of agony crossing the stony expression. "If I don't make it back, tell Annwyl I'm sorry."

Dammit, Keirran, I wanted to yell. *Don't do this.* But my eyes were slipping shut again, and I couldn't force out the words. The Iron Prince turned, the cloak swishing behind him, and walked silently into the tunnel. I tried moving, shouting after him, but the glamour dragging me under finally overcame my will, and I fell into darkness.

CHAPTER TWENTY

EDDIES AND ELEMENTALS

"Master!"

A shrill voice howled right in my ear, jerking me out of the glamour-induced sleep. Mostly awake now, I tried wrenching my eyes open, but sluggishness still dragged at me, and I fought to stay conscious. All the while, the high-pitched gremlin voice buzzed frantically a few inches from my face.

"Master! Master gone! Wake up, funny boy! Wake up!"

I'm trying, I thought irritably, if only to shut the gremlin up. Memory returned in an instant—Keirran using his glamour to put us to sleep; Keirran standing over me with his cold stranger eyes, then walking down the tunnel to confront the monster alone.

Kenzie shifted against my chest, also coming out of the faery slumber. She mumbled something incoherent. I tried, once more, to force my eyes open, feeling as if they had ten pounds of sand in them.

Then Razor gave an impatient hiss and bit me on the ear.

"OW!" My eyes flew open, stinging with the sudden pain, and I jerked back. "Dammit, Razor! Ow!" I swatted at the gremlin, but he leaped to Kenzie's shoulder and hid beneath her hair, peering out at me.

"Boy awake," he buzzed, sounding suspiciously pleased. "Boy awake now...find Master."

I groped for the side of my head, gingerly feeling the damage. Yep, there were several holes in my left ear, no larger than pinpricks, thankfully, but they still hurt like hell. My fingers came away smeared with blood.

"Ethan?" Kenzie turned, her voice slurred. She blinked at me sleepily. "What's going on?" Her gaze drifted to the side of my face, and her eyes shot all the way open. "Are you bleeding? What—"

Puck came into the room, long legs crossing the space in a few strides. "Oy, human!" he barked, sweeping up to the fire. "What's with the ruckus? It sounds like you're holding a cat-skinning competition in here. And you're bleeding. *Again*." He rolled his eyes. "Geez, I can't leave you guys alone for a minute. What happened?"

"It's nothing," I muttered, dropping my hand. "Razor bit me."

"What?" Kenzie shot a fierce glare at the Iron faery, who ducked beneath her hair again. "He bit you? Bad gremlin! Why did you bite Ethan?"

I tried to interrupt, to tell her it was a good thing the gremlin woke me up, annoying as it was, but Puck beat me to it.

"Uh, guys?" he asked, looking around the cave. "Where's Keirran?"

"Master!" wailed Razor, making Kenzie flinch. "Master gone! Find Master!"

I struggled to my feet, shaking the last of the fog from my brain. "Keirran took off," I said, nodding down the tunnel. "Did the whole faery sleep thing to put us out, said he didn't want to drag us in anymore." I glanced at Puck, who looked resigned and annoyed all at once. "How long have we been out?"

"Not long," Puck said. "Just a few minutes. I had just gotten all nice and comfortable, too, when I heard Buzz Saw screeching and came racing back. Sleepy spells don't work well on gremlins, I've found." He shook his head and gave the back of the cave a dark look. "So, I guess we know where our impatient princeling is off to, don't we?"

"Yeah." I raked a hand through my hair, careful not to touch my ear. "He's going to face whatever lives down there alone."

"Oh, that idiot." Kenzie huffed, surging to her feet. "No, he's not! Come on, we have to find him."

She turned and marched determinedly toward the back of the cave, Razor gibbering and bouncing on her shoulder, buzzing encouragements. I wanted to stop her, but she was right; we couldn't let our idiot friend fight whatever was down there alone, no matter what he said.

Making sure my swords were in place, I followed, silently cursing the prince as we approached the looming mouth of the tunnel, icicles dangling from the edge like giant teeth. It was pitch-black through the gaping hole, and Puck sighed.

"You know, this reminds me of a time," he remarked, tossing a ball of faery fire in front of us, revealing a narrow corridor that plunged into shadow, "when ice-boy and I were trapped in an underground crypt together, and he decided to go down another passageway without me. Ran into a horde of tomb guardians and had to play hit-and-run until I could catch up." He scrunched up his face. "Oh, wait. No, that was me. Stupid tomb guardians and their scorpions. Regardless, does that remind you of anyone?" He snorted and continued before we could answer. "Also, does anyone ever consider the consequences of their actions? For instance, what will ice-boy do to me if his kid gets himself eaten by a giant frost worm or something? He'll probably try to hunt me down, war will break out between Winter and Iron, and everyone will put the blame on me. But *noooooo,* no one ever thinks of that."

The tunnel continued deep into the earth. Sometimes it leveled out; sometimes it was so steep we were almost sliding down the ice-covered floor. The faery light threw strange, flickering shadows over the wall, sparkling off crystals and translucent blue-and-green icicles. My breath writhed in front of me, but I wasn't as cold as I knew I should be, thanks to the lingering effects of the flamefruit, I supposed. I was still plenty cold, but it wasn't unbearable. I just hoped we could get out of here before it wore off.

The tunnel finally opened into a massive ice cavern, huge pillars extending up into the darkness. The whole place had a frozen blue-white tint, and it was so frigid I could actually see my breath crystallize into hair-thin shards and drift to the floor.

Puck sent more balls of faery fire into the huge cavern, where they bobbed spastically overhead and gave off a strobe-light effect, making my head hurt. The cavern was a maze of pillars, stalactites and ice boulders, and the dancing shadows made it hard to see what was open space and what was a wall.

"Well," Puck said, his voice echoing into the vastness, "if I was a big nasty giant ice monster, this is where I'd live."

"Yeah," I muttered, squinting into the wheeling lights and darkness. "Let's just hope we can find Keirran before he finds it."

Somewhere in the distance, there was a splintering crash, like a hundred glasses smashing at once.

Puck grimaced. "Too late."

We hurried into the shadows, following the noise, which was hard as it echoed off everything around us. But as we went farther into the cave, we could hear more shattering noises against the rocks and pillars. Puck took the lead, and we sprinted after him, doing our best not to slip, until we turned a bend and came to the edge of an open arena. Crystal stalagmites were scattered about the floor, especially in the middle, but everything else was smooth, glittering ice. Like this was a perfectly flat lake that had frozen over.

In the center, a black-cloaked figure danced and spun amid a flurry of other things that swirled around him. They looked like whirlwinds that had picked up bits of ice and stone and were spinning them in a tight circle. A pair of glowing blue eyes shone from the center of the whirlwinds as they darted around the figure in the middle of the lake.

"Master!" Razor shrieked, his voice ringing through the chamber.

Instantly, several of the whirlwind things broke off, turned and came spinning toward us, making Razor yelp and dive into Kenzie's hair. I cursed and drew my weapons.

"Kenzie, get back," I called, hoping she wouldn't argue this time. She ducked behind a boulder without a sound. The whirlwind things came closer, moving swiftly across the ice, the sound of shrieking wind echoing through the chamber. I narrowed my eyes as it hissed around me, yanking at my hair and clothes. We stood between a cluster of pillars and stalagmites, caging us in on either side, so the only way to Kenzie was through me and Puck. And that was not going to happen.

I brought up my swords as Puck stepped forward and flourished his daggers.

"Well, here they come." The Summer faery shot me a glance and grinned. "Know anything about ice eddies, kid?"

"No."

"Probably for the best. Aim for the middle, watch out for flying rocks and don't drop your swords."

The ice eddies swirled in, whipping the air into a frenzy. One came at me, a cyclone of rocks, pebbles and razor bits of ice. Something struck my arm, tearing a stinging gash across my skin. I smacked down a rock with one blade and lashed out with the other, slicing through the middle of the whirlwind. There was a rush of wind, and the debris spinning around it clattered to the ground. More pressed forward, surrounding me, until I was trapped in the eye of a deadly hurricane. Ice and rock careened around me as I kept moving, kept my weapons spinning in a circle of my own. Rubble clanged off the blades, making my hair stand up, but more stuff hit the swords than me. Most of the time. A pebble struck me in the head once, and I felt a warm trickle creep down my face, stinging one eye. Angrily, I ripped the sword through the offending whirlwind, and the eddy collapsed like a stack of dominoes.

"Whoops! Crap." Puck leaped away, holding a single dagger before him. "Head's up, kid!" he called as the eddy he'd been fighting now turned on me, a dagger whipping through the air in deadly circles. I ducked Puck's blade, scrambling back before it sliced my head open, wincing as a shard of ice stabbed me in the arm.

"Ow! Dammit, Puck!" I raised my sword, knocking the dagger away as it came at my face again. The screech of metal on metal sent a chill up my spine. "Can you *not* make things worse sometimes?"

"What? I never make things worse," Puck replied, stepping forward to deal with another eddy swooshing in from the side. "I make things more *interesting*."

"Yeah, my foot is about to have an interesting encounter with your ass."

Puck laughed. "Ice-boy's been saying the same thing for years, kid. Good luck."

The dagger sliced down, narrowly missing me. As it spun for my head again, I swung my sword at it, putting all my strength into the blow. The two blades met in a screech of sparks as I knocked the dagger free of the whirlwind and lashed out with my second sword, cutting through the middle of the chaos.

As the wind disintegrated, I turned to help Puck, only to see him do a weird, crazy dance that took him through the swirling eddy and out the other side. As he did, his dagger flashed, and the thing collapsed into a scattered pile of rock and ice.

"Well, that was fun," Puck announced. Kenzie came out from behind the boulder, holding Puck's wayward dagger. He took it with a wink. "Appreciate it, human. Nothing more embarrassing than being skewered with your own weapon, right? Well, shall we go help the prince?"

By the time we reached the center of the lake, however, the eddies surrounding Keirran were nothing more than chunks of stone and ice. The Iron Prince stood with his sword out, the last eddy disintegrating at his feet. His eyes were hard, the glowing blue-white of the cold stranger I was beginning to hate. As we came up, his gaze flicked to mine, and that eerie glow vanished, though his face remained blank.

But Kenzie marched right up to the motionless prince and, shocking both of us, shoved him in the chest, knocking him off balance. He stumbled back, barely catching himself, his blank, cold expression shifting to astonishment.

"That was stupid, Keirran," Kenzie said, glaring at the prince, while Razor buzzed and nodded from her shoulder. "What were you thinking? You think you can do this alone? You think we would *let* you just walk out on us? After everything we did to get here? And don't start with that crap about wanting to keep us safe. You should know by now that excuse isn't going to fly." She stepped closer, the tiny form bristling with rage. "And if you *ever* use glamour on me again the way you did my parents, I'm going to kick you so hard Annwyl will feel it through that necklace, I swear."

"Bad!" Razor spoke up, watching Keirran from the curtain of Kenzie's hair. "Bad Master! No leave! Bad."

Wow, even the gremlin was pissed at Keirran. I was going to say something as well, but Kenzie and Razor seemed to be handling it, so I just stood back and watched the show. Keirran grimaced, holding up his hands and taking a step back from the onslaught.

"All right, all right," he said, his expression caught between annoyance and resignation. "I understand. You've made your point, Mackenzie." He sighed, shaking his head. "It seems I'm stuck with all of you, whether I want it or not."

"Damn right you are," Kenzie snapped, Razor buzzing in agreement. "Don't forget it again."

Keirran blinked, giving me a knowing look. I just shrugged. *Yep, that's my girlfriend. And I'm not going to step in front of her for you, either. You're on your own.*

"Well," Puck said cheerfully, lacing his hands behind his head. "Now that we've all kissed and made up, maybe we should focus on what we came for. Namely, the big nasty you all are supposed to fight."

I looked around the cavern. "Where?" I asked, my voice echoing through the vast open space. "This is a dead end. It looks like something might've lived here once, but it's empty now."

"Yes," Keirran agreed, his voice hard again. "There aren't any more tunnels. This is the lowest level of the cave, and those eddies are the only things I've seen. This was a waste of time. Whatever lived here is long gone."

"Au contraire," Puck said, lifting a finger. "You're just not looking in the right direction."

And he pointed straight down, into the frozen lake.

Below our feet, cracked, blurred and distorted by the ice, an enormous shadow lay stretched out on the bottom of the lake. It was probably close to fifty feet long, and though it was hard to see from this distance, I thought I could make out thick stumpy legs, massive shoulders and a broad, armored head. I couldn't tell if it was dead, frozen or just sleeping, but I did know one thing: it was huge.

"You've got to be kidding me," I muttered. Puck shook his head.

"Nope. There's your spirit of the Frozen Wood, right there. So, can we go home now? I was going to say how impossible this task was, but I figured it would be better to let you see it for yourself. Obviously, waking that big guy up would be a bad... Uh, Prince, what are you doing?"

I looked at Keirran. He stood with his eyes half-closed, his hand raised in front of his face. And he was glowing. Like the night in Mr. Dust's office, only this time, instead of the cold, frozen aura of Winter, he flickered and pulsed with light. Like Annwyl, shedding fragments of sunlight, it melted the ice at his feet and turned the air around him to steam. His eyes opened, glowing amber, and his voice was calm and matter-of-fact.

"Waking it up."

He knelt, driving his fist into the ice. There was a flash as he flared painfully bright for a second, cracks spreading out from his hand, and a spear of light shot toward the thing under our feet.

"Well, that's torn it." Puck sighed.

A rumble went through the ice around us, and the ground started to shake. The cracks Keirran had put into the ice widened, spread out, sprouted new ones that raced over the lake. Icicles and stalactites fell from the ceiling, smashing to the ground in ringing cacophonies, and I struggled to keep my balance.

"Right, I vote we do not stand here anymore," Puck offered, and we scrambled away, fleeing to the edge of the lake as sounds of cracking ice grew deafening and the ground began to heave.

The ice exploded, surging up like a frozen geyser, before raining sharp bits of icy shrapnel down on us. A huge, stony foot emerged from the hole, smashing down onto the ice. Another followed, and a monstrous creature of ice and stone lurched onto the surface of the lake, shook an enormous blocky head and roared.

Okay, so it was even *bigger* than I'd first thought, probably stretching close to eighty feet from snout to hindquarters, looming up to an impossible height. It was shaped, vaguely, like some huge bear, with a little porcupine thrown in. Its head, back, shoulders, legs and sides were covered in stone, like a bulky suit of armor, and huge icicles jutted out from its shoulders and down its back, sharp and lethal. Beneath the stony hide, a frozen blue light pulsed through the joints in its armor, and two giant glowing eyes shone beneath its helmeted head.

"Oh, good," Puck remarked as the colossal beast turned toward us, shaking the ground. "We get to fight a mountain."

"Kenzie, take Razor and get back!" I called as the giant creature spotted us and lurched forward with a roar. Its mouth opened, glowing blue light spilling from its jaws, as it breathed a blast of frigid air toward us. We ducked behind a stalagmite as a jagged line of icicles surged up where the creature's breath passed, stabbing into the air. I yelped as a cold, frozen tip jabbed into my arm, ripping my sleeve and drawing blood.

Puck grimaced, peeking out from behind the stone, watching the monster through a cage of ice spears. "Right," he muttered. "So, I'll be the distraction again, while you two decide how we're actually supposed to hurt that thing. Sound like a plan?"

Without waiting for an answer, he darted out from behind the stalagmite, sprinted a few feet away and blew out a piercing whistle.

"Oy, Rocky! Over here! Turn your big stony ass this way!"

The thing roared and blasted Puck with icicle wind, which ripped him apart in seconds. But a flock of screaming ravens emerged from the chaos, spiraling into the air and circling the creature like a dark cloud. It bellowed and shook its head, looking more annoyed than anything, but its attention was not on us anymore.

I drew my swords and took a deep breath. "Let's go."

"Ethan, wait!" Kenzie grabbed my hand while Razor gibbered terrified nonsense from her shoulder. "Don't," she whispered, sounding terrified, while I stared in disbelief. Something had finally given her pause. "You can't fight that thing. It's huge—you'll be killed!"

I glanced at Keirran, who watched us with impassive eyes. He had already made up his mind. He was going to battle that massive, moving fortress, with or without my help.

I sighed and squeezed her hand. "Remember what I said about me standing in front of the dragon for you?" I told her softly, trying to smile. "I wasn't kidding about that." She took a breath to argue, and I quickly overrode her. "I'm doing this, Kenzie," I said, making her slump. "I have to. We can't turn back now."

"Here, then." Bowing her head, she reached around her neck and pulled out Guro's amulet, spinning from its cord. I stared at the disk in surprise; I'd almost forgotten she had it. The metal flashed in the hazy light as Kenzie reached up and draped it around my neck. Her fingers trembled as they brushed my skin. "You need this more than me."

I tucked the amulet into my shirt, wondering if it would really protect me like it did her. Ghostly shadows springing up to deflect lethal sword blows still seemed too good to be true. But right now, I'd take all the help I could get. "Thanks," I told her. "I'll get this back to you later." *If I'm still alive.*

She blew out a shaky breath and leaned forward, hugging me around the neck. "Be careful, tough guy," she whispered in my ear. "Don't get killed. We haven't even had our second date yet."

I held her tightly for a moment, memorizing the feel of her body pressed against mine, three little words dancing on the tip of my brain. I wanted to tell her right now...in case I never got another chance...

No. Not here. I wasn't going to die here. I was going to kill that big ugly bastard and take Kenzie home. When we were safe, back in the real world with no life-threatening faeries surrounding us, I'd tell her exactly how I felt.

After we killed this thing.

Gently pulling back, I met Kenzie's eyes and jerked my head toward the edge of the lake. "Go," I told her softly, and she gave me a desperate look and fled, slipping into the shadows with the gremlin on her shoulder. I swallowed, then looked at Keirran.

"Ready?" he asked calmly.

"If we survive this," I told him, "I'm going to kill you."

One corner of his mouth turned up. "You'll have to get in line, I'm sure."

We charged. Dodging rocks and giant icicles spearing up from the ground, we sprinted across the lake toward the massive creature in the center. The swarm of birds around its head had vanished, and I could just make out a red-haired figure on the thing's enormous skull, a speck of color atop a mountain.

As we approached, the creature spotted us. With a roar, it lowered its head and opened its jaws, bathing us in blue light. "Split up!" Keirran yelled, and we veered apart, just as the blast of frigid air sent a line of jagged spikes down the center of the lake. I dived behind a boulder as the creature blasted me again, nearly impaling me as the huge spines curled around the rock. Peeking around the edge, I saw Puck leap from the blocky head, land on the enormous muzzle and drive his dagger into one glowing blue eye.

The creature bellowed, rearing up and tossing its head, and Puck went sailing through the air. He turned into a raven midfall and flapped away, and as the thing came back down with a crash that shook the entire cave, Keirran darted beside it and cut at its chest with his sword.

The blade screeched off the armored hide, and the raspy echo sent shivers up my back. It didn't seem to have hurt it at all. With a roar, the beast turned on Keirran, smashing at him with a stony paw, and the Iron Prince barely avoided being trampled into gooey paste. It pressed forward, but a big black bird swooped out of nowhere with a screech, flapping right into its eyes, making it flinch for just a second. Keirran dodged back and leaped between two boulders as the beast stomped at him, and the thing bellowed in frustration.

Dropping its head, it opened its jaws and breathed, but this time a cold white mist emerged and rippled over the surface of the lake. I felt the temperature drop, and my skin crawled with cold, even through the effects of the flamefruit.

"Ethan." Keirran appeared beside me, panting, making me jump. "It's no good," he gasped, staring at the monster, still breathing fog over the ground. "Its hide is too tough. I can't get through." He narrowed his eyes at the beast, face darkening. "How are we supposed to kill it if we can't even hurt it?"

"Yeah, well, when I said this was an impossible task, I wasn't kidding," Puck added, dropping beside us. "I think this is some kind of ancient elemental. The rocks aren't a part of the thing. It just uses them for armor. The squishy center is inside."

"So how are we supposed to hurt it?" I asked.

Before either of them could answer, a scraping, rattling sound echoed all throughout the cavern, making the hairs on my neck stand up. The bits of rock, stone and ice scattered over the lake were moving now, shifting and drawing together where the mist touched it. Slowly, they began whirling through the air, spinning faster and faster, until a brand-new group of eddies rose up from the fog and glided toward us.

"Huh," Puck commented. "So that's where eddies come from. Who knew?"

"Great," I muttered, raising my swords as the first of the swirling creatures rounded the boulder. I smacked a rock away with one sword and lashed out with the other, but then two more eddies swirled toward me and I stumbled away, into the open. I looked up and saw the ice elemental opening its jaws....

"Ethan!" Slashing through one whirlwind, Keirran lunged out and tackled me, sending us both sprawling to the ground, just as the blast from the giant elemental ripped through the spot where I had just been standing. Scrambling behind another, smaller rock, we huddled against the stone as the eddies glided toward us and the giant roared angrily behind them.

"This is impossible," I told Keirran as we faced the opponents coming at us once more. Puck, standing in the center of another group of eddies, fought determinedly but had his hands full. I grabbed the prince's shoulder. "Keirran, we have to get out of here. We can't beat this thing. It's not worth dying for."

"Yes, it is." Keirran's voice was steady. "It is for me. Go if you want, Ethan. I can't give up."

He ripped his arm from my grasp, raising his sword as the eddies closed in. I cursed and leaped to help him, fending off rock and ice that spun through the air. There were too many of them, and they just kept coming. Stones and jagged bits of ice struck my skin, tearing me open even as I parried or blocked most.

The ground trembled, and the huge head of the ice spirit loomed above us with a roar. Apparently, it had gotten tired of waiting for the eddies to flush us out. I cursed, scrambling backward as the armored skull swung down and smashed into the rock protecting us from the wind. Stone and ice flew in all directions as the thing pulverized the stalagmite—and most of the eddies—to dust. I turned to shield my face from the explosion, but something struck the side of my head, making me see stars.

When I looked up, I was lying on the cold ice near the center of the frozen lake, completely out in the open, and a mountain of stone and light was standing directly in front of me. Puck had disappeared. Keirran was nowhere to be seen. The thing regarded me with soulless blue eyes, ancient and depthless, a lesser god looking down on an insignificant mortal. For a moment, I hoped it would deem me inconsequential, a speck of dust that couldn't really hurt it, clearly not any kind of threat.

Then it opened its jaws, and I felt the cold blue light wash over me, right before the wind shrieked forward to tear me apart.

I flinched, covering my face and eyes, as useless as that would be. For a split second, I thought of Kenzie and my parents, and how sorry I was that I broke my promise, that I'd never see them again.

The wind screamed in my ears, bone-numbingly cold. I heard the crinkle and snap of ice as the jagged spears surged into the air...but didn't touch me.

Heart in my throat, I looked up.

A dark figure stood between me and the ice monster, one

hand outstretched, the billow of his long coat settling around him. The line of ice spears had split at the point where the figure stood, slicing off to either side. I blinked, both horrified and relieved that he was here, that he had found us.

"'Bout time you joined the party, ice-boy!" Puck yelled from somewhere overhead. The Summer prankster appeared on the monster's head again, grinning down at us. "I was wondering if Furball would ever find you. Hey, remember that time we fought those hill giants throwing boulders at us down Redwater Gorge? This is so much worse than that!"

I scrambled upright as the ice monster roared and blasted us again. But Ash raised his hand, and the wind sheared around him once more, splitting off to the side. I guessed the former prince of the Unseelie Court had a few centuries of Winter magic under his belt; the cold just didn't affect him. The ice monster bellowed angrily, and Ash turned his head and gave me a furious glare.

"Ethan, get out of here, now!"

"No!" I panted, lurching forward, needing him to understand. "We can't leave!" I insisted. "We have to kill it, Ash! Keirran won't give up until it's dead."

"Keirran. Where is he?"

With a roar, the elemental started forward, intending to crush us now that it realized it couldn't breathe us to death. Ice eddies came to life and whirled around it, forming a small but deadly army as they pressed forward. I spotted Keirran then, crouched behind an ice spear, glaring up at the monster as it passed. Ash saw him, too.

"Keirran!" he roared, and Keirran flinched, glancing at him with wide eyes. Ash pointed to the elemental bearing down on us. "Get below it!" he called. "Its underside isn't protected! A strong pulse of Summer glamour to the heart is the only way to take it down!"

Keirran's eyes narrowed. Raising his sword, he darted around the rock and sprinted at the monster.

Ash drew his blade with a chilling rasp. "Go help him," he said, his voice hard and cold. "I'll keep it off you both. Puck!" he called, and Puck's face appeared, peering over the monster's head. "Keep it distracted a little longer! We're ending this now!"

The elemental turned its massive head toward Keirran, but Ash stalked forward, flinging out an arm. A flurry of ice daggers struck the monster in the face, shattering harmlessly on the rock, but the thing turned back with an angry roar and plowed toward him.

Puck dropped to the monster's snout, right in front of its glowing eyes, grinning cheekily. "Hey, ugly, lookee here! I'm doing the Macarena on your nose."

Guess that's my cue. I raced across the ice, right for the mountain looming in front of me. Any other time, it probably would've blasted or stomped me into paste, but it had its hands full at the moment, with Puck dancing on its snout and Ash fending off blasts of icicle wind, hurling his own ice daggers back. I reached the place Keirran stood, in the shadow of the monster's bulk, surrounded by ice eddies. Ash had been right; overhead, the elemental's chest and stomach were open in places, blue light streaming through the cracks and holes in the armor. It was also ungodly cold this close to the monster; each breath stabbed like a knife, and I could see frost creeping over my skin, ice forming in my hair and eyelashes.

"Keirran!" I gritted out, slashing through a whirlwind as I joined him. "Hurry up and kill it! Let's get this done so we can get the hell out of here!"

He nodded, slicing an eddy that came whirling at us. "Keep them off me for a second!"

I lunged forward, protecting his back, as Keirran dropped

his head and closed his eyes. Light formed in his hand, a pulsing globe of pure sunlight, growing hotter and stronger with every passing second. I spun and whirled around him, cutting at the eddies that got too close, wincing each time something hit me. But nothing struck Keirran, who was throwing off waves of heat now, melting the frost on my skin.

"For Annwyl," I heard him whisper, and he thrust his hand up, between the cracks in the armor.

There was a searing flash of light, and a shudder went through the ground. The elemental threw up its head and roared, shaking the cavern, as bits of stone and ice began falling from its bulk, smashing to the ground. The ice eddies shuddered and collapsed into piles of rubble as the monster roared again and started to collapse.

"Keirran!" I spun toward the Iron Prince, but he lay motionless on the ground, all his color washed away. Dodging a huge chunk of armor, I grabbed Keirran's arm, slung it around my neck and hauled him upright. The elemental was crumbling like a cave-in, stone and ice smashing around us. Clenching my jaw, I leaped forward, pulling Keirran out as I did, and the huge bulk of the elemental collapsed with a deafening roar, sending ice and rock flying everywhere. Something hit me in the back and I fell, bringing Keirran with me as I tumbled to the icy ground, stunned.

Gasping, I let Keirran go and rolled to my back, staring up at what was left of the elemental. The cold blue light was gone, and only a shifting mountain of stone remained, spreading over the ice. I was relieved, and at the same time, I felt abruptly guilty. We had just destroyed an ancient force of nature, probably the only one of its kind. And for what? To appease a fickle faery queen who cared nothing for any of us. I had no quarrel with this creature; we had strolled into its home and woken it up when it had been sleeping peacefully, not hurting anything. I wondered if the thing hadn't been try-ing to kill us, would Keirran still have struck that final blow?

I felt tainted. I'd allowed myself to become an assassin of the fey, carrying out their dirty work. I'd sworn I'd never do that. I'd sworn a lot of things, back before I met Keirran. My only comfort was that the prince was family and that Annwyl at least would get to go home.

Keirran groaned and stirred, pushing himself to his knees. His color had returned, though he looked paler than before, faded out and exhausted. He met my gaze and offered a faint smile...right before Ash swept up, hauled him to his feet by the collar and slammed him back against a pillar.

"What have you done, Keirran?"

The dark faery's voice was cold, furious. I scrambled up-right, feeling my bruised, aching body groan in protest, un-sure if I should step in or not. Keirran winced, but didn't try to struggle or break free.

"What I had to."

"You had to kill the spirit of the Frozen Wood." Ash nar-rowed his eyes, unappeased. "You had to wake an ancient el-emental that has been asleep for centuries, fight it in its own territory and destroy it. Because you had no choice."

"You told me how to kill it," Keirran pointed out. "You didn't have to."

"Yes I did. Because I know you. If I hadn't arrived, if I hadn't said anything, would you have stopped? Or would you have kept fighting an unwinnable battle until it destroyed you all?" Ash paused, waiting for Keirran's reply. The prince met the icy gaze for only a moment, then looked at the ground. Ash nodded.

"That's what I thought." His voice, though it had thawed the slightest bit on that last part, hardened again. "Do you realize what you've done? That spirit is what kept the Frozen

Wood alive. With it gone, Mab will lose this territory, either to Summer or the wyldwood. She'll blame Summer for the destruction of her territory, and probably Iron when she hears who dealt the final blow. You've probably started a war."

"It was to save Annwyl!" Keirran's outburst made Ash pause. The Iron Prince glared at his father, his face suddenly tormented, eyes glassy. "It was the only way to get Titania to relent, to stop Annwyl from Fading away completely. I had to do it." His gaze narrowed. "I would've thought that you, of all people, would understand."

Ash sighed, and to my extreme shock, pulled Keirran forward so that their foreheads were touching. "I do understand," the dark faery murmured, and Keirran squeezed his eyes shut. "More than you know. But this wasn't the way, Keirran. You should have come to us. We would have worked something out. But you had to go do everything alone, and now matters are even worse."

Keirran slumped, clenching his fists, but didn't say anything. Ash released him and stepped away, casting a somber look at the mountain of rubble that was once the spirit.

"I have to go to Mab," he muttered as Puck appeared beside him, looking grave. "See if I can convince her not to declare war on Summer or Iron. Keirran—" he stabbed a terrifying glare at the Iron Prince "—go home. Right now. You, too, Ethan," he added, glancing at me. "I'm sure your parents are worried about you."

"No," Keirran whispered, and Ash's icy stare fixed on him. He swallowed, but remained firm. "Not yet. I have to go back to Arcadia, make sure Titania lets Annwyl return to court. Please." He met Ash's gaze, imploring. "Let me do this one final thing. I'll go home after that, I promise. And I'll never leave Mag Tuiredh again."

"I'll take them back to Arcadia, ice-boy," Puck added, his

voice uncharacteristically grim. "And I'll send him home af-
terward. Both of them."

Ash stared at Keirran a moment longer, then sighed. "Fine.
I'll allow it, this once. But you had better be waiting for me
when I return to Mag Tuiredh, Keirran. We are going to
have a long talk. Goodfellow…" He glanced at Puck. "Inform
Oberon we'll be contacting him soon, as well. He'll want to
know about this."

Puck nodded. Ash spared one last look at me and Keirran,
his gaze lingering on the prince. Then he whirled away in a
swirl of black, stalked into the shadows and was gone.

Kenzie. As soon as Ash left, I spun toward the place I'd left
the girl…and nearly ran into her, coming up behind me.

"Oof." She staggered back a pace, but I caught her and
swept her into my arms, holding her tight. She hugged me
back fiercely. Razor peeked out of her hair and grinned at
me, but I ignored him.

"Hey, you," she whispered into my shirt. "Looks like you
managed to slay the dragon."

"Yeah," I muttered, not wanting to say how much I regretted it. That destroying something so ancient and primal,
something that had kept a part of Faery alive, seemed wrong.
Not to mention we might've sparked a war. Pulling away, I
gazed at the mountain of rubble that was once an ice spirit
and grimaced. "We should've never come here."

"Was that Keirran's dad that just left?" Kenzie went on,
looking in the direction Ash disappeared. I nodded. "Where's
he going in such a hurry?"

"Oh, just to visit Mab." Puck sighed, shaking his head as
he walked past. "You know, catch up, have some cookies,
maybe prevent her from declaring all-out war on the other
courts. The usual." He gave me and Keirran an unreadable
look and rolled his eyes. "You two. I swear, this is *so* familiar.

What's that human saying about having a kid that turns out to be just like you?" He snorted. "Well, come on, then. Let's get you back to Arcadia so you can see Titania, and we can put an end to this insanity."

CHAPTER TWENTY-ONE
TITANIA'S DECISION

When we came out of the caves, what Ash had been talking about became abundantly and sickeningly clear.

The Frozen Wood was disappearing. The ice that had coated every leaf, tree, twig and branch was nearly gone, and the snow was melting away, showing patches of bare earth beneath. Water dripped from the branches overhead, turning the ground slushy, and mud sucked at our feet as we walked. Dead animals lay scattered about the wood, some still coated in frozen crystal, but many sprawled limply in the snow. Without the ice keeping them in a state of eternal preservation, they looked dirty and ugly, as did the once-pristine woods around them.

"Mab is going to be pissed," Puck remarked, frowning at the devastation around us. "I hope ice-boy catches her on a good day."

I helped do this, I thought, wrenching my gaze from a scattering of dead birds around the trunk of a tree. My insides turned, making me feel sick. *If Mab declares war on Arcadia or Meghan's court, it will be partly my fault.*

I glanced at Keirran, wondering if he felt as guilty and horrified as I did. His expression was blank, unreadable, even as he faced the fallout of our actions, and I wanted to kick him.

Last time, Keirran. I narrowed my eyes, glaring at the back of his head. *This is the last time you can expect help from me. I know you want to save Annwyl, but this has gone way too far. After this, after Annwyl is home, we're done. Puck was right about you—you're trouble, and I'm not going to get dragged into any more messes because of you.*

"Hey." Kenzie's fingers brushed my arm, interrupting my dark thoughts. "I know that look," she said, peering up at me. "That's not your happy face, tough guy. If your eyes could shoot laser beams, Keirran's head would explode. What are you thinking?"

"Look around us," I whispered and gestured to the body of a stag we'd passed earlier. It had fallen into the mud, its legs rising stiffly into the air. "We did this. Keirran and I are responsible for this. We killed something we shouldn't have, and now look at what's happened."

"So...what? You're blaming him as well as yourself?"

"Mostly him," I muttered, lowering my voice. "But yeah. Myself, too."

Kenzie shook her head. "You and your guilt issues." She sighed. "Not everything that happens is your fault, Ethan. Or anyone's fault. Just because the fey can see you doesn't mean the trouble they cause is on your head."

"This is different," I told her. "I wasn't forced to do anything. This was a choice."

"Yes, it was," Kenzie agreed solemnly. "You chose to help a friend. You chose to go along with this request because it was the only way to save his life. To save both their lives."

"It could start a war."

"There's nothing we can do about that now." Kenzie's voice was relentlessly pragmatic. "You can blame and point fingers and brood on what happened, but it's already in the past, and it won't help anything." Her gaze lingered on a dead fox, a shocking red against a patch of snow, and her lip trembled. Razor peeked out of her hair and wrinkled his nose. "It's over, and we'll just have to deal with whatever comes of it." I started to protest, but she cut me off. "Would you have done anything differently if you knew what would happen? Would you have let Keirran go by himself?"

I slumped. "No."

"Then stop beating yourself up," Kenzie said gently. "And let's just get through this as best we can. We're not out of here yet."

Sometime later, but far earlier than I would've liked, we stood at the edge of the Seelie throne room, peering through the bramble tunnel at the Summer Queen's court.

"Well," Puck said cheerfully, "here we are. And Titania looks like she's in a good mood today—that's always a bad sign." He glanced at Keirran, gazing into the throne room with dark, hooded eyes. "Think I'll wait out here. Having me around might be too much of a distraction for our lovely queen, seeing how fond she is of me." He snickered. "I'll be out here if things get too hairy, or if you need someone turned into a hedgehog."

His voice was sarcastic, but Keirran only nodded, his mind clearly on something else. He began walking toward the thrones, leaving Kenzie and I scrambling to catch up. I glanced over my shoulder once to see Puck, his eyes dark and troubled, ease back into the thorns until he was lost from view.

"Back again?" Titania regarded us disdainfully as we stopped at the foot of her throne. "That didn't take long. And here I was hoping at least one of you would die or become frozen for eternity. How very disappointing."

"We've done what you asked," Keirran said, ignoring that

last part. "The spirit of the Frozen Wood is dead. Now please rescind Annwyl's banishment and let her return to court."

Titania regarded us for a long moment. Then her lips curled up in a pleased smile.

"No," she stated clearly. "I don't think I will."

I felt the bottom drop out of my stomach. Keirran stared at the Summer Queen in silence, but the air around him was turning cold.

"What the hell?" Kenzie burst out, unable to hold herself back. "You said that if we killed this spirit thing, you'd let Annwyl come back."

"No, my dear." Titania settled back on her throne, smiling triumphantly. "I said I would *consider* it. And I have. And the answer is still no."

"You can't be serious! She'll die!"

Titania shrugged. "That is no concern of mine. All fey must Fade eventually. It is only a matter of when." She looked over at Keirran, still standing motionless beside me, and smiled. "I would think you'd be grateful, Prince. After all, the Summer girl isn't who you think she is. Why do you think she was at the river the day you met?" Her smile grew wider, more evil. "Because I told her to be there. I told her to seek you out, to seduce you, win your affections. She was only at those 'secret' rendezvous points because I ordered it. It would have been vastly amusing to have the son of the Iron Queen under my thumb, willing to do anything for my loyal little handmaiden." She chuckled, before her lips curled in distaste and she gestured sharply in contempt. "Of course, the weak-minded girl went and fell in love for real and refused to betray you when the time came. So, naturally, I exiled her for her treason. *That* is the real reason Annwyl has been banished from the Summer Court, Prince. And that is the reason I will never take her back."

Titania settled comfortably on her throne, looking down at us smugly. Keirran was breathing hard, fists clenched, the air around him turning cold. The Summer Queen noticed his reaction and smirked. "I'm afraid your efforts have been all for naught, Prince. Though I do appreciate you getting rid of the Frozen Wood for me. I only hope Mab and the Iron Queen are more forgiving than I."

"Keirran," I warned in a low voice. "Don't lose it."

He lost it.

An explosion of ice, wind and leaves erupted around Keirran, rattling branches and causing everyone to flinch back. The Iron Prince stood with his head bowed, fists clenched at his sides, while magic swirled and snapped around him, whipping at his hair and clothes. I stumbled away as ice spread out from where he stood and iron roots began emerging from the ground like snakes, rising into the air.

"Keirran, don't!" I called, but my voice was lost in the gale. Keirran raised his head, his eyes glowing blue-white, his face fully transformed into the cold stranger I hated.

Titania was on her feet instantly, a cruel, eager smile stretching her lips, as Summer magic rose around her, as well. The rest of the nobles fell back, abandoning the glade, until it was only Kenzie and myself, watching the Iron Prince and the Queen of the Summer Court get ready to duke it out.

"Come, then, Iron Prince," Titania said, raising her hand, and lightning flickered overhead, slashing the sky. "I knew it was only a matter of time before you turned on all of Faery, and your betrayal will not go unpunished. I have been waiting to do this for years."

Keirran thrust out a hand, and the iron roots surged forward, stabbing at the Summer Queen. I tensed, but Titania made a casual gesture, and the ground before her surged forth with plants and vegetation, a virtual wall of vines and roots that swallowed the iron coils and dragged them down again.

"Your horrid Iron glamour has no power here," Titania said calmly. "This is the Summer Court, and within Arcadia's borders, the land bows to me!"

She snapped her fingers, and another tangle of roots surged from the earth, thorny and sharp, wrapping around Keirran. Kenzie gasped as the prince vanished into the crushing branches, but there was a burst of cold, and the roots turned to ice. They shattered, breaking apart like china, and Keirran stepped out unharmed.

Snarling, he sent a flurry of ice spears at the Summer Queen, who laughed and gestured, melting them to nothing. She responded by raising her hand, and a lightning bolt seared across the glade, right for Keirran, who raised his sword just in time. The white-hot beam struck the blade, sending him back a few steps, but he recovered quickly and lashed out again. A screaming gale of ice rushed toward the queen, who raised her arms, and her own whirlwind spun into existence around her, dispersing the wind and sending frozen shards ripping through the trees.

I staggered back, shielding my face as ice pelted my arms, tearing through my shirt. This was crazy. I had to do something before Keirran and Titania tore the court—and everything in it—to pieces. Glancing at the queen, my blood ran cold. She was smiling, her lips twisted into an amused, eager smirk as the wind shrieked around her. She was just playing with Keirran, with all of us. Dammit, I had to get him out of here before she got bored and turned the whole forest against us.

"Keirran!" I lunged forward, grabbing his arm. He spun on me furiously, eyes blazing. Wind and ice shards whirled around us, shredding my clothes and making his cloak snap furiously. "Keirran, enough! This is insane! We have to get out of—"

He threw me backward. I stumbled, but Kenzie darted past me, racing toward Keirran and the gale swirling around him. Titania raised her arm toward the prince, just as Kenzie lunged at Keirran, stepping in front of him and grabbing his shirt.

"Keirran, stop—"

Titania released a bolt of lightning, and in the space of a blink the deadly chain sizzled across the glade, turning everything white for a split second, and slammed into Kenzie's back. My heart stopped as she arched back with a cry, then collapsed against Keirran.

"Kenzie!"

I couldn't think. I didn't even see Titania anymore. I lunged across the clearing and threw myself at Kenzie and the prince. Keirran was gently lowering her limp body to the grass, his face white, as Razor screeched and bounced around in utter terror.

"Oh, God," I heard Keirran whisper as I reached them. "What have I done?"

"Get away from her!" Shoving him away, I knelt and gathered Kenzie to me, cradling her gently. Her head lolled to my chest, and my hands shook as I stroked her face. "Kenzie, wake up," I whispered, feeling my heart lodge somewhere in my throat. "Dammit, don't do this to me. Open your eyes."

She didn't move, and I forced down my panic, trying to think. My trembling fingers touched the skin below her jaw, searching for a pulse, a beat of life. My heart eased slightly. It was there—rapid and frantic, but alive.

"Ethan," Keirran whispered, but Titania's voice rang across the glade, ruthless and unmerciful.

"We are not finished, Iron Prince!" The Seelie monarch still stood in a whirlwind of Summer magic, her hair whipping about and her eyes, scary and cold. "If you dare attack me in my own court, you and your friends will pay the consequences. Turn and face me!"

Keirran looked back at the Summer Queen, but all the fight had gone out of him. The cold stranger had disappeared; the Iron Prince looked pale and grief-stricken now, beaten. But Titania smiled, gathering her magic for another assault; she wasn't going to let him go.

However, as she raised her arm, a flock of screaming ravens suddenly descended from nowhere, flapping around her. At the same time, Puck appeared beside me, dragging me upright with Kenzie still in my arms.

"You know, I thought it was obvious that there are certain things you just don't do!" he shouted, glaring at Keirran. "Things that are too ludicrous for even me to think of! Like, oh, I don't know, picking a fight with the freaking Queen of the Seelie Court! What the hell are you thinking, princeling?"

The cloud of ravens around Titania exploded in a burst of fire and feathers. Puck grimaced and pushed me toward the exit as the Summer Queen's furious gaze found us again.

"Go!" he ordered, giving me a shove. "We have to get out of Arcadia before things get really hairy."

"You will not help them escape, Robin Goodfellow!" Titania called, raising both her arms. Power rippled out from the Summer Queen, causing the very ground to shudder and churn like ocean waves. "I will send all of Arcadia after you if I must! The Iron Prince is mine!"

We ran from the throne room with Puck at our backs. Roars rang out behind us, and when I glanced back, I saw several huge creatures claw their way up from the forest floor. They were vaguely wolf-shaped, but their bodies were made of roots, vines and thorny brambles. Their eyes blazed with green light as they howled and loped forward, following us into the tunnel.

"Oh, goody, she's called in the hounds," Puck remarked as the first of the wolf-creatures stuck its thorny head around a corner and snarled at us. "She's only done that twice for me. You've really pissed her off, princeling."

The wolf leaped forward, and Puck waved a hand, causing part of the bramble tunnel to grow together, blocking its path. It roared and smashed into the barrier, snapping twigs and branches, trying to push through. The Summer prankster glanced back at us.

"You three get out of here," he snapped, nodding down another passage that snaked off into the shadows. "There's a trod to the mortal realm through there. I'll stay back to lead them off the trail. Get going!"

The things on the other side of the bramble wall roared and shook the branches, nearly through. We ducked down the tunnel, following the narrow passage through twists and turns, hearing the howls of the wolf pack and the shouts of pursuing Summer fey echo behind us. I held Kenzie tightly, almost frantic to get her out, to get her back to the real world, where there were no ice spirits or wolf monsters or angry faery queens. She was still limp and unresponsive, her body light and frail in my arms.

Finally, we came to the end of the tunnel, where a small wooden door sat entangled in vines and thorns. They curled protectively around the wood as we approached, but Keirran waved a hand, and they retreated, coiling back and allowing him to yank the door open.

"Go," he said, waving me through. "I'll be right behind you."

I went, holding Kenzie to me as I did. The madness, noise and chaos of Faery was shut out as soon as I crossed the threshold, and the real world finally took its place.

CHAPTER TWENTY-TWO
THE CALM BEFORE

We were back.

Where the hell were we?

Trees surrounded us, dark and tangled. We stood in the middle of a forest, and not the well-groomed woods of a park or even a reserve. This felt like vast, untamed wilderness. Except for the moon and stars through the branches, there was no light and barely any sound. Behind us, a black, narrow hole cut into a rocky shelf, the cave that marked the entrance to the Nevernever and the Seelie Court.

Still panting, I knelt in the dirt, carefully lowering Kenzie to the ground. With trembling fingers, I checked her vitals again, making sure that heartbeat was still there, the pulse that told me she was alive. She didn't open her eyes, however, and dread squeezed my chest with icy talons.

Keirran stood behind me, casting a dark shadow over the girl's slack face. "How is she?" he whispered, his voice subdued. "Will she be all right?"

My vision went red. Lunging to my feet, I spun and drove my fist into Keirran's jaw, knocking him back. He staggered, and I went for him again, yanking him upright and slamming my fist into his stomach, doubling him over with a gasp.

Ramming him into a tree, I hauled back and hit him sev-

eral times, barely aware of what I was striking. Keirran raised
his arms to shield his head, but didn't fight back, which pissed
me off even more. I pounded at his face, slamming him several times into the tree trunk. Razor screeched, landing on my
shoulder and chomping my ear with sharp little fangs. With
a curse, I slapped the gremlin away and slugged Keirran one
more time, this time knocking him off his feet. He landed on
his knees in the dirt, and I fought back the urge to kick him,
repeatedly. But hitting someone while they were down was
going a bit far, even now.

"Damn you!" I snarled as Keirran slowly regained his feet
and slumped against the trunk. Blood streamed from his nose
and mouth, spattering the front of his shirt, and the prince
didn't look at me, staring at the ground between us. "That's
it, Keirran! No more help, no more bargains, no more agreeing to kill ancient spirits! We're done! I don't know you, you
don't know me and you sure as hell don't know Kenzie. I don't
care what you do now, but you are a fucking train wreck. And
I'm done watching everything around you go up in flames,
do you hear me?"

Keirran wiped blood from his mouth and nodded silently.
He looked tired, defeated, but I refused to feel sorry for him.
Not when Mackenzie lay motionless several feet away, struck
down by Titania for trying to stop *him.*

"Ethan?"

The soft gasp pierced my heart, and my anger vanished. I
whirled and flung myself down beside Kenzie, gently taking
her hand. Her eyes were open, though they were glazed and
glassy, and her face was tight with pain.

"I'm here," I murmured. Keirran came up to stand behind
me, out of punching range, I noticed, but I ignored him.
"Can you move?"

"I don't know," Kenzie gasped, squeezing my hand. "Everything hurts."

"We have to get you home." As gently as I could, I shifted my arms beneath her and lifted her as I rose. She whimpered and clutched at my shirt, making my insides twist into near-panicked knots. She needed a doctor, but we were in no-man's-land. How were we going to get back to civilization?

"Here." Keirran stepped away, one hand raised as if sensing the breeze. Stopping beneath a thick pine, he pushed his fingers into empty air and parted the real world like a curtain, revealing the darkness of the Between through the gap. I stiffened, and he turned to me with bleak, haunted eyes.

"I'll take you home, one last time."

The rest of the trip was a blur. I was vaguely aware that we left the Between and took a cab or something to the hospital. Several doctors and nurses surrounded me, asking questions. I answered in a daze and watched them wheel Kenzie away on a gurney, feeling like my chest had been squeezed in a vise. Then she was gone, and I collapsed into a chair, shutting out the world and praying she would be all right.

"Ethan Chase?"

I looked up blearily. A nurse in pink scrubs stood before me, looking kind and sympathetic. How long it had been, I had no idea. "She's awake," she said as I quickly stood up. A couple seats down, Keirran raised his head off his chest, watching us. I'd forgotten about him, too. "We've stabilized her, and she's resting now. She sustained some nerve and tissue damage, and we're keeping her under observation, but she's a very lucky girl."

I nearly collapsed in relief. The nurse smiled. "You can see her now, but keep it brief. Five minutes if you can. She really needs to rest. Has her family been contacted?"

"Yes," Keirran said from the chair, though the nurse didn't even look at him. I felt a pulse of magic go through the air between us, but I was too worried about Kenzie to think much of it. "They're on their way now."

She nodded distractedly, gave me a room number and warned me again to keep it short. As the nurse left, I started down the hall, and Keirran rose from the chair to follow.

I spun on him. Fury blazed up, searing away the numbness. "Where do you think you're going?" I challenged, narrowing my eyes.

He blinked. "To see Kenzie."

I sneered. "Forget it. You're not going anywhere near her, ever again." Another nurse passed us, and I averted my gaze until she turned a corner, before glaring at the prince again. "Get lost, Keirran. Go home."

"Ethan, please. I…" Keirran closed his eyes. "I failed Annwyl," he whispered, his voice breaking. "I've made a mess out of everything. Let me make sure Kenzie is all right, and I'll go. I'll get out of your life forever. You'll never see me again."

Annwyl. Damn. I'd forgotten about her in all the chaos and panic over Kenzie. With no way home now, the Summer faery would Fade to nothing. As would Keirran, once the amulet drained everything he was. No wonder he looked so haunted. He'd gambled everything to get Annwyl home, knowing the consequences would be terrible, knowing they couldn't be together even if he saved her life. And now things were even worse. The courts could go to war, the Frozen Wood was lost, and there was probably some punishment waiting for him for attacking the Queen of the Summer Court. Not to mention Meghan and Ash were going to be furious. And even after all that, after everything we'd fought for, Annwyl was still dying. We were back to square one.

I sighed as some of my anger flickered and went out. I was

still pissed, but Keirran looked about ready to fall apart. I noticed my swords then, tucked under his arm, and scowled in confusion before understanding dawned. He'd grabbed them from me before I entered the hospital. If I had walked through those doors armed, I'd probably be sitting in a jail cell right now. He, at least, had had the presence of mind to glamour them, and himself, invisible.

But that still didn't excuse what he'd done.

"Dammit, Keirran," I muttered, scrubbing a hand over my face. But at that moment, a chill crept up my back, and I looked up, staring past him down the hall.

A shadow hung from the ceiling at the end of the corridor, huge yellow eyes glowing in its featureless face. I tensed and almost grabbed my blades from Keirran's hand, though the second I did they would become visible and then I'd be in trouble. The Forgotten didn't attack, however. Like the other times, it watched us a moment, then slowly eased forward, a shadowy blob against the tiles.

"Iron Prince," it whispered when it was a few yards away, and Keirran stiffened. "We have waited long enough. The Lady wishes to speak to you *now.*"

Keirran took one step toward it, and I grabbed his arm. "Keirran!" I hissed, not knowing why I was stopping him. "Don't be stupid."

"I'm not," he said in a low voice, turning back to me. "Not this time. I have to go to her soon, or the Forgotten will hound me forever. I'm only going to see what she has to say. I'm not going to agree to any more terms or promise her anything. But I have to do this, Ethan." His eyes went dark, and he swallowed hard. "One last thing before I go home... and face my parents."

Reluctantly, I let him go, and he turned back to the Forgotten. "Where is she?" he asked. "The Lady?"

"The faery ring," the Forgotten whispered. "Where the other mortal in your party gained the Sight."

"Ireland," I muttered, frowning. Of course, it would have to be halfway around the world. Not far by trod or Between jumping, I supposed, but plenty far enough.

"Tell her I'll be there soon," Keirran said, and the Forgotten nodded. Melting against the ceiling, it slithered away like a shadow, turned the corner and was gone.

"I'm not going to Ireland," I told him flatly. "Not with Kenzie in the hospital. I'm not leaving her."

"I know," he answered. "I don't expect you to. This is my mess, and I have to do this alone. But I want to see Kenzie before I leave. Say goodbye. She…probably won't see me again."

And neither will I. Pushing that thought away, I went in search of Mackenzie's room, with Keirran trailing invisibly behind.

I had another weird sense of déjà vu as I entered the quiet hospital room, the soft beep of machines the only sound that greeted me. Kenzie lay on a bed in the corner with one arm draped over her stomach, breathing peacefully. Much like last time. I wondered if it was always going to be like this: spending more and more time in the hospital, watching my girlfriend suffer from sickness and exhaustion and magical injuries no normal person would have to deal with. I wondered if my heart would be able to take it.

Razor perched on an overhead shelf like a spindly gargoyle, silent and grim. He eyed me warily as we came in, then turned his attention to Kenzie once more. I hoped the gremlin's presence hadn't shorted out any of the machines, but oddly enough, I was glad that he'd been there, watching her. It seemed Kenzie had picked up a tiny faery champion.

"Hey." Moving to her side, I took her hand. Her eyes were open and alert, though her skin was very pale. Leaning down,

I traced her cheek with my other hand, and she smiled, briefly closing her eyes against my touch.

"Hey, tough guy." Her gaze met mine, weary and a little sad. "Here we are again."

"Are you feeling any better?" I didn't know how one would feel after being struck by a glamour-produced lightning bolt, but I could hazard it wasn't great. Kenzie shrugged.

"Sore, mostly. And drained. The doctors say I have some minor burns, but nothing too serious. They told me I was extremely lucky—most people hit by lightning don't get off that easy." She gave a faint, rueful grin. "I didn't tell them most people don't get hit by angry faery queens, either."

"Mackenzie." Keirran was suddenly at her side opposite me, his eyes bright and anguished in the shadows of the room. "I have no right to ask for your forgiveness," he said, "but I want you to know that I'm truly sorry, for everything. I know that's small consolation now." She took a breath to answer, but he held up a hand. "Your family will be here soon," he continued, to my surprise as well, and his gaze flicked to mine. "I didn't lie about that. Once your parents were contacted by the hospital, the glamour shrouding their minds vanished. They remember everything, up until the night we walked out of their hotel room. I heard the nurses talking to your father on the phone. He's on his way now."

"Oh," Kenzie breathed. "Great. So that means I'm going to have to explain where I was and why I ran out like that."

"Well, that's easy," I muttered, ignoring the sudden dread, the creeping suspicion that Kenzie's father was going to be furious with me. "You can just tell them I kidnapped you again."

Keirran leaned down, placing a hand over Kenzie's arm, squeezing gently. "Thank you," he murmured quite solemnly. "Both of you. For sticking it out with me. It was nice...to have friends for a change. Even if it was for just a little while. I won't trouble you again."

"Where are you going?" Kenzie said, frowning.

"I have to meet the Lady," Keirran answered in a flat voice. "She's called for me, and I promised I would go to her. After that—" his eyes darkened "—I have to return home and face my parents. They've probably heard the news from the Summer Court by now."

"What about Annwyl?" Kenzie whispered.

A shudder went through Keirran, and he dropped his head with a short, breathless sob. "I don't know," he said, one hand covering his face. "I failed her," he whispered. "I don't know what will happen now, what more I can do."

He turned away, hunching his shoulders, and Kenzie's hand came to rest over mine, bringing my attention back to her. "Go with him," she told me.

I recoiled. "What? No!" I leaned down, knowing Keirran could hear me and not caring a bit. "Forget it. He already made his choice, and look where it got us. But that's beside the point. I'm not leaving you, Mackenzie."

"I'll be fine." Her cool fingers brushed the side of my face. "My family is coming. I won't be alone. But, Ethan, you're all he has left, and you're family. You can't send him to face the Lady by himself."

"Dammit, Kenzie." I bent down, pressing my forehead to hers. "No. I don't want to do this. You're more important to me now."

"Nothing will happen to me here," Kenzie whispered back, slipping her fingers into my hair, easing me closer. "Ethan, please. I'm worried for him. I know he's made some stupid mistakes, but he's still our friend, right? What if something happens? What if the Lady betrays him, just like Titania did?" Her voice lowered, meant only for me. "He's probably desperate now that Annwyl can't go home. You have to make sure he doesn't do something really crazy."

Keirran straightened, taking a short breath to compose himself. "I should go," he said. Glancing at Razor, he raised his hand, beckoning him forward, but the gremlin flattened his ears and stayed put. Keirran blinked, then lowered his arm. "You're staying?" he asked in a curiously choked voice. The gremlin garbled something back, and the prince smiled sadly. "I see. Well, it's your choice, Razor."

Kenzie looked at me, eyes wide and pleading, and I whispered a curse.

"Keirran, wait." I rose, wishing I could drive my fist through the wall, wishing I didn't have to make these kinds of choices. "I'm coming with you."

"Ethan, you don't—"

"Shut up." I glared at him. "Don't make me regret this even more. I know I don't have to come along. You're family, and you'll need someone watching your back."

A pair of doctors stopped outside the door, gazing into the room at us. Or, more specifically, at me. Their eyes were hard and wary as they whispered to one another, pointed a finger in my direction and walked away down the hall. I wondered if Kenzie's father had mentioned me and had the sneaking suspicion that they were heading off to find a security guard— or call the police.

"You two better go," Kenzie said as the doctors left. "Don't worry about me. I'll be fine. Keirran, try not to go attacking any more faery queens, okay?"

Keirran bowed to her. "Goodbye, Mackenzie. I'm very glad to have known you." His gaze went to the gremlin, perched above her bed, and a sad smile crossed his face. "Take care of Razor for me. It seems he's chosen himself a new Master."

Razor blinked at Keirran from atop the shelf, huge eyes gleaming, but he didn't say anything.

I bent down, smoothed Kenzie's hair from her face and kissed her. She wrapped her arms around my neck, holding me like she couldn't bear to let go, and for a moment, I let myself forget everything.

Pulling back, I met those deep brown eyes gazing up at me and stroked her cheek. "I love you," I whispered, my voice just a murmur between us. No fear, no hesitation; it was just pulled out of me, unable to stay hidden any longer. Her eyes widened, and I kissed her parted lips once more before straightening. "I'll be back soon," I promised, wanting to do nothing more than sit back down and hold her until the cops showed up to drag me away. "This won't take long."

"Ethan." Kenzie grabbed my wrist as I turned away. Her eyes were bright as I looked back. "I love you, too, tough guy," she whispered, turning my heart inside out. "Be careful. And come back to me."

Footsteps sounded outside in the hall. I glanced up to see the same two doctors enter the room, a uniformed policeman close behind. My stomach dropped, but Keirran, it seemed, was expecting them. He waved a hand at me, I felt a pulse of magic hit my skin, and the world went hazy for a split second. The cop and the doctors blinked and looked around the room in bewilderment, and I realized Keirran had thrown an invisibility spell over me. He jerked his head at the door, slipping around the flabbergasted adults, and left the room. I followed, being careful not to brush against them, until I reached the frame and looked back.

Kenzie's knowing smile met mine across the room. She nodded and winked, then turned her attention to the doctor that approached, demanding to know where I had gone. She gave a very clueless shrug, and I forced myself to turn away, joining Keirran in the hall.

"Hurry," he said, sounding breathless and winded. "The spell won't last long, and I don't have much strength left. Let's get this over with so we can both go home."

CHAPTER TWENTY-THREE
CATALYST

Another trip into the Between. It took a bit longer this time, passing through a landscape of mist and fog, beneath the ruins of an ancient tower, frozen in time.

When Keirran parted the Veil again, we stood at the top of a hill, looking down on the rolling moors, with no artificial lights to be seen. Overhead, the moon was as full and bright as it had been on our last trip here, when Kenzie had made the bargain with Leanansidhe to get the Sight. I desperately hoped she was all right, and wished, yet again, that she'd never made that bargain. That I could have somehow talked her out of wanting to see the fey for the rest of her life. Look where she'd ended up because of it.

"Come on," Keirran said and started down the slope, walking toward a familiar cluster of trees in the distance. The cold moor wind howled through the grass and between the rocks, yanking at my clothes and hair. Keirran had given me back my swords, which were strapped to my waist again, and Guro's amulet lay heavy around my neck, clinking against the iron cross. I found myself thinking that I should've left it with Kenzie; maybe if she'd been wearing it in the Summer Court, the lightning bolt would've missed her.

Could've, would've, should've. I couldn't do anything about

it now. As Kenzie had said, what was done was done, and we couldn't beat ourselves up for the past.

Easier said than done, at least for me.

There was no faery music when we approached the grove this time. No Summer fey dancing under the light of the full moon. However, the faery ring, the enormous circle of toadstools in the center of the glen, was far from empty. Forgotten surrounded it now, dark and blurred, nearly invisible in the shadows except for their glowing yellow eyes. They parted for us without a sound, bowing their wispy heads as Keirran and I stepped through their ranks and walked toward the figure in the center of the ring.

"Prince Keirran." The Lady's low, throaty voice sounded faintly horrified as we stepped before her, hordes of Forgotten watching from the edge of the ring. The faery's shifting eyes barely glanced at me, going wide at the sight of the Iron Prince. "What has happened to you? You feel...empty. Fading. Like my own people."

"Do you remember Annwyl?" Keirran asked, his voice cold. "Do you remember what your people did to her? She started to Fade, and I couldn't allow that to happen."

"What have you done?" the Lady whispered. Keirran gave a grim smile.

"Annwyl wears an amulet now that ties us together, and my glamour sustains her, though it won't for much longer." He narrowed his gaze at the Forgotten Queen. "I find it ironic that I'm going to die, killed by the Forgotten, when all I wanted was to save your people."

"No," the Lady said, one hand going to her chest. "Prince Keirran, there was another way. I made a bargain with Mr. Dust to provide us with the glamour we needed to survive. You could have done the same."

"That wasn't an option," I snapped.

"Really, Ethan Chase?" the Lady said, turning on me. I stepped back; she looked seriously pissed. "And this is better?" She gestured to Keirran, who didn't move. "You would let him die, corrupt his soul, to save a few mortal children?"

"Corrupt his...what?" My stomach went cold. The Forgotten Queen gave me a disgusted look.

"You do not know, do you? The magic on the other end of...whatever he is attached to is not only draining his glamour, his strength and his memories. It is taking his very essence, what makes him who he is. He is mostly human. It is taking his soul." She turned to Keirran as I stood there, reeling. "That is what is keeping your girl alive, Prince Keirran. She has a piece of your soul imprisoned in that amulet, and as long as she lives, you will never get it back."

Guro, I thought, feeling like I'd been punched. *What the hell? Did you know? Is that what you were trying to tell me?*

I looked at Keirran, wondering what he thought of this, but the Iron Prince only shrugged. "It doesn't matter anymore," he muttered, his voice resigned. "Annwyl can't go home. We'll both die soon enough. If the amulet is taking my soul, she's welcome to it."

"No, Prince Keirran," the Lady almost whispered. "There is yet another way."

He looked at her. Wary, I stepped closer, eyeing the Forgotten on all sides, not trusting them or their queen. The Lady ignored me, gliding closer to Keirran, until she stood just a few feet from us. Keirran's face was blank; he'd slipped into the cold stranger persona, not giving me or the Lady anything, even as she reached out to him.

"The exiles and the Forgotten are very similar, Iron Prince," the Forgotten Queen said, gesturing around at the horde of dark, shadowy fey. "The courts have been cruel to us both, dooming the exiles to Fade into oblivion, expecting the Forgotten to do the same. We are both only trying to survive a world without magic. But it is not the Faery realms that are responsible for our disappearance. It is man.

"Mankind has forgotten us," the Lady went on as Keirran continued to regard her without expression. "Many years ago, when I was young, the fey were feared and respected by mortals. They worshipped us, prayed to us, made sacrifices in our name. Not one human doubted the existence of the Good Neighbors, and those that did were quickly reminded what would happen if they forgot.

"But now—" the Lady made a hopeless, weary gesture "—we are all but gone from their minds. Our stories have been sanitized and made into children's tales. The Nevernever still exists on the dreams and fears of mortals, but even it grows smaller with each passing year. For those cut off from the dreamworld, we cannot help but Fade into nothing."

"I know that." Keirran's voice was hard and expressionless. "Everyone in Faery knows that. There's nothing we can do about mankind's disbelief."

The Lady smiled then, and it sent a chill crawling down my back.

"But there is," she intoned. "There is a way to open man's eyes to us once again. The Veil between Faery and the mortal world keeps us hidden. Keeps humans blind to the Nevernever and all the creatures who live there. It separates the two worlds so they can never meet." She raised a thin, pale hand, opening an empty fist. "If the Veil were suddenly…gone, the mortal realm and the Nevernever would merge. The hidden world would no longer be invisible to humans, and once they see us again, truly See us, their belief will save all exiles and Forgotten from the Fade."

"No fucking way!" My outburst made her blink, and I clenched my fists, imagining a world where the fey ran wild, unrestrained. "That wouldn't be salvation—that would be chaos! Complete and utter madness. People would die, go crazy. There'd be worldwide panic."

"Yes," the Forgotten Queen agreed. "Panic, and fear, and belief. The humans would respect us again, or at the very least, they would have to believe what their eyes told them. That the fey are real, that we exist. The Nevernever would grow strong once more, exiles would no longer be in danger of Fading, and we would at last be remembered."

"There is no way to destroy the Veil," Keirran said flatly.

"Oh, my dear prince," the Lady whispered. "You and the courts are not as old as I. You have forgotten the way to tear it apart. It has never been done before, because the catalyst has not been born into this world...until now."

"Catalyst?" I didn't like where this was going. My heart was pounding against my ribs, and a cold chill was creeping up my back. I looked at Keirran, wondering if we could get out of here, but he stood unmoving in the Lady's shadow, his eyes blank.

The Lady's voice went low, soft and terrifying. "To tear the Veil asunder," she crooned, as if reciting something from memory, "on the night of the full moon, one must stand at the site of an ancient power and sacrifice the life of a mortal with the Sight, one who is bound by blood to all courts of Faery. Kin to Summer, Winter and now Iron. With this sacrifice, the Veil will lift, and mortals will be able to see the hidden world, by the blood of the One. Sibling, brother-in-law..." She looked right at me with depthless black eyes. "Uncle."

No. My hands were shaking, and I took a staggering step back, looking around. The Forgotten were closing in on us, stepping across the toadstools into the circle, glowing eyes fastened on me. My stomach turned. *Me.* They wanted me. I was the sacrifice. The mortal whose blood tied him to all three courts. The one who would usher in an age of madness and chaos and terror, when all humans suddenly realized the fey were real.

Screw that.

I drew my swords with a raspy screech as Keirran did the same. I whirled to face the horde, standing back-to-back with Keirran, as the Forgotten glided closer. So many of them. But I wasn't going down without a fight.

"Ethan Chase." From the corner of my eye, I saw that the Lady had drifted back. "I must apologize to you once more. I am saddened that you must die for the rest of us to live, but know that your sacrifice will save thousands of lives. The fey will no longer live in fear. Exiles, Forgotten, even the Nevernever...we will all live on because of you."

The Forgotten were nearly on us, a silent, deadly swarm, and the Lady's words had faded into jumbled background noise. "Keirran," I muttered, reaching for that calm, that eerie peace I got right before battle. The Iron Prince stood rigid at my back, not moving a muscle. "What's it look like on your side? Can we fight our way through?"

"Ethan?"

His voice was strange, almost choked. A shiver went through him, and I glanced back, frowning. "What?"

"I'm sorry."

He turned, just as I did, and ran me through with his sword.

Sound cut out. Movement faded around us. My mouth gaped open, but nothing escaped but a strangled gasp. Keirran, standing very close, stared over my shoulder, one arm around my neck, the other near my gut. I looked down to see his hand gripping the sword hilt, held flush against my stomach.

No. This...couldn't be real; the blade didn't even hurt that much. I looked up at Keirran, still staring at the horizon over my shoulder, and tried to say something. But my voice was frozen inside me.

"Keir...ran." Even that was excruciatingly difficult, and a warm stream of blood ran down my neck from my mouth. *"Why?"* Keirran closed his eyes.

"I'm so sorry," he whispered and ripped the blade from my stomach. *That* brought on the pain I knew I should be feeling, a blaze of agony erupting from my middle, like the ribbons of blood arching into the air. I grabbed my stomach, feeling warmth spill over my fingers, making them slick. I glanced down to see my hands completely covered in red.

This isn't happening. The ground swayed beneath me. I fell to my knees, seeing blackness crawl along the edge of my vision. Looking up, I saw Keirran gazing down on me, the Lady standing behind him. His face was tormented, but as I watched, he closed his eyes and took a deep breath, and when he opened them again, Keirran was gone. The cold stranger stared down at me, his face a mask of stone.

"Goodbye, Ethan," he whispered, and the Lady put a hand on his shoulder and turned him away. I tried calling out, but the world tilted, and I collapsed, seeing only a skewed view of the distant horizon, shrinking rapidly at the end of a tunnel. Somewhere far away, I thought I heard hoofbeats, a faint rumble getting steadily closer.

Then the tunnel closed, the blackness flooded in and I knew nothing more.

★ ★ ★ ★ ★

*If you love Julie Kagawa's cinematic writing,
unforgettable characters and unique worlds,
turn the page to read an exclusive excerpt
from her next novel,*
THE FOREVER SONG,
Book 3 of the thrilling BLOOD OF EDEN *dystopian trilogy.*
Coming May 2014 from Harlequin TEEN.

CHAPTER ONE

The outpost gate creaked softly in the wind, swinging back on its hinges. It knocked lightly against the wall, a rhythmic tapping sound that echoed in the looming silence. Through the gap, the scent of blood lay on the air like a heavy blanket.

"He's been here," Kanin murmured at my side. I didn't have to look at my sire to know what he was thinking. The Master vampire was a dark statue against the falling snow, motionless and calm, but his eyes were grave. I regarded the fence impassively, the wind tugging at my coat and straight black hair.

"Is there any point in going in?"

"Sarren knows we're following him" was the low reply. "He meant for us to see this. He wants us to know that he knows. There will likely be something waiting for us when we step through the gates."

Footsteps crunched over the snow as Jackal stalked around us, black duster rippling behind him. His eyes glowed a vicious yellow as he peered up at the gate, smirking. "Well, then," he said, the tips of his fangs showing through his grin, "if he went through all the trouble of setting this up, we shouldn't keep the psycho waiting, should we?"

He started forward, his step confident, striding through the broken gate toward the tiny settlement beyond. After a moment's hesitation, Kanin and I followed.

Nothing moved on the narrow path that snaked between

houses. The flimsy wood and tin shanties were silent, dark, as we ventured deeper, passing snow-covered porches and empty chairs. Everything looked intact, undisturbed. There were no bodies. No corpses mutilated in their beds, no blood spattered over the walls of the few homes we ducked into. There weren't even any dead animals in the tiny, trampled pasture past the main strip. Just snow, and dark, and emptiness.

And yet, the smell of blood soaked this place, making my stomach ache and the Hunger roar to life. I bit it down, clenching my jaw to keep from snarling in frustration. It had been too long. I needed food. The scent was driving me crazy, and the fact that there were no humans here made me furious. Where were they? It wasn't possible that an entire outpost of mortals would up and disappear without a trace.

And then, as we followed the path around the pasture and up to the huge barn at the top of the rise, we found the townspeople.

A massive, barren tree stood beside the barn, twisted branches clawing at the sky. They creaked and swayed beneath the weight of dozens of bodies, hanging upside down from ropes tied to the limbs. Men, women, even a few kids, swinging in the breeze, dangling arms stiff and white. Their throats had been cut, and the base of the tree was stained black, the blood spilled and wasted in the snow. But the smell nearly knocked me over regardless, and I clenched my fists, the Hunger raking my insides with fiery talons.

"Well," Jackal muttered, crossing his arms and gazing up at the tree, "isn't that festive." His voice was tight, as if he, too, was on the edge of losing it. "I'm guessing this is the reason we haven't found a single bloodbag from here all the way back to New Covington." He growled, shaking his head, lips curling back from his fangs. "This guy is really starting to piss me off."

I swallowed the Hunger, trying to focus through the gnawing ache. "Why, James, don't tell me you feel sorry for the

walking meatsacks," I taunted, because sometimes, goading
Jackal was the only thing that kept my mind off everything
else. He snorted and rolled his eyes.

"No, sister, I'm annoyed because they don't have the de-
cency to be alive so I can eat them," he returned with a flash
of fangs and a rare show of temper. Glaring at the tree, he
stared at the bodies hungrily. "Fucking Sarren," he muttered.
"If I didn't want the psychopath dead so badly I would say
the hell with it. If this keeps up, we're going to have to break
off the trail to find a meatsack whose throat hasn't been slit,
which is probably what the bastard wants." He sighed, giving me an exasperated look. "This would be so much easier
if you hadn't killed the Jeep."

"For the last time," I growled at him, "I just pointed out
the street that wasn't blocked off. I didn't leave those nails in
the road for you to drive over."

"Allison."

Kanin's quiet voice broke through our argument, and we
turned. Our sire stood at one corner of the barn, his face grim
as he beckoned us forward. With a last glance at the tree and
its grisly contents, I walked over to him, feeling the sharp stab
of Hunger once more. The barn reeked of blood, even more
than the branches of the tree. Probably because one whole wall
of the building was streaked with it, dried and black, painted
in vertical lines up and down the wood.

"Let's keep moving," Kanin said in a low voice when Jackal
and I joined him. His voice was calm, though I knew he was
just as Hungry as the rest of us. Maybe more so, since he was
still recovering from his near-death experience in New Covington. "There are no survivors here," Kanin went on, with
a solemn look back at the tree. "And we are running out of
time. Sarren is expecting us."

"How do you figure, old man?" Jackal inquired, following

me to the side of the barn. "Yeah, this is the psycho's handiwork, but he could've done this just for the jollies. You sure he knows we're coming?"

Kanin didn't answer, just gestured to the blood-streaked wall beside us. I looked over, as did Jackal, but didn't see anything unusual. Beyond a wall completely covered in blood, that is.

But Jackal gave a low, humorless chuckle. "Oh, you bastard." He shook his head and stared up at the barn. "That's cute. Let's see if you're as funny when I'm beating you to death with your own arm."

"What?" I asked, obviously missing something. I stared at the barn again, wondering what the other vampires saw that I didn't. "What's so funny? I don't see anything."

Jackal sighed, stepped behind me and hooked the back of my collar, pulling me away from the wall.

"Hey!" I snarled, fighting him. "Let go! What the hell are you doing?"

He ignored me, continuing to walk backward, dragging me with him. We were about a dozen paces away from the wall before he stopped and I yanked myself from his grip. "What is your problem?" I demanded, baring fangs. Jackal silently pointed back to the barn.

I glanced at the wall again and stiffened. Now that I was farther away, I could see what Kanin and Jackal were talking about.

Sarren, I thought, the cold, familiar hate spreading through my insides. *You sick bastard. This won't stop me, and it won't save you. When I find you, you'll regret ever hearing my name.*

Painted across the side of the barn, written in bloody letters about ten feet tall, was a question. One that proved, beyond a shadow of a doubt, that Sarren knew we were coming. And that we were probably walking right into some kind of trap.

HUNGRY YET?

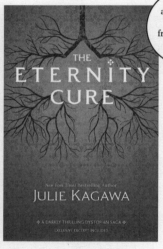

Don't miss the thrilling beginning to The Blackcoat Rebellion

The first move is hers...

PAWN

AIMÉE CARTER

The world is supposed to be equal.
Life is supposed to be fair.
But appearances are deceiving.
And Kitty Doe knows that better than anyone else...

Coming December 2013!

FROM *NEW YORK TIMES* BESTSELLING AUTHOR

GENA SHOWALTER

THE WHITE RABBIT CHRONICLES

Book 1   Book 2

The night her entire family dies in a terrible car accident, Alice Bell finds out the truth—the "monsters" her father always warned her about are real. They're zombies. And they're hungry—for her.

AVAILABLE WHEREVER BOOKS ARE SOLD!